The Silence of the Sea

Also by Yrsa Sigurdardóttir

Last Rituals
My Soul to Take
Ashes to Dust
The Day Is Dark
I Remember You
Someone to Watch Over Me
The Undesired

The Silence of the Sea

Yrsa Sigurdardóttir

Translated from the Icelandic
by Victoria Cribb

MINOTAUR BOOKS

A THOMAS DUNNE BOOK
New York

A THOMAS DUNNE BOOK FOR MINOTAUR BOOKS.
An imprint of St. Martin's Press.

www.thomasdunnebooks.com
www.minotaurbooks.com

The Library of Congress has cataloged the hardcover edition as follows:

Names: Sigurdardóttir, Yrsa, author. | Cribb, Victoria, translator.
Title: The silence of the sea : a thriller / Yrsa Sigurdardóttir ; translated from the Icelandic by Victoria Cribb.
Other titles: Brakid. English
Description: First U.S. edition. | New York : Minotaur Books, 2016. | Series: Thóra Gudmundsdóttir ; 6 | "A Thomas Dunne book."
Identifiers: LCCN 2015040619| ISBN 9781250051486 (hardcover) | ISBN 9781466852341 (e-book)
Subjects: LCSH: Thóra Gudmundsdóttir (Fictitious character)—Fiction. | Reykjavaík (Iceland)—Fiction. | Mystery fiction. | Suspense fiction.
Classification: LCC PT7511.A67 B7313 2016 | DDC 839/.6935—dc23
LC record available at http://lccn.loc.gov/2015040619

ISBN 978-1-250-11555-3 (trade paperback)

Our books may be purchased in bulk for promotional, educational, or business use. Please contact your local bookseller or the Macmillan Corporate and Premium Sales Department at 1-800-221-7945, extension 5442, or by e-mail at MacmillanSpecialMarkets@macmillan.com.

Originally published in 2011 under the title Brakid in Reykjavík, Iceland, by Veröld Publishing

First Minotaur Books Paperback Edition: January 2017

D 10 9 8 7 6 5 4 3

This book is dedicated to
my grandfather, Þorsteinn Eyjólfsson,
ship's captain (1906–2007).

Acknowledgments

Special thanks are due to Michael Sheehan for explaining various points in relation to yachts and sea voyages; Arnar Haukur Ævarsson, first mate, for sharing his knowledge of telecommunications at sea, steering systems, and other aspects of navigation; and finally Kristján B. Thorlacius, advocate to the Supreme Court, for information on the legal side of missing persons' cases. The responsibility for any mistakes is entirely my own.

The Silence of the Sea

Prologue

Brynjar hugged his jacket tighter around him, thinking longingly of his warm hut and wondering what on earth he was doing out here. It just went to show how dull his job was that he should jump at any chance of a diversion, even if it meant having to endure the biting wind. As usual at this late hour, the port he was supposed to be keeping an eye on was deserted, and it suddenly struck him that he didn't know it any other way. He avoided its daytime bustle, preferring it like this—black sea, unmanned ships—as if seeing how it came to life when he wasn't there brought home to him his own insignificance.

He watched an old couple walk out onto the docks, leading a little girl between them. Not far behind them was a young man limping along on crutches, which struck Brynjar as no less odd. Glancing at his watch, he saw that it was nearly midnight. Though childless himself, he knew enough about parenting to realize that this was a strange hour for a toddler to be up and about. Perhaps, like him, these people were braving the bitter cold to see the famous yacht that was due any minute now. Come to think of it, they were probably here to meet a member of the Icelandic crew. Brynjar decided not to approach them in case he was right. After all, they had a reason to be there, whereas he was simply being nosy. Of course he could invent some official business, but he was a hopeless liar and there was a risk the explanation would come out all wrong.

Rather than stand there like a spare part, he walked over to a small van marked "Customs," which had driven onto the docks half an hour ago and parked with a good view of the harbor. With any luck the driver would invite him to sit inside in the warm. As he tapped the window he noticed with surprise that it contained three customs officials instead of the usual one or two. The glass rolled down with a squeak, as if there was grit in the frame. "Good evening," he said.

"Evening." It was the driver who replied. The attention of the other men remained riveted on the harbor.

"Here about the yacht?" Brynjar regretted approaching the van and felt his hopes of being offered a seat fading.

"Yup." The driver looked away and stared in the same direction as his companions. "We're not here for the view."

"A lot of you, aren't there?" Small clouds of steam accompanied his words but the three men took no notice.

"Something's up. Hopefully nothing serious, but enough to warrant dragging us out of bed." The driver zipped up his anorak. "They haven't been answering their radio. Probably a technical fault, but you never know."

Brynjar gestured to the people waiting on the quay. The child was now in the older man's arms and the young man with the crutches had perched on a bollard nearby. "I expect they're here to meet the yacht. Want me to go and check them out?"

"If you like." The man clearly didn't care what he did as long as he kept out of their way. "But I doubt they're here to receive smuggled goods. We watched them arrive and none of them could so much as outrun a wheelchair. They're probably just relatives."

Brynjar straightened up, removing his arm from the window. "I'll wander over anyway. Can't do any harm." He received nothing in reply but a squeak as the window was rolled back up. He turned up his collar. The group on the quayside had to be better company than the customs men, even if they didn't have a warm car to invite him into. A lone gull announced its presence with a squawk as it took off from a darkened streetlight and Brynjar quickened his pace, watching the bird vanish in the direction of the looming black shape of the new concert hall.

"Evening," he said as he drew close. The group returned his greeting in a subdued manner. "I'm the port security officer. Are you waiting for someone?"

Even in the dim light the relief on the faces of the old couple was obvious. "Yes, our son and his family are due in shortly," said the man. "This is their youngest daughter. She's so excited about Mom and Dad coming home that we decided to surprise them." He looked slightly embarrassed. "That's all right, isn't it?"

"Of course." Brynjar smiled at the little girl, who peeped shyly from under the brim of a colorful knitted hat as she cuddled up to her grandfather. "So, they're on the yacht, are they?"

"Yes." The woman looked surprised. "How did you know?"

"She's the only vessel we're expecting." Brynjar turned to the younger man. "You waiting for someone too?"

The man nodded and struggled to his feet. He hobbled over, seeming grateful to be included. "My mate's the engineer. I'm giving him a lift home. Though if I'd known how cold it was I'd have let him take a taxi." He pulled his black woolly hat down over his ears.

"He'll certainly owe you big time." Brynjar caught sight of the doors of the customs van opening, and glanced out to sea. "Well, looks as if you won't have to wait much longer." A handsome white prow appeared at the harbor mouth. The stories he'd heard about the yacht had been no exaggeration. Once the entire vessel had come into view, it didn't take an expert to recognize that she was quite out of the ordinary, at least by Icelandic standards. "Wow." The exclamation was inadvertent and he was glad the customs men weren't there to hear it. The boat rose almost three levels above the waterline, and as far as he could tell she had at least four decks. He had seen bigger yachts, but not often. Her lines were much sleeker, too, than the usual craft that called in here, evidently designed for more exotic purposes than mooring in Reykjavík harbor or braving northern waters; rather, she evoked visions of turquoise seas in balmier climes. "She's a beauty," he murmured, but then he leaned forward and frowned. Anyone would have thought the skipper was drunk; the yacht seemed to be heading perilously close to the harbor wall, moving much too fast. Before he could say another word there was a rending screech. It continued for a long moment, before tailing off.

"What the hell . . .?" The young man on crutches was staring aghast. He sagged toward the harbor wall for a moment, then straightened up and set off with a clatter. The customs officials had broken into a run, and the old couple's mouths were hanging open.

Brynjar had never seen anything like it in all the years he had worked at the port.

The strangest thing was the lack of any movement on board. No figures were visible behind the large windows of the bridge; no crew members appeared on deck, as one would have expected in the circumstances. Brynjar told the bystanders to stay put, adding hurriedly that he would be back. As he raced away he caught sight of the little girl, her eyes even wider than before, but with sadness now rather than timidity.

By the time he reached the other side of the harbor mouth, the yacht had come to rest against the end of one of the jetties. He was just envisaging a long, taxing night filling in forms when the massive steel hull crunched against the timber. The noise was ear-splitting, but over the din he caught a faint cry from behind him and felt a pang for the people waiting in the knowledge that their family and friends were on board. What on earth could be happening? The customs official had mentioned an equipment failure, but surely even a yacht with engine trouble could be steered better than this? And if not, what was the captain thinking, attempting to bring her in when he could easily have idled outside and radioed for assistance?

The bewilderment on the faces of the three customs men was probably mirrored on his own as they made their way warily along the jetty. "What's going on?" Brynjar grabbed the shoulder of the man bringing up the rear.

"How the hell should I know?" Though the man's reply was curt, his voice sounded shaky. "The crew's probably drunk. Or stoned."

They reached the end of the jetty where it had been splintered by the ship's bows, which were no longer streamlined and glossy but scratched and splintered. The shouts of the customs officials had gone unanswered and their leader was now on the phone, conversing in harsh tones with the police. Breaking off the call, he peered up at the bows looming over them. "I suggest we board her. The police are on their way and there's no reason to wait. I don't like the look of this. Fetch the ladder, Stebbi."

The Stebbi in question didn't look too thrilled, but turned and ran back to the vehicle. Nobody spoke. Every now and then they called out to the crew, but to no avail. Brynjar felt increasingly uneasy about the silence that met their shouts and was relieved when the man returned with the ladder. The eldest, who was evidently in charge, led the boarding party. Brynjar was given the role of steadying the ladder while the other three scrambled on board, and was still standing there alone when the police arrived. He identified himself while the officers shook their heads over the situation. Then one of the customs men appeared and leaned over the rail again, looking even more incredulous than before. "There's nobody on board."

"What?" The police officer who had spoken now prepared to climb the ladder. "Bullshit."

"I'm telling you. There's no one on board. Not a soul."

The policeman paused on the fourth rung, craning his head back to see the customs official's face. "How's that possible?"

"Search me. But there's nobody here. The yacht's deserted."

No one spoke for a moment. Brynjar looked back down the jetty at the old couple, the little girl and the man on crutches standing at the landward end. Unsurprisingly, they had ignored his order to stay put. Realizing that the police hadn't noticed them and were otherwise occupied, he decided to handle the matter himself. He started to walk toward them, picking up speed when he saw they were coming to meet him. Though of all those present they had the most to lose, they had no business approaching the yacht. The police must be allowed to carry out their investigation unhindered. "Don't come any closer, the jetty could give way," he called. This was highly unlikely but it was all he could think of on the spur of the moment.

"What's going on? Why did that man say there was no one on board?" The old woman's voice quavered. "Of course they're on board. Ægir, Lára and the twins. They must be there. They just haven't looked properly."

"Come on." Brynjar didn't know where to take them but plainly they couldn't stay here. "I expect it's a mistake. Let's just stay calm." He wondered if they would all fit into his hut. It would be a squeeze, but at least he could offer them coffee. "I'm sure they're all fine."

The young man met Brynjar's eye. When he spoke his voice shook as badly as the old woman's. "I was supposed to be on board." He was about to say more when he noticed the little girl following his every word. But he couldn't stop himself from adding: "Jesus!"

The old man was staring blankly at the smashed bows yawning mockingly over their heads, and Brynjar had to take hold of his shoulder and physically pull him round. "Come on. Think of the little girl." He jerked his head toward the man's grandchild. "This is no place for her. The main thing is to get her out of here. We'll soon find out what's going on." But he was too late; the damage had been done.

"Mommy dead." The child's pure treble was uncomfortably clear. It was the last thing Brynjar—and doubtless the others—wanted to hear at that moment. "Daddy dead." And it got worse. "Adda dead. Bygga dead." The child sighed and clutched her grandmother's leg. "All dead," she concluded, and began to sob quietly.

Chapter 1

The repairman scratched his neck, his expression a mixture of exasperation and astonishment. "Tell me again exactly how it happened." He tapped a small spanner on the lid of the photocopier. "I can't count how many of these I've dealt with, but this is a new one on me."

Thóra's smile was devoid of amusement. "I know. So you said. Look, can you mend it or not?" She resisted the temptation to hold her nose in spite of the stench rising from the machine. In hindsight it had been an extremely bad idea to hold a staff party in the office but it had never occurred to her that someone might vomit on the glass of the photocopier, then close the lid neatly on the mess. "Maybe it would be best if you took it to your workshop and carried out the repairs there."

"You could have limited the damage by calling me out straight away instead of leaving it over the weekend."

Thóra lost her temper. It was bad enough having to put up with this disgusting smell without enduring a ticking-off from a repairman as well. "I assure you the delay wasn't deliberate." She immediately regretted replying; the longer they stood around talking, the longer it would take him to get on with the job. "Couldn't you just take it away and repair it somewhere else? We can hardly work for the smell."

On entering the office that gray Monday morning they had been met by a foul stench. It was surprising no one had noticed it during the festivities on Friday evening, but perhaps that was some indication of the state everyone had been in, Thóra concluded.

"That would be best for us," she continued. "We can manage without it for a day or two." This was not strictly accurate; it was the only photocopier in the office and the main printer to boot, but right now Thóra was prepared to sacrifice a great deal to be rid of the machine and the accompanying miasma. Not to mention the engineer himself.

"You'll be lucky. It'll take more than a couple of days. I might have to order in new parts and then we could be talking weeks."

"Parts?" Thóra wanted to scream. "Why does it need new parts? There's nothing wrong with the workings. It just needs cleaning."

"That's what you think, sweetheart." The man turned back to the machine and poked at the dried crust with his spanner. "There's no telling what damage the stomach acid may have caused. The vomit has dripped inside, and this is a delicate mechanism."

Thóra mentally reviewed the books, wondering if the firm should simply shell out for a new copier. They had been on a roll recently thanks to the economic downturn, which meant plenty of work for lawyers. Indeed, this had happened while they had been celebrating their success with their staff, who now numbered five in addition to herself and her business partner, Bragi. "How much would a new one cost?" The repairman mentioned a figure that was surely a quote for a share in his company, not a new photocopier. Despite their recent success, she wasn't prepared to splash out on such an expensive piece of equipment simply to avoid a slight inconvenience.

Reading her expression, the engineer came to her rescue. "It would be ridiculous to have to fork out for a whole new machine just because of a little accident like this." He put the spanner back in his toolbox. "If you have home contents insurance, it may well cover the cost of the repairs."

"How do you mean? The photocopier belongs to the office."

"No, that's not what I was suggesting." The man's mouth twitched disapprovingly. "The vomit—you know. Your home insurance might pay for the damage you caused when you . . . you know . . ."

Thóra flushed dark red and folded her arms. "Me? How could you possibly think *I* was responsible for this? It has nothing to do with me." Nothing she had said since showing him the machine had implied that she was in any way responsible. But then again, no one else had owned up and it was unlikely anyone would now.

The engineer seemed surprised. "Really? Then I must have misunderstood. The girl in reception mentioned your name."

Thóra was livid; she might have guessed. Bella. Of course. "Did she, indeed?" She couldn't say any more since there was no point arguing with the engineer. It wasn't his fault he had been misled by her malicious secretary. She plastered on her best smile, smothering a desire to storm out to reception and throttle Bella. "Well, you needn't take any notice of her—she's a bit slow on the uptake. It's not the first time she's gotten the wrong end of the stick, poor thing."

Judging by the man's face, he thought they were both mad. "Right, well, I'd better get on. I'll have the copier picked up later today. I suspect that would be the best solution." He picked up the toolbox and clasped it to his chest, apparently eager to return to other, more conventional jobs. Thóra couldn't blame him.

She escorted him to reception where Bella sat grinning behind her desk. Thóra shot her what she hoped was a meaningful look, but saw no sign of apprehension in the secretary's smirk. "Oh, Bella, I forgot to tell you—the chemist rang earlier. The colostomy bag you ordered has arrived. Size XXL."

The repairman stumbled over the threshold in his haste to leave, almost knocking down an elderly couple who had materialized in the doorway. Flustered, they apologized in unison, then dithered outside the door; either they expected someone else to land in their laps or they were getting cold feet. If Thóra hadn't swooped on them with profuse apologies for the collision, they might well have turned away, using the incident as an excuse to back out. She recognized the look on their faces: she had lost count of the clients who'd worn that expression the first time they walked into the office. It was a combination of surprise at being compelled to seek out a lawyer and fear of having to leave the office, humiliated, when the subject of the fee came up. Ordinary people in extraordinary circumstances.

When the awkwardness occasioned by the repairman's departure had passed, Thóra asked if she could help, moving to block their view of Bella behind the reception desk, in a black T-shirt with a picture of the devil emblazoned over her ample bosom and a coarse English epithet underneath.

"We wondered if we could speak to a lawyer." The man's voice was as colorless as his appearance; it was impossible to tell if he had noticed the foul reek. Both looked around retirement age. The woman was clutching a faux leather handbag, the reddish-brown surface worn through here and there to reveal the white canvas beneath. The man's shirt cuffs were a little frayed where they were visible under his jacket sleeves. "I tried to call but there was no answer. You are open, aren't you?"

Bella seemed to think the phone in reception had been connected so she could spend all day gossiping with her friends, especially if they lived abroad, judging by the bills. At other times she generally left it to ring unanswered so she could go on surfing the Internet in peace. "Yes, yes, we're open. Unfortunately our receptionist is ill, which is why no one answered." At worst this was a white lie, since no one could claim Bella was fit for work, though unfortunately in her case the condition was chronic. "I'm glad you decided to come by anyway. My name's Thóra Gudmundsdóttir and I'm a lawyer. We can have a chat now if you like." As they exchanged greetings, she noted that both had decidedly limp handshakes.

The couple introduced themselves as Margeir Karelsson and Sigrídur Veturlidadóttir. Thóra recognized neither name. On the way to her office she observed their puffy features and although she couldn't detect any alcohol on their breath, their appearance hinted at drinking problems. Still, it was none of her business, at least not at this stage.

Declining coffee, they came straight to the point. "We don't really know why we're here," said Margeir.

"Well, that's not uncommon," Thóra lied, to make them feel better. Generally her clients knew precisely what they expected of her, though their expectations were often far from realistic. "Did someone recommend us to you?"

"Sort of. A friend of ours has a business delivering coffee to offices and he mentioned you. We didn't want to go to one of those big, swanky firms because they're bound to be far too pricey. He thought you'd almost certainly be on the cheap side."

Thóra forced a polite smile. The office clearly hadn't made much of an impression on the coffee delivery man and she would stake her life on Bella's being the main reason. "It's true that our rates are lower than the large legal practices. But won't you begin by telling me what the problem is? Then I can explain what it's in our power to do and perhaps discuss a fee for the service you're after."

The couple stared at her in silence, neither willing to take the initiative. Eventually it fell to the woman, after she had adjusted the handbag in her lap. "Our son has disappeared. Along with his wife and twin daughters. We're at our wits' end and need help with the stuff we simply can't cope with ourselves. We have enough trouble getting through the day as it is and dealing with the basic necessities. Their two-year-old daughter's staying with us . . . ."

They were not alcoholics: the bloodshot eyes and puffy features had a far more tragic cause. "I see." She could guess the context, though in general she paid little attention to the news. For the past two days the media had been full of the unexplained disappearance of the crew and passengers of a yacht that had crashed into the docks in Reykjavík harbor. Among them had been a family, a couple with two daughters. Like the rest of the nation, Thóra had been glued to reports about the baffling case, though her knowledge was limited as little of substance had been released as yet. But she did know that the incident was linked to the resolution committee appointed to wind up the affairs of one of Iceland's failed banks. When the luxury yacht's owner proved unable to pay back the bank loan with which he had purchased it, the committee had repossessed the vessel. As a result the yacht had been on its way from the Continent to Iceland, to be advertised for sale on the international market, but this process would presumably be delayed now by repairs and other matters arising from the dramatic manner of its arrival. Apparently there were no clues as to what had happened to the people on board, or at any rate none had found their way into the media. The disappearance of the seven individuals had shocked the nation to the core, but the case had attracted even more attention since the young Icelandic woman married to the yacht's bankrupt owner was a regular in the gossip columns. To judge by the coverage, the reporters possessed almost no hard facts, but this didn't prevent them from speculating, the most popular theory being that the crew and passengers had been washed overboard in a storm. "Are you the parents of the man from the resolution committee who was supposed to be on board the yacht?"

"Yes." The woman gulped. She looked close to breaking down, but managed to carry on. "You mustn't think we've given up all hope of finding them alive, but it *is* fading. And what little the police can tell us doesn't give us any grounds for optimism."

"No, I don't suppose it does." Thóra wasn't sure if it would be appropriate to offer her condolences when they were still clinging to some hope that the family would turn up safe and sound. "We don't specialize in marine claims at this practice, let alone employ an authorized average adjuster. So if that's what you had in mind, I'm afraid I don't think there's much I can do for you."

The man shook his head. "I don't even know what an average adjuster does."

"They're experts in marine insurance, and can advise on claims arising from marine casualties."

"Oh, no, we don't need anything like that, just general assistance. For example, with writing a letter in English. We're no linguists, so rather than make a hash of it ourselves, we thought it would be better to hire someone who speaks the language and knows the ropes to act for us. We also need help with talking to social services about our granddaughter as we're not in any fit state to argue with the authorities at present."

"Are they trying to take her away?"

"Yes, they are. The only thing stopping them is the uncertainty. You see, her parents entrusted her to us before they went abroad, so there's still a chance we're just looking after her for them. But the state is gearing up to take action and we're afraid they may knock on our door any day now armed with a court order." The man broke off, distressed. "Ægir was our only son. Sigga Dögg is all we have left."

Thóra steepled her fingers on the desk in front of her. There was no easy way to break it to the couple that they probably wouldn't be allowed to keep the child. They were too old, and no doubt too badly placed financially. "I really don't want to upset you, nor do I want to give you any false hope that you'll be allowed to keep your granddaughter in the event that your son and daughter-in-law are dead. The fact is that it's extremely unlikely you'd be granted custody. The law isn't on your side, as the permitted age bracket for family adoptions is very narrow and you fall outside it; I'm afraid I don't know of any cases in which the child protection service has made an exception to this rule." When they opened their mouths to protest, she added hastily: "But now's not the moment to discuss this. Do you live here in Reykjavík?"

"Yes. Just round the corner. We walked here," said Sigrídur. "It's still a bit nippy out, though at least it's sunny."

It was extraordinary the details people felt compelled to share when discussing an uncomfortable subject, as if by this they could avoid the topic. Thóra wasn't about to be sidetracked into talking about the weather. "What about your grandchild? Were your son's family based in Reykjavík too?" This time they merely nodded. "It's relevant to the question of which local authority will decide the case. If you like, I can assist you in trying to gain access, and—if you really think it's in the child's best interests—to obtain full custody. But let me repeat that the latter is highly unlikely. There are countless examples of close relatives being denied custody due to their age—it seems horribly unfair, I know."

Margeir and Sigrídur sat as if turned to stone.

"Could I give you a word of advice, ignoring the legal side for a moment? If I were in your shoes I'd try not to worry about this right now. You've got more than enough on your plates and it's important for the little girl's sake that you bear up. Take it one day at a time."

"Of course." The man looked up. "We're well aware of that."

Naturally they knew far more about grief and shock than she did. "You mentioned a letter in English. What's that about?" Thóra hoped this would prove a less emotive issue.

"Our son and daughter-in-law had a life insurance policy with an overseas company," said Margeir. "He gave the papers to us for safekeeping before they set off on their trip and left instructions about what to do in the event of an accident. From the little we can understand, we need to inform the company immediately in the case of death. So we'd like you to write them a letter explaining what's happened."

Thóra considered: why the hurry? "I wouldn't have thought any notification would have to be sent until the initial inquiry is complete. Your son and daughter-in-law are officially still only missing."

"I know. And I can tell you think we're motivated by greed, since the first thing we've asked about is the insurance money." Margeir met Thóra's gaze unwaveringly and she hoped she had managed to disguise the fact that this was precisely what she had been thinking. "But it's not like that. If we're to have any chance of keeping Sigga Dögg, we'll need the financial security that the insurance money would bring. I have nothing but my pension and Sigrídur works part time in a canteen, so it wouldn't be easy for us to provide for the child. The money would almost certainly improve our bargaining position."

"Did you bring the policy documents with you?"

The woman burrowed in her handbag, pulled out a see-through plastic file stuffed with papers and handed it to Thóra. "These are the originals, so we'd need them back. Could you take a photocopy?"

"Not at present, I'm afraid. Our copier's out of order. Maybe later." Thóra hid her blush by bending over the documents. There were two sets: a life insurance policy in the name of their son, Ægir, and another in the name of their daughter-in-law, Lára. The beneficiary would be Lára in the case of Ægir's death and vice versa, but Ægir's parents were named if the prime beneficiary was unavailable. The sums insured were the same in both policies and Thóra raised her brows when she saw the figures. The couple had insured their lives for a total of two million Euros. It would be perfectly feasible to raise a child on that amount. She cleared her throat. "If you don't mind my asking, how come your son and daughter-in-law are insured for such a large sum? Were they heavily in debt?"

"Isn't everyone?" Sigrídur looked at her husband. "Do you know?"

"No. They have a sizeable mortgage on their house, I think, but I have no idea exactly how much. I doubt it's in negative equity, though. They don't live above their means and it's only a terraced house. But you never know—perhaps all the life cover would go toward paying off the mortgage if it was sold. We're living through strange times."

"You do realize that two million Euros is equivalent to over three hundred million krónur? It's highly unlikely they would owe that much on a modest terrace."

"What?" the couple blurted out as one. Margeir stared at Thóra uncomprehendingly, tilting his head on one side as if this would help. Since his world had been turned upside down, this might well have been a more suitable angle at which to view it. "Did you say three *hundred* million? I'd worked it out at thirty something."

"You missed a zero." Thóra reached for a bulky old calculator and tapped in the numbers, then turned the screen round to show them all the zeros. Perhaps they would leap to their feet and head straight over to one of the big, expensive solicitors. But for the moment these were just numbers on a screen. "It's a substantial sum."

Little of any interest emerged after this bombshell. Still dazed by the news, the couple went through the formalities of instructing her and, in spite of the potential fortune that could land in their laps, Thóra offered them the lowest rate. The money would be better spent on the little girl's upbringing or kept safe in the bank until she was older. Besides, the case promised to be rather interesting and at least she would be free of the smell of sick for a few days. Before they rose to leave, Thóra posed a question that she was not sure they would be able to answer. "You don't happen to know why your son and his wife put you as beneficiaries on their insurance policies? You'd have thought it would be more usual to name their daughters."

The couple exchanged glances before Margeir replied. "It's not really a secret, though it's awkward discussing it with strangers."

"I assure you it won't go any further."

"Lára's younger brother is a real dropout, who's always after money to fund his lifestyle. If the girls came into money, Ægir was afraid he'd hassle them or try to scrounge off them, or even wangle his way into becoming their financial guardian. It might sound far-fetched but that brother of hers is capable of anything—even of cleaning up his act for just long enough to appear reliable. But Ægir knew we could be trusted to look after the money for the girls and that we wouldn't let that bastard manipulate us. Lára's parents are another matter. They let him fleece them, so it's clear they'd never have been suitable."

"I see. That does sound like a sensible precaution." Thóra accompanied them to the door and asked them to get in touch as soon as there was any news. In the meantime, she would investigate the life insurance situation.

While they were standing in reception, two men appeared with the photocopier on a dolly and tried to maneuver it round the corner. The reek was more overpowering than ever. "Maybe you could pop into a shop and take a copy of the insurance documents. Our machine is on its way for repairs, as you can see. I could fetch them tomorrow morning, if that would be convenient."

"Yes, of course," replied Sigrídur. "You have our address and phone number. It would be best to ring ahead, though we're almost always in." The couple said good-bye and made their exit before the photocopier blocked their path. Thóra stood there, preoccupied, until she was jerked back to the present by one of the removal men tapping her on the shoulder.

"You might want this." He handed her a sheet of A4. "It was in the machine." He grinned and winked at her before turning back to assist his colleague. Thóra inspected the piece of paper. Although the image was dark, almost black, there was no question of what the flash had revealed. The culprit had leaned on the machine in the act of retching and inadvertently pressed the button. Thóra peered at the dim, blurry outline: Bella. Of course, who else? She turned round to give her a tongue-lashing but the secretary was nowhere to be seen. She could evidently move fast when required.

Triumphant at acquiring this piece of evidence, Thóra marched back to her office. One thing was certain: when Bella came back she would have to be confronted, but until then Thóra needed to get some work done. Thanks to the yacht affair, though, it would be hard to concentrate on mundane matters. It was all very peculiar and the high life insurance policy did nothing to lessen the mystery. Heavy drops of rain began to rattle against the window and gooseflesh prickled her arms as she tried to imagine what it would feel like to be trapped on a boat in a storm, or to fall overboard and struggle to stay afloat, knowing that help was unlikely to arrive. She hoped the passengers would be found alive, adrift in a lifeboat. If not, the odds were that they had met a sudden, tragic end.

She turned to the computer screen. Her current cases could wait half an hour or so; she wanted to refresh her memory of the yacht incident. As she trawled the Internet, it occurred to Thóra that she had failed to ask the couple a crucial question: why had their son gone on the trip in the first place—and taken his family too? It was still winter; hardly ideal cruising season, even on a luxury vessel. And why had the bank's resolution committee allowed one of its employees to make use of an asset for a family holiday? There must be more to this than met the eye.

Chapter 2

Not for the first time on this trip, Ægir felt he had been born in the wrong place; surely he wasn't meant to go through life bundled up against the cold in Iceland? The weather may have been cool for Lisbon, but it was nothing like the arctic conditions at home and he relished the sensation of walking the streets in light clothes. Underfoot were the white cobblestones from which all the city's pavements seemed to be made. There was something oddly pleasing about negotiating their uneven surfaces, though his wife, Lára, would probably not have agreed as she teetered along in high heels at his side, barely keeping her balance. They were wandering the steep, narrow lanes of the old city center, built long before the invention of the motor car. They were a little lost but the square they were looking for was near the riverfront, so they knew they should be heading downhill. Glancing round, Ægir saw that his daughters were lagging behind.

"Hurry up, girls. We're going to be late. I'm supposed to meet the man in ten minutes."

They picked up speed a little, but ten minutes is a lifetime to eight-year-olds, so they saw no need to rush. As usual it was Arna who decided the twins' pace; she had entered the world first and although the order in which they were born was probably coincidental, Ægir often got the impression that they had worked out their roles in the womb. Arna, daring and extrovert, usually charged ahead, while the comparatively reserved and introverted Bylgja took things more slowly. Where her twin rushed in, she would pause to consider. In appearance, however, they were almost identical; had it not been for Bylgja's glasses, it would have been virtually impossible for strangers to tell them apart. "How many stones are there in this pavement, Daddy?" Bylgja was walking behind her sister, her eyes fixed on the ground.

"I don't know, darling. A million and seven. Something like that." Ægir wished he had never mentioned the number of cobbles when they set out from the hotel. He should have known his daughter would become obsessed with the idea, but it hadn't occurred to him that she would actually try to count them.

"Hey! There it is." Lára pointed down a side street. "There can't be many squares that big in the city."

As if they had been waiting for this moment, the girls broke into a run. They were extraordinarily like their mother: their dark wavy hair, green eyes and prominent front teeth, their build, even their hands were miniature versions of Lára's.

A feeling of melancholy stole up on Ægir, though he couldn't put his finger on the cause; melancholy about what lay ahead, perhaps, in the magnificent square that opened out at the end of the street. It could simply have been the awareness that life was perfect right now, that it couldn't get any better, and from now on it could only go down-hill. He was reluctant to let go of the moment. "Do you think we should do this another time?"

"What?" Lára looked astonished. "What do you mean?"

Ægir was sorry he'd mentioned it. Or was he? "I mean, maybe we should just extend our holiday here and forget about the cruise. They don't really need me and I'm sure the crew problem can be sorted out some other way." A strange note had entered his voice; he didn't know where it had come from. A few minutes ago he had been looking for-ward to the voyage, seeing it as a godsend, but now he felt reluctant to leave dry land. Despite its opulence, the yacht didn't actually have much room on board. Besides, they were well off here, with little restaurants and cafés on every corner and no end to the delights on offer. What would they do with themselves all day on the boat? Play cards? He didn't want to leave this bright city that seemed to radiate light. Everywhere one looked there were vibrant colors to raise the spirits; tiled walls in pastel hues that he couldn't recall having seen anywhere else. It must be good for the soul to live among them. How could anyone be unhappy here? Whereas at sea they would probably spend the entire voyage hanging over the rail, being wretchedly sick. What had he been thinking of, volunteering when he learned that one of the crew had dropped out? Why hadn't he just said no and flown home as planned?

His wife and daughters were staring at him. He thought he detected a hint of understanding in Bylgja's eyes, though her glasses were smeary as usual so he couldn't be sure. She lowered her gaze again and resumed her stone counting. "You mean you don't want to go on the boat, Daddy?" Arna turned up her nose. "I told everyone on Facebook that we're coming home to Iceland by yacht."

As if that alone would be enough to clinch the matter. "No, I didn't really mean it." Perhaps he was simply reluctant to meet the captain. Their telephone conversation the previous day had gotten off to a bad start when Ægir had reacted with consternation to the news that the cost of moving the yacht to Iceland threatened to be much higher than expected. The arrangements were his responsibility. He didn't want to go back to his boss with the information that they would now have to hire a local to replace the missing crew member, which would work out to be far more expensive. He had lost his temper when he heard what level of pay the possible replacements were demanding, but the captain had given as good as he got and Ægir had been forced to accept that people were not exactly queuing up to take a short trip north to the ass end of nowhere. At what point in the conversation he had suggested making up the shortfall himself, he couldn't remember, but he hadn't expected to be taken literally, despite half hoping he would. However, when the captain heard that Ægir held a Pleasure Craft Competency Certificate he had latched onto the idea and dismissed all the other man's attempts to retract. He said it made no difference that Ægir had never sailed outside Nauthólsvík bay in Reykjavík; all they needed was to meet the conditions for the minimum safe manning of the ship; the certificate was irrelevant, as was his lack of experience. After all, he wouldn't be on board in the role of skipper, mate, or engineer, if that's what he thought.

Back when he was working toward his pleasure craft certificate, Ægir had entertained no thoughts of becoming a substitute crew member on a luxury yacht. He had been motivated by an old dream of saving up for a share in a small sailing boat, but this had had to go on the back burner since his and Lára's salaries combined were barely enough to make ends meet. The little money they had managed to put aside had been used to pay for his wife and daughters to accompany him to Lisbon for this impromptu winter holiday. There had been no plans for a sea voyage.

The captain had been rather taken aback when he heard there was a family in tow. But by then Ægir had become fired up by the idea; this might be their only chance to sail the ocean in a luxury yacht, and the voyage would also solve a specific problem that had been troubling him. In his capacity as representative of the new owners, therefore, he had presented the captain with a fait accompli; there was nothing further to discuss.

In the meantime Ægir had told his manager on the board of the resolution committee that he himself would assist in bringing the vessel home. His boss had been so preoccupied when he gave the green light that he had dismissed the financial implications, being long inured to far higher sums. He made it obvious during their brief phone call that other, more urgent matters awaited his attention. It seemed that the only reason he had agreed to speak to Ægir in the first place was to find out if he had succeeded in registering the yacht in the committee's name. He had cut Ægir off in mid-sentence, muttering that he would see him when he got back from Spain. In other words, he didn't even remember which country Ægir had traveled to to collect the yacht, let alone realize that he had agreed to his wife and daughters' going along for the ride.

The memory of his boss's lack of concern over his absence only intensified Ægir's odd sense of trepidation about the voyage. By rights he should be bursting with anticipation like Arna. Father and daughter had both been wild with excitement the night before, whereas Lára and Bylgja's response had been more muted. Lára's main worry had been that she wasn't that strong a swimmer, and of course Bylgja had not revealed what was going on in her mind. Eventually, however, Lára had been infected by their enthusiasm and become the prime mover in organizing the trip. She would be terribly disappointed if it didn't go ahead. He would have to shrug off his apprehension, especially now that he was about to meet the captain face to face. He braced himself. "Well, let's go. The man's waiting." Again his wife and daughters looked at him in surprise over this sudden volte-face, but they followed him without a word.

As they drew near the picturesque square, which Ægir had read was the largest in Europe, they were greeted by a warm gust of wind—a harbinger of spring. Ægir's doubts evaporated. In the distance the innocently calm sea sparkled as if to reassure him that everything would be all right. Indeed, what could go wrong? He smiled to himself: What had gotten into him? It would be an adventure, and he had successfully won round trickier customers than this captain in his time. In fact, it was his reputation as an accomplished mediator that had secured him the job of sorting out the red tape surrounding the yacht. He had spent the last two days going from one Portuguese office to another, settling unpaid harbor fees, obtaining licenses and submitting documents to confirm the transfer of ownership.

On the other side of the river, Christ opened his arms to the city. The statue, magnificent on its lofty pedestal, was a smaller scale version of Rio's famous "Christ the Redeemer." "Look, Daddy. There's Jesus again." Arna pointed to the monument. Bylgja shaded her eyes and contemplated it in silence. She had been very impressed when their mother told them that the city's human and animal inhabitants lived under Christ's protection. Ægir didn't know for sure whether his daughters believed in God, but he assumed so. Despite counting themselves as Christian, neither he nor Lára were practicing or ever discussed religion at home, but his parents were churchgoers and he trusted them to talk over such matters with the girls in a tactful manner. "Why don't we have a Jesus to protect Reykjavík?" Arna tugged at her father's sleeve. "Isn't that silly?"

"Yes, probably," Ægir replied distractedly, scanning the square in search of the café the captain had suggested for their meeting.

Once inside the small establishment his eyes took a moment to adjust to the gloom. The captain, who was sitting alone at a table, rose as they approached. He introduced himself as Thráinn. Ægir noticed how calloused the man's hand was, though the captain kept the handshake as brief as possible without seeming positively rude. Perhaps he was ashamed of his workman's fist.

While Lára was at the bar buying soft drinks for the girls, Thráinn asked: "Is the paperwork sorted?" His voice was as brusque as his handshake. "I'd like to sail this evening if possible. The sooner we leave port, the sooner we'll be home."

"I see no reason to hang about. I've got all the documents that were stipulated. If it turns out something's missing, we'll just have to chance it." Ægir drew his chair closer to the table. One of the steel legs had lost its rubber guard and it screeched across the tiled floor.

"Can you be on board by six?" The captain had yet to meet Ægir's eye. "It's as good a time as any and I'd like to leave while it's still light. It gets dark between seven and eight."

"Fine by me." Ægir tried smiling at the man. This was going to be easier than he'd expected. If Thráinn had been intending to renew his objections, he had evidently changed his mind; perhaps he couldn't bring himself to refuse them passage in the girls' presence. "All we need is to buy some supplies. Apart from that we're ready." When Thráinn didn't respond, Ægir decided to plow on regardless. Lára was being served, which meant that she and the girls would be back any minute. "So you're okay about my wife and girls coming along?"

The man's expression did not alter; his eyes remained fixed on something behind Ægir. "I've told you my opinion. I strongly object to taking kids along on this trip. You never know what they'll get up to. As I made clear on the phone, now that it turns out you're not traveling alone I'd rather have hired a local."

Lára and the girls came over, the twins grinning above their glasses of fizzy orange as they took care not to spill the contents. "I'm aware of that," Ægir assured him, "and we'll keep an eye on them. The girls will be our responsibility. So, it's okay, then?"

The man grunted. "Did I miss something? Do I have any choice?"

"No, not really." Ægir took Bylgja's glass and placed it on the table. Arna put her drink down with less care and a small orange puddle formed around the base. Lára wiped up the mess immediately, as if to demonstrate that they would treat the yacht with respect.

"Will you have room for us, Thráinn?" She gave the captain a charming smile. Ægir hadn't been able to bring himself to tell her about their disagreement. For all she knew, the man was well disposed toward them. "I haven't seen the boat yet but Ægir tells me she's amazing."

"Yes, we should have. There are enough empty cabins, if you can call them cabins. They're more like staterooms. The boys and I are so stuck in our ways that we automatically took the crew quarters, so you'll have several cabins to choose from. No one should have any cause for complaint."

"Are there boys on board?" Arna made a face as she released the straw. The day was still a long way off when the girls would go crazy about the opposite sex.

"Well, they seem like boys to me, but you'll probably think they're grown-up men." To Ægir's relief, the captain winked at Arna. Once they were at sea their little teething troubles would no doubt be forgotten. "They're in their twenties." He winked at Arna again. "And both a bit soft in the head."

"Oh." Arna giggled. "What are their names?"

"One's called Halli—short for Halldór, I guess—and the other's known as Loftur, because he's lofty."

Arna didn't understand this attempt at humor and frowned. "He's joking, darling." Ægir put an arm round her shoulders in case she showed signs of answering back. "Loftur's his proper name, and neither of them is really soft in the head." In fact, he hadn't a clue whether the man was joking. Perhaps the boys *were* idiots, though if so he doubted the committee would have hired them. Thráinn, at any rate, came very highly recommended. He hadn't seen the reference himself as he hadn't been involved in hiring the crew, but the committee would presumably have chosen a crack team for a trip with such a valuable vessel at stake. "How's the man who was injured?"

The captain scowled again. "I don't suppose the stupid bastard's having much fun. Broken his leg, apparently. No doubt during a pub crawl, though his friend Halli denies it. That lot can't be trusted to set foot in a foreign port without getting smashed out of their skulls. He's on his way home now, I hear. And you're taking his place." A sardonic smile accompanied his words. "And bringing an army along for the ride."

"Yup. It's your lucky day." Ægir would have liked to say more but bit his tongue. He didn't want the girls to witness a quarrel, even one disguised as pleasantries.

Bylgja sat in silence, watching the captain. The only sound she made was a quiet slurping as she drank her orangeade. She was a pretty sharp judge of character and Ægir longed to know what she was thinking, but it would have to wait.

Ægir and Lára had assumed they had plenty of time to get ready, but in the event the family turned up at the harbor nearly half an hour later than arranged. As a result there was no time to admire the white yacht from shore, though Lára did remark that she was much larger than she had expected. There was a mad scramble to carry the stores on board, but his wife was too anxious about leaving the girls behind on the docks to be of much use. Neither Thráinn nor the two younger men lifted a finger to help. They lounged against the pilot house, watching the family's activities with suppressed grins. By the time the last box was on board, Ægir was in a muck-sweat and longing to root around in their shopping for a beer. But judging by the face the captain had made when he'd appeared carrying a case of wine, this would not be a good idea. At least, not right away.

"Well, well." Thráinn came over to where Ægir stood panting beside the provisions. His gaze fell again on the wine, which happened to be at the front and therefore embarrassingly conspicuous. "It'll make quite a difference to this job to have passengers along for a pleasure trip. I hope you aren't under the illusion that we're your staff." He nodded toward Halli and Loftur, who were looking on impassively. "I know what I said, but you may have to take the odd watch, so it wouldn't do for you to drink too much."

"Don't worry." Ægir didn't intend to let the man rile him. "I won't overdo it, and we'll cook for ourselves. For you too, if you'd like." He hoped the man's attitude would soften; they had a long voyage ahead of them and however spacious the yacht, it would soon become claustrophobic if there was a poisonous atmosphere. He watched Lára and the twins easing their way down into the boat. The gleaming deck emitted a hollow boom as Arna landed, as if the yacht were nothing but a shell—handsome packaging around an empty space. Ægir knew this wasn't true, but the sound reverberated in his head and he couldn't help thinking that under all the surface gloss the yacht was little more than a tub. But since his own experience of seagoing craft amounted to the battered dinghy on which he had taken his competency certificate and a small boat belonging to his cousin, perhaps he simply didn't know how to appreciate quality.

He helped his wife and daughters on board and was surprised to find Lára's palm sweaty, though the temperature had dropped as evening fell. In contrast, Bylgja's hands felt cold and dry.

"Will you look at this?" Lára drank in her surroundings, grinning from ear to ear. She handed him his briefcase, which had been entrusted to the girls at their request, and kissed him on the cheek. "Wow." Seen up close, the ship appeared even bigger and swankier than she had from the quay, though most of the furnishings and equipment on deck were swathed in white covers and there was not actually much to see. Nevertheless, it was possible to glimpse the shapes of the items under the canvas, which gave an idea of how the deck would usually look.

"This is incredible." Lára went forward and peered under a cover draped over what appeared to be a table and a set of bench seats lining the bows. "Look. We can eat out here." She addressed her words to the girls who were gazing around, wide-eyed. Arna seemed as enthusiastic as her mother but Bylgja's glasses gave her a remote look that was harder for Ægir to fathom. Still, he was used to being unsure what was going on in her head. Her features often wore a stony expression, but for the moment she seemed curious about the amenities on board, which was a good sign. Lára had noticed too and cheerfully began to pull the covers off the furniture. "This is going to be great."

"I don't know if that's a good idea. It'll be cold once we're under way and you won't be doing much sitting or eating outside." Thráinn was standing in the doorway of the pilot house. It was admirable how he managed to suppress the irritation in his voice. "Better leave them be as it's a bit tricky to fix the covers so they don't leak."

Lára glanced round with a blithe smile. "Don't worry, we're a hardy lot. I bet it'll be fun to picnic out here, even if it is chilly." She tugged at the cover with renewed vigor and managed to pull it off to reveal a large oval table.

Ægir thought he had better distract Thráinn before the man made some unguarded comment. Lára could be very unforgiving and was quite capable of bearing a grudge for the rest of the trip. "I'll put it back afterward. The girls can help me." The captain's expression did not change. Ægir looked out over the harbor and beyond to the deep-blue expanse of sea that awaited them. "Is that everything, then?"

"Where are Halli and Loftur? I want to see them." Arna addressed this comment to Thráinn. The boys seemed to have vanished.

"Halli's down in the engine room getting ready for departure and Loftur's giving him a hand." The captain raised his eyes from Arna to meet Ægir's gaze. "The yacht's hardly been moved since the trouble began with the owner, so I had them check the engine even more thoroughly than usual. We don't want to break down in the middle of the ocean now, do we?" The question did not appear to be rhetorical.

"No, I don't suppose we do." A gull took flight from the smooth surface of the sea beside the boat, spreading its long wings to soar lazily over the harbor. Ægir realized he was still clutching his incongruous briefcase, which made it look as if he was about to take himself off to his office and stop getting under the professionals' feet. He was unwilling to put it down, though; the deck was slippery and there was a risk it might slide overboard.

"By the way," said Thráinn, sounding disgruntled, "the Internet doesn't work and neither does the satellite phone. Weren't you supposed to take care of that? At least, I was told you were here to deal with that sort of thing." He glowered at the briefcase as if it were to blame. "Not that it's essential to have it working—but it would be better."

Ægir took his eyes off the gull, realizing to his chagrin that he felt guilty, as if Thráinn were a strict teacher and he had failed to hand in his homework. The briefcase only heightened the impression. "I'm afraid I didn't manage to sort it out. The owner owed the telecom company a fortune and they were reluctant to open a new account for us unless the debt was paid off. They were being completely un-reasonable and would probably have backed down in the end, but I didn't have time to argue. To arrange it for this trip I'd have had to find another service provider and I have to admit that, not knowing the ropes out here, I didn't have a clue."

"You could have asked me. I'd have found out for you." Thráinn glared at Ægir, then at the clock. "Well, too late to worry about that now. We'll be off shortly. You'd better find something to hold on to at first. You'll soon get used to the motion but there's no point taking a tumble." He disappeared into the pilot house.

Ægir hurriedly stowed his briefcase in a safe place amidst the pile of shopping, glad to be rid of it. He rubbed his upper arms: the air was growing colder and his thin sweater provided little warmth. His wife and daughters were sitting on one of the padded benches in the bows. Lára was tentatively stroking Bylgja's hair as the girl snuggled up to her chest, apparently intent on the other yachts moored in a seemingly endless row along the docks, but since he couldn't see her face, her eyes might have been closed behind her smeary glasses. He went over to them and when Lára looked up he kissed her on the brow.

"What do you say, girls? How do you like it?" He ran his eyes over the sailing boats that Bylgja was studying and couldn't help marveling at how much money there was in the world and how unevenly it was distributed. "It won't be like this all the way. We're heading north, so it may get a bit rough."

"This is fantastic." Lára shifted Bylgja's head. As she smiled, tiny wrinkles appeared round her eyes. Ægir found them charming, though to her they were a source of endless grief. She pressed her lips to Bylgja's head and spoke into her hair. "By the time we're out on the ocean we'll have developed our sea legs and the motion will seem like fun." She gave her a smacking kiss.

Ægir put his arms round Arna and they sat in silence, watching the activity on shore. Halli came out on deck and jumped up onto the docks, where he cast off the moorings before hopping back down. Again, the hull emitted a booming echo. He disappeared below and shortly afterward the yacht moved off.

She glided smoothly downriver to the sea. In the evening sunlight the city appeared tranquil, the warm pastel hues of the buildings lovelier than ever. "Aren't you excited, little Miss Speccy?" Ægir took hold of Bylgja's soft chin and turned her face toward him. She met his gaze with a woebegone look.

"Who'll take care of us now, Daddy?" She pointed to the huge Christ monument which was rapidly receding into the distance.

"Jesus, of course. He takes care of everyone, doesn't he? Wherever they are."

"He won't look after us at sea. He only looks after the city."

Ægir smiled. "No, he doesn't. He protects everyone, no matter where they are." Ahead the ocean waited, vast, rough and pitiless. For the first time in his life he wished he were religious, that he believed in something. Who *would* watch over them at sea?

"Hey, are you okay?" Lára reached over and squeezed his shoulder. "You look so sad."

He shook off his sense of foreboding, making an effort to appear happy. "What? Of course. Everything's fine." She didn't seem to believe him, but turned back to the view without comment. He tried to snap out of his gloom; it would be absurd not to make the most of this moment. It would be fine. According to the captain, the voyage was about one thousand six hundred nautical miles, so if all went according to plan they should reach Iceland in five to six days. The weather forecast wasn't bad and there was no reason to believe this would be anything other than an enjoyable experience. The time would pass quickly enough. Besides, what could possibly go wrong?

Chapter 3

Winter refused to relinquish its grip. Spring kept making fleeting appearances only to vanish again almost immediately, the brief thaws merely serving to kindle false hopes and remind people what they were missing. Thóra shivered as she stood down by the harbor, waiting to meet a representative of the bank's resolution committee and look around the yacht. Her thin summer coat provided little protection against the north wind, which succeeded now and then, with admirable persistence, in whipping up drops of moisture from the sea, leaving an unpleasant tang of salt on her lips.

"Oh, why haven't I been to the hairdresser?" Thóra's hair, unusually long for her, kept whipping over her face and plastering itself against the lip-gloss which she now regretted having applied before she got out of the car.

"How should I know?" Bella was coping better with the gale than Thóra. No doubt her khaki army jacket was made of thicker fabric than her boss's coat, and the bulging pockets must have provided good ballast. And her hair was so short that she probably couldn't mess it up if she tried, even with her hands. Only the enormous baubles dangling from her ears rocked to and fro. "When's this bloke coming, anyway?"

"Soon." It was worse than traveling with her daughter and tiny grandson. *Are we there yet?* She should never have given in to Bella's nagging. She was still furious with the secretary about the photocopier, and the fact that Bella couldn't care less only made her angrier. In point of fact, Thóra herself hadn't given in; it was Bragi who had insisted that Bella should be allowed to tag along to see the yacht. Thóra had consented with bad grace, aware that this was his revenge for the previous month when she had persuaded him to take Bella to the district court. Thóra had been expecting an important client and the only ploy she could think of to remove the secretary from reception was to ask her to assist Bragi with his case. According to him, far from helping she had contented herself with sitting beside him, alternately fixing the judge and the counsel for the prosecution with a menacing glare. In spite of this they had won, and Bragi, in his modesty, put it down to Bella's presence, saying that from now on he would always take her along as a mascot when there was a lot riding on a case.

"There's something spooky about that boat. Did you hear about it?" Bella spat in the direction of the yacht, much to Thóra's disgust, but missed her target and the gobbet of saliva floated briefly in the sea before dissolving.

"What do you mean?"

"There's something weird about it. I read it online. Apparently you shouldn't even go on board." No doubt Bella was referring to the sensationalist article Thóra had also skimmed over. The report, if you could call it that, had implied that the ship was under a curse, which had supposedly originated when one of the shipbuilders had had an accident and bled everywhere. From then on the calamities had multiplied during her construction: a welder had lost a hand, an engineer was severely burned, and other such incidents. Just before the yacht was launched the owner of the shipyard had committed suicide, and as if that wasn't enough, on her maiden voyage one of the passengers fell overboard and drowned. There were no sources cited, though, and Thóra regarded the accounts as dubious, to say the least. Even if the stories contained a grain of truth, it was clear that they had subsequently taken on a life of their own; and, understandably, they had affected the sales value of the yacht. When the last owner bought her with a loan from the bank that had now repossessed her, the price had been fifty percent lower than at her launch ten years earlier. By then she had passed through four pairs of hands and as many name changes. The most recent owner, not to be outdone, had rechristened her *Lady K* after his wife, Karítas, which Thóra found a bit tasteless. She hoped the next purchaser would keep up the tradition and change the name. She didn't know Karítas personally but the woman was a regular in the gossip columns thanks to her glamorous lifestyle and penchant for designer clothes. Significantly perhaps, as long as all was going well there had been no hint in the Icelandic media of any curse on the yacht; they had simply lavished praise on her magnificence and high price tag.

"You shouldn't take any notice of half the stuff you read online, Bella. The journalist responsible for that piece was probably just desperate for material because the investigation's not getting anywhere. He must have googled the yacht and found all sorts of nonsense. Why on earth did you come along if you believe that crap?"

"Are you kidding? I came *because* of the curse." Bella studied the vessel, her face unreadable. Thóra shook her head; there was no end to the girl's idiosyncrasies.

A small car pulled up nearby. It was dirty and missing a hubcap. Thóra watched it closely, though she did not for a minute expect it to contain the man from the committee. As the driver's door was flung open, a Coke can tumbled out and was instantly snatched away by the wind. It was still clattering over the tarmac when the driver himself emerged: a smart young man in a suit, who made a startling contrast to the scruffy vehicle. He strolled over to them. "Sorry I'm late. Been waiting long?" Avoiding their eyes, he busied himself with extracting a bunch of keys from his coat pocket.

Thóra's innate courtesy kicked in: "No, not at all. Don't worry about it." What she should have said was that they had nearly died of exposure during the twenty minutes they had been hanging around out here, but it would be better to keep the man sweet. "So you're Fannar?"

The young man nodded. "Wow. This boat is something else. Every time I see her I'm struck by how awesome she is." He put a hand on the rail of the gangplank, swung athletically onto the steps and gestured to them to follow suit. "Come on. See for yourselves." His black coat flapped like a cloak.

Bella scowled as only she knew how, obviously unimpressed by such acrobatics. Thóra, on the other hand, copied his move as if there were nothing to it, then picked her way up the steps and down onto the ship's deck. A heavy thud on the gangplank behind her indicated that Bella was on her way. The deck was larger than Thóra had expected: it occupied two levels, divided by the pilot house. The upper or foredeck extended to the bows, the lower or aft deck to the stern where there were hatches that looked as if they gave access to the sea. In addition to these main decks, there were two smaller platforms on the upper levels, one just large enough to hold a Jacuzzi. The pictures in the papers had failed to do justice to its opulence, and Thóra felt faintly bemused as she surveyed her surroundings. This was a fairy tale vessel, yet somehow the glitziness didn't appeal to her. But then she had no experience of yachts in the circles she moved in, so she couldn't imagine what life on board was like. Her thoughts automatically turned to the missing passengers. Perhaps that was why she wasn't blown away by the boat like Fannar; in Thóra's opinion there were plenty of other things in life that fell into the "awesome" category. If anything, she found the surroundings unsettling; a shiny white setting for pain and misery, like an operating theater. She hadn't a clue why that image should have sprung to mind. Perhaps it was because of the events she was now trying to piece together.

"I'm assuming the police have been over the whole place with a fine-toothed comb." She glanced around her but couldn't see any obvious signs of a recent investigation.

"The police, the Marine Accident Investigation Board, and a representative of ours as well. I was sent to accompany him, so I know my way about." Fannar stuck a key in the lock of a door that presumably led to the pilot house and passenger area. "Enough to realize that nobody knows what the hell happened here and I doubt they'll ever find out. Unless your attempt to solve the mystery for Ægir's parents uncovers something the others overlooked." His grin showed how little confidence he had in that happening.

"Did you know Ægir at all?" Thóra didn't really expect him to say yes. He was so breezily cheerful that it seemed impossible the two men could have been close.

"Yes, of course I did—we worked in the same office. But we weren't involved in the same projects, so I can't say I knew him well. Though well enough to find the whole thing totally bizarre. He wasn't the type you'd expect this to happen to." Fannar made a wry face. "He was a family man, you know. He rarely came out for a drink with us; he was always in a hurry to get home."

Thóra resisted the temptation to point out that there was little correlation between being a responsible family man and suffering an unexplained accident at sea. It seemed inappropriate too to refer to his colleague in the past tense, though she had to admit it was perfectly understandable. "Of course there's still a chance that he and the other people on board will be found alive. It's faint but we can't rule it out."

Fannar gave her a look as if she wasn't quite right in the head. "Maybe," he said skeptically, then added: "Let's hope so. Of course, it would be best for everyone if you could solve the mystery and find them alive."

"Yes. Though I fear the chances are slim." She didn't need Fannar's mocking grin to tell her that the prospect was highly unlikely. Where on earth was she to begin, and what was she actually looking for? Her job was to prove to the overseas insurance company that although their bodies had not been recovered, Ægir and his wife Lára were dead. It was unlikely that the proof would turn up on the yacht, and even if it was there she might easily overlook an important piece of evidence. She knew nothing about boats and the answer to the riddle almost certainly lay in conditions at sea: a storm or a leak, for example.

"If it's any help, the Marine Accident Board were perfectly happy for you to get involved," said Fannar encouragingly, which was an improvement on his earlier derision. "When I went over to fetch the keys, the guy I talked to even said he hoped you'd spot a new angle that the people who deal with this stuff every day might have missed. He doesn't believe this was your standard accident and thinks the trouble with the experts is that they'll try to fit this into a conventional box. He also said that this isn't a unique case—this kind of thing happens fairly frequently but no one ever manages to find an explanation that satisfies everyone. People come up with all kinds of theories but none that are obviously right."

This did little to raise Thóra's morale. Looking round, she saw

Bella picking her way gingerly across the deck toward them. "Did he happen to mention any theories about this incident?"

The key seemed to have jammed in the lock and the young man jiggled it to and fro until finally it turned. "No, and I didn't like to ask. But the opinion going round the office is that they must have freaked out—thought the boat was sinking and flung themselves overboard, thinking it was their only hope. But nobody can imagine what would have made them crack up like that. Sunstroke, maybe."

"Is that plausible?" Thóra peered around. "I doubt people would jump into the sea if there were lifeboats available." She couldn't see them anywhere, though they should still be in place according to the report Fannar had sent that morning. "Have they been removed?"

"No, they're still here. See the container that looks like a barrel lying on its side?" Thóra followed his finger and nodded. "The life raft's inside that. There are four of them. One on each side, this one, and then one in the bows. They haven't been touched, as far as I know. Maybe they panicked and couldn't work out how to launch them. It seems a bit odd, to say the least, that the yacht should have been deliberately designed to disguise the life-saving equipment. I suppose it didn't go with the décor. And perhaps the passengers didn't take the time to study the safety procedures before they left port."

Thóra turned to Bella. "Take some pictures of that barrel, would you? There are three more that you'll find if you do a circuit of the ship. And photograph the instructions that should be displayed near them, and any lifebelts, that kind of thing." The presence of the life rafts on board was the clearest indication that something extraordinary must have happened. Thóra tried to envisage the kind of circumstances that would force her to abandon ship with her children in the knowledge that another child was waiting at home. Her own daughter, Sóley, was a similar age to the twin sisters who had in all likelihood perished with their parents. Her son, Gylfi, was almost twenty but still a child in her eyes, for all that he was a father himself.

She tried to picture herself seizing the two of them by the shoulders, forcing them to the side and urging them to throw themselves into the icy waves with her. No, it didn't make sense. You didn't need much knowledge of the sea to realize that there would be little hope of survival. And she doubted sunstroke would make that much difference.

"Come inside. That's where things really get spectacular." Anyone would have thought Fannar was trying to sell her the yacht. "Check this out. Smarter than any hotel, don't you think?"

Thóra nodded distractedly. Rather than being impressed she was struck by the stale air inside, mingled, she thought, with a faint trace of perfume. "Is there a funny smell in here?"

Fannar sniffed. "Hm, you may be right. Like soap or something. Maybe they've been cleaning in here, though I can't think who would have arranged that without my knowledge." His nostrils flared as he inhaled. "Nope, it's gone. But don't take any notice of me; I haven't got much sense of smell." He was right; the scent was no longer there.

While she recognized that the interior was extremely stylish and finely crafted, Thóra's attention was mainly drawn to the signs of human occupancy. An open paperback lying face down on the table beside an armchair upholstered in black leather; a DVD case and some magazines on a coffee table toward the back of the room. Beside them were a wine glass and an open bottle that had rolled over. The dried-up spillage had stained the glass table-top pink. Items of clothing lay in a heap on a chair, presumably placed there by the police during their search. "Can I touch this? Are the police coming back to conduct any further examinations?" No sooner had she spoken than she noticed the white fingerprint powder coating the surfaces.

"No, they're not coming back; they spent almost an entire day here. You can poke around wherever you like. At least, nobody warned me not to touch anything. It's not as if it's a murder scene. I gather they're treating it as an accident. Or at most, a missing-persons case."

The boat kept up a continual gentle movement and Thóra noticed the wine bottle rocking slightly without moving from its place. From the description of the yacht's collision with the docks one would have expected the bottle to have rolled off the table onto the floor. The police must have replaced it there during their inspection. "Wasn't everything sent flying when the yacht crashed into the jetty?" Two paintings, one of which looked like it might be of Karítas, hung askew on the walls.

"Yes, it certainly was. There was stuff littered all over the place. I saw the pictures taken at the beginning of the investigation and it was a real mess in here." Looking round, he added: "Actually, the yacht's furnishings are designed to resist fairly heavy seas before they start falling over or being knocked off the walls, but it's a different story with the passengers' own belongings."

Thóra ran her gaze around the room. "What happened to the pictures that used to hang here?" The dark wood paneling on two sides bore traces of missing frames. "Might they have fallen off and not been replaced?"

"No, the former owner took them down and had them valued when his money troubles began. The yacht was on the market with all her contents, but this was at the height of the crash and even the people who could afford expensive toys like this weren't in the mood for buying. It didn't help that the boat was mortgaged to the hilt and the bank hadn't agreed to a sales price. The loan didn't cover the pictures, though, so the guy was free to sell them and I gather they went for a small fortune. Apparently they included some serious art. But the sale didn't raise enough cash, so toward the end he must have sold off paintings from his other homes too. It's unbelievable how quickly even a vast fortune like that can vanish into thin air. Must be a traumatic experience."

"No doubt." Thóra may have lacked the imagination to visualize the lives of the super-rich but she had no trouble guessing what it would feel like to lose a fortune. It was easy to grow accustomed to money; quite another matter to lower your standard of living. One didn't have to be rich to know that.

"I took the pictures you wanted." Bella reappeared, her cheeks ruddy. She glanced round, evidently unimpressed. "God, this is tacky. I thought this boat was meant to be classy." She examined the portrait of Karítas. "Look at that bimbo. I went to school with her, she was a total moron."

Thóra couldn't suppress a grin when she saw the indignant expression on Fannar's face. But experience had taught her that it wouldn't pay to allow Bella to make any further comments; she had a tendency to be foul-mouthed, especially when least appropriate, and Fannar didn't seem the type to appreciate it. "Where are the guest quarters? Should we maybe look at them next? Bella, could you take some pictures in here, including the belongings left behind by the passengers?"

Thóra and Fannar descended below decks to the cabin area. As he had pointed out, the bedrooms were more lavishly appointed than in any hotel, at least the type of place Thóra frequented. According to him there were four luxury staterooms, as well as five cabins for the crew and chambermaid, and another adjoining the engine room for the engineer. There had been no maid along on this trip, since it wasn't a conventional cruise, so her cabin hadn't been used. However, two of the staff cabins did show signs of occupancy, and Fannar told her the engineer's quarters had also been slept in. Two of the guestrooms had clearly been used, while the other two had not been touched. Fannar confirmed that the married couple had occupied the master suite; not that Thóra had really needed to ask, since the clothes overflowing from the suitcase on the floor could only have belonged to Lára.

Two identical coloring books and a jumble of wax crayons littered the unmade bed. Picking up the books, Thóra flicked rapidly through them. The girls had managed to color in a fair amount. The first page of each was labeled with their names, Arna in one, Bylgja in the other, and both girls had taken a great deal of trouble over this mark of ownership. From what Thóra could tell, they had each begun with the first picture and progressed in order through the book, and both had finished twelve and embarked on the thirteenth. When the books were compared, it transpired that all the pictures had been colored in almost exactly the same. The thirteenth stood out as neither girl had had time to complete it. It showed a jolly elephant balancing a large ball on his extended trunk, his childish appearance in shocking contrast to the unknown fate of the little girls who had begun to bring him so vividly to life. They had each colored in the ball and half the cloth on the elephant's back.

In one place Bylgja had drawn something in the margin, perhaps while waiting for her sister to catch up. Thóra had trouble working out what the girl had intended to depict; she seemed to have drawn a

ring around a long-haired woman with a gaping mouth and sprawl-
ing limbs. The lines were black but the woman's dress was green and
she was surrounded by blue. Giving free rein to her imagination,
Thóra saw it as a person falling, viewed through a lifebelt. But no
doubt she would have interpreted it quite differently if she had come
across the book in other circumstances. Closing it, she laid it back
on the bed with the other one.

The door of one of the closets stood open, revealing a densely
packed row of dresses. Thóra couldn't resist a closer look, although
the clothes could hardly have belonged to Lára. They were all designer
pieces that probably cost more per garment than Thóra's entire wardrobe. She thought about all the hassle involved in owning clothes like
that; the endless trips to the dry cleaner and constant fear of damag-
ing the expensive fabrics. Indeed, she noticed some stains on the skirt
of one of the dresses; clearly even these exclusive garments were not
immune to accidents. She thanked her lucky stars that she didn't have
to lug around a suitcase full of designer gear, however much she enjoyed looking at it.

Something shiny caught her eye in the murky depths of the closet.
Thóra removed a long dress from its hanger and saw that a pair of
glasses was tangled in the fringe on the hem and hung from the skirt
like an abstract ornament. The lenses appeared intact, but the glasses
looked rather small to have been worn by the boat's former mistress.
"Do you know who these belonged to?" She held up the dress to show
Fannar her discovery.

He shook his head. "Not a clue. Maybe Karítas wore reading
glasses."

"They don't seem quite her style." Thóra inspected the small red
frames. She thought she had better return the dress to its place and
leave the glasses where they were. They couldn't be very important:
people didn't jump ship en masse on account of a lost pair of glasses.
They had probably been dangling there long before the missing family
even came on board. She shut the wardrobe door and continued her
exploration.

Again she came across an empty wine bottle, this time lying on the
floor beside the bed. It appeared that someone had been drinking

during the trip. Apart from that, the contents of the bedroom were very ordinary, at least those that belonged to the missing couple. The interior design was another matter, as imposing and ostentatious as the rest of the ship's furnishings. The dark, polished mahogany gleamed in the glow of the spotlights recessed into the ceiling.

The en-suite bathroom was in chaos, with cosmetics, towels, bathrobes and bars of soap scattered all over the place, presumably as a result of the collision. She made do with peering inside but saw no point in picking her way through the mess just to admire the bathroom suite and mixer taps. The cabin told her nothing except that the couple had been comfortably accommodated on board, at least for most of the time. Personally, however, she wouldn't have chosen to sleep in the bedroom of a woman she knew, if only by repute. It felt uncomfortable, especially when the closets were still full of her clothes and there was a box on the pretty dressing table that could only have belonged to her. Ordinary people like Ægir and Lára did not carry heavy, elegant jewelry cases with them on holiday. But when Thóra took a quick look inside, it turned out that Karítas had filled it with photos, postcards and other mementos of her life and travels rather than valuables. Thóra closed the case again. The former owner's young wife could hardly be implicated in the mystery, and while she may have been a favorite of the tabloids, Thóra did not have the stomach to snoop around in her private affairs. Even so, on her way out of the bedroom she couldn't help staring at the giant mirror that covered most of the wall and picturing Karítas admiring herself in it. This was unfair, given that Thóra had no idea what she was really like, and she resolved to make an effort to be more impartial next time the young woman entered her thoughts.

The two girls had slept in the smallest of the guest cabins, next to their parents. The instant Fannar opened the door they were struck by a pungent smell of strawberries, so sickly sweet that Thóra had to turn away. "A shampoo bottle burst in here," he explained. "I can't imagine why anyone would want their hair to smell like that but maybe it's not as overpowering once it's been rinsed out."

The girls had shared a double bed. Two cuddly toy rabbits lay abandoned amidst the tangle of bedclothes. Thóra was overwhelmed with sadness at the sight. To enhance the poignancy still further, it appeared that the twins had stuck a photo of their little sister on the headboard; a child who would one day grow up to thank her lucky stars that she hadn't been old enough to accompany them on the voyage. Lifting the corner of the picture, Thóra saw that it had been fixed up with blu-tack, which suggested her guess was right. Karítas did not seem the blu-tack type. She picked up a pink Hello Kitty sock and put it on the bed. "God, this is harrowing."

"I know." Fannar sounded sincere. "It would be best if they were found alive. Adrift at sea. Or maybe they've run away to another country."

"Done a bunk?" The possibility hadn't even occurred to Thóra. "Has anyone seriously suggested that?"

Fannar turned pink, obviously regretting having blurted it out. "No, not really. I've heard whispering at the office but it's nothing. Someone was talking crap about Ægir, saying maybe he'd been embezzling funds from the committee and had done a runner. That he'd faked his own death and was living it up abroad."

"Is that likely? I'd have thought you kept strict tabs on the assets the committee repossesses or has at its disposal."

"Of course we do. It's just gossip. Ægir didn't embezzle any money, that's for sure. The management will have carried out a thorough check, and if any misconduct had come to light it would have been all over the office. It would be impossible to hush it up—it would have leaked out somehow."

Thóra looked back at the photo of the little girl on the headboard. "Irrespective of the money, I would stake my life on the fact that they didn't deliberately disappear. People don't leave a child behind—they either take all or none of them. And what about the crew? Is he supposed to have dragged three men into exile with them?"

"It was just a stupid theory, as I said. Firstly, Ægir didn't steal anything and secondly, as you say, it doesn't make sense."

Thóra peered under the bed and, spotting the other sock, felt an impulse to pair them. As she bent down, she took the opportunity to change the subject. She didn't want to discuss the family's tragic fate with a big-mouth like Fannar. "What's the committee going to do with the yacht? Won't the repairs cost a fortune?" The sock was just out of reach, so she had to contort herself still further.

"Yes." From where she was kneeling, Thóra saw Fannar come two steps closer. "The way things have turned out, it would have been better to leave her berthed in Portugal. They'd get a better price for her on the other side of the Atlantic these days, but even so the amount wouldn't be enough to cover the repairs."

"Why do you think you'd get more for her in America than Europe?" Thóra glanced round in search of a pen or some other implement.

"There's a chance her reputation won't follow her over there. Most European brokers know her history and that affects the price. In their eyes what's wrong with her can't be mended. Whereas in the U.S. and Central or South America, she'd have a clean slate."

"I don't suppose this latest incident has helped at all." Having failed to find anything with which to hook the sock, Thóra almost wrenched her arm out of its socket stretching under the bed. She brushed the sock with two fingers. Now all she needed was to reach a tiny bit further and pinch it between them.

"No, that's clear enough. And now that Ægir's not here, the problem's landed on my desk. I should be grateful really, as it represents something of a promotion for me."

Thóra stretched her fingers out in vain. "Did you take over from him, then?" She was now so obsessed by the idea of retrieving the sock that she couldn't give a damn what Fannar thought of her crawling around on the floor. She had to pair those socks and wouldn't leave until she'd succeeded.

"Yes. I'd just finished a sale, so it was perfect timing. At least it'll be interesting. The curse may sound ridiculous to us but sailors are notoriously superstitious and if her reputation carries across the Atlantic, I'm in deep trouble."

At last Thóra got hold of the sock. The muscles in her armpit were burning but she didn't want to lose it again, so she looked under the bed to make sure of her grip.

What she saw caused her to start back so violently that she bashed her head. The pain was excruciating but her attention was distracted by the pounding of her heart, which felt as if it would burst its ventricles. "Christ." She rubbed the sore spot.

"Did you bang your head?" Fannar sounded concerned. "Can I see? Are you bleeding?"

Thóra showed him the back of her head and felt him parting her hair in search of a wound. "What happened?"

"I misjudged the space." She wasn't going to tell him what she thought she'd seen. Especially not now that Bella had appeared in the doorway. No doubt the hallucination was the result of all Fannar and Bella's talk about a curse. That was all. There was no denying that the atmosphere on board was a little creepy, but that was only natural given recent events. Unsolved mysteries were grist to the imagination's mill, she knew that. It had been nothing but her mind playing tricks on her. What else could explain the little feet she thought she'd seen on the other side of the bed, in Hello Kitty socks?

Chapter 4

"I want to stick the picture of Sigga Dögg here. Then we'll see her every time we go to bed and can kiss her good night." Arna held the photo of their sister up to the headboard. "Is that in the middle?"

Lára came over to the foot of the bed. "Yes, that's perfect." She sat down beside her daughters. "Lift it off so I can fix it." She stuck small grayish lumps of blu-tack under the corners and pressed them firmly down. "There." She put the packet of blu-tack back in Bylgja's school bag and closed it. "You must do some homework tomorrow. I promised your teacher you'd keep up while you were on holiday, and this extra cruise is no exception." She leaned back a little to see how the photo looked. Her two-year-old daughter beamed back at them, happy and carefree, sitting on the swing Ægir had installed in the back garden. Gazing as if hypnotized by her little daughter's round face, Lára felt suddenly sad. It was probably the aftereffects of the unsatisfactory phone call to her in-laws, who were looking after the child. She had rung them from on deck just after the yacht left port so they could all say good-bye to Sigga Dögg before they lost reception. But, as was only to be expected, the little girl hadn't grasped what was happening. Now Lára wished she had said more and made a greater effort to help the child understand. She should have told her how much they all loved her and that she should be a good girl. A good person.

Lára shook herself. She was being melodramatic, and besides it was too late to start having regrets now as, according to the captain, they wouldn't have reception again until they were within a few nautical miles of the Icelandic coast. And since Ægir hadn't managed to organize a satellite phone connection on board, there would be no more conversations with Sigga Dögg on this trip.

"Mommy, I've got a tummy ache." Bylgja was lying beside her sister, her glasses perched crookedly on her small nose, looking even paler than usual. Lára only had to compare her with her sister to realize that this was not down to the mood lighting in the cabin.

"You're seasick." Arna gave her sister a disgusted look. "You're going to puke your guts up."

Lára laid her hand on Bylgja's forehead: it was damp. She had no idea if there was a cure for seasickness. They should have read up on it before setting off, but the voyage had been sprung on them with so little notice. Doubtless this would not be the only such problem to arise but it couldn't be helped. Surely the captain must know how to deal with all kinds of contingencies, including nausea? "Just because you feel queasy it doesn't mean you're going to throw up, darling." Bylgja looked relieved at this piece of spurious wisdom. "Now, wait here and I'll bring a wet flannel to put on your forehead. Maybe you should drink a little Coke too. It can help when you're feeling sick."

"No, thanks." Bylgja grimaced; she didn't like the idea of swallowing anything. "My tummy feels strange." She met her mother's eyes imploringly. "I don't want to puke my guts up."

"No one likes being sick, darling. If you stay lying down, I'm sure it won't happen." She fetched a flannel from the bathroom, grabbing the small bin just in case. She wasn't feeling too well herself; the drone of the engine and the rolling of the ship caused a sensation not unlike breathing in cigarette smoke when one had a hangover.

"Bylgja thinks we're going to sink." Arna's voice held the aggrieved note that both resorted to when complaining about each other to their parents, though, to be fair, Arna did this rarely and Bylgja almost never.

Lára was aware that her smile failed to reach her eyes. She too had been assailed by a vague sense of unease. It was only natural, given that this was her first time at sea apart from a few ferry trips to the Westman Islands. Their surroundings were unfamiliar; she had swapped the security of dry land for life on shipboard. There would

be no going to a hospital if anyone fell ill out here. No dentist if they
developed a toothache. And no shop to run out to if they realized
they'd forgotten something. But that wasn't the worst; the worst
was the seemingly infinite vastness of the Atlantic. Lára had often
seen maps of the world that showed the size of the oceans relative to
the landmass, but representations like that simply could not do justice to the huge flat expanse that now confronted them on all sides. Sea,
sea, endless sea. They had better notice if someone fell overboard, or
that person wouldn't have a snowball's chance in hell of being rescued. "Of course we're not going to sink. Nothing can happen to a
boat like this." Seeing that the girls were unconvinced, she added: "I
asked Captain Thráinn and he said this boat is unsinkable. So you
needn't worry—about anything." That seemed to work. She wished
she believed her own words.

Bylgja closed her eyes behind her wonky glasses and lay back on
the pillow. Arna darted her a rather resentful look, fiddling with the
Snakes and Ladders game she had been hoping to play before lights
out. "Read your book, darling. Bylgja needs to rest now but she'll
be fine in the morning." Lára lifted the glasses gently from Bylgja's
face and placed them on the bedside table.

"What about you? Won't you play?" Arna already knew the
answer: Lára had many excellent qualities as a parent but playing
games with her daughters was not one of them.

"No, darling. I'm going to see Daddy for a while, but we'll come
down and check on you before you go to sleep." She kissed them both
on the cheek, adding to Arna in an undertone: "Come and find us at
once if Bylgja starts throwing up. We'll be on deck." From the doorway, she blew them each a kiss, then added a third, directed at the
picture of Sigga Dögg. The toddler stared back at her from the glossy
paper with lifeless eyes, her fat fingers clasped firmly around the ropes
of the swing.

"Do you know anything about seasickness?" Lára flopped down beside Ægir on the padded bench on the foredeck. He had opened a
bottle of red wine and rustled up two glasses. "I think Bylgja's suf-

fering. Or heading that way." She ran her hands through her hair and sighed. "You can pour me a little wine—or a lot, actually. I'm feeling a bit woozy myself but it can't hurt."

Ægir half-filled their glasses, as they had learned on the wine course Lára had given him as a birthday present. "All I know is that there's no cure, except to get some fresh air, I think, and stay on deck." He couldn't remember where he had learned this, as there had been no mention of seasickness on his sailing course. He sipped his wine. "God, that's good. We chose well there." He looked forward to being able to allow himself such luxuries more often; most of their money worries were now over and the prospect of a comfortable future lay ahead. Growing older wasn't as bad as people said.

Lára followed his example, but took a much larger gulp. "Should we fetch her? She could lie here beside us. She was asleep, though, or just dropping off, so maybe it's not such a good idea." She replaced her glass on the table. It had a wide bowl and an unusually long stem; presumably not cheap—probably ludicrously expensive. "Maybe I should ask Thráinn's advice?"

"Oh, no." Ægir put his arm round her. "Leave him be for now. He might want to join us and I can't face having to deal with him at the moment. Let's just enjoy being alone together."

It was very dark; next to nothing could be seen beyond the rail. The night might have been concealing anything; they could have been on shore were it not for the slapping of the waves and the soothing pitching of the yacht. Lára averted her gaze from the blackness and concentrated on Ægir's dimly lit face. "Bylgja's afraid the yacht's going to sink." She tried to laugh as if it were funny but could hear how fake it sounded. "I told her there was no chance. I am right, aren't I?"

"Of course you are." Ægir ran a finger down the stem of his glass, making it squeak. "I mean, there are circumstances in which the yacht could founder, but we're talking major storms or collisions with other ships, that kind of thing." He realized this was not what Lára wanted to hear. "But there's no likelihood of that on this voyage. None at all."

Lára was reluctant to pursue the subject. She didn't want to look out into the encroaching darkness either, to be reminded of how alone and abandoned they were. It would have been different if she could have hoped to see the lights of other ships or stars twinkling between the clouds. They had seen any number of larger and smaller vessels as they left the coast of Portugal, but the further they had traveled from land, the fewer other ships they had seen, until at last they might have been alone in the world. "I'd have preferred to sit on the aft deck." She glanced up at the large windows of the pilot house. "It makes me so uncomfortable to think of those three up there spying on us."

"They're not." Ægir turned to look at the pilot house, which was on the level above them. "Take a look. There's no one there. I think Thráinn's gone to bed and Loftur's reading in the saloon, so Halli must be manning the bridge alone and it's not as if he has to stand at the helm, staring ahead. It's all more or less automatic."

No sooner had Ægir turned away from the bridge than Halli's dyed thatch of hair appeared. Lára couldn't discern his face properly but she could tell that he was watching them. "He's looking our way." She murmured the words as if afraid he could lip-read. "What on earth's the matter with him?"

"Stop it. He can't even see us. He's inside a brightly lit room and we're outside in the dark. Just because we can see him doesn't mean he can see us." Nevertheless Ægir blew out the tea light in the little candleholder he had found in the galley. "There, now it's impossible for him to watch us. I can scarcely make you out and you're right beside me."

Although what Ægir said sounded sensible, Lára could have sworn that Halli was peering at them. "He makes me uneasy somehow. I was trying to catch his attention earlier but he pretended not to notice and didn't even look round. He never speaks either, just stares when he thinks we're not looking. He does it to the girls, too, and it makes my flesh crawl. His expression's so sinister—as if he'd like to throw them overboard."

"Stop it, will you? He's just an ordinary bloke who doesn't have much time for kids. I've yet to meet a young man who dotes on them if he doesn't have children himself. You'd be more worried if he was over keen."

Lára bit her lip but couldn't tear her eyes away from that white head. She didn't relax until he had vanished from the window. Then she took another sip of wine and leaned against Ægir. "What do you think it's like to be stinking rich and live like this all the time?"

"All right, I suppose. Though it must be stressful, too. Imagine what the guy who owns this boat felt like when his world came crashing down. It must have been horrendous. Especially as he must have been aware that no one manages to amass a second fortune like that."

"Did he lose the lot?"

"I doubt it. It's unbelievable how many smokescreens people like him manage to erect when it comes to money. Stashing it away here and there, using all kinds of shell companies and front men, so it's impossible to get to the bottom of it all. What we have managed to recover from his bankruptcy suggests that he's got a fortune hidden away somewhere. Probably in so many different places he's lost count." The yacht gave a sudden lurch before resuming her former lazy rocking. Ægir had to grab the back of the bench to keep his balance. "Apparently his wife Karítas possessed some information that she was prepared to share with us on condition that she got to keep what was registered in her name. But she changed her mind—no doubt in return for a substantial bribe. Or maybe she had nothing to gain because it turned out that the whole lot was in her husband's name after all."

"She changed her mind?" Lára loosened her grip on the table edge. "How terribly convenient."

"You're telling me." Ægir took another sip of wine, with a look of satisfaction that even the darkness could not hide. "In spite of that we've managed to seize a considerable proportion of the guy's assets. Like this yacht, for example. At least he can't cruise around in luxury any more, with staff to cater to his every need. But I bet he's still pretty comfortably off. Our life is a hard grind by comparison."

"Her dresses are still hanging in the closets in our cabin. I was going to unpack but there's no room to put anything away. Do you think she minded losing all those clothes? I'd have taken them with me."

Ægir drained his glass, leaving only the dregs behind. "The yacht was sealed off without warning. They didn't have time to remove any belongings. Anyhow, I bet she's got so many clothes she wouldn't even notice. Having said that, Thráinn did mention that the seal had been broken when he came on board, though nothing appeared to have been taken. The lock was intact, so whoever meant to break in probably gave up. Maybe he was disturbed or lost his nerve."

"Unless it was Karítas or her husband. Someone with a key." Lára took another mouthful of wine, shooting a quick glance at the bridge: Halli was nowhere to be seen. "Though come to think of it, it can hardly have been her or she'd have taken the clothes."

"I doubt Karítas needs those dresses. I'm sure she's perfectly well off."

"Just because you're rich doesn't mean you don't have clothes that you're really attached to and want to wear again and again. Especially evening dresses like those." Reaching for the bottle, she took Ægir's glass and refilled it almost up to the brim; she had learned less than him on the wine course. "Do you think I'd fit into them? If I get bored perhaps I could amuse myself by trying them on."

"I think you should leave them alone." Ægir took the glass back, looking a little disapproving when he saw how full it was. "I'd rather we didn't touch more than necessary." He smiled. "Just the essentials, like these glasses. We couldn't have drunk fine wine like this out of coffee mugs."

A loud knocking sounded above their heads, causing Lára to jump so badly that she slopped her wine and nearly swept everything off the table. "What on earth was that?" Looking up, she saw Halli standing at the window, banging on the glass. He beckoned to them.

Ægir raised his brows. "What do you suppose he wants?"

"There's only one way to find out." Lára stood up. "Bring the bottle; it's getting chilly out here. Let's go inside after we've spoken to him. We'll be more comfortable in the saloon. And we won't have to put up with his spying any more."

"Have you forgotten that Loftur's lying on the sofa in there?"

"We'll scare him away by coming over all lovey-dovey." She grinned and gave him a long hard kiss on his unshaven jaw, until she was forced to do a sudden sidestep by the plunging of the yacht. Apparently the sea didn't approve of such intimacy.

"I told you we'd be on deck, darling. Why didn't you go there?" Lára tucked Arna into bed and picked up her book from the floor, where it must have fallen when the little girl nodded off.

"I couldn't remember if you said you'd be at the front or the back, and I didn't dare go out and end up on the wrong side. I thought I'd better find the captain and ask him for help. But he wasn't there, only Halli."

"That was a good idea." Ægir stroked the hair from Bylgja's brow and felt it with his hand. "She hasn't got a temperature; she just feels a bit clammy. Maybe it's passed. She hasn't thrown up, has she, Arna?"

The other girl shook her head. "She was asleep. I was going to wake her up but I was afraid she'd puke all over me. That's why I ran—I didn't want to leave her alone here too long. Not with that woman."

"Woman?" Lára felt Arna's forehead, to check if she too was coming down with a fever. Perhaps both girls had caught a bug during the holiday. "What woman?"

"The woman in my dream. She wanted to hurt me. And Bylgja."

"You were dreaming. There's only one woman on board, and that's me. You don't think I'd hurt you?" She pressed the tip of her daughter's nose. "Never in a million years."

Her words had no effect. "She doesn't want us here. Maybe it's her bed." Arna sat up. "Can we sleep with you?"

"Hey, it was just a dream, dear. No one owns this bed, except maybe the people at Daddy's office. And they don't mind in the least if you sleep here. No mysterious woman has any say in the matter. If you close your eyes, I'll sit here beside you until you go to sleep. But the moment you open them, I'm going. Deal?"

Arna agreed and after turning out the light Lára sat down beside her. Ægir tiptoed over to the door, bracing himself against the wall in the steadily increasing swell. As he pulled the door quietly behind him, Lára opened her mouth to ask him to leave it open a crack but changed her mind; the door would only bang if it was left ajar. She put her arm round her daughter and before long the girl's breathing was deep and regular. Unable to bring herself to get up straight away, she stayed on, listening to the girls sleep. When she finally eased herself carefully to her feet, Arna stirred, frowning as if she was having another nightmare. Lára considered staying with her but then Arna quietened down again, and Ægir was waiting above. Pausing in the doorway, she wrinkled her nose. She smelt a waft of strong, heavy perfume that seemed to emanate from the corridor. But that couldn't be right, because when she stepped out of the cabin to sniff the air, the scent seemed fainter outside. And when she checked again it had gone.

She shrugged, closed the door to the girls' cabin and made her way out along the narrow, dimly lit corridor.

Chapter 5

There were few things Thóra found more tedious than cooking. In this she differed from most of her friends and their husbands, who seemed to have become increasingly interested in food over the years. One had even bought tickets for Thóra and her partner, Matthew, to attend a cookery course as a Christmas present and seemed very pleased with her own idea. They had dutifully attended the course, which was called Middle Eastern Magic, but the instructor had failed to infect them with any enthusiasm. By the end of the classes they were as clueless as they had been at the beginning, apart from having learned how to prepare a decent couscous. This proved rather embarrassing when the friend in question demanded to be invited to dinner to taste the fruits of her gift. As the only Middle Eastern restaurants in Reykjavík were takeaway kebab shops, they decided to buy an Indian meal, shove it in a pan and serve it with couscous. Then they looked up an appropriately Arabic name for the dish on the Internet. Their friends were impressed, especially with the Al-Jazeera Chicken. Thóra's only worry was that their deception had succeeded too well and that she and Matthew would receive another cookery course for Christmas next year.

The course had made no more difference than the countless recipe books and magazines they had acquired over the years. Thóra was quite simply a hopeless cook. As a result, the other members of the household—apart from her grandson, Orri—rallied around the task of feeding the family. Sadly, these attempts proved no more successful than her own. Sóley showed the most promise but lacked the patience to cook proper meals. She was mainly into baking muffins, but while the family's eating habits left a lot to be desired they had not yet sunk so low as to eat cake for supper. Besides, the kitchen always looked like a bombsite after Sóley had been at work. Thóra's son, Gylfi, and his girlfriend, Sigga, had reached an age when they would soon be setting up home together, so they should have shown more interest in cooking, but no such luck. They were also the fussiest eaters, vegetarians one minute, on a raw food diet the next, if not both at the same time, and everyone had long ago given up trying to remember which craze they were following—they couldn't always remember themselves. This evening they had taken Orri and their faddy eating habits to supper with Sigga's parents, so it shouldn't have been difficult to decide what to make. If only the fridge hadn't been empty.

"How about Chinese?" Thóra closed the fridge. "We can order or have noodles."

"Takeaway." Matthew started clearing away the knives and forks he had just laid on the table. They had become pretty adept at using chopsticks by now. "I can't eat any more pot noodles. Not this year, anyway."

"I could bake something." Sóley looked up from the homework she was trying to finish before evening. She was supposed to hand in a page on occupations in India for her social studies class, but the sheet of paper in front of her was blank apart from drawings of elephants, tigers and snakes which had at best a tenuous connection to the topic.

"No, really, there's no need." When he saw Sóley's hurt expression, Matthew clearly regretted having jumped in so quickly. "All I meant is that you need to finish your homework and that's more important than supper right now. You can do some baking on the weekend if you're still in the mood. How about chocolate licorice whips?" He knew these were her proudest achievement, though her pride was not necessarily justified by the outcome. "How would you like to take a little break and come with me to fetch the food?"

Sóley was quick to push aside her zoologically inclined essay on Indian society, and Thóra felt a warm glow of pleasure at how well these two got on. Gylfi and Matthew were friendly enough but they weren't especially close. If her children had rejected Matthew, it would have been the end of her relationship with him, at least in its current form; the happiness of Sóley, Gylfi and now Orri took precedence. That's just the way it was and so far no one had had any cause for complaint, least of all Matthew who entirely respected her priorities. Thóra tried to ensure that their life did not entirely revolve around the younger generation, and she and Matthew were quite good at making private time for themselves, but this had become harder since her ex-husband had taken it into his head to start working alternate months in Norway. She made an effort to be understanding about this since Hannes had been forced to start again after their divorce, and had been saddled with a hefty mortgage as a result of buying in the middle of the housing bubble. Working abroad meant he could pay off some of his debts. The upshot was that the children now spent half as many weekends as before with their father, but this was compensated for by the fact that her parents had moved out at long last. They had finally managed to solve their money troubles by selling their timeshare in Spain, which they had had little use for anyway. With the departure of Thóra's mother, however, the family had lost the cook they so badly needed.

After Sóley and Matthew had left to fetch the takeaway, Thóra pulled out the file on the yacht. She was filled with a profound desire to solve the mystery, but knew she was unlikely to succeed. The vessel itself had fired up her imagination as much as the unknown fate of those on board. She was fairly down-to-earth by nature, yet she simply could not shake off the image of those little pale legs. It wasn't that she believed there had been anything supernatural about the vision; on the contrary, she was sure it had been conjured up by her own brain. The passengers may have vanished but the signs of their existence were so ubiquitous on board that it had been easy for her mind to fill in the gaps.

Before Fannar had said good-bye on the dockside, he'd told her Ægir's boss would do everything in his power to help solve the case. The man felt partly responsible for what had happened since it had been he who sent Ægir on the fateful voyage. Thóra had asked Fannar to find out if his office had any documents that she could have copies of, in addition to the damage report compiled by the committee following the yacht's arrival in Reykjavík. He had promised to look into the matter but Thóra hadn't really expected to hear any more. Yet she had hardly sat down at her desk before her cell phone rang: Fannar, calling to say they were making up a file for her. She had collected it from the committee offices on her way home.

The sheaf of documents that she pulled out of the envelope was not particularly thick. There were several pages on top containing lists of those who had crewed the yacht at various times. They were in French, so had presumably been acquired from abroad. This figured, since the yacht had been registered in Monaco until the committee repossessed it in Lisbon. As she perused the lists, Thóra could tell from their names that the crew members were of various nationalities, few of them French. She paused at one that had been highlighted: *Halldór Thorsteinsson*. An Icelander. Clearly she needed to talk to this man.

The Halldór in question had only worked on the boat for three months. It was a short spell of duty compared to others on the list, but he must be well acquainted with the yacht nonetheless. Of course, there was always the possibility that he had either resigned or been sacked, which would be unfortunate since it might affect his testimony if he held a grudge against the former owner or other crew members. Still, he would almost certainly be able to fill her in about safety procedures, life-saving equipment and any other aspects she needed to have straight before she laid the matter before the insurance company. Any gaps in her report would lead to delays; it was a common tactic by insurance companies to reply by questioning a particular item and then, when that query had been answered, to flag up another, and so forth. This could hold up proceedings by months, so it was vital to present a well-argued case from the beginning.

Following the crew lists she found the yacht's registration certificate, which confirmed what Thóra already knew, that Karítas and her husband had not been the first owners and that they were responsible for christening her *Lady K*. The name still struck Thóra as crass. She wondered if she would have done the same, but *Lady T* sounded even more absurd. Turning back to the crew lists, she noticed that Halldór had worked on the vessel while it was owned by Karítas and her husband. It was probably irrelevant, but she made a mental note.

Her attention was also caught by an inventory of the yacht's furnishings, if that was the correct term for ships' contents. The letterhead on the document belonged to an overseas ship broker who apparently specialized in the sale of maritime vessels, and the value of all the items was noted over many pages. The document was dated a little over four years ago, so it would not necessarily be representative of the yacht's present contents. Thóra raised an eyebrow as she read. Never had she imagined that everyday objects could be so expensive: a sofa that cost more than her car; knives that were worth more than the entire contents of her own kitchen, including the table and chairs. The inventory also contained gadgets, instruments and other equipment associated with sea travel, such as Jet Skis, wetsuits and fishing gear. She had noticed the Jet Skis, in a storeroom with a hatch that opened to give access to the sea, but she didn't remember any diving suits or fishing rods. This might not mean anything, as they had made a whistle-stop tour of numerous storerooms and cupboards, and there must be plenty she hadn't seen. Thóra supposed it was always possible that somebody had walked off with the stuff, since it was certainly valuable enough to tempt a thief. She hadn't been particularly surprised to discover what the angling gear was worth because Matthew had recently developed an interest in salmon fishing and the price of the equipment he coveted had made her eyes water. She hoped to God he would steer clear of sailing.

The contents of the next page brought her up short. It was blank apart from one line: the name Karítas Karlsdóttir, a telephone number and an e-mail address. She frowned, surprised that this information should have been included, and wondered if it was by accident or design. Reaching for the phone, she tried the number—but it had been disconnected. Similarly, when she tried to send an e-mail it bounced straight back. The details must have been included in error.

She was still thoughtfully contemplating the pile of documents when Matthew and Sóley got home with the food. Throughout supper her mind kept returning to the yacht and the papers and she responded automatically to Sóley's comments without taking in what she said.

After supper, Thóra resumed her reading. She was longing to discuss the case with Matthew out of earshot of Sóley, but had to wait until they left the table and her daughter returned to her homework. For all she knew the little girl might be turned off boats for life if she got wind of the yacht affair. Ever since seeing a news item about a flight attendant who saved a child from choking on a gobstopper, Sóley had refused to touch boiled sweets—and that had been three years ago. "What do you know about boats, Matthew?"

"Next to nothing. They're used to catch fish, carry freight and travel by sea or on inland waterways." He smiled. "Any help?"

"Not exactly."

"Why do you ask?"

"I've taken on a case connected to the mystery yacht. I was allowed on board this morning, and the atmosphere was really eerie. Maybe it was just because I'm unused to boats in general, let alone luxury yachts. But that's not the main point. The case involves a life insurance claim and it's bound to be trickier to pursue than it would be for a death in normal circumstances."

"I imagine you'd need to know quite a bit about boats."

"Maybe, maybe not." Thóra fetched her laptop. As it was early in the month, Gylfi had not yet managed to use up all their foreign download credit, which meant they were not restricted to browsing Icelandic pages. "Do you think it's common for people to vanish from a boat and never be seen again?"

Matthew shrugged. "It's not unheard of but I've no idea how common it is. I remember one story that had a big impact on me as a boy, though I can't vouch for it. It was about a ghost ship that went on sailing the seas long after her crew disappeared. I can't remember her name, though. Why don't you try searching online? If nothing comes up, presumably that'll mean this type of incident is unusual or a one-off. Though I don't really see how that'll help you."

"I'm just curious. I can't get that creepy atmosphere out of my mind." She paused before adding: "I can't really describe it but I felt as if the people were still there, as if they didn't realize they were supposed to have vanished. Silly, isn't it?"

"Yes and no." Matthew didn't smile, clearly not finding the idea all that ludicrous. "There can be an odd feeling associated with a place where someone has recently died. In my experience it can muddle your thoughts and give you odd thoughts. When I visited a murder scene for the first time, in the police, I caught myself hearing nonexistent noises and thinking someone was touching me. It was only because I was new to the horror of it all."

Thóra felt comforted. It sounded sensible; although she had seen a few scary things—including dead bodies—in her line of work, she was hardly an old hand and her mind simply hadn't been able to process the unfamiliar situation in a rational manner. In other words, she wasn't going mad—or hopefully not. It was a pity she couldn't ask Bella if she'd had a similar experience, but that was out of the question: Thóra was not prepared to expose any weakness that Bella might exploit.

She searched for information about Karítas's foreign husband, Gulam. It was unlikely to help, but she wanted to know more about the background to the case. The Icelandic papers had carried reports of his bankruptcy because of his links to the local banking crisis, but business news bored her so she had only skimmed the headlines at the time. When she tapped his name into the search engine, remarkably few results came up considering the scope of his activities. Presumably he was keen to keep a low profile. It seemed he was a major investor in other people's companies rather than an empire-builder on his own account, and this allowed him to operate largely under the radar.

The articles that did come up divided roughly into three categories: Icelandic schadenfreude over his financial collapse, passing references to his investments in international business news items, and finally foreign gossip columns about the jet set in which he featured more or less as an extra. Thanks to Karítas's presence, these stories tended to find their way into the Icelandic news, where the couple's importance was inevitably exaggerated. Icelanders were fascinated by any of their countrymen who moved in exalted circles abroad, especially if they had done well for themselves, and that was certainly true of this young woman who seemed, moreover, to enjoy basking in the limelight.

It was this third category that drew Thóra's attention most; she had felt a certain curiosity about the woman since Karítas had indirectly entered her life. These articles made no mention of the stock market or share prices, focusing instead on gala dinners and glitzy parties, largely from the point of view of which designer labels the guests were wearing. Gulam was not a big enough fish to earn the couple a starring role; when they appeared in a picture it was almost invariably as a filler at the end of a series of photos. Gulam never appeared without Karítas on his arm and Thóra suspected that without her the photos wouldn't have been published at all. His Icelandic wife was unusually glamorous, but where she could easily have been a model with her statuesque physique, her husband was short and squat with a fleshy face and a comb-over that must have been the first thing she saw every time she looked down at him. Nevertheless, one would have thought he was a fairy tale prince by the way she clung to him in all the pictures; her slender arm, in a succession of expensive dresses, crooked round his plump, black-sleeved elbow. The contrast was striking: where he was pallid and invariably dressed like an undertaker, she was perma-tanned and clothed in vibrant hues; where he was balding, she had a long, thick mane of blond hair, generally worn loose. His jowls were flabby, her cheekbones high. He shunned all ornament, she was adorned with jewels on every available part of her body. Where his teeth were small and not particularly well cared for, hers were large, straight and a brilliant white, as if ordered from a catalog. It was hardly surprising that she was always baring them in a grin for the photographer, while her husband scowled. Their union was a true marriage of opposites.

When it became clear that her trawl through the celebrity news was not throwing up any leads, Thóra abandoned this tack and started searching instead for information about Karítas herself. A stub article in the Icelandic media revealed that she was nearly thirty years younger than her husband and had met him while she was working for a Reykjavík hotel where he had been a guest. Her exact position was not specified, but three months later they were married; he for the third time, she for the first. She had no children from this marriage or any other relationship. Another article claimed that when her husband was threatened with bankruptcy, Karítas had demanded a divorce. Thóra vaguely recalled having seen a headline about this when she was at the supermarket. The divorce can hardly have come out of the blue since it was painfully obvious what had attracted her to her husband in the first place. It was the same old story, and all talk of love at first sight rang rather hollow; strange how Thóra had never heard of any marriages between beautiful young women and penniless older men. Still, what did it matter? People were attracted to different things; as long as the arrangement made both parties happy it didn't do any harm, whatever their motivation. But in this case their happiness had been short-lived: Karítas had sued for divorce after only four years of marriage.

However, further searches indicated that the couple must have sorted out their differences since they had not apparently separated after all. Thóra suspected that the fact there was nothing left in the coffers for Karítas's settlement had played its part, though it was rumored that her husband had concealed a considerable sum from his creditors, including the Icelandic bank's resolution committee. No doubt sticking with him had seemed preferable to going back to her job at the hotel. The narrowness of Iceland's social circle was its main drawback: after featuring in the celebrity gossip columns it can hardly have been a tempting prospect for a young woman to return home so ignominiously. Initial reports that Karítas intended to cooperate with the bank had proved unfounded, but when the media subsequently asked questions, they received few answers. Karítas had been uncontactable when the yacht story broke; in fact, she seemed to have vanished off the face of the earth. A representative of her husband had announced that she was staying in Brazil to avoid the press furor, but her mother, who lived in Iceland, was unable to confirm this.

"Matthew." He was glued to his laptop. "Have you heard any talk at the bank about the couple who owned the yacht? I know the guy didn't do business with you directly, but is there any water-cooler gossip about them? About where Karítas might be living at the moment, or whether she's intending to shed any light on her husband's business arrangements?"

It took Matthew a while to work out what Thóra was talking about. Although he had made great strides in the language, it sometimes took him a moment or two to switch from German to Icelandic mode. "Yes, I've heard things, though nothing worth repeating. The women tend to gossip about her; the men, about him."

"What do they say?"

"Nothing very interesting. He's supposed to have squirrelled away a fortune in assets, which no one's managed to trace despite an exhaustive search, and apparently she doesn't want to come home because she won't be able to flaunt her wealth any more if they have to keep a low profile. The word is that she's afraid of being questioned by the financial authorities or special prosecutor. I don't know how seriously to take that, though. It's probably just speculation."

Thóra considered. "I'm going to try and contact her parents or siblings. They may know how I can get hold of her. I bet she'd be able to provide some useful background on the yacht. Maybe there was a problem the crew weren't aware of when they set out. Karítas and her husband hadn't used the boat for a while before she was confiscated—perhaps because of a fault."

"Or because a boat like that costs millions of krónur a day to run. They've had to tighten their belts in the recession like everyone else." Matthew yawned. "Why on earth would she talk to you, anyway?"

Thóra closed her laptop. "I doubt she'll have the slightest interest in doing so. But it's worth trying." She stretched lazily. "Is her husband a criminal?"

"What do you mean? The kind with a gun or the kind with a credit rating?"

"A gun."

"I doubt it. What makes you think that?"

"I just find it incredibly convenient that she should disappear completely at the time most convenient for her husband. One minute she's on her way home to testify against him; the next, she's vanished. I started wondering if she might actually be dead. Supposing they've bumped her off? It's quite a while since the press last managed to take any pictures of her, though they've been pulling out all the stops over the last few days. Whatever her financial woes, it's unlike her to lie low—she's usually so eager to be seen in the media. So maybe it's all connected. The documents from the resolution committee included a piece of paper with her name and an out-of-date phone number and e-mail address, which started me thinking. Perhaps they're onto something that they can't reveal for reasons of bank confidentiality, and her details were a hint to steer me in the right direction."

"I find that highly unlikely." Matthew looked incredulous. "Just because you're given a piece of paper with a woman's name and contact details, it doesn't mean she's dead. Anyway, you'd be a fool to speak to her family if you do believe she's been murdered. What are you going to do? Ask her relatives to pass on a message, and assume she's dead if you don't hear back?" He smirked. "Not exactly brilliant, is it?"

"No, I didn't mean it like that. It would be enough to meet one close relative for a chat. If it turns out the family hasn't heard from her, then that would support the idea that there's something wrong. After all, it's one thing not to talk to the press, but quite another to leave your loved ones in the dark. If there's any truth in the quotes from her mother in the papers, she doesn't have a clue where Karítas is. On the other hand, it's perfectly possible that they know exactly where she is and will be able to put me in touch with her. Which is what I'm hoping for."

Matthew shook his head, still unconvinced, but at that moment Gylfi and Sigga appeared with Orri asleep in his father's arms. Sigga took the little boy from him and carried him into the bedroom, but Gylfi hovered. It was obvious that he was bursting with news. "Dad rang from Norway."

"Oh?" said Thóra. "How's he?"

"He's had an idea. A brainwave, actually." Gylfi perched on the arm of Thóra's sofa. Recently he had shot up to his full height, though he had yet to fill out. Before she knew it, he would be an adult. "He's met a guy in Norway who works for an oil company and apparently he could sort out a job for me if I wanted."

"A job?" Thóra sat bolt upright. "This summer, you mean?"

"Yes. And winter. It's insanely well paid."

"Just hang on a minute." There were so many questions racing round Thóra's head that she didn't know where to start. "I thought you were going straight to university after you'd finished school. This is a crazy idea, isn't it? And what about Sigga? She's got a year left of sixth form—are she and Orri supposed to go with you or stay behind?"

"Sigga can take her final year by distance learning. And I'd be up for taking a gap year. It would give me time to work out what I really want to study. We'd save some money too. I said the pay was unbelievable, didn't I?" There was no mistaking his elation; he looked ready to go online and buy his ticket right away.

"Wages may be high in Norway, but the cost of living is astronomical. All your money would go to day-to-day expenses. I mean, what do you think it costs to rent a flat there?" Thóra racked her brain for a way of dampening his enthusiasm, of making him wake up to the fact that this was an appalling idea. The last thing she wanted was to lose them to a foreign country, though she had been aware for some time that it would not be long before he, Sigga and Orri moved out to set up their own home. She had even assumed it would happen soon after he started university that autumn, but it had never crossed her mind that they might take Orri to live abroad.

"That's what's so fantastic. Dad's got this big flat, which he only uses every other month. We could share it with him when he's there and the rest of the time we'd have it to ourselves." Gylfi beamed. "It's a brilliant arrangement. And the job's awesome. I'd work for two weeks, then have three weeks off."

Thóra exclaimed: "That can't be right. What kind of job is it anyway?

"On an oil rig. They fly you out there by helicopter." He couldn't stop grinning at the thought.

"I see." She didn't know whether to laugh or cry. Of all her ex's idiotic ideas, this took the biscuit. Gylfi on an oil rig. He had hardly ever left Reykjavík, let alone experienced the sort of conditions he could expect on a floating steel platform in the middle of the Arctic Ocean, or wherever this oil rig happened to be. "You know, Gylfi, this is a terrible idea." She looked to Matthew for support but he didn't say a word, and his face was unreadable. "The reason it's well paid is that it's incredibly dangerous, and anyway you're far too young and inexperienced. The journey alone would be too risky. It's out of the question."

The smile fell from Gylfi's face. "It's not 'out of the question.'" He stood up. "Anyway, it's not up to you. I'm going to put together a CV and send it to Dad to pass on to the guy. There's no guarantee he'll agree to take me on, but if he does, I want to do it." Gylfi's eyes sought out Matthew but he encountered the same shuttered expression. He turned back to his mother: "You'll just have to get used to the idea. Why are you always so negative?" He stomped into his room.

Thóra sat in silence, trying to bring her emotions under control before she spoke. "What the hell's he going to do on an oil rig? He can't even fill up the car with petrol; he always gets the attendant to do it."

Matthew shrugged. "I expect there are plenty of jobs for lads like him. I think it might do him good."

Thóra glared at him. "You can't be serious?" But he clearly was. It looked as if she was the only person opposed to the plan. She would have to find some way of stopping it on her own—prevent her son from taking on a job that could well be the death of him and would, moreover, rob Orri of the stability Thóra believed she herself represented in his life. Although Gylfi and Sigga were good parents and keen to take proper care of their son, they lacked the necessary maturity to raise a child. She was brought up short by the realization that she had become a mother at about the same age. That had worked out all right. Great, now even her own brain had turned against her.

She opened her laptop again, angry with everyone and everything. She didn't want to waste any more energy thinking about it now, since the chances were that Gylfi would have changed his mind by morning. To distract herself, she started searching for instances of abandoned ships.

The results turned out to be quite a mixed bag.

Chapter 6

The weather had deteriorated overnight and the yacht kept plunging, at the mercy of the waves. Heavy, dark clouds obscured the sun, presaging a downpour, and the sea had changed from blue to a threatening gray, reflecting the leaden sky. The mood on board was similarly muted, the girls scowling with boredom. It appeared the voyage was not going to be the adventure they had anticipated.

"Why are the waves white on top, Daddy?" Bylgja sat peering out of the window in the saloon where the family were gathered.

"Because when the sea rears up like that the water mixes with air. And that's good for the fish because they get their oxygen from the sea." Ægir didn't actually know why—he had never gone in for natural history—but thought this sounded plausible. Arithmetic and mathematical problems were more in his line; a logical discipline with no room for exceptions. "Careful, sweetheart. Try to choose a route where there's something to hold on to." He watched his daughter walk unsteadily across the saloon toward the sofas. The yacht pitched and rolled violently; they had all lost their footing at some point that morning. Ægir guessed he himself probably looked as sick as the rest of the family. They were trying to put a brave face on things but their stomachs revolted at every new movement.

Lára was prostrate on a sofa, her face buried in her arms. She had complained of a headache and been unable to eat much breakfast. The girls in contrast had tucked in as if they didn't know where their next meal was coming from, and Ægir hoped this meant their nausea had passed, at least for the time being. Seeing how wan and lethargic they looked now, however, he realized he had been optimistic. This time Bylgja was not the only one to be subdued; Arna seemed little better.

"Does my head look bigger than normal?" Lára shifted one hand. Her head appeared its usual size; the only difference was the red mark left by her arm across her cheek.

"No, it looks perfectly normal to me." Ægir breathed out sharply to combat a sudden stomach cramp.

"I think it looks bigger." Arna had leaned forward to get a better view. Lára groaned.

"You know what we should do?" Ægir slapped his knees in an attempt to summon up the courage to move. "We'll feel better if we go out on deck. Remember what Thráinn said? Fresh air works wonders and I reckon it wouldn't do us any harm to try it. Afterward we'll have a nap and wake up feeling like new." The captain had not in fact mentioned anything about lying down, but Ægir felt confident that it would help. Nothing on the sailing course had prepared him for this. At the time he had thought of asking one of the instructors about seasickness but had been reluctant to expose his lack of experience, which was ridiculous considering that most of the other people on the course were amateurs too. No experienced sailor would need a pleasure craft competency certificate. "Come on, then."

Their movements were slow. Ægir had to help Lára to her feet; her eyes were glassy and flickered as if she was having trouble focusing. "I think I'm dying," she mumbled in his ear as he helped her outside. "Aren't there any drugs you can take to stop this torture?"

"I'm afraid it may be too late now. But perhaps we should take some pills before we lie down. I'd throw up if I tried to swallow one at the moment, however small they were." Ægir paused to undo the catch on the door to the deck. It had taken him a while to get used to the fact that all the outside doors were fastened with catches both inside and outside, but he had finally learned not to grab the handle and jerk it in vain until he remembered. "Halli's out there." Ægir peered through the porthole in the door at the back view of the young man who was leaning over the rail. The smoke from his cigarette scarcely rose above his head before the wind snatched it away.

This was just as well, as Ægir suspected that in their present state cigarette smoke would be the final straw. He opened the door, keeping a tight grip on it.

Halli turned his head. "Morning." He had still been in bed when they themselves got up, but now he was standing there with his short white hair flattened in whorls, his eyes a little puffy with sleep.

They exchanged greetings, the girls barely audible over the roar of the wind and waves, Lára hoarse and throaty. Only Ægir managed to sound more or less his normal self. "We're hoping some fresh sea air will perk us up."

"Well, watch out. It's very windy." Pinching his cigarette stub between finger and thumb, Halli flicked it into the sea. "People can be blown overboard—kids especially." The girls were uneasy under his gaze. Ægir felt Bylgja's small paw slip into his hand and clasp it tight. "I'll look after them." He reached for Arna's hand as well. "How long does it take to get used to it? The seasickness, I mean."

Halli shrugged unsympathetically. "I wouldn't know. I've never been seasick."

Ægir choked back the urge to swear at him. "And you've never seen anyone else suffer from it?"

"Yeah. I just don't remember how it turned out. Anyway, you look pretty chirpy for people who are sick—you should be hanging over the rail, chucking up your insides."

"Please, not another word." Lára clamped her lips shut as soon as she had spoken. She retched as Halli headed past her on his way inside, but managed to hold it down.

"Deep breaths, darling. He's gone and there's nothing but clean sea air." Ægir kept a firm hold on his daughters although they seemed eager to pull free now that Halli had gone. "You must hold my hands—you heard what he said. We don't want you to be blown into the sea." Immediately the small fingers ceased their wriggling.

"There's something wrong with that man. It's as if he had a grudge against us." Lára inhaled deeply.

"He's just a bit uncouth." Ægir practiced breathing steadily and it seemed to work. The discomfort in his abdomen abated slightly and the pain in his temples dulled. "Try to breathe like this, girls. It'll help."

"If I breathe like that I'll have to close my eyes and I don't want to." Bylgja was even paler now than when they had first come outside. "If I do, I'll see that woman."

"What woman?" Ægir bent down, taking care not to release Arna's hand.

"The woman in the picture. I dreamed about her and if I close my eyes, I'm afraid I'll dream about her again."

"What picture, sweetheart?"

"The one in the saloon. In the frame on the wall." Her glasses were covered with tiny droplets from the spray that splashed over them at regular intervals.

Ægir tried to think which picture Bylgja could be referring to. He had limited interest in people, unlike Lára who could spend hours poring over pictures of strangers in the tabloids. She also spent an excessive amount of time on Facebook, studying her friends' photos, a habit he found incomprehensible. "What's she talking about, Lára?"

"The painting of Karítas. The wife of the man who used to own the yacht. It's on the wall beside the television. You *must* be off-color if you haven't noticed it." She gave a ghost of a smile, which made her look a little less wan. "Or are you so mad about your wife that you don't have eyes for any other woman?"

Ægir didn't know how to reply. He was afraid of agreeing in case that would be the wrong answer. Instead, he turned back to Bylgja who was pulling at his hand. "The woman with the necklace, Daddy. In the painting. She was wearing it in my dream. But her face looks different somehow."

"The necklace, right." Ægir had even less interest in jewelry than in people. He squeezed Bylgja's hand. "We often dream about things we've seen during the day. That's why the woman turned up. It's perfectly safe to close your eyes, darling; dreams can't hurt you. They're only thoughts—thoughts that are a bit muddled because we're asleep and our guard is lowered." He was about to add that it was like being drunk—when common sense goes out of the window and all kinds of foolish things seem like a good idea—but he caught himself in time. It would only have confused her.

"I had a nightmare about that woman too. I told Mommy last night." Arna looked up at her father, who smiled and pressed both their hands. Instead of returning his smile, she added anxiously: "My friend Helga says dreams are trying to give you a message. If we both have the same dream it must mean something. Perhaps the woman's hiding on the boat."

"I very much doubt it. You have the same dreams because you're twins. You think alike even when you're asleep. It's not the first time, is it?" He received no reply because at that moment the door suddenly opened outward with a crash.

Halli appeared in the gap and pinned the door back with one foot. "Take these. They might make you feel better." He held out his fist and waited for them to come over. "They're seasickness tablets I found in a cabin. Thráinn says they're all right. The plasters work better but we couldn't find any."

Lára took the pills. "Thanks." She examined them, before closing her fingers over them. "I hope they work fast." Halli shrugged, removed his foot and let the door swing behind him. They heard the catch snap back. "Oh, great. Are we locked out now?" Lára asked.

"No," Ægir reassured her. "The catches inside and outside both work on the same hinge. I've tested them." He had been afraid the girls might be locked in or out; you never knew what they would get in to when they wanted attention. "Now, how about grabbing a few more lungfuls of air, then going inside and taking the pills? I'm sure they'll go down better if we wash them down with a drink." He expanded his chest as far as he could and exhaled gustily. As he repeated this, he fixed his gaze on the heaving sea in the hope that it would help. But he couldn't interpret the movements of the waves and brace himself for what was coming next; their behavior was too unpredictable. One minute everything appeared calm, the surface of the sea smooth; the next, the ship was tossing about like a cork.

He wondered how deep the water was at this point but couldn't come up with a plausible figure. They had left the continental shelf behind some time ago, so it might be several kilometers to the ocean floor. Or perhaps not that much. Again he was stymied by his lack of knowledge about the natural world. It was the sort of fact that he should probably have picked up along the way but his mind was blank; perhaps even at its deepest it was only a few hundred meters down to the seabed. He hadn't the faintest idea. It had probably never formed part of the school syllabus. In any case, what did the depth of the ocean matter? If you sank, you sank; you would be just as dead whether you ended up a hundred or a thousand meters down.

Such reflections were hardly designed to raise the spirits, so Ægir banished them from his mind. There was no point letting his thoughts run away with him. He knew from experience that if he gave his worries free rein they could take on extremely colorful forms. Like the time he had let himself be talked into scuba diving while on a beach holiday with some university friends, long before he met Lára. The first day's training had consisted of a short course in the swimming pool. But that night while his friends snored away, oblivious to the danger they were about to expose themselves to (and at considerable expense), Ægir had not gotten a wink of sleep. Countless possible variations of death in a diving accident passed through his mind as he tossed and turned, until eventually he decided it would be best not to go on the dive. But the following morning, unwilling to lose face in front of his friends, he had agreed to go out on the boat after all.

When it came to it, he had not done badly at all, perhaps because he had already resigned himself to drowning in the clear, aquamarine water. The instructor had even singled him out for praise because he had kept his head and remained relaxed during the dive. The only time he had come close to panic was when they reached the bottom and, viewing the alien surroundings and strange life forms through his goggles, he had experienced a strong aversion to the idea of leaving his bones there. However, by concentrating on taking deep, regular breaths through his mouthpiece, he had managed to master his fear. It was not until his ascent, when he saw the approaching light above him, that he was seized by an uncontrollable urge to breathe through his nose and had to force himself to look down and wait until he had reached the surface. A further shock had come when the instructor swam with them to the place where they could see the sea-bed fall away into true darkness and barren depths. It had made his flesh creep. Why was he thinking of that now?

"Let's go inside." Lára pulled at him. "If I inhale any more, my lungs will fill up with salt."

"Let's go, Daddy," Bylgja pleaded. "I don't want to stay out here any longer." Ægir tried to hide how fervently he agreed with her. Suddenly, he felt a longing to sweep up his daughters in his arms and lock them as deep inside the yacht as possible. Keen as he was to avoid ending up on the sea bed, his fear that his daughters might share the same fate was infinitely stronger.

Later, Ægir thought the pills had probably helped. They had managed to take them before anyone was sick and that may have made all the difference. The Coke was tepid, and barely drinkable, but Ægir had insisted they each finish a can, if only to have something to throw up if worst came to worst.

"Is that the picture you were talking about?" Only now had his wooziness receded sufficiently for him to notice his surroundings. He pointed to an offensively ornate gilded frame containing a canvas of a young woman, presumably Karítas. The rather kitsch subject matter was totally out of kilter with the frame, which would have been more appropriate for an old master.

"Yes. Beautiful, isn't she?" Lára was watching him beadily for his reaction.

"I can't really tell from here. She's all right, I suppose."

Lára reached out a foot from the armchair where she was sprawled and gave him a little kick. "Don't talk rubbish. Take a better look."

Ægir rose with difficulty. He felt weak, as if after a strenuous effort, perhaps as a result of constantly having to ride the waves. "The things I do for you." The twins looked up from the coloring books that had been hurriedly purchased for them in Lisbon. They had recovered much quicker than their parents and had soon grown bored of lying on their sofa. Karítas's eyes seemed to follow Ægir, growing slightly larger once he was close to the painting. Although there was no denying that the young woman was gorgeous, she was not Ægir's type: too perfect, too manicured, too conscious of her own beauty. Too plastic. Or at least that was the impression she gave. Her hair was what Ægir had chiefly noticed when he leafed past pictures of her in the papers. From what he recalled it was extraordinarily thick and healthy, perhaps the only part of her that hadn't been artificially enhanced. The artist had clearly been of the same opinion, judging by the painstaking care he had taken over this feature. While the rest of the painting was executed in a rather perfunctory fashion, her blond mane cascaded over her shoulders in perfect waves which may well have been due to artistic license. Ægir couldn't remember whether her hair had been straight or wavy in the photos he had seen. The light paint tones were fairly successful in capturing her natural color, so different from the bleached-out effect that so many young women seemed to favor these days. But the other colors in the painting were cruder and more garish, like the huge red jewel in the necklace Bylgja had mentioned, which looked more like a Christmas-tree decoration than a precious gem. The same applied to her clothes and the matching nail polish on her fingers and toes. Her tanned skin also seemed too uniform and flat, as if her slender limbs had been modeled on those of a Barbie doll, with unnaturally smooth joints. There was a hint of Barbie, too, in the way her bust was completely out of proportion to her slim figure.

He bent closer to examine the necklace, puzzled as to why it should have made such an impact on the women in his family. The chain was a simple affair of gold or white gold and the massive red jewel in its heart-shaped setting nestled between the sitter's splendid breasts. It was studded all around the edge with white stones that Ægir took to be diamonds. Suspended from the bottom of the heart was a blue teardrop—presumably also precious. "What are red gems called again?"

"Rubies," Lára replied, with surprising promptness for one who did not own much jewelry herself and as a rule took little interest in it. She had a few pieces she'd received as Confirmation gifts, as well as a ring and necklace he had given her when they were courting. Later she'd told him that it was a testament to the strength of her love that their relationship had survived those presents. He had not seen her wear any proper jewelry for years, not since the twins were born by Cesarean section, when she had put on the necklace and forced the ring onto her swollen finger in the belief that they would bring good luck. Perhaps she hadn't needed any luck since then, but Ægir found himself wishing suddenly that she had brought them along on this trip.

"There was an article on that necklace in *The Week*. It cost her husband a fortune and she's never parted from it. He gave it to her as a wedding present."

"What?" Ægir swung round. "You mean I was supposed to give you a wedding present? For some reason I thought the guests took care of that."

Lára grinned, looking much brighter. "No. Anyway, don't ask me. Maybe it's a custom among the super-rich abroad. Don't worry, you didn't commit any faux pas. Though, strictly speaking, according to Icelandic tradition you should have given me a bridal gift the morning after. Still, it's not as if the wedding night was our first time and I needed some sort of reward." She sat up properly. "So, what do you think of her? Be honest."

"Nice looking, but not my type."

"Yeah, right." Lára's disbelief was obvious. The girls looked from one to the other, waiting eagerly for their father's reaction.

"No, I mean it. She looks too perfect to be any fun. Besides, beautiful people tend to be a bit odd; everyone treats them differently, so they never develop their inner self." As he turned away from the painting he felt the woman's eyes boring into his back. "I'm not saying it applies to everyone and it's not based on any kind of scientific evidence, but I'm sure it's true. She lacks some quality."

Lára looked delighted. "You're a pretty good judge of character. From what I can gather she's a complete airhead. In interviews she comes across as really shallow and conceited."

Arna was reproachful. "You're always saying we're beautiful, Daddy. Does that make us bad?"

His daughters' little faces under their soft, fine hair were the most beautiful he had ever laid eyes on. But that beauty lay in their small imperfections: the slightly too-big teeth, the crooked smiles, the freckles and uneven eyebrows; Bylgja's smeary glasses that she had wiped with her fingers after coming inside.

"As I said, the rule's not infallible. Far from it. But people who think about nothing but their appearance soon lose their charm. Not you, though. Never you."

"Good." Arna seemed satisfied.

Bylgja was pensive. She was holding a red wax crayon, which lay quite still in her unusually steady hand. "The woman in my dream wasn't bad, just unhappy. Maybe it wasn't her."

"Or I've got it all wrong and she's actually a really nice person." Ægir grinned. "It wouldn't be the first time I was mistaken."

The red crayon sank toward the half-completed picture. "I hope so, Daddy. I hope she's nice." Bylgja began coloring again. The red wax covered an ever-larger area of the page; from where Ægir was standing it looked as if the crayon was slowly bleeding to death.

Chapter 7

It turned out that it was far from unheard-of for people to vanish without trace at sea. The stories Thóra discovered online kept her glued to the screen for ages, so it was not only exasperation with her menfolk that kept her up long after everyone else had gone to bed. The fascination of the stories lay in the very aspect that presented the greatest problem for her; without exception they remained unexplained. The fate of the *Lady K*'s crew and passengers would no doubt be the same: to live on as characters in a tale of mystery, their names and the other facts of the case gradually forgotten.

The most famous example she came across was the disappearance of the crew and passengers of the *Mary Celeste*. In 1872, a month after leaving New York bound for Genoa in Italy, the brigantine was found abandoned and adrift under full sail in the Atlantic. One of the lifeboats was missing but the ship was still seaworthy and contained six months' supply of food and water. Neither the cargo nor the personal belongings of the eight-man crew and two passengers had been touched, but the ships' papers were missing, with the exception of the captain's log, though unfortunately this shed no light on what had happened. The story of the *Mary Celeste* was uncomfortably similar to that of the *Lady K*, not least because the captain's wife and one-year-old daughter had been on board. It was as if the crew and family had vanished into thin air. No reason for this had ever been found and the mystery remained one of the most perplexing in seafaring history.

But the stories Thóra unearthed were not only historical; there were also more recent cases, including five in the last ten years. The most striking was the disappearance of three people from the yacht

Kaz II off the coast of Australia in 2007: the boat had been in perfect condition when found and everything looked normal on board, apart from the absence of the crew. There was food on the table, a laptop was switched on and the engine was still running. Moreover, the life jackets and other safety equipment were all in place and there were no signs of violence or robbery. The only real difference from the situation on the *Lady K* was the discovery of a video camera on the *Kaz II*, containing films taken of the crew before they vanished. Of course, now that Thóra came to think of it, it was quite possible that a similar find had been made on the Icelandic yacht, since at least one of the passengers must surely have had a camera or camera phone. She would have to ask the police. Admittedly, the films from the *Kaz II* had not helped to solve the riddle but it might be a different story with the *Lady K*.

Thóra was less interested in the articles that dealt with the disappearance of entire ships' crews than she was in the large number of articles and reports about individuals who had vanished without trace from cruise-liners. Apparently, this occurred on average about ten times a year, which was not really that often considering the enormous volume of cruise passengers, but it was striking nonetheless. The statistics were of secondary importance to Thóra, though, compared to the fact that the missing people's relatives tended to hit a brick wall when it came to payment of their life cover. The insurance providers refused to pay out on the grounds that it was impossible to prove the insured party's demise, and this argument seemed to satisfy the courts. This did not bode well for Ægir's parents, though with any luck the fates of Ægir and his wife would be deemed sufficiently different to avoid the same outcome. Where one person might conceivably have absconded to start a new life abroad, it would seem far-fetched to claim a conspiracy involving seven people. In addition to which, it was unthinkable that anyone could have jumped ship and survived since the yacht had been a long way from land for most of the voyage, unlike cruise ships, which tended to call at a string of ports.

"What time are you meeting the old couple about the life insurance case?" Bragi came over to join Thóra by the coffee machine where she was helping herself to her second cup of the day.

"Two. Why do you ask?" She added a splash of milk.

"Oh, I was wondering if you could take a look at some correspondence I've entered into in relation to a case that looks as if it's heading to court. You might be able to see a way to soften up the litigants. I've run out of ideas and would welcome your insight." He pushed the button to release a stream of black liquid into his cup. "I'd have copied it for you but . . . well . . . and I'll need to review it myself before lunch."

"I'll take a quick peek now."

Bragi nodded, pleased. "By the way, any idea when we can expect the photocopier back? The situation's getting me angry. I almost went down to the stationery shop to buy carbon paper, then realized it probably wouldn't work in the printer."

"Hasn't it occurred to you to print out two copies?" Thóra grinned and took a sip of coffee. "But I agree. The situation's intolerable; I'll check what's happening. In the meantime, why don't you get Bella to pop out to the copy shop for you? Preferably with one sheet at a time. The whole thing's her fault, so it would be only what she deserved."

She went back to her office to ring the workshop. As she picked up the receiver, she decided to call Karítas's mother too on the off-chance that, in spite of Matthew's dire predictions, the woman might prove amenable. It couldn't hurt to try.

Bella slammed the door so hard Thóra thought the car would fall apart. It was still cold outside; on the news that morning they had forecast snow in the north, though spring was supposed to be just around the corner. For some unaccountable reason Thóra had been anticipating a good winter followed by an early spring, though this had not been based on any meteorological evidence or gift of prophecy. The bitter wind now blowing her hair in all directions reminded her yet again how wrong she had been. She could hardly see a thing but managed with difficulty to drag her hood over her head, which considerably improved visibility. They had succeeded in arranging this meeting with surprising ease and were now standing outside Karítas's mother's house in the suburb of Arnarnes, south of Reykjavík. Thóra had tracked down the woman's name online, then looked her up in the telephone directory and tried calling her. She had drawn a blank, however, when it came to Karítas's father. Her patronymic was Karlsdóttir, but there was no Karl registered on her mother's phone number. Perhaps her parents were divorced or her father was dead. At any rate, her mother was evidently lonely enough to view a meeting with a lawyer as a welcome diversion.

"God, what a hideous house." Once again, Bella seemed unaffected by the wind as she stood on the pavement, critically surveying the property in question. It was a Spanish-style villa and Thóra had to agree that it looked totally incongruous in the Icelandic climate.

"Shh!" Thóra made a face at the secretary. "She might hear us."

"Are you joking?" boomed Bella, peering around. "I can hardly hear you in this gale and you're standing right next to me."

"All the same." Thóra was about to ask Bella to watch her tongue when they went inside, but decided not to bother. It wouldn't do any good. She was hoping the secretary's presence might come in useful, since she and Karítas had been in the same year at school. When Bella had let this slip during their visit to the yacht, Thóra had failed to follow it up, assuming that Karítas was irrelevant to the case. It had also seemed unwise to encourage Bella to talk in front of Fannar, since the secretary had looked as if she had some inappropriate comment on the tip of her tongue. Later, however, after finding the page with Karítas's contact details, Thóra had asked Bella about their acquaintance, only to receive an angry lecture on how the fact that they were in the same year at school did not mean they were friends or had known each other at all. Thóra had waited for Bella to simmer down, then tackled her again.

She turned out to remember Karítas well, which was hardly surprising given that the other girl had been the queen bee of the school. Far from belonging to the same gang, however, Karítas had hung out with the cool kids, Bella with the misfits. Not that Bella had put it quite like that but Thóra could read between the lines. "Do you think her mother will remember you?" They entered through a wrought-iron gate far too fussily ornamental for its Icelandic setting. A paved path led down to the house, which stood on a plot by the sea.

"No way. I bet she'd like to forget those days. She didn't live in a posh house like this then. From what I remember Karítas and her mother lived in a small flat that probably belonged to the council. Her mother used to work in the local shop."

"Things have obviously looked up for her since then." Thóra lowered her voice as they approached the front door. "Remember to drop in casually that you used to know her daughter," she whispered, "but for goodness' sake don't badmouth her. Pretend you were her number one fan."

Bella snorted disgustedly but didn't refuse outright as Thóra had feared. In the large white concrete tubs flanking the entrance, the yellowing stalks of last summer's flowers poked up out of the dry earth and trembled in the wind. Thóra thought statues of lions would have been more in keeping. She rang the bell, adding as an afterthought: "Otherwise I'll never take you out with me again, not even to the recycling center."

"Is that supposed to be a threat?"

Before Thóra could reply the door opened and a woman emerged. "Oh, do come inside, quick. There's such a draft that everything will go flying." She beckoned them in with a tanned, somewhat leathery arm, jingling with gold bracelets. They didn't look genuine but then Thóra was no judge. "I was smoking out of the downstairs window when you rang the bell. Come in, come in."

Thóra and Bella hurriedly closed the door behind them and the three of them crowded into an entrance hall that was surprisingly poky in comparison to the rest of the house. Thóra was afraid of elbowing the owner in the jaw as she removed her coat; a bad start like that could ruin everything. "What a beautiful house." She followed the woman down the hall. In fact, the décor was not at all to her taste, but she knew that there were people who regarded gilt and velvet as the height of sophistication. The hallway and sitting room were so cluttered with occasional tables, vases, pictures, shelves and knick-knacks that Thóra pitied the poor woman having to dust them all. On closer inspection, she realized the place could do with a good cleaning, but she didn't dare spend too long examining the surfaces in case it looked rude. Perhaps the woman's cleaner had left, which was not unlikely if she was dependent on her daughter for money.

"Do sit down. I'll bring us some coffee." While she was out of the room, Thóra and Bella had a good look around. To judge from Bella's expression, she was even less impressed with the furnishings and ornaments than Thóra. Her upper lip curled as if she had noticed a bad smell. Really, it was hardly possible to imagine less suitable surroundings for Bella. Her attention was fixed on the photographs of Karítas, alone or with her husband, which no doubt brought back teenage memories she would rather forget, even though—interestingly—the pictures all dated from the time after Karítas had married into the jet set. There were none of her as a child or teenager.

"Here we are." The woman bore in a silver tray laden with rose-patterned china cups and a large matching coffee pot. There was even a cream jug and a sugar bowl with a dainty silver spoon. "Would you both like some? I'm dying for a cup myself, though I'm trying to give up as my blood pressure's sky high at the moment." Thóra and Bella had both nodded while she was sharing this information, so she poured them each a cup as well as one for herself. "Now, which of you is Thóra?"

"Me," Thóra blurted out loudly in her eagerness not to be confused with the secretary. "I'm Thóra—I spoke to you on the phone. This is Bella who works for us."

The woman extended her hand to Bella: "Hello, do call me Begga." Still maintaining eye contact, the woman studied her intently. "I recognize you. Do I know you from somewhere?"

"I used to live in the same neighborhood as you when I was a kid. Karítas was in my year at school. You probably remember me from those days."

Begga instantly became very twitchy, clearly uncomfortable at being reminded of her former life, and Thóra cursed herself for not considering this possibility. "Bella happened to mention to me that she remembered your daughter because she was so stunning. Still is, of course."

The woman relaxed a little. The same could not be said of Bella, but at least she refrained from making a face. "Karítas was always special. Even as a baby she looked like an angel." Her mother smiled fondly at the memory. The lipstick she had applied, perhaps in their honor, had bled slightly into the small lines that fanned out from her mouth, making her appear older than she probably was. While it couldn't be said that her daughter took after her in looks, there was a certain resemblance, particularly about the eyes, though the woman had troweled on such a ridiculous amount of makeup that it was hard to tell what she looked like underneath. Perhaps she had been a beauty in her youth and found it difficult to reconcile herself to aging. Her legs were still slim and elegant, a fact she was apparently aware of as she was dolled up in a knee-length skirt and high heels that were far too smart for the occasion. In comparison to her legs the rest of her body appeared almost bloated, and she seemed to be in low spirits. "I can't begin to describe how much I miss her. We're so close. It was always just the two of us. Her father was never in the picture and that made us all the more important to each other. We're more like best friends than mother and daughter." Begga's tone sounded increasingly hollow.

"I can believe it," said Thóra. "Does she stay here with you when she's in the country?"

"Usually, yes. If she's alone. They own this house, though I live here—as a favor to them really. Otherwise they'd keep getting burgled. But when Gulam's with her, they stay at a hotel. Not that he comes very often—or at all nowadays. It's hardly surprising." Begga tossed her head. "Even Karítas can't face it any more."

"You mean because of the business with the bank?" Thóra didn't dare breathe a word about debts or bankruptcy for fear the woman would take offense.

"Yes. It's so awful." Begga took a sip of coffee, and when she put down her cup there was a scarlet smear on the rim. "I can't discuss it for obvious reasons—you never know what might get back to that vile special prosecutor. How could they dream that a man as rich as Gulam would commit fraud for money? He has absolutely no need to, I assure you." She sniffed and ran a hand over her badly styled hair. "Not that I suspect you of being in the pay of that prosecutor. You both seem far too nice."

That the woman could mistake Bella for a nice person was testimony to how few visitors she received. She must have a tough time of it socially if she had shed her old friends and acquaintances, only to discover that she was not welcome among the new Icelandic elite. Too obviously nouveau riche herself, she would serve as an uncomfortable reminder to others in the group that they were no better.

"Karítas is okay, isn't she? Financially, I mean." Incredibly, Bella managed to sound genuinely concerned.

Begga paused to consider for a moment, then waved a hand over her shoulder as if dismissing her troubles. "Well, don't spread it about but Karítas is fine. It isn't like when ordinary people go bankrupt; she and Gulam have all sorts of funds and that sort of thing, but they've had some problems as a result of this cash-flow crisis—you know, all that unpleasantness caused by those Lehman brothers. It's so unfair, really, because if they'd been allowed to take out more loans, it wouldn't have been an issue. If you want my opinion, it was nothing but jealousy. They had so much that people were determined to take it away. But fortunately it didn't work. Not completely."

Thóra assumed an expression of sympathy. At least Begga won points for mistaking Lehman Brothers Holdings for a couple of fraudsters and trying to blame the whole disaster on them. "As I explained on the phone, we're here to ask you a few questions about the yacht that Karítas and her husband used to own. We don't actually know anything about their finances, though naturally we're pleased to hear they're doing well. The thing is, as you've no doubt heard, the yacht turned up empty the other day, minus the crew and passengers who were supposed to be delivering her to this country. I'm working for the relatives of the missing family." The woman's face revealed scant pity for the victims, so Thóra tried another tack. "I gather that even without this tragedy the yacht would have been hard to sell."

"Oh?" Begga raised heavily penciled, over-plucked eyebrows. "Was she damaged? Karítas and Gulam shelled out a fortune for her back in the day."

"Yes, she was crippled, but after this latest incident it's her reputation that's likely to bring down her price. Apparently they're a superstitious lot in the seafaring world."

"Will Karítas lose out as a result of this?" Anxiety shone from the woman's eyes as she glanced at them both in turn.

"No, not exactly." Thóra took extra care over the phrasing of the next part, as she didn't know whether the woman was aware of the change of ownership. "The bank's resolution committee has repossessed the boat. I gather that part of Karítas's husband's loan was used to pay for the yacht, which gave the bank a claim to her. You know what financial institutions are like . . ." She stopped herself from adding "ruthless," in case it seemed over the top.

Begga nodded but seemed distracted. "Yes, I knew about that. Karítas was staying with me when she heard." She paused. "I do believe it was the last time she was in the country. It was the final straw really as she was already in a state about whether she should divorce Gulam. And it didn't help that the authorities here wouldn't stop pestering her and kept summoning her to interrogate her about their finances." She looked disgusted. "Can you believe it? As if there was anything more private than one's personal finances!" Without waiting for an answer, she continued: "It was driving her frantic; she even considered handing over all her papers, just to get some peace. Then the news came about the yacht and I swear I thought it would push her over the edge. But she's got a backbone, has Karítas, so she simply left the country. Of course I miss her terribly but it's better for her to stay away until all this fuss has died down."

"Do you have any idea where she went?"

"She went to Lisbon, where the yacht was moored. She needed to pick up all kinds of stuff that was on board—personal belongings that the bank had no right to confiscate. She has a maid she could have sent instead, but she wanted to go through everything personally. The maid isn't exactly the sharpest knife in the drawer, so I can understand why Karítas preferred to do it herself."

"Is she still in Lisbon? Do you think she'd be prepared to talk to me on the phone? I don't suppose there are many people who know as much about the yacht as she does, so there's a chance she might be able to help me piece together what happened to the crew and passengers. Perhaps she could tell me if there was a lifeboat on board that other people didn't know about, for instance, or testify to the fact that there wasn't one. There's also a chance that Karítas knew about some fault that the crew were unaware of. I could use any information that would lend support to the idea that there was a problem with the boat. The case I'm dealing with concerns a life insurance policy that will only be paid out if it can be proved that the people who were on board are dead." She deliberately avoided referring to Ægir or his family by name in case Begga had heard about them on the news and realized that he had worked for the resolution committee.

A grandfather clock chimed once to mark the half hour. Looking at her watch, Thóra saw that it was only twenty past ten. Clearly, the dusting wasn't the only thing that required attention around here. Begga was suddenly keen to offer them more coffee. They accepted, and then, ignoring the woman's evasion tactics, Thóra repeated her question.

"I don't know if she'll talk on the phone. She's been badly burned by all this and I think she's afraid her phone's bugged. I mean, she hasn't rung me once since she left, though usually she makes an effort to stay in touch." She began to rearrange the cups and pot on the tray, turning them all to face Thóra and Bella. "I am her mother, after all."

"Where is she now? I promise you we have absolutely nothing to do with the Financial Supervisory Authority or any other official body." Thóra put down her cup, taking care to position it correctly on the saucer.

"In Brazil. I think." Begga watched Bella drain nearly a whole cup in one go. "I got a postcard from her this morning. She's sent me cards before on her travels. On my birthday last year, for instance. She was in America at the time."

"Could we see the one you received this morning?" Bella came straight to the point and Thóra could have kissed her.

"No, I'm afraid not." Begga was affronted by the request. "It's private and I really don't see what it could have to do with the yacht."

It would be odd, to say the least, to send a private message on a postcard that anyone could read, but there was no easy way of breaking this to Karítas's mother, and not even Bella could bring herself to do so. Besides, the woman was right; the card had nothing to do with their business. "Have you been on board the yacht yourself?" Thóra deftly changed the subject.

"Yes. Twice, in fact." Begga reminded Thóra of her cat at its smuggest. "It's absolutely amazing," she added, on an indrawn breath, leaning back a little and fluffing up her hair, inadvertently revealing gray roots.

"Did anyone happen to mention the life-saving equipment while you were on board? Did Karítas or her husband point it out to you?"

"I haven't met Gulam that often and when I did we didn't discuss the yacht. For one thing, my English isn't good enough, and anyway the subject wouldn't have crossed my mind. The few times we've been together since Karítas married and moved out, I've tried to discuss more important matters, like whether they're planning to have children. I keep hoping she'll come home for a long holiday or that I'll be able to visit her abroad for more than a few days at a time, but it never seems to be the right moment. Her husband's always so preoccupied with business and I suspect him of wanting to have Karítas to himself. Understandably, of course." She gave a cloying smile. "But he didn't always get his own way as I do perhaps have more of a claim on her when it comes down to it. After all, she is my daughter." She apparently regretted having said anything negative because she added hastily: "Don't misunderstand me; it's not that I bear a grudge against him. Not at all. Gulam's a wonderful man and quite devoted to Karítas. She can have anything she wants."

"He's a bit old. Isn't that kind of weird? He must be about your age." Again, Bella took it upon herself to ask the difficult question. Wham bam. Straight to the point.

Begga's smile didn't reach her eyes. "He's a little older than me. But it's quite different with men. They're slower to mature than women, so an age gap like that can work perfectly well." An embarrassed silence ensued; clearly none of them believed that men lagged almost thirty years behind women in maturity. "In any case, there was no need to make a fuss about life-saving equipment. That yacht's unsinkable." She gave them a scornful look. "And it didn't sink, did it?

I don't know what safety equipment could have stopped those people from going missing." There was no reply to this, so Thóra and Bella simply sat there sheepishly. This seemed to cheer the woman up. "Not that I had the time or inclination to do anything but enjoy myself while I was on board. I don't know when I've eaten so well or drunk so much good wine. It was as if the meals arrived on a conveyor belt." Again she looked like the cat that got the cream.

They continued chatting until the clock struck eleven (at ten to, of course). Little of importance had emerged so Thóra seized this opportunity to end their visit and thanked Begga for her hospitality. They were walking away from the house when Begga suddenly called after them: "If you do manage to get in touch with Karítas, you might ask her to give me a ring. I need to get hold of her rather urgently about a small misunderstanding over the property tax."

Thóra turned and looked back at the woman standing in the porch of her daughter's house, a house that must have required endless outgoings that Begga almost certainly couldn't afford on her own. Perhaps a smaller home and a larger social circle would have been preferable if the daughter had really wanted to make her mother happy. "I'll do that. Of course."

They carried on walking but did not hear the door close. No doubt the woman was still standing there, watching them leave, as if to eke out this unremarkable visit. Thóra felt bad as they drove away.

"What's the betting that Karítas's old man has killed her to prevent the divorce or shut her up?" Bella abandoned the attempt to fasten her seat belt and turned to face Thóra. "Postcard, my ass. Anyone can send a postcard: *Having a great time in Rio—kiss, kiss, Karítas.* I bet he just copied a sample of her handwriting, then used Google Translate to put it into Icelandic. Think about it—no one's seen her since she went to fetch the stuff on the yacht." In spite of her dislike, Bella had clearly been following the news about her old schoolmate with avid interest.

Thóra was no gambler but she wouldn't have taken that wager even if she'd been an inveterate risk-taker. "Let's hope that's not true." If only for her mother's sake.

Chapter 8

"God, this is good, if I say so myself." Lára spoke with her mouth full, but swallowed before continuing: "To think that only this morning I was sure no food would ever pass my lips again." The family had spent most of the day languishing in the enormous bed, the girls sandwiched between their parents, each with a book that they glanced at whenever they weren't dozing. Ægir had nodded off a few times himself, only to awake again immediately, without knowing why. Lára, meanwhile, had slept like a log for at least two hours, untroubled by her husband and daughters' movements. The pills had made them so drowsy and lethargic that they had wasted the whole afternoon, but thanks to them they were now feeling almost as well as before they had left harbor. Almost—but not quite.

They were all seated in the galley apart from Loftur, whose turn it was to stand watch on the bridge. The family had taken so much trouble over the meal that anyone would have thought it was a celebration. No sooner had the girls revived than they were itching for a distraction, so they were given the task of setting the table for supper. They took the job seriously, unearthing a white tablecloth, stiff with starch; linen napkins which they inserted into silver napkin rings that could have done with a polish; and elegant glasses to match the rest of the tableware. Ægir brought out some wine to complete the party atmosphere. Thráinn had immediately accepted their invitation to dine with them, perhaps because the girls asked him and it was harder to say no to them. Halli had refused at first, but relented when Thráinn dismissed his talk of grabbing a sandwich to eat in his cabin. It was difficult to tell if he regretted his decision but although he hung his head and stared at his plate for most of the meal, he did at least seem grateful for the food.

Lára and Ægir had taken care of the cooking, sitting down once they had searched the fridge for something they felt up to digesting. The outcome of their efforts lay before them in large dishes. "Cheers." Ægir raised his glass and waited for the others to follow suit. "Pity we didn't have the sense to bring along a few bottles of white. We should have known there'd be fish."

"That's all right." Thráinn took a deep gulp. "We're not fussy, are we, Halli?"

"No." The young sailor was as taciturn as ever. Perhaps it was his age, or simply that he was unused to having families on board. Ægir would have felt the same if a family of four had invaded his office. Halli sipped his wine, but did not look particularly appreciative. Maybe he was more of a beer drinker; after all, he was considerably younger than the other three adults.

"It is okay for you two to have a little drink, isn't it? I mean, if you're on duty?" Lára forked up another piece of fish.

"Sure. We're on autopilot and cruising at a gentle speed. We go as slowly as possible at night, but make up for it during the day. Since we're just pottering along at the moment it doesn't matter if we have something to drink. I'll be my usual self when I take over the watch later. Don't worry—it takes more than a couple of glasses of wine to get me drunk."

"Who sails the boat at night?" asked Bylgja.

"We take it in turns to keep watch, but there isn't much to do. We just lie on the couch within reach, and plot our position at hourly intervals in case anything goes wrong."

"Like what?" Arna looked up from the search for fish bones that had delayed her from starting her meal. Her tuna steak had been shredded to pieces.

Thráinn looked ill at ease; evidently he hadn't been prepared for the question. "Well, mainly it's so we'll know where we are if there's a power cut and the GPS drops out. But if the electricity *did* go, it's unlikely to be serious, and it's not going to happen anyway. And even if something else went wrong, we'd be all right; in the worst case scenario we'd have to request assistance from another ship."

"But there aren't any other ships out here." Bylgja was eating more dutifully than Arna and had more color back in her cheeks, perhaps because she had succumbed to the sickness first. Neither had mentioned Karítas or nightmares again, which was a relief. "We haven't seen any and can't hear any either."

"They're out there even if we can't see them. The sea's very, very big. But if you're interested I can show you the equipment on the bridge that tells us what vessels are nearby. We've got radar, too, of course."

"To find our way?" Bylgja looked up from her plate.

Thráinn smiled. "Yes, you could say that. Radar shows us what's in the sea around us so we don't collide with anything."

Lára topped up Thráinn's glass. Until now the men had behaved as if the family were not there. They would reply if asked a direct question but never volunteered any comment. Halli and Loftur were still rather aloof but Thráinn at least seemed to be thawing. "Have you crewed this yacht before?" Although she didn't let on, Lára was hoping they might be able to share some indiscreet tidbits of gossip about Karítas. She had read so many articles and news items about her in the tabloids that she almost felt she knew her.

"No, I'd never set eyes on the boat till the other day. I must say I wouldn't have minded sailing her round the Med in summer. Or the Caribbean." Thráinn peered out into the darkness. It had begun to rain as they sat down to eat and the drops rattled on the windows, making it feel quite cozy inside. "Though I gather it's almost a charity gig to crew these yachts; they don't pay half as well as the trawlers. People with money tend to be pretty tight with the purse strings."

"What about you, Halli?" Ægir made an effort to include the young man in the conversation.

"Yes." It looked as if this monosyllable would be their only answer, but suddenly he added: "Only for three months. That's why I'm here; they thought it would be better to have someone who knew their way around."

"Wow. What was it like?" Lára hoped it wasn't embarrassingly obvious what she was fishing for. "It seems amazing that a yacht like this should have belonged to an Icelander."

"It depends what you mean by belonged," interjected Ægir. "The yacht was registered in her husband's name. Or rather a company owned by her husband." He couldn't work out what his wife was up to but saw that his comment had annoyed her.

"You know what I mean." Lára turned back to Halli. "What was it like?"

Halli dropped his gaze to his plate and toyed with a lone potato. "Oh, you know, nothing out of the ordinary."

"But it *must* have been out of the ordinary." Lára tried and failed to make eye contact with him. "Do tell us. What was Karítas like, for example? And her husband?"

"They were just like anyone else. That's all I can say. I had to sign an agreement not to discuss my time on board, especially not the guests or owners, so I can't really talk about it." He cleared his throat. "Mind you, it might not count any longer, now that they're bankrupt. I wouldn't know. But it doesn't make any difference, because nothing interesting happened, so there's nothing to say."

"Are you going to tell me they made you sign an agreement not to share your knowledge of the engine either?" Thráinn folded his arms. "Anyone would have thought so, judging by how little you seem to know what you're doing." He winked at Lára without Halli noticing. The young man flushed to the roots of his white hair.

"Were there any children?" Either Arna hadn't grasped the part about the confidentiality clause or she dismissed it as irrelevant.

"He doesn't know, darling." Ægir worked with confidentiality agreements every day at the committee and the subject made him uncomfortable. It was to the young man's credit that he wanted to keep his promise. Such matters ought to be honored, and Ægir tried to convey as much to Lára by sending her a sobering glare. She ignored him.

"Yes, he does. He can answer yes or no, can't he?" Arna put down her fork and returned to the attack. "Were there any children?" She had inherited her mother's friendly interest in people, whereas Bylgja took after her father. So alike on the outside; so different inside.

"No." It was unclear whether Halli was answering or trying to put a stop to any further questions.

"You could at least tell us if you enjoyed it." Lára wasn't going to give up so easily.

"No." At first the others weren't sure whether he was refusing to answer or referring to his experience, but his next comment removed all doubt. "I wasn't happy on board and I was in two minds about accepting this job when it came up."

"Oh." This was not the reply Lára had been hoping for. "Were you seasick?"

For the first time since they had embarked, they saw Halli genuinely amused. "No. I wasn't seasick."

"What was wrong then?" Lára pretended not to notice when Ægir trod warningly on her foot.

"There's something weird about this yacht. I can't really explain. There's just something wrong with her." He gave Thráinn a nasty smile. "The captain was a real loser as well, not that that's unusual."

Thráinn snorted. "Rubbish. As if you know anything about a boat like this. You've only been at sea for what, three, four years? This yacht is one of the finest vessels I've ever sailed and I know what I'm talking about."

Halli turned red again, this time from anger, not embarrassment. "I didn't criticize her performance, did I?" He took a slug of wine. "It's the atmosphere. There's something creepy about her and I'm not the only one to think so."

"Really?" Ægir said, then wished he hadn't. This conversation was the last thing the girls needed to hear. They were sitting rigid with attention, hanging on every word instead of eating their supper.

"Some of the other crew members told me the stories that were going round about her. They were all the same. I'm not particularly superstitious but all that talk about a curse made me uneasy. It was obvious they weren't joking." Halli broke off abruptly and concentrated on shoveling the last potato into his mouth. "Thanks for the food." He stood up and went out.

Ægir walked into the pilot house and was surprised yet again at how different it was from what he had been expecting when he first came aboard. It reminded him more of a radio repair shop than the bridge of a ship, with its rows of computer screens and gadgets, all with a mysterious role to play. The only detail consistent with his preconceptions was the handsome wooden wheel below the window, though Thráinn had told him on the first day that it was only there as backup in case the automated navigation system failed. Generally, if the crew needed to steer the ship manually for any reason, they would use a joystick that was no bigger than the controller for a computer game. In addition to all the navigation equipment, the yacht had a sizeable telecommunications system, and although Ægir didn't trust himself to repeat Thráinn's explanation of how it all worked, he remembered more or less what role each system played. Still, he hoped he would never have to operate any of the technology in here; if he did, there was a risk the yacht would end up sailing in circles.

"Isn't it hard to keep an eye on all those screens and monitors?" Ægir plonked a cold beer on the table that stood in the middle of the pilot house. It was covered with a non-slip cloth and had a raised chrome edge around it to prevent objects from sliding off in heavy seas. The bottle was wet with condensation, so he took care not to place it too close to the chart that was spread out on the table. He had seen similar charts on his sailing course, covered with lines and numbers that he had understood when sitting in the classroom but which now seemed to bear little relation to the sea they were supposed to represent. "I brought you a beer. Thought it would be okay since Thráinn's relieving you soon."

"Thanks." Loftur reached for the bottle, after what looked like an internal struggle about whether to keep up his surly manner. "I've had just about enough anyway. The goddamn radio's playing up and I can't fix it. It's doing my head in." He took a swig of beer.

"What's wrong?"

"Endless goddamn interference, a couple of weird calls." He nodded toward what looked like an ATM machine, from which a strip of paper protruded like a tongue. "There was an alert on the NAVTEX about a container falling off a freighter not far from here. That may have something to do with it."

"What's the NAVTEX?" Ægir went over to the machine and read the short English text on the printout, which was accompanied by a sequence of numbers and letters.

"It receives messages about navigational alerts, like weather warnings, ice reports and notifications about other hazards such as drifting containers—like now."

"We're not in any danger, are we?" Ægir's tone was ironic as he assumed the answer would be no. Loftur seemed far too relaxed and would surely have fetched Thráinn if it were serious. Ægir took a sip of cold beer.

"No, I shouldn't think so." Loftur's attention was fixed on the radar. "Have your wife and kids gone to sleep?"

"Well, Lára hasn't, but the girls are in bed. She's reading to them in the hope that there won't be a repetition of last night's bad dreams. I must say, I wouldn't mind turning in myself though we've been lying down most of the day. This sea air's making me sleepy." Ægir toyed with the beer bottle. "Are you a family man yourself?"

Loftur looked up from the radar, and at first it seemed as if he had taken offense at the question. Perhaps he didn't like discussing his private life with strangers, or maybe Ægir had touched a nerve. Young though he was, he might recently have split up with a girlfriend. Ægir immediately regretted having asked, but he must have misread Loftur's reaction because the other man eventually replied: "No, not yet."

The yacht dived suddenly and as she came up there was a resounding thud that made the entire vessel shudder. Ægir had to grab the table to keep his balance. The sea had been relatively quiet for the last hour, so he had been completely unprepared. "Whoa!" As he straightened his knees, he noticed that Loftur was unaffected by the movement. Next minute all was calm again and the yacht righted herself. "Can any of those smart gadgets give advance warning of that kind of thing?"

"If you mean can I warn you when a wave's coming, the answer's no. Your best bet's to look ahead over the bows." Loftur glanced over his shoulder at the various monitors. "If you want to have a look around, it's fine. Just don't touch anything."

Ægir didn't want to decline the invitation and point out that Thráinn had already shown him the ropes. He was afraid this would be interpreted as a lack of interest and expose his true nature, that of the wimpy office worker. Besides, it would be a pity not to respond to the man's friendly overtures now that he seemed to be coming out of his shell at last. "That's the radar, isn't it?" Ægir asked, standing in front of a large, multi-colored screen whose function he knew perfectly well. The screen showed a disk with a radial sweep that revolved slowly, trailing an illuminated area that gradually faded away.

"Yes." Loftur came over. "It shows the magnetic waves of the radar spreading out from the yacht's transmitter. If they hit anything, they bounce back and it shows up on screen. We're in the middle of the circle, here." Ægir nodded, feigning ignorance, and Loftur continued: "As you can see, there's nothing in the vicinity, which is pretty unusual, and I was beginning to wonder if we'd drifted off course—if the GPS was programmed wrong."

"What did you conclude?"

"That we're on course. It's just a coincidence."

"Could the radar be malfunctioning? Could there be ships out there that aren't showing up?"

"I doubt it. It's not exactly a busy sea route, so it's probably not significant. We'll see other vessels once we enter the fishing grounds. The sea underneath us is dead; all the life has been hoovered up. It's kind of depressing."

"What about the container? Would it show up?"

Loftur shrugged. "Depends how high it's riding in the water. The radar waves have to bounce off something and if the container's mostly submerged, they wouldn't pick it up. Actually, it would be better if the sea was rough, because then it would move up and down with the waves and be more visible."

He showed Ægir another screen. "This is the echo sounder. It's no use here as the ocean's so deep, but it's an important instrument when you're sailing in shallower waters."

Remembering his earlier musings, Ægir asked: "How deep *is* the sea here?"

Loftur bent over the screen and pointed: "About 3,200 meters. At that depth sunlight doesn't penetrate to the seabed, so the life forms are really strange. It's amazing anything survives down there at all. The pressure is almost three hundred times what it is on the surface. It's too far down even for deep-sea fish." Loftur looked out of the window, as if he expected to see something in the darkness. "Deep-sea fish are bizarre enough as it is. I've never seen it myself, but occasionally they get caught in the nets and blow up like balloons because of the change of pressure. I expect the same would happen to us if we were dragged out of the earth's atmosphere."

Ægir recalled a picture he had seen of a fish with a lantern dangling in front of its jaws. It had been a deep-sea species that used the light to lure in other curious fish, before snapping them up. He didn't dare mention it in case the fish was fictional, a maritime hoax invented by sailors to trick landlubbers like him.

A rasping sound came from the speaker grille at Loftur's side. "There the bugger goes again." He stooped slightly toward it. For a while they heard nothing but the raindrops on the windows and their own heavy breathing. Then the machine crackled again and this time it was accompanied by another noise, which reminded Ægir of the popping of air bubbles when he'd been diving.

"Is that the radiotelephone you were talking about?" Loftur nodded, his attention riveted to the machine. "Is it making those noises because it's broken?"

The radio was now completely silent. "Well, I think it's faulty. You shouldn't hear a thing unless someone's transmitting. But no one would waste time transmitting stuff like that. I don't know—it's a VHF 16 channel with a very limited range, barely as far as the horizon. Maybe we're receiving feedback from a message that wasn't intended for us. There's no vessel within thirty nautical miles according to the AIS, so I suppose it's possible." He noticed that Ægir was looking blank. "All vessels are equipped with a transmitter that sends out information about which ships are in the area, where they're headed, their position, and so on. The AIS is an automatic tracking system that receives all transmissions within a radius of thirty-five nautical miles. The Coast Guard and harbor authorities use it as well, to keep an eye on marine traffic."

The radio emitted more static and they both stared at it. "Perhaps the radio transmitting the message is faulty?" Ægir felt absurdly pleased when Loftur looked at him with a hint of respect. "You know, maybe someone's trying to send a message but failing because there's a glitch at his end."

"That could be it." Loftur seemed about to say more when the noises began again. This time instead of crackling they heard the sound of air bubbles and what may have been a human voice, but it was so distorted that it was impossible to tell. Silence fell again. Yet it was not complete silence; Ægir had the feeling that the channel was still open, as if the person at the other end was sitting there, staring at the transmitter. Loftur snatched up the microphone. "Hello." There was no answer. "Hello. This is the *Lady K*. Our position is 316 nautical miles northwest of Lisbon. Please identify yourself. Over." Although Loftur had a thick Icelandic accent, his English was perfectly comprehensible. There was no answer. "Please identify yourself. Over." Still no answer. Loftur replaced the microphone. "It must be some idiot messing about."

"A idiot with access to a radio, though." Ægir tried to sound jovial, to lighten the atmosphere. The air felt oddly charged; perhaps someone was in trouble but unable to call for assistance due to a broken radio. It might even be a yacht like theirs, with children on board. "Should you try again?"

"*Lady K*." They both froze and stared at the loudspeaker. Now the sound was crystal clear, with no crackling or air bubbles, just those two words, unmistakably the name of their yacht. "*Lady K*," it repeated, and Ægir felt a cold shiver down his spine. The voice sounded vile, oozing malice, as if uttering an obscenity. The words were pronounced without haste or any hint of desperation, each letter enunciated precisely. Whoever it was, this person was not in any trouble. The radio fell silent again, and this time it was obvious that the channel had been switched off.

Ægir looked at the beer in his hand and decided against drinking any more. Given the way his imagination was working overtime, the alcohol obviously wasn't doing him any good. Seconds ticked past, the radio now silent, and the whole thing began to seem ridiculous. Of course it must be some idiot mucking about, as Loftur had said. He glanced at the young mate, intending to smile or crack a joke, but stopped short. Loftur's expression was not unlike the one he himself must have been wearing a moment ago; naked fear. Ægir was badly shaken to see this taciturn man looking so scared, and he remembered what Halli had said over supper about the yacht's being cursed; that explained a lot, though it did nothing to console him.

Their attention was suddenly attracted by a bleeping from the radar—too fast and too urgent. A winking black blur had appeared on the screen right beside the yacht, where a moment before there had been nothing.

Chapter 9

"I recommend you apply to the district court for Ægir and Lára's property to be declared their estate. Perhaps not today or tomorrow, but soon, unless the situation changes significantly. If the court rules in your favor, a decision will be made about when they're presumed to have died." It was clear from their faces that Sigríður and Margeir were upset by Thóra's suggestion, but she plowed on regardless. She had suggested meeting at their house rather than her office for precisely this reason. They would cope better with the harsh facts in familiar surroundings. "It's covered in the first article of the 1981 Missing Persons Act, the purpose of which is primarily to safeguard the interests of the individual who has disappeared; that is, to protect their property and other rights. I will then present all the facts relating to the disappearance to the court, and the judge will decide whether the evidence is satisfactory. You probably won't be made to pay costs, as cases like this are covered by legal aid."

"That's a relief. As you're aware, we don't have much money, so if the case went against us we'd have problems paying." Margeir waved his hand as if to draw attention to the small, plain flat. Thóra had already noted that the furniture was old but well cared for. In the sitting room a boxy television set stood on a crocheted cloth, which fell in a neat white triangle over the edge of the table. Family photographs, old and new, had been arranged on either side of the TV, the cheerful smiles of the subjects looking utterly out of place in the gloomy atmosphere. There was a vase containing what looked like supermarket flowers on the small, old-fashioned dining table, and Thóra guessed they had been sent with condolences by a friend or relative. The petals were drooping, their beauty wilted, their purpose done, but no one had thought to throw them away. Everywhere there were signs of mourning.

Thóra paused briefly before carrying on. She wanted them to absorb the message, and to keep it separate from the next matter she needed to raise. "But there are other things you should bear in mind. I went over the terms and conditions in Ægir and Lára's life insurance policies and see nothing to preclude their being paid out. There are no clauses about death having to occur after a certain period, as is common in these contracts, nor is there anything about the right to make a claim being declared void if the insured party commits suicide. I know this isn't suicide but it would complicate matters if the insurance company tried to claim that it was. The case is not straightforward, however."

"Isn't it?" said Margeir, though he didn't appear all that interested.

"No. For example, the rule is that the insurance company has to be notified without delay if an event occurs for which a claim is to be made: in this instance, Ægir and Lára's deaths," said Thóra. "The notification would have to be accompanied by more or less the same proof as that required by the district court, so at least that simplifies matters. But the most likely scenario is that the insurance provider will reject the initial claim. It's very common—there was a recent case here in Iceland. A man disappeared when sailing a yacht from America to Iceland and the foreign insurance company refused to accept that he was dead. So the case went before the district court here in Iceland, which ruled that the man was missing presumed dead, and after that the insurance company was forced to pay out his life cover. I'm confident that your case would go the same way, which would mean that the court would examine the facts, but also that relatives and anyone else who might possess any relevant information could potentially be summoned to appear."

"Would the case have to be heard overseas, what with it being a foreign company? I'm not sure we'd feel up to appearing before a foreign court." Margeir sounded oddly detached, as if he were reciting lines from a play.

"No, the Icelandic court has jurisdiction in cases in which the missing person was most recently domiciled in this country, regardless of where the insurance company is based. So it would go before the Reykjavík District Court." Thóra awaited further questions and when none were forthcoming, she carried on: "I know it's a lot to take in and that this isn't the best time, but I propose that I set about obtaining the documentation required by the insurance provider, then inform them of what's happened. There's no point delaying. If Ægir and Lára do turn up safe and sound, hopefully that will happen sooner rather than later, and in that case we'd simply send the company a correction. If the cover had already been paid out, it would have to be returned—subject to a reasonable depletion of the sum, which would be non-refundable."

"We're not planning to use the money; we told you that the first time we met." Sigríður ran a hand through her hair, which looked greasy and unwashed. There were two obvious stains on her shirt and her jeans could have done with a wash as well. Margeir's gray stubble and dirty hair gave him the look of a man recovering from a serious illness. There was nothing to choose between them for suffering. "The money belongs to Sigga Dögg; we'd only use it for her upkeep. And to pay for all the legal proceedings you're describing."

"That won't make much of a dent in the money."

"Won't it?" snapped Sigríður. Margeir laid a hand on his wife's knee, as if afraid she would offend Thóra. But Thóra knew it wasn't personal; the woman was angry with the world in general. Sigríður continued: "You mentioned proof that would have to be sent with the letter. What did you mean?"

"Documents showing when they left port, the route information they supplied on their departure from Lisbon, the weather conditions, where the yacht was last sighted with the crew and passengers on board, and so on. We'd also have to send a report detailing any signs that might indicate that the yacht had been abandoned in a hurry or that the passengers had been washed overboard, along with other material relating to the inquiry, which I should be able to obtain from the police. If they're unwilling to cooperate, I'll have to apply for a court order to compel them." The couple looked even more disheartened. "Don't worry. I'll take care of all that. You have enough on your plate."

"You can say that again." Margeir made no attempt to play down their distress. "We're on the verge of . . . well, I don't really know what."

"Of madness," said Sigrídur emphatically. She flushed a little, then went on, candid in her grief: "The worst thing is hearing about the case on the radio and seeing it in the papers. I keep thinking about all the news of deaths and accidents I've heard over the years without really comprehending the pain they bring. Of course you think: *Poor things*, but it never occurred to me that this would happen to us—that *we*'d be the 'poor things.' " She sniffed loudly and sat up straighter. "But luckily the news has quieted down a bit now. And there's another thing; I know it's futile, but I can't stop brooding over how it came about in the first place. They'd never intended to sail home." Her eyes slid sideways, as if she couldn't bring herself to look at Thóra while getting this off her chest. Perhaps she was ashamed of these thoughts, though they were only natural in a grieving woman. "If that crew member hadn't injured himself, they'd have flown home as planned. And if Ægir hadn't taken that sailing course—no one could understand what had gotten into him at the time—he'd never have been asked to step in." Her eyes welled up and she broke off briefly. "And I would still have a son and a daughter-in-law and the twins." Margeir sat very still, staring into space. No doubt the same thoughts had been running through his mind, but he preferred not to share them with a stranger.

Thóra picked up a brightly colored Duplo brick and handed it to the little girl who had sidled up to her. The child stared down at it as if expecting it to do something entertaining. Thóra knew she was two years old—it felt like only yesterday that her grandson, Orri, had been the same age. There was an air of sadness about the girl. "And how has she taken it?" Thóra smiled warmly at Sigga Dögg, who looked surprised. "Is she too young to grasp what's happened?"

"She hasn't a clue what's going on. She cries for her mother every night." The woman shivered. "I don't know what to do. How do you explain something like that to a baby? We had a visit from a child psychologist and a social worker but neither of them could give us any advice."

"It must be very unusual. It's not every day that almost an entire family goes missing. Perhaps they don't know how to deal with it." The child held out the brick to Thóra, having decided it was no fun, and she took it back. "I mean, I can't begin to put myself in your shoes, so I can't claim to fully understand. This is a tragedy no one should have to go through. Maybe it's a good thing she's too young to comprehend what's happened." Thóra couldn't tell from the grandmother's expression whether she agreed or not. Her face looked as if it had been turned to stone; as if the corners of her mouth were doomed to turn down for the rest of her days. It was harder to interpret her husband's state; if anything, he appeared even more destroyed. "Have you had any further thoughts about her future? I imagine you still want access, at the very least."

"Of course," replied Sigrídur. "But we still haven't decided whether we should apply to keep her. Of course it's what we really want, but we appreciate that there's no guarantee we'd be granted custody, or that it would be deemed in her best interests. As I told you on the phone, the social workers came round yesterday and again this morning, and we feel as if they hold all the cards. They'll take her away, regardless of what happens about the money, and leave us empty-handed. It doesn't look good. They haven't had the guts to break it to us yet but I can see it in their eyes." Sigrídur looked at the little girl, who was still gazing silently at Thóra. "Sadly, there are no uncles or aunts; Ægir was an only child and Lára had no siblings apart from that no-good brother of hers. It would be out of the question for him to adopt Sigga Dögg. And Lára's parents are no better off than us, they say they can't take her. Naturally we've been to see them and talked a great deal on the phone, but Lára's mother is so distraught she can't even have Sigga Dögg round to her house for a few hours. I know it's not fair to the child but I can't help praying every night that we'll be allowed to keep her. I've handed in my notice at work, and together we could give her all our attention." She wiped the corners of her eyes angrily, as if furious with her own grief. "She's named after me. It'll be so unfair if she's taken away from us. If she vanishes from our lives as well, it'll be as if we never had any children. As if those pictures were only borrowed." She gestured at the framed photographs.

The child extended her hand for the brick again and Thóra laid it on the little palm. She had a sudden urge to take in the child herself, to guarantee that her grandparents would be allowed access. But it was only a momentary impulse; a decision like that couldn't be made in a hurry, quite apart from the fact that Thóra was in no position to add a small child to her household. "As soon as you're ready, I'll look into it for you. Even if they allow Sigga Dögg to stay here for a while, you won't have long to make up your minds. Once Ægir and Lára are declared dead, you can expect the child protection authorities to take up her case." She couldn't say any more than that. While she was fairly confident that the formalities relating to the will and Ægir and Lára's life insurance policies would eventually be dealt with in a reasonable manner, a question mark hung over the child's fate. In her opinion, the best solution would probably be for the child to be adopted by a nice young couple and for her grandparents to be allowed regular contact with her, though it was unlikely to be frequent enough to satisfy them. She decided to turn to more pressing matters. If they asked her to act for them in their application for custody or access, the little girl's case would of course take precedence, but right now there were other concerns. "If you can face it, I'd be grateful if you could answer a few questions relating to the points I need to cover in my letter to the insurance provider." They both agreed, apparently relieved by the change of subject.

"Had Ægir or Lára been diagnosed with a critical illness, either recently or before they took out their life cover? If they failed to disclose any information about their health when they took out their policies, it could invalidate them. Any recent illness could be used to cast suspicion on their deaths."

"They were both very fit. Never suffered a day's serious illness." Margeir sounded as if he knew what he was talking about. "Neither of them smoked and they only drank in moderation," he added, as if that alone were enough to provide a watertight bill of health.

"Good. Could I have the name of their GP in case I'm asked for documentary evidence?"

"I don't think we know which practice they went to," replied Sigrídur. She looked at her husband hopefully, but neither could answer.

"It doesn't matter. I can probably find out from their local health center. Let's turn to the incident itself. Was there no suggestion at all before they set out that Ægir and his family might sail home to Iceland?"

Margeir appeared irritated but when he spoke his voice was as flat and empty of feeling as before. "Not a word. They would have told us. After all, we were taking care of their daughter. No, I'm positive it wasn't planned."

"People often discuss possibilities, then change their minds—they could have toyed with the idea before deciding against it. But it's good to hear they didn't. It'll support your claim that Ægir was forced to step in." Thóra was keen to remove all doubt; she didn't like to raise the matter, but the insurance company's potential assertion that the family had arranged their own disappearance would be undermined if it could be proven that the voyage had been a last-minute decision. Conspiracies required considerable preparation; it was highly unlikely that they could be organized at extremely short notice. Either the decision to vanish without a trace had been made before they left Iceland, or they had made no such plan. In any case, the idea was patently ridiculous. What kind of person would abscond like that and put his parents through such anguish? The same anguish that Lára's parents must be experiencing right now. "Is it at all conceivable that they were considering returning by sea but forgot to tell you?"

The woman plucked at a loose thread on her shirt cuff. Her nails were badly bitten and her hands veiny; her fingers a little crooked, perhaps from arthritis. "Obviously we can't answer that. Look, I don't know what you've been told; all I can say is that if they were intending to come home by boat, they didn't breathe a word about it to me. Not a word." She glanced at her husband for corroboration.

"Nor me." His voice was firm now. "And they had plenty of opportunities to raise the idea. Presumably they didn't because it was never part of their plan." From his body language, it appeared he had a better command over his feelings than Thóra had imagined.

"Fine. I wouldn't worry about it." Thóra regretted having created any doubt in their minds. They had enough worries as it was. "Did they send you any e-mails or other messages that would confirm their travel plans? With phone numbers, for example, or information about the hotel they'd be staying at, in case of emergency?"

"We're not on e-mail," Sigrídur replied, "but Ægir gave us a list of dates and hotels, as well as their cell phone numbers. They were very anxious because it was the first time they'd left Sigga Dögg on her own. The list is still on the fridge. Do you want me to fetch it?" Thóra nodded and the woman rose to her feet with an effort. As she went into the kitchen she held a hand to her hip as if it was painful. The sight did nothing to boost Thóra's confidence about their chances of gaining custody. But her spirits rose when she saw the list, because it supported the current interpretation of events. The family had been intending to fly home and resume life as normal after their holiday. The neatly written itinerary with the phone numbers of the two hotels they would be staying at, one in London, the other in Lisbon; their flight numbers and departure and arrival times—this was all evidence that they had wanted to be absolutely sure they could be contacted and that Ægir's parents would be in no doubt about where to find them at any given time. They gave her permission to take the note away with her, as long as she promised to return it afterward.

"Did you hear from them at any point while they were away? Before they left port, for instance?"

"Oh, yes," said Sigrídur. "They rang often. The last time was to tell us they were coming home by ship. They'd actually embarked by then and were just leaving harbor. I spoke to them both. Ægir gave me a brief account of how it had come about but they were mainly ringing to speak to Sigga Dögg." She reached down and picked up the little girl. "They said they'd ring back before they lost their signal but they never did. I don't know why. Maybe they lost reception sooner than expected. I've no idea how far out at sea cell phones stop working."

"Neither have I." Thóra had hoped to hear that they'd been in touch with Ægir or Lára during the voyage, via satellite phone or radio. That would have made it easier to ascertain when the family had gone missing. But it couldn't be helped; doubtless the police had information that would narrow the time frame, like the captain's communications with shore.

Sigga Dögg laid her cheek against her grandmother's chest and cuddled up to her. After a bit of wriggling to find a comfortable position, she turned her head to watch Thóra. The toddler's large gray eyes observed her intently, though it was unclear what she was expecting. Perhaps she thought Thóra was yet another social worker come to give her a test or ask her questions—not that she seemed capable of answering; she hadn't said a word since Thóra arrived. "Has she started talking yet?"

The girl's grandfather answered. "Oh, yes. She can say plenty. Though she's been much quieter since . . . you know. She understands more than you'd think. Actually, that's why we're unhappy with what the experts have been saying to her. You'd have thought professionals like them would know better."

"What do you mean?" Thóra was puzzled. "Are you saying you've witnessed inappropriate behavior?"

"No, we weren't allowed to be present during yesterday's visit." He reached out and gently stroked Sigga Dögg's leg. "But it doesn't alter the fact that she's suddenly started coming out with things she can only have heard from other people, and since it wasn't from us, it must have been those jumped-up government flunkies. We haven't felt up to receiving visitors, so she doesn't really see anyone else." He withdrew his hand. "Not that we've had to turn many away."

"What's she been saying that's led you to that conclusion?"

They both pursed their lips as if reluctant to answer. Then their eyes met and Sigríður silently urged Margeir to speak. "Things connected to the accident. Things she can't have made up herself. A two-year-old knows nothing about d-e-a-t-h, let alone d-r-o-w-n-i-n-g." He laboriously spelled out the words. "She must have heard that from someone else and, as I said, there aren't many obvious candidates."

Thóra's mind kicked into action. Was it possible that the child had heard this not from the social worker or psychologist, but from her parents? Could they have been plotting in front of the little girl? It was just conceivable that it might emerge now, when the child grasped that all was not well with her parents and sisters. Thóra opened her mouth to ask a leading question but couldn't frame one. If Lára and Ægir were lying on a beach somewhere, soaking up the sun, then his parents were plainly not in on the secret. Their grief was too real, their bewilderment too palpable for them to be acting a part. The more she thought about it, the more impossible it seemed. No one would do that to their parents or child. "Children are easily distracted," she said. "I'm sure she'll soon become interested in something else." She caught the little girl's gaze. "Maybe pussycats? Do you like pussycats? I've got one. She's rather fat."

Sigga Dögg raised her head from her grandmother's chest, her lips slightly parted, a trickle of saliva glistening between them. It looked almost silver in the strange light from the window.

"Mommy."

Thóra felt the blood rise to her cheeks. What had she been thinking of to talk about cats to a child in this situation? She knew nothing about child psychology, despite having almost completed the practical when it came to her own children and grandchild. That clearly wasn't enough, however. "Yes, sweetheart." Unsure what else to say, she hoped the child would stop talking, or that one of her grandparents would jump in. But they sat in silence, perhaps disconcerted by how much they had revealed to a virtual stranger.

"Mommy got water in mouth." The little girl's own mouth turned down. "Oh, dear."

Thóra coughed, flustered. She glanced at Sigríđur and Margeir. "Is this what you meant?"

They nodded, their eyes perturbed. "There's more," said Sigríđur, almost in a whisper. "Just wait."

The child didn't seem to notice that she had her grandparents' full attention. She sat with eyes wide open, gazing at Thóra who had the feeling that the little girl was frustrated at being unable to communicate what she wanted to say. "Oh, dear. Poor Adda and Bygga." She stuck out her lower lip to indicate sadness. "Bad water."

Thóra wasn't sure if she had heard right; it sounded as if the little girl was referring to her sisters Arna and Bylgja. "Bad water?"

The child nodded. "Poor Adda and Bygga." She inclined her head toward Thóra, the gesture uncomfortably adult in such a young child. "Big bad water. Water in mouth."

Thóra's cell phone bleeped in her bag; a pale blue light was visible through the opening. Profoundly grateful for the interruption, she fished for it apologetically. The office number flashed up. She put it on silent, though the screen continued to glow. "It doesn't sound as if she's repeating anything that adults would say."

"Well, who else could she have gotten it from? She hasn't met any other children since . . ." Sigrídur clutched her granddaughter tight as if she was afraid Thóra would snatch her away. Her voice was shrill and she placed her hands solicitously over the little girl's ears to protect her from hearing her agitation.

"Is it possible she could have heard someone discussing the family's fate and is trying to understand it in her own way?" The big water must surely mean the sea and water in mouth could be a child's understanding of drowning, though a two-year-old couldn't be expected to comprehend such a word.

"I wouldn't know; as far as I'm aware no one's discussed it in front of her. But whatever's behind it, it's terribly distressing. She woke up crying last night, stammering these words between sobs and calling for her mother. The same thing happened this morning. She's quiet now, but last night she was out of her mind with terror. What can you say to a child who calls for her mother, when no one knows what's happened to her?"

"I can't begin to imagine." Thóra realized it was time to call a halt. These people were seething with suppressed rage and grief over what had happened and with anxiety about the future. It must be a terrible strain to live with such uncertainty. She pitied the psychologist and social worker who had to advise them. "Look, I know it's naive of me, but I really hope they're found drifting in a lifeboat somewhere and that everything will soon be back to normal."

They regarded her suspiciously at first, then seemed to accept that she was sincere. Margeir stretched. "So do we." He clenched his fists until the knuckles whitened. "As you can no doubt imagine."

The phone on Thóra's lap had gone dark. When she darted a glance at it, it flashed once to indicate a text message. "Excuse me." It might be Bragi or one of her other colleagues needing to get hold of her urgently. But the message was from Bella: *Saw online body turned up—prob from yacht.*

Instantly all hope of finding them adrift in a lifeboat vanished.

Chapter 10

Thóra was far from satisfied when she hung up. It wasn't that she had expected to be supplied with exhaustive detail about the body that had been washed ashore but she had hoped to get a little more for her trouble. In the event, the news Web sites proved more informative. The police had stonewalled all her inquiries with: *I'm afraid we can't reveal any information at present.* She was still in the dark about the gender and age of the deceased, and could receive no confirmation that the body was even connected with the yacht.

"Who is it? Do you know?" Bella appeared in the doorway and leaned against the frame, holding a steaming mug of coffee. The aroma wafted across the room, and Thóra realized she was in dire need of caffeine. For a split second it crossed her mind to ask Bella for a sip, but she was not that desperate.

"They refused to say." Thóra turned back to her computer and checked in case there was any more news. There wasn't.

"Those bloody cops are useless." Bella scowled.

"Oh, I expect they're just following protocol; no doubt they have to notify the next of kin before they can discuss it with all and sundry." Thóra's thoughts flew to little Sigga Dögg, who probably had a greater interest than anyone in knowing the identity of the body. But then again, the crew members might also have children who were now waiting in fearful suspense. The papers had just published the names of the missing men but not their family circumstances. No doubt those would follow in the next reports, along with the promise of interviews with loved ones desperately waiting for news. She had tried Googling their names but they were too common, though one had been familiar: Halldór Thorsteinsson, the sailor who had worked on the yacht for a three-month period while it was owned by Karítas and Gulam. It must be the same man—anything else would be too much of a coincidence—so that ruled out the possibility of picking his brains about the yacht's life-saving equipment or what he thought had happened.

Thóra was torn between hoping that the body was not from the yacht and praying that it was. At least the recovery of a body would make it easier to secure the insurance money. Presumably it would also be a comfort of sorts for the families if the remains of their loved ones were found. Though what did she know? If it were her children, would she want closure or would she rather cling to hope for years, for the rest of her life even? On balance, she'd probably prefer to live with the uncertainty. "I can't put my finger on it, but I get the impression from the news reports that it's a man. There's something about the way it's phrased. Even though it's the twenty-first century, people still write differently about women—with more delicacy somehow."

"Is there a picture?" Bella's eagerness struck Thóra as tasteless.

"No, of course not." No online media source had published any photos with a direct link to the incident; one showed the crippled yacht moored in Reykjavík harbor; another the coastline where the body had been discovered; the rest made do with vague sea-related visuals. The police had managed to evade the vigilant eyes of photographers while carrying out their duties, helped by the fact that the beach where the body had washed up was well off the beaten track. It was located some way to the south of the village of Sandgerdi, on the western tip of the Reykjanes peninsula, about forty-five kilometers south of Reykjavík. Anyway, even if reporters had stumbled on the scene, it was unthinkable that any news site would publish a picture of the corpse.

"I reckon it's a woman." Bella slurped her coffee. "And I bet I know who."

"Well, it wouldn't take a clairvoyant. Lára was the only woman on board."

"I don't mean her. I think it's Karítas."

Thóra looked up from the screen. "What on earth makes you say that? That would be really weird."

"Well, firstly, I'm sure she must of snuffed it."

"Must *have*," Thóra corrected her automatically—it came from living with three children. She might get away with it this time but it was excruciating when she caught herself doing the same to clients or colleagues. The worst occasion was the time she had corrected a judge. She was still convinced her client had received a heavier sentence as a result.

"Must of, must have. Whatever."

"Never mind that, why do you think so?"

"I've been combing the Internet for any news or blogs mentioning Karítas. However hard I search, I can't find a single photo or any other information about her since she left for Portugal to sort out her stuff. Which is kind of suspicious."

"She's hardly big enough news for the papers to go chasing her halfway round the world in hope of a story. Surely she's simply lying low in Brazil like her mother said? Just because she's managed to disappear so effectively doesn't mean there's any cause for concern. She hasn't been gone that long."

"I have zero concern for her. I couldn't care less whether she's lying in a body bag in the morgue or on a sun-lounger somewhere in South America." Bella's tone belied her words. People rarely forgave others for what they did to them when they were children, and the secretary wasn't exactly the magnanimous type. "I'm not just talking about the Icelandic sites—I'm talking about the Internet as a whole. There's a ton of pictures and websites recording that she attended various parties, but they all pre-date her visit to Portugal. What's more, there were two fairly recent articles that mentioned her old man and his agreements with his creditors, but not a single word about her. If you ask me, that's fishy. I can't believe she'd voluntarily steer clear of the limelight, wherever she is. She gets off on the attention." Bella gulped down her coffee with an exaggerated relish that made Thóra green with envy. "She's a goner. Her old man's killed her."

Although the possibility had already occurred to Thóra, it sounded implausible when spoken aloud. Indeed, she now understood Matthew's skeptical reaction when she had voiced a similar idea. "We know nothing for certain about this woman apart from one thing: it's not her body. It just doesn't fit. For one thing, if her husband had killed her, how could she have been on board?"

"Maybe he'd hidden her body on the yacht and the passengers found it, freaked out and threw it overboard. Then maybe they regretted it and tried to recover her body but something went wrong and they ended up in the sea themselves."

Thóra bit back a mocking riposte. Ever since she had started working on this case, Bella's attitude toward her had been unusually mellow. Their relationship had been strained for a while, and this armistice made a welcome change. It felt like ages since Thóra had been able to relax at the office without worrying about what the secretary might be plotting behind her back, so she had everything to gain by keeping the peace. She had even refrained from giving Bella too much of a hassle about the photocopier, which they were having no success in recovering from the workshop. "Who knows? Maybe."

Bella frowned. "Or maybe an alien swallowed her whole and puked her up in the sea just off Reykjanes—by total coincidence." Her gaze was fixed provocatively on Thóra's. "I know when you mean what you say and when you don't. I'm not a total idiot. If you think my idea about Karítas is bullshit, just say so."

"I don't know what's bullshit in this case, Bella. That's the trouble. I'd be surprised if you were right, but then I'd probably be surprised by all the possible alternatives. The explanation's bound to be extraordinary, so there's no need to take offense."

"I'm not offended." Clearly, she was. Her coffee was no longer steaming and the delicious aroma had gone, to be replaced by the familiar smell of stale vomit. Though it had faded, the miasma still seemed to linger and Thóra was beginning to wonder if it was in her imagination. If so, she would never be rid of it. She wrinkled her nose.

"Could you give the workshop a ring about the photocopier? I've tried calling but they seem very relaxed about the parts that are supposedly on their way. If we keep bugging them maybe they'll make more of an effort to chase them down." It went without saying that Bella was better qualified for that role than anyone else in the office. "If you can get the copier back by the end of the week, I'll install that high-speed broadband you keep going on about."

Bella screwed up her eyes, apparently regarding this as an unfair exchange. But in that she was wrong; they'd had no plans to upgrade their connection, so Bella only stood to gain by making an effort. After all, she was the only employee who complained about the current connection speed and download capacity, and they all knew that the secretary's desire for an upgrade had nothing to do with work. Indeed, that was why Thóra and Bragi had been dragging their feet: it would be extremely embarrassing if the firm ended up being investigated by the police for illegal downloads on an industrial scale.

"Okay. Deal. But I haven't been going on about it—only asking." Glowering, Bella took herself off, no doubt to seek out the most powerful upgrade on offer but hopefully also to launch a major campaign of harassment against the repair shop.

Thóra had difficulty concentrating after Bella had gone. She still had to collate a lot of documents to enclose with the notification to the insurance provider but simply didn't know where to begin. It didn't help that if the newly recovered corpse turned out to be Lára or Ægir, this would render some of the paperwork unnecessary. There was a possibility the postmortem might reveal the cause of death to have been a disease, as it wasn't out of the question that the crew had fallen ill or been poisoned. She picked up the phone to dial the number of her ex-husband, Hannes, then changed her mind. This was not because she thought he would take her request badly—on the contrary, he was usually helpful on the rare occasions she sought his advice on medical matters. Since the divorce this was about the only subject they could discuss without constantly having to watch their words as if negotiating a minefield. No, she was afraid of losing her temper with him over his ridiculous notion of sending Gylfi to an oil rig in the middle of the Arctic Ocean. Even if she had deliberately sat down and made a list of all the ways Hannes could possibly screw up as a parent, this would never have crossed her mind. An oil rig. She sighed aloud and replaced the receiver. The conversation would only descend into an insult match and she would never get round to asking about infectious diseases. Besides, it was unclear what good a list of them would achieve. They would still be left with the problem of why the passengers were unaccounted for, since surely there was no illness that triggered a longing to fling oneself into the sea.

Thóra refreshed her browser and realized a new article had been posted about the body.

It was high time Brynjar changed jobs, and no one knew this better than him. He was finding the night shifts no easier now than when he had started work as a port security officer five years ago, back when he still believed he would get used to them. It had never been his plan to get stuck in this job; he'd only meant to bridge the gap after dropping out of university, earn a little money before enrolling in a course that suited him better. He'd intended to use the nights to ponder his future, but now, some thousand night shifts later, the only conclusion he'd reached was that he didn't want to work here any longer. The arrival of the yacht had opened his eyes: no doubt the people on board had believed, like him, that they had their whole lives before them, but they were wrong. He didn't want the life he was living now to be his lot forever, but only he had the power to change it. He'd become socially isolated, as if he lived in a different time zone from his friends, and if he didn't take action soon he would end up a lonely old weirdo, interacting only with the undesirables who roamed Reykjavík's streets by night.

Like these two. "You shouldn't be here. This area is restricted." He walked briskly toward a couple who were staggering along the quay. The girl was wearing high heels, hopelessly inappropriate to the terrain, which made her walk like a zombie, at least when viewed from behind. Her companion was little better, though he couldn't blame his footwear. Brynjar hoped he wasn't the type who became violent when drunk. He'd had enough of those.

The girl turned, bleary-eyed, her lipstick smeared. "Eh?" She called to her companion who had continued walking. "Lolli! Talk to this bloke." Her tongue sounded thick and swollen in her mouth.

"You what?" The man appeared older than the girl, probably around Brynjar's own age. He swayed as he tried to get his bearings. "Who are you?" He paused to do battle with the forces of gravity. "Wanna party?"

"Sure, why not." Brynjar beckoned them over. "Come on, or you'll end up in the sea."

"The sea?" The girl didn't seem to know where she was. "Whaddya mean?" she slurred. "We're going to a party."

"There's no party here. If that's what you're looking for, you'll have to head back into town—or home."

"No. There's a party. We saw it." The man had reached the girl's side and was leaning on her. They seemed steadier like that than separately.

"Then you must be seeing things. There are no buildings here, just boats. And no parties."

The man smiled idiotically. "Yes, there is. We could see it." He turned and pointed into the air. "On that posh boat over there."

Brynjar realized at once which vessel he meant; the couple would hardly describe the fishing boats or trawlers as "posh." He must be referring to the yacht that was berthed in the Coast Guard area. "There's no party there. You'll have to leave. Come back tomorrow when you're in a better state."

"There *is* a party. I saw it. One of the guests was on deck." The girl sounded like a spoiled child who got hold of an idea and wouldn't let go. "You can't ban us from going to a party."

"You're mistaken. There's no one on board and no party. That ship is damaged; no one would throw a party on board." Brynjar felt his heart begin to pound, pumping the blood round his body in readiness for danger. "I repeat, you'll have to leave."

"There *is* someone there." The girl swung her head clumsily to her companion, stumbling as she did so. Brynjar put out a hand to prevent her from falling flat on her back, but the man didn't notice. He seemed in an even worse state than when Brynjar had first spotted them. Initially he had contented himself with watching them from his hut, hoping they'd turn back and spare him the bother of dealing with them. He didn't recall noticing any movement on the yacht, though come to think of it the couple had stopped and stared at it when they first entered the harbor area. The girl had nudged the man and pointed, but Brynjar had assumed she recognized it from the news. It went without saying that he would have shot out of the hut the instant he spotted an unauthorized visitor on board. It must have been an illusion.

"I think I'd better go home." The man's face had turned gray. "I don't feel well. I reckon I'm seasick. Is the dock moving?" Brynjar couldn't be bothered to point out that they were standing on solid concrete. The man was leaning most of his weight on the skinny girl, who was not amused. "Thanks, mate, it was cool—be seeing you." He had forgotten who Brynjar was. They tottered away, in spite of the girl's protests that they were missing out on a "wicked boat party."

When he was sure they had really gone, Brynjar finally braced himself to look over at the yacht. She was listing a little toward the dockside, presumably as a result of the damage she'd sustained when she hit the jetty. Was it possible that a drunk had climbed aboard without his noticing and was now wandering about on deck? He couldn't see any movement, or hear any sound but the quiet lapping of the waves, but there was a chance someone might be standing out of sight. They couldn't be below decks unless they had broken in, since all the doors were securely locked. Perhaps the drunk had left or passed out, if he or she was ever there in the first place. Still, Brynjar was duty bound to investigate, however little he relished the task. He started walking.

Recently the yacht had dominated conversation in the coffee breaks between shifts, so Brynjar had heard all the tales about her supposed curse. While he didn't necessarily believe such nonsense, he couldn't ignore the fact that there was an odd atmosphere about her, one which couldn't be put entirely down to the lurid stories or the unknown fate of her passengers. He had witnessed with his own eyes the way the birds shunned her, never perching on her, not even flying over her if they could help it. Of course it could be—must be—coincidence. And yet. The night after she had been moved to her current mooring he had noticed several fish floating dead in the water by her hull. This was abnormal; he couldn't remember ever having seen more than one dead fish at a time before. As his job demanded, he had made a note of the incident and learned the following evening that a team from the Matís food research institute had collected the dead fish for testing. Brynjar's informant had added that although some of the white coats put it down to pollution or poisoning, people in the know believed it was linked to the yacht.

There was no sign of any figure on deck. Switching on his torch, he shone it along the ship but could see nothing but fleeting shadows. "Hello!" His shout pierced the stillness but faded instantly. The ensuing silence felt heavier, more tangible, as if it resented the disturbance. "Hello!" Brynjar called again, wondering how often he would have to repeat this before he could be said to have done his duty. There was no answer. He took a step backward to get a better view and began to shine his torch back and forth along the white aluminum hull, at which the shadows resumed their jerky dance. He tried to illuminate the waterline to check that the uninvited guest hadn't fallen overboard but could see nothing unusual. A red Coke can was floating lazily beside the ship; otherwise the sea looked as if it had been vacuum-cleaned. When he directed the beam further away he noticed a narrow white ribbon of mist curling in over the surface of the water from the harbor mouth, only about a meter above sea level. While it was not particularly common, he had often experienced misty conditions in the harbor before without being alarmed. But this time it was different. He didn't want to be standing beside this notorious ship if the mist thickened into a fog and closed in on him, reducing visibility to zero. Enough was enough.

He hurried back toward his hut, not looking round even when he thought he heard a whisper from the deserted yacht. He couldn't make out the words but was fairly sure that, despite their similarity, there were two voices. Female, but not those of grown women; more like children. Two children. Twins. His mouth felt suddenly dry and the torch weighed heavy in his hand. He stopped and strained his ears, though his brain was screaming at him to keep moving. He could hear nothing now, yet that did little to lessen his terror. He hadn't a clue what he was afraid of; until now children had roused little emotion in him, and certainly never fear. Perhaps it was the mental image of the dead sisters roaming the yacht in a vain search for their parents or a way out, forever trapped aboard the vessel that had robbed them of their future. Brynjar started walking again. One thing was certain—he wasn't putting a word about this in his report, or people would think he had finally cracked.

He quickened his pace and once safely inside the hut locked the door behind him for the first time since he'd started the job. Then he rang the police and reported a possible break-in on the yacht, not mentioning the voices. If something untoward was happening, let the police sort it out.

He *really* needed a new job.

Chapter 11

The young man on the other end of the line sounded subdued and distracted. He was the only Snævar Thórdarson in the telephone directory whose occupation was listed as ship's engineer. Thóra had been running out of ideas about who to ask for background information on the yacht when she suddenly remembered the crew member who had dropped out, and Fannar had supplied her with his name. With any luck, she thought, his account of the accident that had caused him to be left behind might also come in useful for her report.

Snævar readily admitted that he was meant to have sailed with the *Lady K* to Iceland but his replies to Thóra's questions, though so swift and to the point they almost seemed rehearsed, were not actually much help since his involvement in the preparations for the voyage had been minimal. At first she found it odd that his answers should be so fluent, but it turned out that he had already given the police three separate statements.

When Thóra persisted, Snævar became more uncomfortable, especially on the subject of how Ægir had come to take his place on board; but then, it can't have been much fun to be the indirect cause of a whole family's disappearance. He started off trying to give a sober, factual account, but as he progressed he became increasingly choked up with emotion.

"I'm still in shock, to be honest. I'm not usually easily upset, but when I saw the yacht sail straight into the docks with none of the crew doing a thing to prevent it, I knew something was seriously wrong. I was so nearly on board myself. It should have been me, not that couple and their poor little girls."

"Disasters are impossible to predict; you can hardly blame yourself

for what happened. This time you were lucky, and others less so."
Thóra was aware of the futility of her words; his conscience would
continue to gnaw at him whatever she said. "Why were you on the
docks when the yacht was due in? Surely that wasn't by chance?"

"I'd come to pick up Halli. We were mates; he's the one who sorted
out the job for me. We were both between tours on the trawler
and he thought it would be a good idea to take me along. They were
dead keen to hire him because of his previous experience, so he
had no trouble fixing it for me. Personally, I wasn't that bothered, but
I didn't mind going. You know—the pay was all right and I reckoned
it might be a laugh if Halli was going, too. We could have a bit of an
adventure; the flight was free and we could hit the nightlife in Lisbon. But even that went wrong, though the first couple of days were
awesome."

"Because of your accident?"

"Yes. Breaking a leg is no joke. And it was a real bummer for Halli
to have to go through it all with me."

"May I ask what happened?" Silence greeted her question. "You
don't have to tell me unless you want to, but if you don't I'll simply
have to find out by other means. It's vital for me to know why Ægir
ended up on the boat if I'm to sort out his and his wife's affairs. May
I remind you that they have another little girl, and for her sake it's
essential that the settlement of their estate goes through as smoothly
as possible. Which means we need to clarify the sequence of events."

"All right, I can tell you what happened." He briefly turned his head
away from the receiver to cough. "Though I don't really like talking
about it because the accident was so stupid."

"Most accidents are, so you needn't worry about that."

"Maybe not." He took a deep breath, then the words came out in
a rush as if to give them less time to leave a bad taste in his mouth. "I
was drunk. Totally off my face, and I tripped and fell down one of
those really steep streets in Lisbon. Actually, I was lucky it didn't turn
out worse because I rolled quite a long way and nearly ended up getting run over. If I had, it might have changed everything for the better. At least, that's what I keep telling myself."

Thóra could think of nothing to say. If Snævar had been killed, his friend Halldór would almost certainly have pulled out of the voyage, and then the captain wouldn't have been able to get away with using Ægir as a replacement. The committee would have been forced to hire two new crew members instead. Still, it was no use crying over spilled milk.

"And there's another thing," Snævar continued. "I don't know if it has any bearing on this case, but I was pushed. The Portuguese doctors didn't want to hear it—no one was listening to me because I was totally out of it. But I *was* pushed. It all happened very fast, but I'm almost a hundred percent positive."

"If you could give me some proof of the accident, I'd be very grateful. Regardless of whether you were pushed."

"What, you want my leg?" It must have been meant as a joke, though Snævar did not sound particularly amused.

"Actually, I was thinking more along the lines of hospital notes or maybe a signed statement from you."

"I can give you a statement but I might need your help to put it together. I don't have any documents, though; the whole thing was handled by the Social Insurance office. If you like, I can ring them and ask if they have the papers. It's not as if I have much else to do at the moment. If they can't help, you'll just have to contact the hospital in Lisbon."

"Okay. When would suit you? Is there any chance you could come to my office tomorrow or the day after, so I can type it up? And it would be helpful if you could have a word with the Social Insurance people first." Thóra was pleased with the way this phone call had panned out, though she hadn't had high hopes beforehand. "On a tangent, since you knew Halli, I wanted to ask if you have any idea why he originally quit after working on the *Lady K* for such a short time. Could it have had anything to do with inadequate safety procedures? Or a problem with the yacht's engine?"

"Oh, it was nothing like that. According to him, everything was fine. All the equipment was present and correct, and the engine was as good as new; he had no complaints on that score."

"So what was it?"

"I gather it was to do with the captain. Halli said he was a complete jerkoff and really tightfisted. I haven't crewed any yachts myself but according to Halli, the way it works is that at the end of every tour the captain is given a tip that he's supposed to share with the crew. But there are two kinds of captains—those who divide the money equally between all the crew members and those who take sixty percent to share with the mate and chief engineer, then give what's left to the rest of the crew. It might not sound so bad but when you're working for the jet set there can be as many as twelve employees sailing the boat, cooking, cleaning and working as waiters. Then it really matters how the tip's shared out. The *Lady K* usually had a staff of ten and the officers took twenty percent of the tip each, leaving the rest of the poor sods to share the other forty percent. Halli was employed as an engineer, so he was one of the unlucky ones. We're not talking peanuts, either. The tip was often higher than the wages—and tax-free, too." That sounded a bit dodgy to Thóra, but she refrained from commenting. "Under normal circumstances Halli would only have done two tours with a captain like that. But he stayed on a bit longer because he got the impression that the Icelandic woman who owned the yacht liked having him around so she could chat to him in Icelandic—you know, take the piss out of the guests without them understanding. But of course that wasn't enough in the long run, so Halli left. Quit as soon as he found another position."

"Did he stay in touch with Karítas afterward?"

"Are you joking?" Snævar laughed, genuinely this time. "It wasn't that sort of relationship; you've got it all wrong if that's what you think. The crew doesn't really mix with the owners and guests on vessels like that. Halli may have enjoyed a laugh with Karítas, but not every day. As far as I can remember, he only saw her once after that, from a distance. He caught sight of her on the deck of the *Lady K* when she was moored off some island in the Med just after he left—he was working on another yacht by then. Not long afterward he quit the luxury yacht business and went back to the trawlers."

"So he wasn't in contact with her on Facebook?"

"He wasn't on Facebook." Of course not.

"Tell me something." She hesitated for fear Snævar would lose patience and refuse to come to the office if she kept him on the phone too long. "What do *you* think happened? You've been on board, so you must have more insight than most into what might have become of them."

Snævar hesitated before answering; perhaps he was trying to run through all the alternatives he'd considered. "Look, if one or two or even three of them had vanished, there would be all sorts of possible explanations. But all of them? There aren't many answers to that. The only sensible theory I can come up with is that they believed the yacht was sinking and thought their only chance was to abandon ship. Maybe they were afraid she was about to blow up, though it's unlikely the crew or captain would have thought that. They would have known better. In fact, they're trained in risk assessment, so I'm guessing the crew weren't around when it happened. I have no clue what became of them—I still can't come up with a plausible explanation."

"Let's just say they did believe she was sinking—why wouldn't they have launched a lifeboat?"

"How would I know? Maybe they didn't think they had time. Maybe there was another boat nearby that picked them up."

"One final question. What could cause a crew or passengers to misread the situation so badly? Is there an alarm that would go off if the hull was holed, for example? I'm wondering if the system could have malfunctioned and given them the wrong message."

"Naturally, there's an alarm system on board, but even if it went off by mistake, the crew wouldn't just jump overboard. The passengers, maybe—but not the sailors. They'd check what was up and wouldn't abandon ship unless she was literally in flames. Either somebody forced them to leave the yacht or they died by some other means. Nothing else makes any sense."

Thóra thanked him and said good-bye, satisfied even though she was none the wiser.

Although the police were very understanding, Thóra had a tough time persuading them to answer any of her questions. She supposed they would need to double-check what information could be released to her. But at least the officers she spoke to seemed to appreciate the gravity of the situation and were keen to make things easy for her out of sympathy for Ægir's parents and their little granddaughter. Admittedly, eyebrows were raised when she mentioned the life insurance policies, especially when it came to revealing the level of cover. She could have kept quiet about it, but that wouldn't have been in her clients' long-term interests. She persisted for a while in trying to find out whether the body recovered from the sea had any connection to the yacht, but gave up when she realized the police's patience was wearing thin.

"I appreciate that you can't hand over the papers today, but would you be able to give me an idea of what there is? I'm particularly interested to know if the ship's documents were on board and, if so, which ones?" She decided to mention a few essential items but avoid listing them in detail in case she left something out. "I'm particularly interested in the official logbook, any other logbooks and any certificates of seaworthiness. As well as any compliance certificates connected to the yacht's safety equipment."

"That I can tell you." The detective to whom she had finally been passed unwrapped a piece of chewing gum and put it in his mouth. "I'd offer you some if it wasn't nicotine gum. I've just given up smoking. Apparently you just get addicted to this stuff instead but it's not as bad for you as cigarettes, or so they claim." From his expression it would obviously be some time before he became reconciled to the flavor. "Most of the ship's papers were on board and we should be able to release copies to you shortly. Just bear in mind that there are a few pages missing here and there, so the versions you receive will be incomplete."

"Pages missing?" The ship's documents were official papers that the vessel was required to carry by law. Removing material from them would be highly irregular. "Were they the ones relating to the Iceland trip?"

"Yes, in all likelihood. Though there's no way of telling when they were torn out; it may have happened before the captain took over, in which case they wouldn't have included his notes. The problem is, we don't know when the captain disappeared. There are a few entries from the beginning of the voyage, but it looks as if some of the older ones—if that's what they were—have been ripped out. At any rate, the pages haven't turned up. There's no telling whether it's significant, but it certainly looks odd."

Thóra jotted this down. "Next, have you had a chance to examine any cameras or phones? It would help my report if I could establish when the passengers were indisputably still alive."

"No." The detective kept chomping at the gum, his jaw muscles bunching.

"Do you have any idea when you might have a chance to look into it?"

"Never."

"Never?" Thóra was taken aback.

"That's right." His facial muscles relaxed as he shifted the gum to lodge under his upper lip. "There were no cell phones or cameras on board."

"Isn't that a bit odd?"

"I don't know. They probably took all that stuff with them when they abandoned ship, or didn't bring any along in the first place—though I admit that's unlikely."

"Very." Thóra hastily scribbled "phone" and "camera" in her notebook, followed by three question marks. Ægir and Lára had included their cell phone numbers on the list they gave his parents, so they must have intended to take them. And Lára had rung them from on deck, hadn't she, as they were leaving port? So they could hardly have forgotten them in the hotel, or anywhere else in Lisbon. The crew must have had theirs with them too—there was hardly anyone under seventy who didn't own a cell phone these days. It was more than a little suspicious. "Another thing that would be helpful, if it's available, would be the data from the yacht's GPS system. Though I can't work out what format I could access it in."

"We've already plotted their course using the GPS data. If we're permitted to release this to you, it would probably make sense to give you a printout of the maps. That would save you the effort of duplicating our work."

"That would be great. Then there's one further matter and after that I promise not to bother you any more for the time being. Do you have a summary of the yacht's communications with shore or other vessels after she left port, including the dates and times? If I don't submit exhaustive records, I'm afraid the insurance company will take advantage of the fact to delay proceedings."

"Hmm. Good question." He pushed his tongue under his lip to reassure himself that the gum was still there. "That's a bit of a funny one too, actually."

"Oh?" Thóra's first thought was that the yacht's communications system must be missing. Nothing about this case was quite as it ought to be.

"Either the radiotelephones broke down or gremlins got into them during the voyage. Or so we gather from what the captain wrote in the logbook. The satellite phone wasn't working either, though according to the captain's notes that was because they hadn't set up an account for the trip. We're in the process of examining both radios but we do know they were working when the yacht left port. At least, the captain ticked the box stating that they had been tested and were in working order. What hasn't yet emerged is whether they were sabotaged or it was simply coincidence that both broke down."

"Don't they have two radios precisely to avoid that kind of communications breakdown?"

"Possibly, but I gather they also have different ranges. The short-range radio or VHF can only communicate with nearby ships but there is also a long-range one, although I'm not really clued-in on the technology. At any rate, they managed to make contact at least once. The connection was poor so the message was a bit garbled, but about thirty hours out of port the captain spoke to a mate on a British freighter. The conversation took place in English, so there may have been a misunderstanding due to language difficulties, but we aren't ruling out the possibility that the message was correct."

"What was it exactly?" Thóra resisted the urge to cross her fingers.

The detective dislodged the gum from under his lip and began to chew with renewed vigor. "The captain asked the British ship to report the discovery of a body on board to the Icelandic authorities because their own long-range radio was broken and their satellite phone was out of action. From what the English mate could understand, the body was female. Their conversation touched on some other matters too, which I'm not presently able to divulge. Going by what was said, it seems unlikely the woman was Lára, though we can't completely rule it out. And whoever it was, we have absolutely no idea how she died." The policeman stopped chewing and regarded Thóra levelly. "In other words, since we've found no trace of the dead woman, we may be dealing with not seven but eight missing people."

Chapter 12

"It'll have to wait till morning." Thráinn hauled himself back on deck after leaning so perilously far over the rail that Ægir moved instinctively closer to grab him if he fell. "I can't get a good enough view. It looks like it's that sodding container, or at least part of it. You should have called me sooner, Loftur. When there's debris like that in the sea you're lucky if it shows up on the radar, as you should know. We might have been able to avoid the collision if we'd spotted it at the point when it became visible. This isn't what we need right now."

"It was too late." Loftur looked shamefaced. "We hit it almost immediately after the radar picked it up. I was keeping an eye out but then he came in and distracted me." He indicated Ægir, his expression distinctly unfriendly.

"Don't try to blame it on him." Thráinn wiped his hands on his trousers.

Ægir ignored them, not wanting to create trouble between the two men. The outcome was inevitable; sooner or later they would make up and then they would both resent him even more than they did before. He bent over the rail and peered into the gloom below, where he could see the gleam of water but little else. "Won't it have drifted free by morning?"

"Maybe. That would be the best outcome." Thráinn turned to Loftur. "I think we should let her drift tonight rather than trying to hold our position. But Halli had better keep watch with me in case there's any more wreckage about. You go to bed and we'll take it in turns to keep an eye on the bugger and see if we can get any sense out of the VHF. The transmission you heard was probably someone repeating a warning about the container." He looked over the side again. "With any luck it'll break away during the night; if not, we'll sort it out by daylight."

Loftur nodded, still looking sullen. The moment they spotted the container he had sent Ægir to wake the captain. The thud when they struck it had not been loud, nor had it noticeably checked the vessel's progress, but Loftur was alarmed and insisted on putting the engines in neutral until Thráinn had assessed the situation. The captain had taken it seriously too, which did nothing to reassure Ægir. If Thráinn was worried, there was every reason to be afraid: he didn't seem the type to make a fuss about nothing.

"If we're just going to idle, I could take the watch with you." Ægir let go of the rail and instinctively stood up straighter. "Wouldn't that make more sense? Loftur and Halli need their sleep and this may be the only time on this trip that you can trust me with a night watch." The two men said nothing; their expressions were hard to read. "If it turns out that you do need to sort it out tomorrow, wouldn't the sleep do them good? We can always wake them if anything happens." Still neither man broke the silence. Loftur was apparently waiting for Thráinn to come to a decision, but it was unclear whether he hoped the captain would choose Ægir over Halli, or vice versa.

A wave drove the flotsam against the side and another low boom broke the silence. Ægir couldn't help wondering how strong the hull was and how many blows of that magnitude it could withstand. Perhaps his idea of taking the watch was foolish; if the yacht was holed his presence on the bridge would be worse than useless. Even as these reservations occurred to him, Thráinn accepted his offer with a decisive nod. "If anything goes wrong, Loftur, we'll wake you or Halli. With any luck the current will carry it away and solve the problem for us, so there's no need to have two men on watch. It's probably an unnecessary precaution, but you never know when it comes to junk like this."

"No problem." It wouldn't be the first time Ægir had stayed up all night. "I'll just nip below and fetch my book."

Lára was asleep in the cabin with the duvet bunched up around her. Her breathing was heavy and her eyelids flickered as if in a dream. Ægir perched gently on the side of the bed and whispered that he would be on the bridge for the rest of the night. She murmured something incomprehensible and turned over. He doubted she had taken in the message and wondered if he should wake her, but then she might not be able to get back to sleep and would lie awake for the rest of the night. On his way out he stuck his head into the girls' cabin and saw that they were lying oddly entwined in the middle of the double bed. Sigga Dögg beamed at him from the headboard as if to reassure him that everything would be all right; she would watch over her twin sisters while he did the same for the yacht.

He closed the door, plunging their cabin back into darkness.

Ægir hesitated and considered opening the door again, either to turn on the light or at least to leave it open a crack so that the blackness would not be so profound. But neither was a good idea. If he turned on the light, the girls might wake up, and the constant motion of the yacht would make the door bang if he left it open. After a brief pause he set off down the corridor, only to stop by the door at the end. Everything looked as it should; the ceiling lights glowed dimly and all the doors were closed. They fitted so tightly that not a sound could be heard from the cabins and even the drone of the engines seemed more muffled down here than in any other part of the yacht. Even so, Ægir couldn't rid himself of the unsettling feeling that he was abandoning them somehow. Perhaps it was instinct warning him to make the most of every second he could spend with them while they were on board this boat. As if the future was measured in minutes, not years.

Thráinn was waiting for him in the pilot house. His back was turned and Ægir had the impression that he had been speaking into the radiotelephone but was now trying to hide the fact. "Was there another message?"

"What?" Thráinn frowned as if he didn't understand the question. Then realizing what Ægir was referring to, he said: "You mean on the VHF? Oh, no." He ran a hand lightly over the screen. "It seems to be buggered—at least, I'm having trouble getting through. It's a pain in the arse that the long-range radio's playing up as well. I expect what you heard before was the result of a short circuit. Maybe a fuse has blown and affected both radios. On the plus side, it means you won't have to worry about them. You won't hear a peep out of them, not until I've given them the once-over tomorrow with the boys. The problem's too complicated for me to fix tonight."

"I won't mind that." Ægir stared at the VHF, fervently hoping the captain was right; the last thing he wanted to hear when he was alone was that sinister voice echoing through the bridge. The captain's explanation struck him as a little odd, though; how could a short circuit cause the ship's name to be transmitted over the loudspeaker? But the man must know what he was talking about. Ægir couldn't afford to start doubting his expertise at this stage.

He watched as the captain checked the screens, and wondered about the man. He still hadn't come to any conclusion about his character; one minute he was friendly, the next gruff. Even his age was hard to guess. His appearance offered only vague, contradictory clues; thick, dark hair contrasted with a lined or weather-beaten face, and his powerful frame made his height even more striking; Ægir only reached up to his ears. His arms were tanned a dark brown and the back of his right hand was crisscrossed by a network of mysterious white scars. Perhaps they were an accumulation of many different small cuts. Ægir was too ignorant about life at sea to know whether they went with the territory. As he stood beside this big, strong man it occurred to him how sheltered his own life had been—how different from the life of a sailor. Every morning he went to the office where the greatest peril he faced was paper cuts, while this man wrestled with unpredictable currents and ferocious storms. There must have been times when he doubted he would make it home alive. Nothing like that had ever happened to Ægir in his line of work. He cleared his throat. "Do you want me to start outside or inside?"

"Probably best if I take the outside watch to start with."

"Anything in particular I should keep an eye out for?"

Thráinn surveyed the bridge. "Well, there's no need for you to touch the console since we're idling, so I won't waste time teaching you how to use the equipment. If anything happens, just come and get me."

Ægir was left alone in the pilot house. His book seemed to have lost all its power to entertain and he could barely make out the print in the semi-darkness anyway. Despite Thráinn's absence, Ægir couldn't bring himself to occupy his seat like a fully grown man playing at being captain. Instead, he huddled in the corner with his feet propped on a side table. He put his book down, not even bothering to check whether it was open at the right page. It didn't matter, as he was unlikely to return to it during the voyage; if he didn't feel like reading it when alone on night watch, when would he?

It was going to be a long night. He sat with his hands in his lap. Outside there was nothing but impenetrable darkness; there were no stars and the moon was hidden by cloud. Night in the city was nothing compared to this dense, unrelieved blackness. It seemed almost palpable; if he thrust his arm far enough over the rail he imagined he would be able to feel its texture, yielding and slippery, like cold slime. Rising, he moved into the circle of light in the middle of the room. Mercifully, the VHF remained dormant but that malevolent voice still rang in his ears.

He regretted not having asked if it would be all right to step outside now and then for a breath of fresh air or a drink. Surely it would only take him a couple of minutes to dash down to the galley and grab a can? He longed for a cold beer but decided against it, not because he was indirectly in command of the ship but because he was afraid it would make him drowsy. For some reason he felt a strong aversion to sleeping alone in here. No doubt it was the fear of being caught by Thráinn.

The galley lights came on after an instant's delay. He hadn't noticed the humming of the fridge before; perhaps it was because everything was quieter now. He was assailed by a sudden feeling of loneliness and wondered if he should wake Lára to keep him company, but dismissed the idea at once. If he did, the girls would be alone while their parents slept off their fatigue in the morning, and it would be unforgivable to leave them unsupervised on deck. Though they were growing up faster than he liked, they were still young and foolish enough to do something silly.

The fridge, a big double-door model, was half empty. The supplies they had lugged on board could not fill the deep shelves and it was almost alarming to see how little they had to eat. Supposing they ran out of food before the voyage was over? Then again, they had the world's biggest larder right underneath them, so they were unlikely to starve. He pushed aside a bottle of ketchup in the hope of finding a can lurking behind it. No such luck. The same went for all the other possible hiding places in the roomy interior. For a moment he was glad Lára wasn't there to tick him off for failing to replace the can he had taken out earlier. It was an endless bone of contention between them; they both took drinks out of the fridge, but he took it for granted that she would replace them. And the last thing he wanted right now was a tepid Coke. How stupid to have a big fridge like that with no ice-maker. That would have saved the day.

Feeling grumpy, Ægir fetched a Coke from the larder, but his spirits revived when he caught sight of the huge chest freezer whose existence he had forgotten. They had chucked a couple of loaves in it to ensure they would keep for the entire voyage, along with some packets of chicken breasts and mince. He had been in a hurry at the time, so couldn't recall if he had seen any ice cubes, though he did remember that the former owners had left the freezer stuffed to the brim—they had barely been able to squeeze their own food in on top—so it was quite possible there was ice in there somewhere.

The large lid creaked as he opened it. He was met by a puff of arctic vapor and recoiled for an instant before bending over to root around among the frozen contents.

At first he was able to shift the packets without much effort, but couldn't find any ice cubes. Determined not to give up straight away, he carried on digging, deeper and deeper, hampered by increasingly numb fingers. While he rummaged, he reflected on the inadequacies of freezer design; it was impossible to reach the contents at the bottom of the cavernous chest except by removing the upper layers. He was only halfway down when he encountered a black bin-bag, which seemed to fill the rest of the interior. He prodded it in the faint hope that the owner of the yacht had been planning a mega party and had bought in several kilos of ice for the occasion. Unsurprisingly, this turned out to be overly optimistic. Whatever the bag contained, it was much larger; the entire carcass of a suckling pig, perhaps, or a side of beef. Snatching back his hand, he blew on his fingers. He would have to make do with lukewarm Coke.

Food packets of various sizes were now heaped at either end of the chest and Ægir set about replacing them. It wasn't easy as the freezer had been crammed to bursting. As he tried to stuff some fish fillets down beside the bin-bag, his hand was forced up against the cold plastic, making him uncomfortably aware of its contents. Withdrawing his arm slowly, he peered into the chest, from which a cold mist rose as if it were exhaling. What the hell had he touched? It wasn't a side of beef, that much was certain. Nor a suckling pig either. It had felt almost like rigid fingers. Waving the vapor away, he tried in vain to make out the shape of whatever the black plastic was covering. He felt an urgent desire to slam the lid, take his Coke and return to the bridge without exploring any further, but he couldn't.

In the lull before he acted he was acutely aware of his solitude. He yearned for the warmth of Lára's body under the thick duvet and the sound of her gentle breathing. The last place on earth he wanted to be was here, with whatever was in that bag. Suddenly, losing patience with himself, he tore open the plastic where he had touched it.

The light picked out a white finger, sparkling slightly with frost, tipped with red nail varnish.

They jostled for space in the small larder, nobody wanting to stand too close to the freezer. "What are we going to do?" Lára's voice was husky from sleep, her hair tousled, her cheek still creased by the pillow. Loftur and Halli were in much the same state, also newly woken, though they succeeded better in keeping their cool. "What are we going to do?" she repeated in a trembling voice. "We can't sail home with a dead woman in the freezer as if nothing had happened."

"Who do you think it is?" Thráinn bent over and peered into the chest. The contents were just as Ægir had left them; no one apart from the captain had liked to touch the bin-bag after Ægir had opened the lid to convince them it wasn't a delusion.

"I'm not sure I want to know," said Halli. "And personally I have no desire to see the woman's face. What difference would it make, anyway? It wouldn't be anyone I know." He shuddered. "At least I hope not."

Lára chewed her lip. "Answer me, somebody—what are we going to do?"

Ægir opened his mouth to speak, then changed his mind. He hadn't the faintest idea; besides, Thráinn was in charge, so it was his problem. He didn't envy the man; he was finding it hard enough to get a grip on himself let alone take responsibility for other people. Ever since he had realized what was in the bag, he had been obeying a stream of orders issued by his brain without any apparent intervention from his conscious mind: close the lid, fetch the captain, wake Loftur and Halli, and take them up to the bridge without disturbing his wife and daughters. Lára had, in fact, woken up, but the girls were still sleeping peacefully.

Thráinn spoke then with a firmness that brooked no disagreement. "We won't do anything. Just close the freezer and hold to our course. If we try to deal with this ourselves, we'll probably end up destroying vital evidence."

"Shouldn't we call the police and ask them to come and remove the body? We could wait for them, or maybe sail to meet them." Lára hugged her cardigan more tightly around her in the chill from the freezer.

Thráinn snorted. "We're not waiting for the police. Where do you think they'd come from? We're in international waters, hundreds of miles from any police station or any country's jurisdiction." This was true—Ægir had noticed from the course plotted on the chart in the pilot house that they had long since left Portuguese waters.

"So what, then? Are you suggesting we do nothing at all? Aren't there any laws in force at sea?" Lára darted a glance at the freezer and shuddered. She had been unable to bring herself to take more than a brief peek inside; the only reason she had followed the men into the larder was to avoid being left alone in the galley.

"Of course there are laws." But Thráinn didn't elaborate, or explain how they were supposed to comply with them or organize an investigation. He must know, though; even Ægir had been given a brief overview of international maritime law on his sailing course. Perhaps Thráinn simply wanted to shut Lára up. Ægir decided not to intervene. He could always explain the situation to his wife once they were alone together. But in the event there was no need because Thráinn took pity on Lára and clarified: "We have no choice but to hold to our course. Close the lid. I'll report the body and we'll continue to Iceland as planned. When we get there the authorities will take over. This is an Icelandic ship and when in international waters you're under the jurisdiction of the flag you sail under." He addressed his next comment to Ægir. "All the papers are definitely in order, aren't they? You haven't bungled the registration of the yacht like you did the satellite phone?"

Ægir met his eye and didn't require a mirror to guess that his own expression must be idiotic. "Yes, I mean no. She's Icelandic now." He sincerely hoped he was right. After all, he had never registered a ship before and it hadn't helped that the documents were all in Portuguese or French. He could conceivably have made a mistake, though everything should be in order.

"Just as well. Otherwise it's possible we'll be turned back."

"Where to?" Lára looked at him in alarm. "Portugal?"

"Yes, or Monaco where the yacht was last registered. That's a risk if the change of ownership hasn't gone through and she's not registered as Icelandic."

"But . . ." Loftur broke off as suddenly as he had interrupted.

"But what?" Lára sounded as if she feared even worse was to come. Though what could possibly be worse?

"No, I was just thinking." Loftur looked embarrassed as all eyes turned to him but realized he had better continue despite his reluctance, since Lára looked quite capable of extracting his words by violence. "That body must already have been in the freezer when we embarked. Mustn't it?"

"Obviously." Ægir was disappointed by the banality of the observation. Against his better judgment, he had been hoping for more, for the insight of a sailor with experience under his belt. "No one's missing from our group." He added hastily: "And *we* didn't bring a body on board with us." He remembered that Thráinn had seen them stashing food in the freezer and wanted to remove all suspicion that he and Lára might have put the bin-bag in there.

Loftur nodded. "In which case the body was on board before the ship was registered as Icelandic. Does that make a difference?"

Thráinn's lips thinned. "There's no way of knowing. It could have been brought aboard somewhere else entirely. Icelandic jurisdiction only covers crimes committed on Icelandic vessels in international waters, so if it happened in territorial waters, I'd be duty bound to report to that country. The rule applies to all countries with a coastline, so the nationality of the ship is of secondary importance in those circumstances." He reached out and closed the lid. "Look, there's no point discussing it any further as we haven't a clue how, when or where it happened. Or even if a crime's been committed. There may be a perfectly natural explanation."

"A natural explanation?" Lára sounded a little bolder now that there was no danger of inadvertently catching sight of the corpse. "What could possibly be natural about finding a body hidden in a binbag in the freezer of a yacht?"

"Well, maybe not." Thráinn left the larder and beckoned to the others to follow. "But that doesn't alter the fact that I'm in charge and I'm going to turn the matter over to the Icelandic authorities. I'll report the incident, then leave it in their hands."

Lára realized it wouldn't be in their interest to object. Thráinn wanted to carry on, as they all did. In Portugal they would be taken in for questioning and maybe even banned from leaving the country until the investigation was over.

"I'm going to try to make radio contact," Thráinn announced. "You two go below and get some kip," he said to Loftur and Halli, adding to Ægir: "I won't be requiring your assistance again anytime soon." Ægir didn't reply; it would be a long time before he offered to stand watch alone again. There was something very wrong with this yacht.

Once in bed he and Lára lay staring at the ceiling, unable to sleep. They hadn't discussed the body since coming below, just brushed their teeth and got ready for bed as if nothing had happened. They exchanged inconsequential comments in a way that made Ægir feel as if he was acting in a bad play.

"I know who it is." Lára didn't turn toward him.

"Oh?" Ægir lay very still. "Who?"

"It's Karítas. I recognized her scent just before the lid was shut."

"Somehow I doubt a corpse smells the same as a living person. Your mind's playing tricks on you."

"It wasn't the smell of decomposition, it was perfume. The bottle's in a drawer in the dressing table. It was the same scent."

"Surely millions of women wear that perfume?"

"No. It's a very exclusive brand that I've never come across in any shop. That's why I had a sniff. I was curious because I'd never heard of it."

"I suspect that's because they sell it in the kind of luxury stores abroad that we never go into. For all you know it may be popular with rich ladies. Perhaps the woman's one of the hundreds who must have been guests on board over the years." Ægir closed his eyes. "Though the body can't have been there for that long. If the previous owners had hidden it in the freezer, they'd surely have disposed of it at sea, which means it must have ended up there fairly recently." Ægir opened his eyes wide again. Whenever he closed them he couldn't get the image of the blue-white hand out of his mind. "Or just before the yacht was confiscated." After a brief, pensive silence, he continued: "Unless they hid it there when the yacht was in port. The seal was broken, remember? Maybe someone smuggled the body on board— someone with keys, because there was no sign of a break-in. That doesn't leave many suspects—apart from the couple who owned the yacht."

"Not Karítas—she's lying in the freezer."

"You can't be sure. In spite of the perfume."

"It wasn't just the perfume. When Thráinn was poking around down there with the wooden spoon I could have sworn I caught a flash of red. I didn't realize until I smelt the perfume, but it must have been the necklace. The red jewel in the painting."

Ægir gave up. He couldn't be bothered to argue with her by pointing out that Karítas's necklace was not the only object in the world that was red. It wouldn't make any difference. Whoever it was, Karítas or some other unidentified woman, she had been doomed to a premature death and an ice-cold grave.

Chapter 13

Breakfast tasted odd; perhaps it was the atmosphere. No one mentioned the events of the previous night in the girls' presence, but they seemed to sense the tension between the adults. They pushed their cereal around their bowls, saying little and asking no questions. When the occasional spoonful found its way into their mouths, they chewed it for an unusually long time. Heavy rain beat on the windows and the yacht was rocked by the violence of the weather so that all loose objects had to be fixed to the table.

"I've got more seasickness pills if you want them." Thráinn's attention was fixed on his half-eaten slice of toast. He looked weary and the dark circles under his eyes hinted at a bad mood, though one wouldn't have known it from his tone.

"We might well take you up on that." Ægir hadn't experienced any discomfort until now, but at the mention of seasickness he became aware of an uneasy sensation in his stomach. If the ship carried on pitching and tossing like this all day, one if not all of the family would be retiring to bed.

"Take them now rather than waiting until you feel queasy. It can't do you any harm." Thráinn lifted his toast as if to take a bite, then put it back on his plate. He took a gulp of coffee from a heavy mug that even the rolling of the ship had failed to stir. "It would be better to have you fit later on if we need to tackle the container. With the weather this bad, it'll take three men, and Loftur could do with some shut-eye; we were up nearly all night trying to get the communications system to work."

Lára's eyes widened when she heard this. She had said to Ægir earlier that morning that none of them should go out on deck in this weather. The risk of being washed overboard was too great. He squeezed her thigh to reassure her that she needn't worry. "Don't you want a rest yourself?" he asked Thráinn. "Weren't you on watch all night? It's okay by me if we wait a bit before taking a look."

"Okay by me, too." Halli was the only person whose appetite seemed unaffected. He reached for a slice of toast and began, with difficulty, to spread it with a thick layer of cold, hard butter. "I'll take a look in the meantime and try to work out what to do. There's no rush—even if we do manage to free it now, we're not going anywhere in a hurry while the sea's this rough. We can idle a bit longer. It won't change anything."

"Maybe not, but I want to sort this out as soon as possible. There's no point hanging about and I can't pick up the transmissions from shore well enough to get a weather forecast. The NAVTEX issued a storm warning but there's no telling how long it'll last. It could be several days. The forecast has changed since we set out so I have no idea how it's going to develop." Thráinn swallowed another gulp of coffee. "There are raincoats in the store cupboard—unless you've brought your own." Neither Ægir nor Halli had had the foresight; Ægir hadn't anticipated a sea voyage, and Halli had probably assumed that all the gear would be provided. The idea of having to don someone else's smelly raincoats made the prospect of going out on deck even less alluring and Ægir's appetite dwindled to nothing.

"I think it's ridiculous to go outside in this weather." Lára pushed Ægir's hand off her thigh. "It'll end in disaster." Her gaze strayed to the larder door, which was now secured with a padlock. Thráinn must have locked it during the night to prevent the girls from accidentally looking in the freezer, and perhaps also to ensure that none of the adults tampered with the evidence. "Why can't we just accelerate and leave the wreckage behind?"

Thráinn's expression did not alter; he merely contemplated Lára with weary, dispassionate eyes. "Because it's risky. The debris could get caught up in the propeller or damage the hull and I don't suppose you'd find that much fun. The fact it hasn't already floated away suggests it's caught, maybe hooked onto us, and that worries me. You have no reason to doubt my judgment on matters like this." Apparently realizing how harsh this had sounded, he tried to mitigate the effect: "But you needn't worry about us going out on deck. I wouldn't take your husband if I thought there was any danger."

"I once saw this guy get swept overboard. Talk about unlucky. A big wave came and . . . whoosh. He was gone." Halli spoke with his mouth full, having emptied his plate again. "But that was in a much worse storm than this."

Lára narrowed her eyes at him. "Poor man! What happened to him?"

Halli shrugged. "Dunno. We never saw him again."

The twins were gaping. "Did he die?" said Arna.

"No, he didn't die," Ægir interjected quickly, before Halli could scare the living daylights out of the girls. "He was picked up by a lifeboat from a passing ship." His daughters seemed to accept his improvised happy ending. Indeed, they often seemed to believe what suited them. "Now finish your breakfast. I don't suppose it's a good idea to take seasickness pills on an empty stomach." He glared at Halli to stop him from contradicting the rescue story. The young man looked mortified, as if he wished the floor would swallow him up; his blush was even visible between the roots of his dyed hair. Ægir ignored Halli's discomfort and concentrated on his daughters. "Finish your milk but leave enough in your glasses to wash down the pill."

"Ugh." Bylgja made a face. "It was disgusting. I don't want another one."

Ægir was so relieved by the change of subject that he didn't bother to point out that the pill was flavorless. "Finish your breakfast." The talk of the unfortunate man who had been washed overboard was an uncomfortable reminder of what lay in the chest freezer behind the larder door. His mind was haunted by dead white fingers clutching at thin air. Somehow, not seeing the whole body made it worse. He leaned back in his chair and put the last piece of toast in his mouth. He would have more success in making them eat if he set a good example but the bread was as dry and unappetizing as when he'd taken the first bite and the butter tasted like rubber. Perhaps he was fated to find everything he ate equally off-putting for the rest of the voyage. So much for luxury: inedible food and secondhand raincoats.

"Did you make contact yesterday?" Ægir had to raise his voice to make himself heard over the crashing waves, wind and rain. Contrary to his hopes, conditions were even worse on deck than they had appeared from inside. The only ray of light in the darkness had been the raincoats, which turned out to have hardly been worn. He and Halli had been offered a choice of gear, all of it virtually untouched, presumably because the yacht had chiefly been used for cruising in warm waters. "Did you receive any clearer instructions about what we should do?" Difficult though it was to carry on a conversation against the wind, this might be his only chance. Some of what he wanted to discuss was not for the girls' ears and he would rather keep Lára out of it too, as far as possible. She had been badly shaken by the turn of events.

"I couldn't get through to the Icelandic Coast Guard," Thráinn replied, "but I managed to raise a British ship on the VHF. I couldn't hear much because of all the static but I'm pretty sure they got the message and will pass it on to the Icelandic authorities. With any luck we'll manage to get the long-range radio working, so I can call home myself and repeat the message. Still, we'll hold to our course regardless, as I said last night." Thráinn no longer looked like a ghost; he seemed to have been revived by the roaring elements. There was color in his cheeks and his eyes were alert. The same was true of the well-rested Halli who looked full of beans, as if he was positively eager to do battle with the forces of nature. The difference between these two men and Ægir could not have been starker; they relished hard physical labor and a hint of danger, whereas he preferred to work in a safe indoor environment.

"You didn't tell them about the container and the fix we're in?" Ægir received a slap of spray across his face, and the salt stung his freshly shaven cheek. Volunteering to replace the injured crew member was without a doubt the most serious error of judgment he had ever made. He managed to banish this thought by concentrating on the idea of going home. All they had to do was hold out until they reached Iceland, where a new and better life awaited them.

"No. It was more important to pass on the other message. I didn't want to risk confusing them. Besides, what are they supposed to do? Is your committee prepared to pay to have us rescued?"

"Probably not." Ægir took hold of the long pole with a hook on the end that Thráinn now handed him. The wet wood felt slippery in his hand. "But you reckon they understood and will report the news about the body?"

"I hope so, but I can't be sure. We'll just have to wait and see; hopefully we'll find out sooner rather than later. It all depends on how successful we are in repairing the long-range radio—or the VHF, for that matter. Then at least we'd be able to make contact with other vessels. Fortunately, the navigation system seems to be unaffected, which suggests it's not caused by an electronic fault. To be honest, I don't know what the hell's going on."

"Want me to take a look at it?" Halli was holding open the lid of a white chest while Thráinn pulled out various pieces of equipment. He had a job keeping his grip on the lid in the buffeting wind. "I know a thing or two; I was going to train as an electrical engineer once."

"That would be great. But Loftur seems to know a bit about radios too and he was stumped." Thráinn straightened up, keeping one foot on the tools he had taken out so they didn't roll away. "Maybe it's just a coincidence—the storm pissing us about." He handed Halli two poles similar to the one Ægir was holding and took two more for himself. "I hope this'll be enough." He also picked up a tangle of straps from the deck and held it out to the others. "Put this on. I don't think your wife would be too pleased with me if you were washed overboard, and I can't afford to lose you either, Halli."

Ægir put down the pole and untangled the straps, which turned out to be a harness for attaching to a safety line. Copying Halli, he eventually managed to pull it on after a clumsy struggle. It appeared that Thráinn didn't intend to fasten himself to anything, although Ægir had noticed more harnesses in the box. Perhaps it was beneath his dignity. Although the harness was rather uncomfortable he felt much better for wearing it and would be even happier once it was clipped to the lifeline. His courage rose and he no longer dreaded what was to come. "Right." He picked up the pole and his new sense of daring was bolstered by the heft of the powerful implement in his hand. Perhaps he was in the wrong profession at home, and would have done better to choose a job that tested his physical endurance and manliness rather than his knowledge of debit and credit. The gust that buffeted him sideways as he thought this jerked him smartly back to reality. In weathering it, he banged his elbow so hard that his funny bone screamed in agony. The deck was running with water, which made crossing it treacherous, and his raincoats acted like a sail. He took care to tread down heavily to keep his balance on his way to the rail. It was as if the wind was intent on knocking him over but couldn't decide in which direction.

"Clip this through the loop." Thráinn handed Ægir a hook, then fastened the other end of the lifeline to a steel ring on the rail. After that, he took a firm grip on the line where it hung down from Ægir's body and yanked it. He did not offer Halli the same treatment. "Ready?" Both men nodded. They now embarked on an operation that Ægir found baffling and counter-intuitive for much of the time. The aim was to push the debris away from the ship, ascertaining, as they did so, whether there was anything lurking under the surface that might damage the propeller or rudder when they started moving again. But no matter how hard they strained and how far over the rail they hung, nothing worked: the rusty, slimy container refused to budge. It made no difference whether their efforts were co-ordinated or not. The wreckage clung like a limpet to the side of the yacht, and the only visible change was that several cardboard boxes bobbed up and floated alongside it.

"It looks as if the bloody thing's come open." Thráinn pulled in his pole. "Fucking hell."

"Is that bad?" Ægir hauled in his pole, too, glad of a chance to rest his arms.

"Potentially." Thráinn wiped his forehead to stop the water streaming into his eyes. "It depends what's inside and which way the doors are facing."

"Can this piece of junk really be caught on something?" Halli spat out a mouthful of briny saliva and nearly had it blown straight back in his face. "There's something fucking weird about this."

Thráinn wiped his forehead again. "I don't know what's going on down there. There shouldn't be anything on the keel for it to snag on. Unless there's a hole. You did check below yesterday, didn't you?" This was directed at Halli.

"There was nothing wrong. Not then, anyway, and I doubt the hull's been holed since. We'd have noticed. The container's just too bloody heavy and we can't get a proper purchase on it from up here. You can't see a fucking thing either." He bent over the side again, using the pole to give the wreckage another prod. "I'll go below when we're finished here and do another check."

"Are you positive it was only one container?" Ægir scanned the heaving sea as it dawned on him that there could be more debris on the way. "And where's the ship that lost it? Surely it's their duty to recover it or make sure it sinks?"

Thráinn and Halli exchanged mocking glances. "It doesn't work quite like that." Thráinn gave Ægir's shoulder a punch. "Not such a dumb question, though. According to NAVTEX there was only one container. If more had fallen overboard, there'd have been another alert. So, no need to worry about that, just concentrate on finding out how we can get rid of this bugger without doing any damage."

"Shouldn't we simply chance it? Start sailing and see what happens?" Ægir was desperate to prevent the captain from saying the words he dreaded most; that they should launch a dinghy and try to take a closer look. The deck felt as secure as a padded cell compared to the thought of braving the ferocious sea in a flimsy little tender. He was suddenly aware of the seasickness pill lodged in his throat, refusing to slide down into his stomach.

Thráinn shook his head without speaking. Halli vacillated at his side, then spoke up when it appeared that the captain was not going to. "I reckon we've done what we can from up here. The weather won't make any difference." He tapped his pole lightly on the rail. "Why don't we go inside since this obviously isn't going to achieve anything? I'll check the engine room and the bottom deck. If everything's okay down there, maybe it wouldn't be such a crazy idea to get going again."

Ægir was facing into the wind, which made it difficult to see the men's faces. The gale seemed to be growing stronger and the drops that lashed his face were halfway between rain and hail. Turning away from the weather, he saw one of his daughters watching him through a porthole. The glass was covered with spray so he couldn't see which of the twins it was; Arna, or Bylgja without her glasses. The little face looked somehow different, more dejected than a child's face should, unless it was a distortion caused by the streams of water coursing down the glass. He hoped her father's performance on deck was not the cause of her misery. His heart grew heavy and the bravado that had been fueling him until now evaporated. "I'm all for going inside." His voice betrayed neither agitation nor eagerness; he was simply stating a fact. The wind snatched the hood from his head and water trickled down his neck, forming an icy river down his spine. The cold triggered a mental image of the thin hand in the freezer and suddenly he could do no more. "I'm completely exhausted."

His words seemed to galvanize Thráinn, though it was possible he had been intending to call it a day anyway. They unclipped the life-lines and stowed the equipment and poles in the box without speaking, too exhausted to yell above the noise of the wind. When they entered the storeroom where the raincoats were kept, Halli was the first to break the silence. It was as quiet as a church inside after the roaring of the storm. "I reckon my raincoats are even wetter on the inside." He wrestled with the trousers, which clung obstinately to the legs of his jeans. "Don't know why I bothered putting them on."

"This stuff's crap. Useless in these conditions." Thráinn beat most of the water from his jacket and hung it up. "We'd have been better off wearing this thing." He yanked at the leg of a wetsuit hanging from one of the pegs. An oxygen cylinder, mask and buoyancy compensator were stowed underneath. "Then you wouldn't have needed the lifeline either."

"No, thanks." Halli grimaced. "No one'll ever talk me into diving. It's unnatural to breathe underwater."

"Me either." Thráinn's voice sounded as worn and hoarse as it had at the breakfast table. "I've never understood the attraction."

Ægir stopped rubbing at the wet patches on his sleeves. At last here was a chance to prove himself braver than these men. "I can dive. I even have a certificate." He omitted to point out that it was a certificate for beginners, which had involved little more than learning how to expel water from one's mask.

"You can dive?" Thráinn eyed him with an expression he didn't much like, as if the captain was investing his words with a deeper meaning than he would wish. Halli also stood and stared at him for a moment, then caught the captain's eye.

"Er, yes." Ægir hesitated. Didn't they believe him? Was he so pathetic in their estimation that they believed he was capable of making up a lie like that to impress them? "I went on a course a few years ago while on holiday abroad."

"Then isn't it time you gave it another go?" Thráinn poked the oxygen cylinder with his toe; it didn't budge. "There's no point trying to see what's happening from up on deck but it would be child's play for a diver. How about it? It should only take a few minutes."

Once again Ægir was conscious of the pill burning his dry throat. What kind of moron was he? He had absolutely no desire to plunge into that angry gray sea, which had nothing in common with the warm turquoise waters where he had learned to dive. Here he would be enfolded in an icy grip about as comforting as the embrace of the body in the freezer. He gulped and the pill shifted infinitesimally further down his throat. He was transported back to the time he had lied to some boys he used to look up to as a kid, by claiming that he could jump between two garage roofs. They had taken him at his word. He had climbed up onto the neighbor's garage and tried to leap over to the next one, about ten meters away, as he claimed to have done often, aware all the time that he would never make it. He had spent the rest of the summer stuck at home with a broken leg. Had he learned nothing since then?

Ægir's thoughts returned to that summer as Halli and Thráinn lowered him into the sea. If the worst happened, broken bones would be the least of his problems. His only comfort was the knowledge that he was attached to the rail, so he could be hauled up in case of emergency; a fact he kept repeating to himself in the hope that it would help him master his terror. There had been no lifeline when he leaped off that garage years before. But this consoling thought evaporated the instant his feet dipped into the pitiless sea and the cold began to tighten its iron grip on him. It was no better when his whole body was submerged. His teeth chattered uncontrollably, preventing him from yelling with all the breath in his lungs that he wanted out. He was here now and would simply have to complete his task; even as he told himself it should only take about five minutes, he knew he was lying. Checking the pressure gauge, he saw that there was still enough air in the tank, which was hardly surprising as he had barely had time to use any. Why couldn't the cylinder have been empty? Then no one could have expected him to do this.

He deflated his buoyancy compensator, the BCD, a little and began to sink. Such was the shock of the cold when the surface closed over his skull that he felt as if he'd been hit over the head with a plank. Everything went silent and he realized he was holding his breath, so he concentrated on his respiration for a while. In. Out. In. Out. After a minute or two he was breathing instinctively, which was a relief. Yet it was as much as he could do right now, with the murky gray waves heaving just above his head, to focus on not panicking. He tried to calm himself, this time by closing his eyes and listening to his own breathing magnified by the mask. Feeling slightly better, he resolved to get on with the job, but even as he moved, warning bells began to go off in the most primitive part of his brain.

This would end badly.

This would end badly.

This was bound to end badly.

He opened his eyes.

Chapter 14

"I want eight *eyeses*." Orri did not explain his choice of number. Perhaps it was the highest he knew.

"What do you want with eight eyes, darling?" Thóra parked in the only free space in front of the nursery school. "Isn't two enough?"

"I want to see lots and lots." Orri gazed out of the window, his face thoughtful. The view outside offered little to engage the interest of a four-year-old, even if he had quadruple the number of eyes; only some spindly poplars, not yet in bud.

"I'm not sure you'd see any more with eight eyes than you do with two." Thóra got out and opened the door for the little boy. "And I bet it would be much harder to get to sleep at night if you had to close all those eyes."

"I want eight *eyeses* anyway."

Thóra unfastened his seatbelt and moved aside so that he could climb out. "There isn't any room for them, darling. Your face isn't big enough."

"Spiders are small but they've got eight *eyeses*."

That explained it. "Spiders have eight legs, not eight eyes." The wind shook the poplars, rattling a few dry leaves left over from summer. As she led Orri to the entrance they were met by a crescendo of noise created by dozens of parents tugging anoraks off whimpering children, mingled with the shrieks of those who were already playing inside. When Thóra opened the door, she felt like following Orri's example and putting her hands over her ears. Stooping down to him, she freed one hand and whispered: "It's a good thing you haven't got eight ears, sweetheart, or you'd need eight hands."

As she got back behind the wheel and slammed the car door, she experienced a familiar pang of guilt. Was the child really all right in the care of non-family members? It wasn't that she suspected the staff were anything but kind—quite the contrary. It was the sheer number of children that worried her; at home there were five of them to see to Orri's needs but at nursery school the ratio was almost reversed. Still, it couldn't be helped. She should be grateful for all the time she got to spend with her grandson, unlike many grandmothers. For the moment, at least. Gylfi was still obsessed with the terrible oil rig idea and it was becoming infectious. Only this morning she had heard Sóley asking her brother whether summer jobs were better paid in Norway. And considering how keen Matthew was on the idea, it wouldn't surprise her if he sent in an application next.

"Any more news about the body?" Thóra hung up her jacket, trying to mask her surprise that Bella should not only have arrived punctually but already be seated at her computer in reception.

"No idea." Bella didn't raise her eyes from the screen. The bluish glow illuminated her broad, chalk-white face, rendering her pallor more corpse-like than ever. "But there's no point wasting any more time thinking about it. I've already told you—it's Karítas."

"Well, perhaps." Thóra closed the cupboard and picked up her briefcase. She hadn't told Bella what the police had disclosed about the possibility that a dead woman had been found on board. She didn't quite trust her, though as far as she was aware the secretary had never leaked any information. In any case, the details were as yet unconfirmed, so there was no need to give Bella further grounds for believing that Karítas was dead. "Why are you here so early?" Perhaps the secretary was so gripped by the case that she felt compelled to come to work before the day's regular business began.

"I owe money on my home Internet account." Bella flung Thóra a scornful look. No doubt it was meant to convey that they didn't pay her a wage fit for a human being. But to earn that, of course, one would have to do some actual work. "I've put in a bid on eBay that I want to keep an eye on. The time's nearly up and I don't want anyone jumping in at the last minute and outbidding me."

Thóra paused and turned. "You say you can't afford to pay for the

Internet, yet you're always shopping online. If I were you I'd concentrate on paying off those little debts first."

Bella rolled her eyes. "They're not 'little.'" She fiddled with the mouse and puffed out her cheeks. "Look, I'm doing deals, okay? If I buy this box for the right price I can sell it on afterward for a profit. So I'm making money, not spending it."

"Box?" Thóra was puzzled. "What kind of box can you buy and sell for a profit?"

"Batman Legos. Arkham Asylum."

Thóra didn't trust herself to repeat this. "How can it be an investment to buy boxes of Legos?" Perhaps Bella had finally gone round the bend, but, then again, it was probably no worse than putting one's money in Icelandic shares if the experience of the last few years was anything to go by. "Is it a collector's item?"

Bella nodded. "Yes, and this bloke obviously has no idea what he's got his hands on." She grinned and squinted at the eBay screen. "The packaging is intact, all the booklets are included and there isn't a single piece missing. There were seven figures in the box."

Thóra gave a tentative smile, unsure whether seven represented an unusually large or small number. "Good luck." She decided this brief insight into Bella's world was quite enough to be going on with and went into her office. If she had found a box of Legos at home she would doubtless have handed it to Orri, probably even helped him tear open the packaging. Unable to resist the temptation, she pulled up eBay to see what all the fuss was about. When she finally managed to track down the precious box it turned out to be a real anti-climax. It consisted of a small Lego figure in a Batman costume, a selection of his enemies and some bricks for building a house or prison. An investment was not the first thing that sprang to mind. Noticing that the auction was due to close in half an hour, she felt tempted to outbid Bella by a fraction, just for the hell of it, but didn't have the heart. Instead, she knuckled down to work.

After spending half an hour studying the laws relating to life insurance and missing persons, and reading the Reykjavík District Court's verdict in the case of the Icelander who had vanished from a

sailing vessel, she was still unsure what to advise Ægir's parents about
how long the process might take. All she could say with confidence
was that it would take time and, if no new evidence emerged, the
case would probably be delayed by the court. The one encouraging
sign was that the life cover had eventually been paid out in the case
of the missing Icelander. If she presented sufficiently careful arguments, the same result could probably be achieved for Ægir and
Lára. She rang the police to chase down the documents she'd requested and to her delight was informed that after lunch she could
pick up all the papers they were currently prepared to release. However, they warned her to ring ahead to avoid a wasted journey as
they were busy and unsure when they would have time to make the
copies. Before hanging up, she asked if there was any new information about the person who had been washed up on shore but was
told again that they were not prepared to release a statement as yet.
Well, all would be revealed eventually and in the meantime she could
occupy herself by working on the letter and report for the insurance
company.

The document soon filled up with a feeble attempt to explain a set
of circumstances so implausible that there was a risk her letter would
be dismissed as a bad joke. After wrestling for ages with a recalci-
trant sentence, Thóra gave up, stood and stretched. It troubled her
that she didn't know why Ægir and Lára had insured their lives for
such a vast sum. Ægir's stepping into the breach to replace the injured
crew member also struck her as highly irregular. When she had spoken to his manager on the phone, it turned out that the man had a
vague memory of agreeing to the suggestion in order to cut costs, but
when she pressed him for a concrete figure that she could quote in
her report, he hesitated. In point of fact, the saving had been negligible; the cost of around a week's wages for one foreign sailor, possibly with a bonus, and a flight ticket home. Ægir's boss admitted that
this was an insignificant amount in the context, and therefore an unnecessary economy. He concluded by saying what she did not want
to hear; that it had been Ægir's personal decision to make up the
shortfall as he had been very keen to make the voyage. In other words,
it had been his idea.

This was the weakest link in the entire case. It would have been better, from Thóra's point of view, if Ægir had been given no choice in the matter. As it was, his decision raised the possibility that the family's disappearance had been premeditated. If she subsequently discovered that their debts were sky high, there was a risk the circumstances would appear even more dubious, so she had better find out the worst as soon as possible. Sitting down again, she picked up the phone to Ægir's parents and asked them if they could discover how much their son and daughter-in-law owed the bank, as well as any other financial institutions and the tax authorities. The old couple balked at this, pleading ignorance and raising so many potential objections that in the end Thóra extracted their permission to dig out the information herself. She was unlikely to succeed as they still needed a court order to declare Ægir and Lára dead before the family would be permitted to administer their estate. As a last resort, they might have to search their house for receipts or paying-in slips. Sigrídur, who had answered the phone, received this suggestion with even less enthusiasm, and the upshot was that once again they agreed that Thóra should undertake the task. If it did come to that, Sigrídur asked Thóra to fetch more clothes and toys for Sigga Dögg because she and her husband still couldn't bring themselves to set foot in their son's house.

Thóra was about to fetch herself a coffee and check on the results of the eBay auction when the phone rang. "Some old woman for you." Bella's voice was replaced by that of an older lady who introduced herself as Begga, Karítas's mother. "You came round to see me, remember? You left your card in case I needed to get in touch."

"Of course. Hello. How are you?" Thóra asked.

"Oh, fine," the woman replied, sounding falsely hearty. "I just wanted to let you know that I heard from Karítas yesterday." Unable to think of an immediate response, Thóra allowed a silence to develop, which the woman obviously found uncomfortable. "You asked after her? I just thought you'd like to know."

"That's right, I did. And I'm very pleased to hear this news. I'd begun to wonder if something had happened to her, though I didn't like to mention it." Thóra hoped her surprise was not too obvious.

She had thought it more than likely that the body purportedly found on board had been that of Karítas, whether because of Bella's insistence, or because Karítas was the only woman connected to the case apart from Lára. The police had now confirmed that the body which had been washed up was not Lára.

Begga let out a short laugh, almost a giggle. "To tell the truth, I was getting a bit worried myself. But it turns out she's absolutely fine and there's nothing wrong."

"Did you happen to ask if she'd be willing to have a quick chat with me? I can ring her if she's abroad; I wouldn't want her to have to pay for the call."

"Oh, she wouldn't mind that." Begga's confidence rang hollow; evidently she no longer knew what her daughter could or could not afford. "I did mention it but unfortunately she couldn't answer because she had to dash. I'll bring it up next time I hear from her, which should be soon now that she's got Internet access again."

"Internet access?" Thóra wondered if Karítas was in the same mess as Bella but avoided referring to it, so as to preserve the illusion of a luxurious lifestyle that Begga was keen to maintain. "Has she been away from civilization then?"

"Yes, she's been on the move. Trying to get her bearings. You know."

Thóra didn't know. When she had problems, she couldn't afford to take off to the Galapagos to work them out. "But she's home now?" she said, then added quickly: "Which is where?"

Begga tittered again. "Oh, I might have known you'd ask that. But, seriously, she's in Brazil—I think. The subject didn't actually come up but they own a house there and although it's autumn now, it's warmer than here. So I assume that's where she is."

"Do you have her phone number?"

There was no laughter this time. "No. She didn't tell me and I forgot to ask. She changed her number when this whole thing blew up because the Icelandic press wouldn't leave her alone. She even got rid of her cell phone—can you imagine? But unfortunately I didn't ask and I don't actually know if she has a cell phone now. It was such a brief conversation, as I said."

"So you didn't see what number she was calling from?"

"Oh, no, she didn't call. This was on Facebook. Didn't I explain?"

"I must have misunderstood." This struck Thóra as decidedly odd. If she hadn't spoken to her mother for weeks she would almost certainly have found the time to have a proper chat with her, on the phone rather than through social media, though that didn't necessarily mean anything. On the other hand, if someone was posing as Karítas to throw dust in her mother's eyes, the conversation would have to be kept as short as possible and naturally could not have been conducted over the phone. The longer the communication, the more chance there would be of making a mistake—particularly if Google Translate was involved. She longed to ask the woman if they had discussed anything personal, anything that no one else would know. But that would only worry her and it would be a pity to undermine her obvious relief over the Facebook exchange. "Did she say anything in particular, apart from that she was okay?"

"Not really. Just that she was fine and the weather was good. Then she asked about the weather in Iceland. I don't remember the details."

"No, of course not. It's great that she's safe and let's hope she contacts you again soon. When she does, perhaps you'd remember to mention my request?" Suddenly it dawned on her—if someone was impersonating Karítas, that person must be an Icelander. Google Translate was all right as far as it went, but a foreigner wouldn't be able to put together so much as two sentences without betraying him- or herself. "I forgot to ask last time, does Karítas have any Icelandic friends who visit her abroad?"

"Well, not many. She's always so rushed off her feet when she's abroad that she has no time to socialize with friends from before. She hardly even has time for her old mother." Begga laughed again, failing miserably to sound amused. "The only Icelanders she associates with when she's traveling are the ones who work—or used to work—for her. If I recall, there was once an Icelander crewing the yacht, and she had an Icelandic maid or PA or whatever you call them. She's always been well disposed toward her country and people, which is why all the negative press about her and Gulam since the crash is so unfair."

"Do you happen to remember the name of the PA who worked for her? Is she the girl who accompanied her to Portugal?" Thóra jammed the receiver under her chin and reached for a pen. She turned over the page where she had been writing notes on the case of a family who were about to lose everything they owned. It seemed singularly appropriate as the family's misfortunes were the result of financial shenanigans by the global super rich—unscrupulous rogues like Karítas's husband. "Since I can't speak to Karítas directly, I could try to get hold of the PA. Is she with her in Brazil, by any chance?"

"I don't think they're together, though Karítas didn't say. At least, she said she was alone, but then perhaps she doesn't count the staff—she's as used to having help as we are to having dishwashers. And I wouldn't describe my dishwasher as company."

Thóra was unlikely to start comparing people to household appliances any time soon, but she checked her impulse to retort as much. "If she's not in Brazil, there's a good chance she's here in Iceland. That would be even better, and all the more reason for me to try and track her down."

"Well, I don't know what she'd be able to tell you. The people who work for Karítas and Gulam have to sign a strict confidentiality agreement and I'm sure she wouldn't want to break it. Mind you, I wouldn't put it past *her*. I always found the girl impossible but Karítas couldn't see it. I even offered to help out myself so she could get rid of her, but Karítas didn't want to. She didn't want to take advantage of me or hurt the girl by giving her the sack. She's always been so kind-hearted."

Thóra chose to put a different construction on this: Karítas obviously didn't want her mother tagging along on their trips abroad. "You don't happen to remember her name?"

"Aldís. I don't know her patronymic." Well, that was a great help. After Thóra had said good-bye, she discovered that there were 219 women called Aldís in the telephone directory, and no clues to help her identify the right one. At a loss for ideas, she tried logging into Facebook to see if Karítas would accept a friend request, though Thóra's own page was neglected and contained little of interest except an album of pictures of her kids that she'd posted when she joined, so there was little reason for Karítas to want to befriend her.

With any luck, she would be one of those people who accepted all requests indiscriminately, but if she sifted her friends carefully, Thóra was unlikely to make the grade.

Karítas's page turned out to be public, so Thóra was able to examine it without hindrance. The first thing she checked was whether Aldís was among the hundreds of friends the owner of the page had deigned to accept, but she was nowhere to be found. That told its own story about their relationship; staff obviously didn't count as friends—any more than dishwashers would. There was little else of interest on the page apart from the photo albums. They contained such a vast number of images that either the woman must employ someone to upload them for her, or else the busy schedule described by her mother was pure fiction. Thóra decided to scroll through them in the hope of finding a picture of Aldís and any other information about her. After several hundred photos, however, her interest waned. They were generally taken at gatherings of smartly dressed people, the women drooping under the weight of their jewelry, their emaciated figures hardly built to carry such burdens. Despite the silver trays of canapés none of the photos showed any of the women eating, whereas the opposite applied to the men; they came in all shapes and sizes, and were often caught by the photographer in the act of stuffing their faces.

A few photos featured Karítas either alone or with her husband in more informal surroundings. What they all had in common was that they were carefully posed to show off her figure to the best advantage. She never had a hair out of place or appeared in casual clothes. Even stranger was the fact that although it was clear from the background to many of the pictures that Karítas had traveled all over the world, the photographer apparently had no interest in anything but people. People, people, people and more people.

Just as Thóra was about to give up, she came across a picture of Karítas getting dressed with the help of a young woman who was carefully zipping the evening gown up her employer's long, slender back. Only part of her face was visible but there was no mistaking the fact that the girl looked as if she wished she were elsewhere. The caption read: "Late for the charity ball in Vienna—Aldís saves the day!" Her last name was missing but at least Thóra now knew what the girl looked like. Perhaps her full name would emerge if she checked through the rest of the photos. The prospect wasn't exactly tempting; she'd had quite enough of this display of narcissism, so she picked up the phone and put a call through to Bella. As an Internet addict, the secretary should be grateful for the assignment. Before raising the subject, Thóra asked about the Lego set but learned that some bastard had jumped in at the last minute and massively outbid Bella.

"Oh, dear. Better luck next time." Thóra hoped this was what Bella wanted to hear. All she got back was a grunt that was impossible to interpret. Thóra received the same reaction to her request that Bella trawl through Karítas's Facebook page. When she hung up, Thóra still wasn't sure whether the secretary had agreed to the task, but then that was par for the course.

The photo of Karítas dressing with Aldís's assistance was still up on her screen when Thóra turned back. She stared at it, sighing in exasperation and slowly shaking her head over the whole affair. Although she might have been reading too much into what she had seen and heard, she had come to the conclusion that Karítas was a nasty, social-climbing snob. She had risen from rags to unimaginable riches and handled the transition badly—unless she had always been a bit of a bitch, which was certainly the impression Bella gave. On closer inspection, Thóra found the expression of the girl who was taking care not to pinch her employer's skin in the zip even more informative. At first glance her face betrayed irritation and suppressed anger at having to fuss over this spoiled princess. When Thóra zoomed in on the image, however, she saw something more telling: Aldís's expression revealed not just anger but hatred.

Chapter 15

Visibility in the depths was minimal. The beam of Ægir's diving torch swung around wildly as he juggled it in his inexpert hands. The constant motion of the surrounding water seemed menacing, as if anything could happen. His one experience of sea diving had had nothing in common with this sense of infinite vastness; on that occasion he had felt fine and succeeded for the most part in forgetting the fragility of his existence. But now his heart was hammering in his chest and he had to focus on every breath he took, on remembering to inhale sufficient air through the mouthpiece and telling himself that everything would be fine as long as he kept his head. But he couldn't make himself relax. With every loud breath, impregnated with the taste of plastic, he grew increasingly panicky.

He hoped the sight of the surface just above his head would have a calming effect, but the light aroused in him an uncontrollable desire to breathe through his nose. He looked down again so quickly that he felt the bones of his neck creak in the numbing cold. The sound was muffled, and seemed to travel through the water at a snail's pace. Why hurry? No one was listening. The yacht too emitted a constant creaking, perhaps caused by tension in the aluminum, and this was even less likely to soothe Ægir's taut nerves. What if there was a problem with the ship's hull? Would they insist that he went down again with tools to repair the damage? He pushed away this thought by squeezing his eyes shut and inhaling three times. As the air bubbles rose past his ears he envied them for being on their way to the surface. Then he opened his eyes wide and steeled himself. The sooner he set to work, the sooner he would escape this hell.

He tightened his grip on the torch, doing his best to hold the beam steady. Once he had gotten the knack, he swept the light back and forth in search of the container that must be somewhere nearby. Thráinn had not wanted to lower him too close in case his equipment snagged on it or was damaged. Mindful of the captain's words, Ægir wondered what would happen if the air cylinder caught on the container when he swam closer to investigate. Would he be able to free himself? It was one thing to don the gear with help on deck; another to remove it underwater in a frenzy.

The beam landed on the floating container and Ægir kicked himself cautiously forward using his fins. He did what he could to illuminate the entire structure but the water was cloudy and his torch inadequate for the task. Although he reminded himself that everything appeared much larger through his diving mask, it was nevertheless clear that he had underestimated the size of the container from on deck. The captain had known what he was talking about; there was every danger that the massive steel crate would smash the propeller or rudder if it collided with them. The container was leaning against the ship, as if hooked onto it by the corner. One of the double doors at the end had opened and was hanging down, while the other still appeared to be tightly shut. Doubtless that was why the thing hadn't sunk; air must be trapped in the corner on which they had been expending most of their energy. And when he saw the structure from the side, it was easy to see why they hadn't been able to push it away; while they had been shoving against the part that was visible from above, the lower edge of the same side had been wedged against the hull.

Even from this new perspective, he found it hard to judge whether it would be safe to set the yacht in motion again with the wreckage still clinging to her side; he would have to consider the bigger picture. Although he himself would not like to be dragged over the rough steel surface of this huge contraption with nothing but his flimsy wetsuit for protection, he thought the ship would probably not sustain too much damage from metal grinding against metal. So as long as it didn't hit the propeller or rudder, they might be able to risk sailing full steam ahead.

He was moving his legs with slow deliberation, yet found himself

approaching the container much faster than he liked. Suddenly he had
to free one of his hands from the torch to stop himself hitting the side.
His palm made contact with icy steel while his legs kicked frantically
against the current. The open door stirred beside him as if in a gentle breeze. Shining his light into the black opening, he glimpsed brown
cardboard boxes, still marked for the recipient with white sticky
labels that were beginning to peel off. Ægir shifted his hand to get a
better grip. Foolish though it was, he was afraid of being sucked into
the container, afraid of perishing inside it with the goods that would
never now reach their intended destination. He jerked the line
round his waist to reassure himself that it still connected him to the
world of the living. It was still securely fixed, but this did nothing to
raise his spirits; the line would be of little use if he became trapped
down here.

Still, he was not here to investigate the contents of the container
or to let his imagination run away with him; he was meant to be inspecting the hull for holes and searching for a way to detach this vast
piece of flotsam—a feat even the powerful current had been unable
to achieve. He felt like an ant faced with moving a mountain.

He made a half-hearted effort to drag the container away from the
side, but although the open door stirred a little, the rest did not budge.
It would take a stronger man than him—a team of men, more
like. He had nothing to brace against either, which rendered his effort pitifully feeble. At the second attempt he put more of his strength
into it, but the result was the same, the door flapping slightly but the
rest not shifting so much as a centimeter away from the hull. It didn't
help that he had to hold onto the torch at the same time, but he didn't
dare search for a fastening on his belt to which he could attach it. All
his attention was fixed on avoiding the sharp metal edges of the crate.

Then, out of the blue, he had a brainstorm that was both simple
and obvious. If he opened the other door, the container would fill
with water and the air that was holding it afloat would disperse. Then
the bugger should sink and they would be able to continue on their
way. The only difficulty might lie in unfastening the bolts, especially
if they had warped. He would have to dive down to the handle in the
middle of the door and undo the catches on the locking bars. The

task shouldn't be beyond him, but Ægir couldn't work out how he was to achieve it with one hand while the other was occupied with holding him steady. He was still too terrified of being sucked inside to let go for a moment. As it was, his grip on the door would be weakened by having to clamp the torch under one arm.

He would just have to work it out as he went along. Deflating his buoyancy compensator a little, he descended until he reached the handle, which fortunately looked in fairly good shape. Then he gripped the torch under his arm and hung on for dear life to the side of the door. His feet drifted slowly into the black aperture and he kicked with all his might to pull them out. To prevent this from happening again, he took the time to adjust his position until he could press his body against the closed door. That way he would be supported by the metal while he worked.

It was a struggle to turn the lever one-handed, without the advantage of body weight. The muscles of his upper arms ached, already sore from wielding the poles earlier that morning. He felt as if that had been hours ago, if not yesterday, but then every minute of the dive was like an hour on the surface. Taking a deep breath, he exerted all his strength. The handle screeched and to his wild elation it yielded and turned all the way. He had managed to unlock the door. But his joy was short-lived and his mind and body froze at the sudden realization that the container might sink before he managed to swim clear. The door would fly open and the wreckage would plunge into the depths, taking him with it, screaming into his mouthpiece. In desperation, Ægir shoved himself off as hard as he could and eventually felt reassured that nothing of the kind was going to happen. His fear had probably been unnecessary, but it had opened his eyes to the potential hazard.

He swam cautiously back and pressed his body against the door. He tried to tug it toward him but no matter how hard he strained, nothing worked. The resistance of the water and weight of the door made it impossible for him to budge it. There was no point continuing; he was quite simply incapable of achieving the feat on his own. But disappointment was a luxury he could not afford. He must finish the task he had undertaken; even if he couldn't free the container from the hull, he still had to ascertain whether it would be safe to set the yacht in motion again. To do so, he would have to swim along and underneath the keel.

Ægir checked his pressure gauge and saw that it registered over a hundred bars, but all that told him was that he was fifty bars away from the needle dipping into the red, at which point he had to return to the surface. He shook inwardly with idiotic laughter at the thought that he hadn't a clue what the figures meant. The fact that he was no longer conscious of the cold—hardly a good sign—filled him with even more mirth. But if he laughed aloud he would spit out the mouthpiece and drown, and this had the effect of sobering him. He deflated his BCD again and sank deeper. There was no point wasting time; the sooner he swam underneath, the sooner he would be restored to his family and his proper element.

The idea of swimming on his back struck him as most appealing because that way he would be able to look up and wouldn't risk catching his air cylinder on the bottom of the container, but he wasn't sure it would be physically possible. To be on the safe side, he descended further than necessary; he had no desire to go down this deep but it would at least mean he was further from the dangers above. His ears popped and he pinched his nose to relieve the pressure. Sore ears would be a small price to pay compared to what he faced now, but he would still rather avoid the ill effects. He wanted nothing to spoil his euphoria once he was safely back on board.

In any event, the air tank turned out to be too heavy. Despite all his efforts to swim on his back, he kept rolling over and losing control. He would have to reconcile himself to gliding along on his stomach, looking up at regular intervals to examine the keel for damage. Every time he did glance up, the adrenaline pumped through his veins at the realization that he was rising ever higher and closer to the container. But by concentrating on swimming a little deeper, he managed to steer clear of it.

All of a sudden he jerked to a halt. At first he thought he had been run through by a steel spar or sharp splinter of wood and flung out his limbs, unable to control himself. He floated upward in the commotion, breathing rapidly, unable to see for the bubbles all around him. When his air cylinder bumped into the container he froze momentarily before managing to get a grip on himself. The realization that he was still holding the torch brought him to his senses and he worked out that the reason for his abrupt halt had been the tightening of the line around his waist. So he hadn't gone completely mad. With unsteady fingers, he transferred the torch to his left hand and used it to fend himself off while he fumbled at his waist with his right hand. The lifeline was taut, which meant either that they wanted him to come up or that it had entangled with some impediment on the way.

Clearly, he could go no further. One option would be to unfasten himself from the line and continue without it, but it would be difficult to swim back against the current. If the men on deck didn't spot him, he might drift away and never be found again. It was out of the question. Life was too precious—both his own and the lives of his family. Who gave a damn what the others thought of his performance? Just let them try and do better themselves. He craned his neck as far as he could to peer into the distance. The beam couldn't penetrate the murky water, yet he glimpsed what looked like the end of the container and darkness beyond it, which meant that he had in fact made it all the way. This cheered him a little. Now no one could find fault with his attempt to solve the problem. The thought lent him courage and he decided to try to ease the container away from the hull from underneath. Swimming to a point he guessed was somewhere near the middle, he positioned himself so that he could brace against the ship's keel and then pull at the lower edge of the crate with all his might.

He trapped the torch between his thighs and bent double so that his feet were on the keel and his hands clamped around the edge of the container. Then he tried to straighten out his body while pushing against the metal, but the wreckage still wouldn't budge. His further attempts produced nothing but a dawning sense of surprise at his own determination. He had forgotten everything else in the struggle but reality returned with a jolt when he finally abandoned the endeavor. His sense of time was muddled; he hadn't a clue how long he had been wrestling with the crate or how many minutes he had been underwater. His pressure gauge registered sixty bars and he felt a sickening stab of fear. He had probably used up too much oxygen and would have to return to the surface immediately. As calmly as he could, he turned and began to battle against the current, grateful now to have the container overhead since it made his progress easier. But the torch was a nuisance as he really needed both hands free, so he tried to tie it to his belt in such a way that it would shine upward. That way he would still be able to see but would be in a position to grab any available handhold on the bottom of the container.

Too scared to release his grip on the metal, he fumbled one-handed at his belt, with disastrous consequences. Finally, believing that he had secured the torch, he risked letting it go, only for it to drop away from him. Panic seized him as he watched the beam descending slowly and inexorably through the gloomy water. Suddenly it illuminated a white arm floating in the depths below him. The iron taste of blood filled Ægir's mouth; he had never experienced such a powerful impulse to look away but he couldn't. For an instant the torch beam lit up the water around the arm and he glimpsed part of a body; a thin, twisted torso clad in drab-colored material that billowed gently like a jellyfish. The head was at an odd angle to the body, so Ægir could only make out the profile. But it was enough to see the eye staring through the tendrils of long hair that waved upward as if reaching out to him.

Everything went black, and Ægir felt the blood flooding into his fingers and toes. Instinctively, he began to fumble his way, panic-stricken, in the direction he had been heading. He was moving probably twice as fast as before and for all he knew he had not taken a single breath during the entire maneuver—or flight—that brought him unexpectedly to the end of the container. He sucked the mouthpiece hard and the chemical taste of compressed air filled his mouth as it poured into his lungs. Vile as it was, it felt so good that he allowed himself the luxury of taking several more breaths before inflating his BCD with steady fingers and beginning his ascent. His relief was so great that he almost lost control and it took all his willpower not to rip off his mask, he was so desperate to breathe naturally again. When his head finally broke the surface, he felt an uncontrollable urge to scream.

The rope ladder was still hanging in its place and Ægir clung for dear life to the bottom rung as he spat out his mouthpiece and fully inflated his BCD to keep him afloat. Only as he hauled himself out of the sea did he remember the weight of the air cylinder and for an instant wondered if he would make it. The way up offered life, while there was nothing below but a cold grave, so up he would go. He flexed the chilled muscles of his upper arms and heaved himself upward groaning with the pain of it. Had the woman he saw in the water been a hallucination? Now that he had escaped the ocean, it all seemed so unreal that he was no longer sure. Yet it must have happened.

"This is the best beer I've ever tasted. Pass me another." Ægir emptied the bottle as he sat there wrapped in a blanket, which seemed to be having no effect. He didn't usually drink before midday but now all he wanted was to get plastered. Strange though it might seem, the chilled beer was exactly what he needed and it made no difference that he shook like a leaf with every gulp. His body did not seem particularly grateful, but he couldn't give a damn; any more than he had cared about the fuss Lára had made. She had freaked out when they came inside and explained why he was in such a state. She exclaimed that he had betrayed her and the girls by taking such a decision without consulting her, and generally behaving like a selfish shit, either because he was an adrenaline junky or out of a pathetic desire to please the others. And so it went on. In his present state there was no question of persuading her to listen to reason; he couldn't move from the galley chair where he sat shivering. Keen not to miss anything, the girls had remained behind when their mother stormed out. They were sitting opposite him, their large dark eyes filled with wonder. It was a sign of the state he was in that he didn't mind their witnessing such an unpleasant scene.

The one part he was determined to keep to himself was the woman; it would be too difficult to explain through chattering teeth. In any case, it had almost certainly been a hallucination brought on by excessive loss of body heat, and he didn't want to detract from his own heroism by telling a story that would make them shake their heads and roll their eyes when he wasn't looking. He had gotten out alive—nothing else mattered. For now.

"Are you cold, Daddy?" Bylgja received a jab from Arna's elbow for asking such a stupid question. Her glasses were knocked askew and she winced.

"I'm so cold that if I tried to pee, it would come out as ice cubes." Ægir took another swig of beer from the newly opened bottle that Halli had passed him.

"Did you see any fish?" Arna leaned forward over the table and rested her head in her hands, stretching her eyes into slits. "You should have caught them."

"I didn't see any fish. It's too cold even for them. They're all dead of cold, I reckon."

Thráinn did not look amused. He stood on the other side of the galley, propped against the sink with arms folded. "I'm not sure I follow. You managed to undo the bolts but failed to open the door? And you saw no sign of any damage?"

Ægir nodded, his head jerking in time to the shaking of his body. "No. I couldn't see any holes. There were scratches all over the place, but none of them looked deep enough to be dangerous. I unlocked the door but I couldn't open it, not on my own. Perhaps it would be possible to attach a rope to it and drag it open with a concerted effort from on deck. I don't know. But it can't be done from below."

"Not by the likes of you, at any rate." Halli winked at Thráinn. Spray had plastered the white hair to his forehead.

Loftur, who had joined them while Ægir was underwater, added with a sneer: "I thought everything was supposed to be so light underwater. Obviously not light enough."

"Oh, shut up. If you're such tough guys how come you're not strapping on tanks yourselves and going to sort it out?" Ægir took another swig. Losing his temper had warmed him up a little. "I'm just describing the situation. I haven't a clue how to solve the problem. You're the sailors. You sort out this mess instead of giving me a hard time."

"You've had enough beer." Thráinn pushed himself suddenly

upright. "Why don't you go and talk to your wife? She didn't look too happy when she ran out. Then you'd better take a hot shower and get into bed. It's the only way to beat the cold."

"Mommy got mad." Arna grinned. "She won't want to talk to you yet." It was obvious that Arna wanted to stay and listen to the grown-ups quarreling. It didn't often happen, so the opportunity was too good to miss. "I'd wait if I were you."

Bylgja looked reproachful. "She wasn't angry, Daddy, just upset. When you were away so long, she thought you'd fallen in the sea. She looked out of the window and could only see two men—not you, Daddy—and she thought you'd drowned. She sent us below so we couldn't watch. I wish I'd seen you come up again."

Ægir discovered that his lips were dry. When he ran his tongue over them, he tasted salt. "Mommy'll get over it."

"I want to try being that cold." Arna leaned even further over the table. "If I ate a ton of ice cream and chewed loads of ice cubes, would I be as cold as you?"

"Yes, I'm sure you would. But I don't recommend it."

"There is no ice cream." Thráinn took the rest of the six-pack from Halli and put it back in the fridge.

"There is," Arna retorted obstinately, unwilling to bow to the captain's authority. To her eyes he was just another bossy grown-up. "I saw ice lollies in the freezer when we put our food in there. Can I have one, Daddy?"

"No." Ægir put his beer down with a clunk. Her question had jolted him back to reality and the predicament they were in. "Let's go below and find Mommy. Thráinn's right." He met the captain's eye, then his gaze traveled onward to the larder door. At that point, the effects of the alcohol wore off completely. The padlock was lying on the floor and looked as if it had been clipped through. It had been intact and locked when they went out on deck. He coughed. "Have you been fiddling with the lock?" He nodded as casually as he could toward the larder. The three men shook their heads. "Somehow I doubt Lára or the girls did that."

Arna and Bylgja stared at him uncomprehendingly. "Did what?"

"Nothing." Ægir watched Thráinn walk over and open the door.

He caught a quick glimpse as the captain slipped inside and gasped when he saw the state the larder was in. The freezer lid was open and the food that had been in the top of the chest was scattered all over the floor. Ægir had no need to see inside the freezer to realize that the body was missing. The captain's expression was enough.

What the hell was going on? Actually, he knew where the body had ended up; the woman in the sea had been no hallucination. What an idiot he was not to have mentioned it immediately; now his story would seem both unconvincing and suspicious. Who could have thrown the body overboard and why? It wasn't him, and presumably neither Thráinn nor Halli could have done it without the other noticing. Which did not leave many people. He stared at Loftur, who immediately averted his eyes.

Chapter 16

The dog-eared bundle of photocopies on the desk in front of her showed evidence of rough handling. When she unfolded them she discovered flakes of tobacco and fluff that suggested they had been stuffed into a less than pristine anorak pocket. "Thanks for bringing these. It must be difficult getting around in weather like this with your leg in plaster." She smoothed out the papers and had a quick leaf through them. At first sight everything appeared to be present. She looked up at Snævar and smiled. "Did you have much trouble getting hold of them?"

"Oh, no, not really. I looked through my junk and found these hospital forms. Halli must have chucked them in my bag when he packed it for me. I fetched some documents from the Social Insurance office too, in case you needed something official. I've nothing better to do at the moment. They probably won't be much use to you; they're just payments linked to my European Health Insurance card, but there's also a bit about what they did at the hospital and so on. Anyway, you've got them now. Give me a shout if there's anything else I can do for you. It makes a nice change to be busy."

"You obviously won't be going to sea for a while. Do you have any idea when your leg will have healed?"

"No, but hopefully in a couple of weeks." Snævar shrugged, and the stretched-out neckline of his garish sweater gaped to reveal a white T-shirt. He was wearing dirty tracksuit bottoms that in no way matched the shapeless, bobbly acrylic sweater. His dark hair, though shaven to within a millimeter of his scalp, smelt as though it was in need of a wash, and a close encounter with a razor around the jawline wouldn't have hurt him either. Thóra tried to avert her attention from the young man's slovenly appearance. After all, the way he looked now was probably not habitual. It must be difficult to find trousers with bottoms wide enough to fit over the plaster cast, and taking a shower couldn't be easy either. "I go to sea every other month. The accident happened during my time off, so I'd better be cell phone again before my next tour or I'll be off work for another two months. Unless I can make a deal with the bloke who works opposite me."

Peering under the desk, Thóra noticed that his plaster cast was wrapped in a plastic bag from Ríkid, the state-run off-license. "Well, you certainly won't get far like that."

"No." He smiled briefly without showing his teeth. "Do you know whose body it was on the beach?" Evidently he did not have much time for small talk. Thóra understood his concern; his friend Halldór was one of the few likely candidates.

"Yes. It wasn't your friend." Earlier that morning Ægir's father had rung to let her know that the police had told him the body was not that of his son or any other family member. The postmortem had confirmed this and the person in question's next of kin had been notified. Since a statement would be issued to the press at midday, Thóra thought it wouldn't matter if she revealed the man's name to Snævar. "It was the mate, Loftur." She observed his relief, followed almost instantly by apparent shame at his selfishness; naturally it was still a tragedy, whoever was involved.

"You didn't know him?" Thóra asked, though the answer was obvious from his reaction.

"No. Never met him, as far as I know. But I'm not very good with faces. We may have worked on a short tour together, though I don't think so."

"So you didn't see him in Lisbon?"

"No. Nor the captain either. I had my accident before they arrived, though of course I'd have met them if things had gone according to plan. I think I know who Loftur was, though. At least, I've heard people talk about him."

"Oh? What have you heard?"

"Nothing bad, far from it. I forget exactly what it was but nothing

like that. Just that he was a bloody good ship's mate. He passed his
certificate quite young, if I remember right." Snævar raised his eyes
to the ceiling in an effort to recall. "That was it—they said it was a
pity he turned his back on the fishing industry because he was very
promising. He used to work on the same trawler as me but quit just
before I started. He got on the wrong side of the first mate or something stupid like that, and people were wondering what he'd do instead. That's all, I think."

"Did your friend Halli know him?"

Snævar shook his head slowly. "I don't think so, though I can't be
sure." He craned his head so far back that Thóra had a momentary
fear that his Adam's apple would pop out of his neck. "God, it's all
so awful."

"It certainly is." Thóra watched him return his head to its normal
position, wondering if people like him coped better with grief than
those who wore their hearts on their sleeves. But going by Snævar's
expression, she thought maybe the silent type found it harder. "I suppose you realize that this greatly reduces the chances of finding the
others alive."

He rolled his eyes. "None of them are alive. I don't know how anyone could believe they were."

Thóra folded her arms. "I'm inclined to agree with you, but it's incredible what people can endure."

Snævar shook his head. "There's no chance they're drifting somewhere in a lifeboat, if that's what you think. It would have capsized
long ago."

"I suppose you're right." Although she did not say as much, Thóra
thought Snævar's response to the news that the dead man was Loftur indicated that he too was holding out hope that Halli was alive.
But he had a point; they must all be dead by now. The official search
had been called off; there were no more helicopters hovering over
the sea where the yacht had passed. Instead they were combing the
beaches—in search of the dead, not the living. "When did you last
hear from your friend Halldór? Ægir and his family called Iceland as
the yacht was leaving port in Lisbon, but nothing was heard from

them after that. Did Halli get in touch with you after the voyage had begun?"

"No," Snævar said without hesitating. "Before he left he brought me painkillers, Coke, sweets, and so on. Then we said good-bye at the hotel the day he was supposed to sail. I didn't hear from him again after that. He was great; bought me a plane ticket home and all that. We didn't have our laptops with us so I couldn't do it myself but luckily there was a computer in the hotel lobby. I really don't know how I'm supposed to repay him; I don't want to get in touch with his family yet in case they're still hoping he'll be found alive. I'd rather wait a bit. But I'm afraid I'll forget and then they won't understand what's going on when his credit card bill arrives."

Thóra had noticed the travel documents as she leafed through the pile of papers, and quickly turned back to them. She found a receipt from Expedia for a flight to London and another onward to Iceland. The name of the card holder was Halldór Thorsteinsson. She showed it to him. "I'll return this when I've taken a copy and then you'll have the receipt to remind you." She put the papers down again. "One question that might sound a bit daft. Did Halldór have a cell phone? Or a camera?"

Snævar looked at her as if she was an idiot. "Of course he had a phone. But I'm sure he didn't have a camera. At least, I never saw him carry one. If he'd wanted to take a picture, he'd have used his phone. Though why he'd have wanted to take one, I don't know." He tilted his head on one side. "Why do you ask?"

"Oh, it's only—they didn't find any phones or cameras on board, which seems rather odd. If they abandoned ship in a hurry you'd have thought at least one of them would have left their phone behind, not to mention if they were washed overboard." She changed the subject. "Did it never occur to you to sail home yourself? To take the boat instead of flying, so you didn't have to hang around in the hotel? Your leg wouldn't have prevented you from taking your turn on the bridge, would it?"

"I wouldn't have been much use for the first forty-eight hours but after that I could have helped out, as you say. I went home after three days and the flight was just as tiring as if I'd taken a watch on board. It's a nightmare traveling in this state but it's not as if there's any physical effort involved in sitting on the bridge. Once I was alone I remember being pissed off that Halli and I hadn't slept on the yacht instead of wasting money on a hotel. I was sure they'd have given me a ride home if I'd been on board already. Though now I'm thanking my lucky stars I wasn't, as you can imagine."

"Was sleeping on board an option?"

"Yes, why not? We had the keys and no one would have complained. We were supposed to start making her ready and running checks on the engines and equipment before the others arrived, so I can't see why anyone would have kicked up a fuss."

"You didn't ring the captain to suggest it?"

"No. He was so pissed off that I couldn't face talking to him. I've learned it's pointless trying to reason with people when they're angry. Halli did mention it in passing but the captain wasn't having it. Anyway, by then it had been decided that the family should go instead. I have to admit I'm glad I didn't try harder—the pain in my leg is nothing compared to what Halli must have gone through."

Thóra brought out a file containing the documents that the police had released to her late the previous day. "If you don't mind, I'd like to ask your opinion on something." She showed him the file. "This is the route that was programmed into the yacht's GPS." She ran her finger along a line that followed a rather circuitous course between Lisbon and Reykjavík. Then she turned over the next two pages, which showed, on the one hand, a blown-up picture of the route within Icelandic territorial waters and, on the other, some circles the yacht had made not far from her destination. "I can't get hold of the man who gave me this but the way I understand it, the yacht started sailing in circles around about here." She pointed at the first blown-up page. "I take this to be the date, which would mean that she made these maneuvers about twenty-four hours before she careered into the harbor. Have you any inkling what might be going on here?"

Snævar, looking surprised, studied the chart. "I suppose it's possible that the autopilot developed a fault or the rudder jammed, though that's pretty unlikely. The captain would never have let her sail round and round like that before he took action. It's more likely that someone fell overboard and they were looking for him. Or her. Or them."

"That's what occurred to me, too. It's a pity the printout doesn't say who it was."

"The navigation system isn't that sophisticated."

"I was joking." Thóra turned over to the enlarged chart. "What about the final part of the voyage? That looks odd too. If I have this right, there's a change of course as the yacht approaches Iceland and she's brought in very close to the shore at Grótta before heading back out to sea where she sails in another large circle before making a beeline for Reykjavík harbor. This is a blown-up picture of her final movements."

Snævar pored over the chart. "What's this?" He pointed to the text at the top of each page.

"I'm guessing they're the dates which tell us when the course was plotted on the GPS."

Snævar seemed to agree. "In other words, someone must have been alive on board as the yacht approached land?" He pointed at the date on the second chart.

"Yes. If my interpretation's correct." Thóra ran her finger along the line of the ship's course. "Is it possible that this person abandoned ship near Grótta and went ashore there? Do you know anything about the currents in that area?"

"Jesus." Snævar ran both hands through his hair with such force that he pulled his eyes out of shape. "Jesus."

"I know." Thóra's initial reaction had been the same, not least because it would considerably complicate her case. How was she to persuade a judge to rule that Ægir and Lára were dead if there was a chance they could have sneaked ashore? In fact, any of the people on board could probably have abandoned the yacht at that stage. All of them, even. Except Loftur, of course. Unless they had all lost their heads for some reason and drowned right by the shore. But that did not tally with the fact that Loftur's body had turned up on the Reykjanes peninsula, some forty-five kilometers to the south. It could hardly have been carried all the way there from Grótta, which was a small isthmus crowned by a lighthouse that jutted out from the coast of Seltjarnarnes, Reykjavík's westernmost suburb. "What's the sea like off Grótta? Is it possible to swim ashore there?"

"Yes. No. I really don't know. It would depend how strong a swimmer you were and what the sea was like. You'd have to ask someone who's experienced at swimming in the sea." Snævar was apparently still having trouble getting his head around this latest development. "Jesus. I wouldn't trust myself to do it."

"How about in a diving suit?"

He smiled. "You're asking the wrong man. I tried it once and it wasn't for me. I'd never dive in the sea round Iceland, though maybe it wouldn't be a problem for a pro."

"Another question. Is there any reason to sail close to land there? To avoid reefs, shallows or currents, that sort of thing?"

"Nope. None at all."

"Okay." Thóra ran her finger round the loop that extended from near the lighthouse at Grótta and out into Faxaflói bay to the north of Reykjavík. "What about this? Do you have any idea why the yacht didn't make straight for port?"

Snævar shook his head. "No. I can't make head or tail of it. It's crazy. Completely crazy. Unless someone fell overboard again. But that wouldn't explain this loop because the circle's too wide and doesn't go back over the same area. It's just mental."

"That's what I thought." Thóra pulled the file back toward her. "Could someone who doesn't know how to use the system enter the coordinates? Does it work like the GPS in a car?"

"No. That is, the GPS works the same but you'd need to know how to set the autopilot—the specific system they had on board. If not, you wouldn't be able to make it do tricks like that. Well, unless the strange maneuvers were caused by the fact that the person fiddling with the system didn't know how it worked. I suppose that's possible."

"Yes." Thóra was thoughtful. "What about someone who has a pleasure craft certificate? Would he know how to use the system?"

Snævar snorted contemptuously. "No. They learn nothing with those courses. They don't even teach them about magnetic variation when they're plotting their coordinates on a chart. *You* would have as much chance of working it out as some genius with a pleasure craft certificate."

That ruled out Ægir, as well as Lára and the twins, of course. Not to mention Loftur.

Which only left Thráinn and Halli.

Google Translate had its uses. Thóra had tried typing in the comments that the doctor or nurse had scribbled on what she took to be Snævar's admission form for the casualty ward in Lisbon. One box turned out to be marked *Description of Incident*, and when to the best of her ability she typed the text it contained into the translation program, her curiosity was piqued. It emerged that, when being admitted, the seriously intoxicated patient had claimed that the person who pushed him had been an Icelander. He had not known who it was and when asked if it had been his companion, Halldór, he had denied it and begun to ramble incoherently. The doctor's verdict was to postpone reporting the incident to the police until the patient was sober enough to make sense. Since there was no further mention of this in the accompanying documents, it was impossible to tell what the outcome had been. Snævar had not said a word about his assailant being an Icelander when describing the events to her.

Thóra rang when she guessed he would have reached home, to avoid catching him in a bus or taxi. People tended not to talk as freely on the phone when strangers were listening. After apologizing for bothering him again so soon, she described the contents of the hospital report. "Do you remember it at all?"

"Yes. Vaguely." Snævar sounded rather embarrassed.

"Do they quote you correctly? That you were pushed by an Icelander?"

"Well . . . That's what I thought at the time, but I wouldn't stake my life on it. I was pissed out of my mind. But I'm fairly sure the man who pushed me said something in Icelandic just before the blow sent me flying."

"Surely it must have been Halldór? You were out together that evening, weren't you?"

"No way. He was inside paying the bill. I'd gone outside for some fresh air—I was totally wasted, like I said. So it definitely can't have been him."

Thóra was silent for a moment. "Was it reported to the police?"

"No. I couldn't face getting involved with the police in a foreign country, and nothing would have come of it anyway. What were they supposed to do? Take his fingerprints from my jacket?"

"Was the hospital satisfied with that?"

"Yes, they were just relieved to be able to discharge me. Halldór stayed with me overnight and in the morning I got him to lie to them that I was going home that day. I couldn't be bothered to go back for a checkup either. They'd sorted out my leg and there was nothing more to do but wait until the bones knitted. They swallowed the story and gave him the forms to hand in at home."

"Then why have I got the originals? Haven't you been to see a doctor since you got back?"

"No." Snævar sounded even more sheepish than he had at the beginning of the conversation. Thóra felt like his mother. "I keep meaning to go."

"You should do it. I'll photocopy these and return the originals to you. I could have them dropped off at your GP's office you like." But Snævar asked her to give the papers to him and Thóra suspected he would delay the doctor's appointment as long as possible, probably until it was time to remove the cast. Or perhaps tough guys like him removed it themselves. "Tell me another thing: do you have any idea when Loftur and Thráinn arrived in Lisbon?" Given that there were no direct flights between Iceland and Portugal, it was unlikely there would have been many Icelandic tourists around at that time of year. And it was extremely implausible that Ægir and his family would have attacked a fellow countryman who they didn't even know.

"They were supposed to arrive three or four days after us, I think."

"When was that?" Thóra dug out the copy of Snævar's flight ticket to Lisbon and compared the date with that of his hospital visit. They were three days apart. "The day after your accident?"

There was a pause as Snævar apparently searched his memory, then he replied: "Yes, I have a feeling it was the day after." He paused again.

"I can't remember the dates for the life of me. Wait a minute. Yes, they were supposed to arrive on the afternoon of March 3. So that was probably the day I broke my leg."

Thóra checked the date on the hospital admission forms: March 3. So it was conceivable that either Thráinn or Loftur might have been involved. She decided to ask Bella to type the hospital report into Google Translate in case the nursing staff had recorded any further details about Snævar's statement. Since his own memory of the events was hazy in the extreme, they might have more luck in finding out the story there. She thanked him and rang off.

All this was very bad news for her case; there would be no call now to refer to the hospital report or attach it to her summary as she had intended. In fact, she would be better off persuading Snævar to go to his GP and get a signed letter stating that his leg was broken and avoiding all mention of the mysterious Icelander who might have caused his fall. If the insurance company got their hands on the report, they could well use it to concoct an explanation for Ægir and Lára's disappearance. It would be a simple matter to claim that they had planned it all in advance and that their decision to take the boat home was no coincidence: Ægir must have pushed the man deliberately in order to take his place on board. Highly improbable as it sounded, the theory couldn't be ruled out entirely. Oh, why was nothing ever simple?

Thóra sat up and stretched. Perhaps there were jobs for lawyers on the oil rig.

Chapter 17

A twitching tail was the only sign of life from the cat on the window-sill. She glared out into the garden where the gale was flattening everything in its path. Storms and rain were beneath her dignity; she might have been lashing her tail to show her disgust at the elements for daring to behave in this way.

"Cats are rubbish." Sóley watched the animal, bored. Mother and daughter were lying on the sofa together, Sóley with a library book open on her stomach. "They never do anything."

"They do lots of things." Thóra felt compelled to stand up for their pet. "But only what *they* want to do, not what you want." She gave Sóley a gentle kick. "Don't be mean to the poor kitty. It's not her fault the weather's like this." Sóley was supposed to be playing in a football match later that day against a team from Egilsstadir, in the east of Iceland, but their flight had been canceled. She and her friends had been convinced they were going to thrash the other team, so they were crushed by disappointment. "In fact, I'm sure she's as disappointed as you. She wanted to go exploring but I was afraid she'd be blown out to sea."

"I can't stand the wind either. Why does wind have to exist?" Sóley seemed to be burdened by all the world's injustices today.

"Perhaps it was invented to drive sailing ships in the old days—or windmills," Thóra suggested. Sóley rolled her eyes to indicate that these were nothing compared to a match in the junior girls' fourth division. Thóra sat up and hugged her daughter. "Well, it's lovely to have you here even though you're in grumpy." She disengaged and stood up. "And don't you dare dream of applying for a summer job in Norway."

"Talking about me?" Gylfi came in yawning. Sigga had taken Orri to a birthday party at a relative's house but the youthful father had announced that he had a cold and didn't want to infect the horde of children. Thóra had bitten back a comment, recalling how Matthew had been driven to distraction by the children's parties they had held for Orri. She didn't know which annoyed him most, the noise of the kids or the chattering of the mothers. So she could well understand Gylfi. More to the point, she had recently taken the decision not to interfere in his relationship with Sigga. Although they all lived under the same roof, the young couple had to learn to sort out their own affairs without her constantly acting as referee.

"No, we weren't." Thóra smiled at him. "Norway can come up in conversation without its having anything to do with you." She studied him, aware that he was transforming with terrifying speed from the child she had brought into the world. There were still glimpses of the old Gylfi in the young man before her, but the next stage in his development to adulthood would doubtless be even more dramatic, and Thóra realized that if he did go abroad for a year, he'd probably be unrecognizable when he returned. Perhaps that was why she was digging her heels in. She wanted him to grow up, to live his life, take risks. But she didn't want to miss it, any more than she would want to watch him walk the tightrope without a safety net.

"You do know how close Norway is, don't you, Mom?" Gylfi had obviously read her mind.

"No." She would just have to face facts. The little family would move abroad and learn to stand on their own two feet and she would have to resign herself to going through airport security every time she wanted to visit her firstborn and her grandchild. "How close is it?"

Gylfi looked evasive. "I'm not absolutely sure. But it's not far. And you can visit Duty Free."

So if they did go, at least she'd have the compensation of cheap alcohol and chocolate. "Great. I hadn't thought of that." Gylfi's relieved smile indicated that he had failed to detect the sarcasm. "When are you expecting to hear?" They might turn him down and then all her worrying would have been for nothing. She had heard that people spent most of their time getting anxious about things that would never happen, but then again the statistic probably applied to people like her mother who were forever lying awake at night, fretting over the silliest things. Whatever was reported on the news immediately constituted a major risk to her mother's loved ones. In her mind, a national campaign against speeding meant that her family were all more or less doomed, either because they might suddenly take to driving recklessly themselves or because they would fall victim to some crazed road hog. When the president of the Ukraine was poisoned with dioxin, her mother was convinced that Thóra would accidentally buy a canned drink destined for a foreign dignitary and suffer the same fate, and so on. No wonder Thóra had kept her parents in ignorance of Gylfi's plans; she had enough trouble coping with her own anxieties without having to put up with her mother's as well.

"I'm not sure. If I don't hear by the beginning of next week, Dad's going to call them for me. He's got the flat all ready for us, apparently, so we could go over as soon as school finishes. It won't take us long to pack."

Thóra closed her eyes and counted up to ten. Her son had never packed so much as a pair of socks himself; she had always done it for him. But it was not this that caused the anger to flare up inside her, since she had only herself to blame. No, her main gripe was with her ex-husband. Why did he have to give his opinion? If he had kept out of it, no one would ever have dreamed of such an idea; Gylfi would now be applying to university and Sigga would be enjoying the fact she was a year younger and still in the sixth form. But in fairness Thóra knew her ex meant well; doubtless he was lonely in Norway and wanted the company of his only son. It couldn't be easy to spend every other month alone in a foreign country. "You can't plan a long stay abroad at such short notice. Don't forget that although you two may be able to rough it, the same isn't true of Orri." She made an effort to compose her features. Lecturing the boy and laying down the law for him was exactly what she had promised Matthew not to do. Gylfi was responsible for his own life and the sooner she accepted the fact, the better. Perhaps she should be directing her anger at herself, not his father. She had often wished her son would take more risks, live life to the full. "Anyway, we'll see. There's no need to make a fuss about it now."

"There's no need to make a fuss about it at all," muttered Gylfi, flopping down on the sofa where Thóra had been lying. Sóley didn't react, as if it was nothing to her that her brother and nephew were leaving the country.

The cat turned her head in a leisurely manner and yawned at the brother and sister, utterly indifferent to any undercurrents.

A metallic female voice announced a storm warning for the southeast Iceland shipping area. Thóra had lost count of the number of times she had heard these words but only now that she had become interested in boats did the full implications sink in: she thought about those out on the ocean, pictured waves breaking over bows, vessels plunging in the heaving waters. One thing was certain; she had no inner sailor struggling to escape. "Turn here." She directed Matthew down to the harbor side. "He's going to meet us by the yacht." She glanced at the clock on the dashboard and saw that they were early. "Let's park and wait. He's bound to need help getting up the gangplank so it would be better to go together."

"The lock can't have been much good if someone's managed to break in." Matthew backed into a parking space to give them a view over the harbor. "And it's asking for trouble, leaving the ship unguarded at night over the weekend." Fannar had rung Thóra to tell her that a port security officer had reported a break-in on board the previous night. The police had found no sign of any theft or vandalism, and after performing his own inspection Fannar had concurred with their findings. Yet from his tone it was evident that he was concerned about this burglary in which nothing had been stolen. Thóra was pleased he had rung her and even happier when he offered her the keys in case she wanted to survey the scene for herself. She accepted with alacrity and asked if he would mind her taking along Snævar, the crew member with the broken leg, who might well notice some detail that those unfamiliar with the vessel had overlooked.

After the briefest pause, Fannar had given his consent and told her where to pick up the keys.

"Do you think it's all right for me to come too?" Matthew asked. The water streaming down the windscreen blurred their view of the yacht, making it look as if she was moving.

"Of course. You're here as my assistant." Thóra turned on the windscreen-wipers. "I'm sure it'll be good to have you there if Snævar needs help. I tend to forget about things like that and would probably charge off without thinking and leave him behind."

Condensation crept up the glass and Thóra was about to ask Matthew to switch on the heater when Snævar appeared in an old banger that could have done with a clean. "I thought fishermen were well paid." Matthew couldn't disguise his disgust as the car drove up. It was covered in dents, some of them rusty.

"Maybe he's a rally driver."

"I doubt it." Matthew's expression didn't alter. "Rally cars have souped-up engines. That's nothing but a rust-bucket. It wouldn't make it a hundred meters from the starting line."

"Shh. He might hear you." Thóra watched as Snævar opened the car door and, after a considerable tussle to pull a plastic bag over his cast, clambered out. They walked over to the yacht together and waited while Thóra dug out the keys. She was struck by how out of place the elegant vessel looked in the dismal rain, as if she should have been protected by covers. The lavishly appointed interior only intensified this impression, especially when Snævar managed to locate the light switch. However, the dim illumination did little to enhance the expensive furnishings, whose sheen was now obscured by a layer of dust. Thóra looked around, wondering what it would be like to be cooped up in here for days at a time. Of course it was impressively spacious in comparison with most yachts, but even so there was not much room; staying here for long periods would probably be like living under house arrest in a small chateau. "Is it really much fun cruising on a boat like this?"

Snævar didn't seem to understand what she was getting at. "Oh, yes, I expect so. I mean, I don't actually know what it's like to be a passenger, but I bet it's cool to sail her. Whether you're crew or passenger, the main thing is that you enjoy sailing in the first place."

"You said the crew didn't mix with the passengers or owners, so where do they hang out? Is there a special deck where the staff can sunbathe and let their hair down?" Thóra tried to remember how many decks there were but couldn't picture the layout. She knew there were more than two, though, so it seemed reasonable that the crew would have one to themselves.

Snævar burst out laughing. "The crew don't spend their time sunbathing, if that's what you think. They work flat out pretty much round the clock and grab sleep whenever they can between watches. The kind of people who'd pay a fortune for a fancy vessel like this aren't going to fork out for an extra deck for the staff. And who can blame them?"

Matthew seemed more impressed with the yacht than Thóra. Then again, he was seeing her for the first time, unaffected by the sadness that she felt about the fate of the passengers. She couldn't gush over the design or craftsmanship when everything reminded her of that little girl who was now almost certainly an orphan. "How fast does she go?" Matthew ran his fingers over the window frame, which he seemed, for some inexplicable reason, to find interesting.

"Around sixteen knots, I imagine. Though she'd rarely cruise at that speed. She'd make around twelve as a rule."

Thóra allowed her gaze to wander, bored by the talk of knots and certain that any minute the conversation would turn to engines. "I'm going to take a look around, see if I can spot anything unusual. It'll be quicker if we split up, and you'll be in better hands with Matthew." Leaving them in the saloon, she made her way down to the bedroom wing, if that was the right word. No doubt the sleeping quarters should be referred to as cabins but her own term seemed more appropriate for rooms that large. The moment she entered the corridor, she regretted her decision. Turning on the lights made her feel a little less uneasy, though they flickered alarmingly; as they had approached along the dock Snævar had remarked that the yacht's batteries might be running low since the engine had not been used for a while. The corridor was empty and all the doors were closed, which made it seem all the more sinister, and Thóra couldn't shake off the fear that the person who broke in might be lurking behind one of the doors. She tried to dismiss this thought as nonsense—the police could hardly have overlooked the presence of a burglar.

Pulling herself together, she started checking the cabins, one by one. She couldn't remember exactly what they had looked like before this peculiar break-in, but they appeared to be completely untouched. It wasn't until she opened the door to the master cabin that she realized something was amiss. She stood in the doorway, surveying the scene, before hesitantly stepping inside. The door slammed behind her. Thóra jumped, her heart racing, but forced herself to carry on. She knew the door had only slammed because of the movement of the boat; she had even expected it. This was a perfectly normal ship, she told herself; a terribly smart one, but only built of steel and aluminum. No different from her car, or her toaster; neither of these frightened her, so there was no reason to behave as if this yacht bore her any ill will. Yet even so she couldn't quite rid herself of the uncomfortable sensation that there was something evil in the air.

There was no obvious sign of any illegal entry in the master bedroom. The bed had been made in a perfunctory manner, and a large bath towel hung from the back of the chair by the dressing table, but apart from that everything looked the same. Only the couple's belongings had been removed, which may have accounted for the change she sensed. She turned a slow circle in the middle of the room but could detect no difference. The yacht must have sent her imagination into overdrive again. She refused to let her mind stray to the child's feet she thought she had seen last time. Instead, she went over to the imposing wardrobe and forced herself to open it. She could have spared herself the effort. Everything looked exactly the same as before. The other closets also turned out to be packed with clothes, elegantly displayed on citrus-wood shelves and in compartments, or suspended from substantial hangers on rails that she would not have been surprised to learn were made of silver. The feminine garments emitted an overpowering floral fragrance that made her feel slightly queasy. A single unused hanger formed an odd contrast to all the rest.

If Karítas had really gone to retrieve her clothes from the yacht when it was berthed in Lisbon, she had either abandoned the effort or only coveted one particular garment.

In the double wardrobe that had evidently belonged to Karítas's husband, Thóra caught sight of a dial behind a row of shirts. Pushing the shirts aside, she discovered a sturdy-looking safe built into the back of the cupboard. Naturally it was locked and Thóra knew better than to turn the dial on the off-chance. But this did not prevent her from speculating about what it might contain; cufflinks sporting diamonds the size of cherries perhaps, or bundles of banknotes. Since neither Ægir nor his family were likely to have been able to open the safe, it could not possibly be concealing any evidence of relevance to the inquiry, but Thóra suspected that its contents, rather than any clothes or personal effects, were what had drawn Karítas to Portugal. No doubt it was empty now. After checking the remaining drawers, which contained rolled-up ties, socks and belts, she turned her back on the closets.

As she was berating herself for her own foolishness, she realized what had been niggling at her. It was nothing remarkable—the wooden box on the dressing table was missing. It had contained nothing but photographs and bits of paper that Karítas had wanted to keep for whatever reason, perhaps as mementos of the high life, and who would be interested in that? Hardly the police. Thóra went over to the dressing table and peered in the drawers and cupboards, in case the box had been tidied away. It was nowhere to be seen. She couldn't imagine why anyone would break into a luxury yacht to steal an item like that with all these other valuables lying about. The only people who could possibly be interested in its contents were tabloid journalists, and she doubted that even they would resort to burglary.

There was nothing much to see in the corridor, so Thóra felt she had done her duty there. She hurried out, switching off the light with her back to the darkness, then hastily climbed the stairs in search of Matthew and Snævar. She finally tracked them down in the bowels of the ship, where they were investigating a garage-like storeroom, which housed Jet Skis, fishing tackle and other equipment she could not identify. On the wall there was a large hatch that could presumably be opened outward when people wanted to use these toys. Judging from the interest with which Matthew was examining the Jet Ski, they were no longer searching for signs of the break-in, or had at least allowed themselves to be sidetracked. Though, to be fair, Snævar was standing by the hatch, resting his injured leg and apparently inspecting the catch. As Thóra stepped in, the yacht rocked without warning and she had to grab the door frame to prevent herself from falling. Her palm came away smeared with thick grease.

"How are you getting on?" She walked past Matthew, barely glancing at the Jet Ski, and headed for the large sink on the wall behind him. "It looks to me as if there's a box missing from Karítas's dressing table. It contained nothing of obvious interest, so I don't understand what the thief was up to. Perhaps he thought it was a jewelry case, but I checked inside the first time we came on board and found only personal papers." She rubbed her hand under the freezing jet of water and watched the sink fill as if the plug was down.

"Perhaps he thought it was a jewelry case and grabbed it. All the same, it's strange that he didn't open it." Matthew frowned. "It doesn't sound very convincing. Surely the police must have taken it when they were here this morning? Perhaps they wanted to empty the yacht of valuables in case of further break-ins."

"Then why only take that box?" Thóra inspected her hand and decided it was clean. She watched the water slowly drain away and when the sink was almost empty, tried to pull out the plug to speed things up. The filter underneath was clogged with blond hairs. She showed it to the others. "Who on earth would have been shaving or cutting their hair down here?"

Snævar looked round and shrugged. "Anyone. One of the crew, maybe. It's probably been there for ages. I doubt the guys who sailed her home would have come down here to use the sink. It's not as if there's any shortage of basins or bathrooms elsewhere."

Matthew made a face; he was fastidious about hair in plugholes. "Put it back. It can hardly have anything to do with the burglar."

Thóra did so, then dried her wet hands on her trousers. Her attention shifted to Snævar, who was attentively examining the hatch again. He unfastened the heavy steel catch, reached for the handle and eased the door out with a creaking sound. "What are you doing?" For a split second Thóra almost thought he and Matthew were planning to go for a Jet-Ski ride.

"I can't quite work this out." Snævar pointed at a slender nylon rope, one end of which was tied to a ring on the wall, while the other ran out through the hatch. "This line can hardly have been hanging outside while the yacht was moving. I'm just going to check it out. Perhaps it's attached to a float, or something connected to these Jet Skis." He waited until the hatch was almost horizontal, giving them a view out over the harbor where the surface of the sea was jumping under the relentless pelting of the raindrops. There was no float visible; the rope simply disappeared into the dark water. "Could you help me a sec?" Snævar said to Matthew. "I'm having trouble bending. Let's haul it in."

Matthew hurried over and took a firm grip on the rope. A look of surprise crossed his face. "Either it's stuck or there's something heavy on the end."

Snævar scowled. "There can't be." He stooped, with difficulty, and gave the rope an experimental tug. "You're right." He straightened up. "I don't know what the hell it could be. The line must have been left outside the hatch by mistake and snagged on the keel or something." He scratched his chin. "We'd better not try and sort it out ourselves. They'll find out what's going on when they take the yacht to the shipyard for repairs."

Matthew jerked the rope. "It's not fixed. There's something on the other end."

Thóra craned her head out and stared down to where the line vanished into the water. "Could it be a net? Perhaps they were trying to fish."

Snævar's expression showed what he thought of this theory.

"I think I've got it." Matthew heaved, coiling the slack around a low steel post as they hauled in the wet rope. Finally, they glimpsed a bundle of pale-green canvas attached to the nylon line with a steel hook.

"What the hell is that?" Snævar asked. Once Matthew had managed to drag it up to the hatch, Snævar reached out and seized the tarpaulin. With a concerted effort they swung the load on board and stood there panting, surveying their catch.

"Do you think it's advisable to open it?" Thóra had taken two steps backward when the entire bundle came into view. Of course, she could be wrong but all the signs pointed to its containing a body. As the seawater poured from the waterproof surface onto the gleaming metal hatch the canvas formed more and more closely to its contents and the shape bore an ominous resemblance to the last thing they wanted to find.

Neither Snævar nor Matthew answered her. Instead they stared in shock at the dripping tarpaulin. Then Snævar broke the silence. "I'm going to take a look." He bent down, slowly and carefully, and tackled the rope and clasp with practiced ease. Now nothing remained except to pull the folds of canvas apart. "Shit." He looked at them, exhaling. "I don't know what I'm doing. Do we want to see this?" Neither Thóra nor Matthew replied. Snævar lowered his eyes to the bundle and breathed out again with determination. Then he whipped the canvas aside, only to throw up all over the body of his dead friend.

Chapter 18

"Did you always want to go to sea?" Still furious with Ægir, Lára was ignoring him and focusing her attention instead on the young man who was sitting in the saloon with them, playing a game of patience. Thráinn had gone to find out if Loftur knew anything about the disappearance of the woman's body, and Ægir suspected that Halli had been ordered to keep an eye on them in the meantime, in case Lára was implicated. Nobody had informed her of the woman's fate as yet. It had been tacitly agreed that this should be Ægir's job, but there was little he could do when she wouldn't even look at him. He knew her well enough to understand that she was not angry so much as upset, as Bylgja had said, which was harder to deal with. What made it worse was that he knew she was in the right; he should never have taken a risk like that without consulting her. Even so, he felt it was unnecessary to kick up such a fuss about what might have happened, given that everything had turned out all right. As so often when they quarreled, he had no idea how to behave; whether to try and bring her round or obey her command to leave her alone. On occasions like this she sometimes said one thing and meant another, but at other times she meant exactly what she said. He still hadn't learned to read the signs. Generally, whatever he said only made matters worse, so the best course was to hold his tongue and wait out the storm. Consequently, he was keeping unusually quiet now while Lára focused on Halli, who did not seem to be enjoying the unexpected attention. The conversation limped along, since all Lára actually knew about Halli was that he was a sailor and this imposed strict limits on her search for a suitable topic.

"To sea? Uh, I don't know." The hectic color in the young man's cheeks owed nothing to the temperature in the saloon, which was on the chilly side, though none of them had remarked on the fact or dared ask Thráinn to turn up the heating. "I suppose so."

"Are you from the countryside?" Lára smiled, pretending not to notice his reluctance to engage with her.

"Nope. Kópavogur."

"Oh." Lára fiddled with her hair and racked her brains for something else to say. "Are you a family man?"

"No, not yet." Halli sneaked a look under one of the piles and risked taking off the top card. "It'd be difficult, what with me spending so much time at sea."

Lára seized on the fact that his answers had become less monosyllabic, spying an opening to penetrate his shell. "Wouldn't you like to change jobs, then?"

Halli made a dismissive noise. "And do what?" He gave Lára a puzzled glance. "It's perfectly possible to work at sea without being away as much as I am." He immersed himself in his game of patience again, once more stealing glimpses under the piles. "The big trawlers pay better but then the tours are longer. And it depends what the catch is like too, of course; you can be lucky or unlucky. That's true whatever the size of vessel."

"Are you saving up for something?" Lára smiled encouragingly, though he didn't seem to notice. "Are you maybe thinking of putting a roof over your head?"

"What? What for?" The color in Halli's cheeks deepened. "No. I'm saving up for something else."

Ægir felt an urge to come to his rescue by changing the subject but all that came to mind was the question that had been consuming him ever since he had found the body. "If the British ship has reported the discovery of the woman's body, won't there be a big furor when we get home? Police interviews and all that?"

"Probably." Apparently Halli wasn't going to take advantage of this conversational lifebelt. "I guess we'll soon find out."

Ægir hastily interjected again, before Lára could pounce from the sidelines with further personal questions. "How can we let them know when we're arriving in port if the radiotelephone can't be repaired?"

"We'll show up on their radar as soon as we approach land. If they received the message I expect they'll have a reception committee waiting. We won't be allowed to go straight home, that's for certain. So you can forget about smuggling your wine ashore."

Ægir's heart sank. This was not what he wanted to hear. He could think of nothing he wanted less than a homecoming marred by police interrogations and a customs clampdown. His dream of being greeted on the threshold by the familiar smell of home, of sleeping in their own bed, faded. Why the hell hadn't they simply flown back? Taking advantage of his silence, Lára leaped in and returned to her line of questioning. "Anyway, what were you saying—what are you saving up for?"

From Halli's expression one would have thought Lára had asked him to strip off. Ægir was astonished that she should be oblivious to the fact that this diffident young man had no wish to talk to her at all, let alone answer such personal questions. Usually she was much more adept than Ægir at reading social situations. Perhaps her fury with him had blunted her instincts.

"I'm saving up for a motorboat. With a mate of mine."

"Great." Ægir smiled encouragingly at Halli who had given up on his game of patience, in spite of his cheating. The yacht bucked and rolled, and Ægir doubted he would ever want a motorboat, even if he were offered one for free. He was fed up with the sea, with the constant wallowing and pitching, and was pretty sure that his former dreams of owning a share in a small sailing boat would never be resurrected now. The money would go toward something else: a new car, foreign holidays, some decent jewelry for Lára; anything really, so long as it had nothing to do with boats. It was ironic then that he seemed to have developed his sea legs at last, thanks no doubt to the captain's pills, and the ship's incessant rocking no longer bothered him the way it had for the first two days. He had begun to ride the waves instinctively, as if he and the yacht were one. Perhaps he would find that the land was moving up and down when and if they reached Iceland. The smile faded from his face as he tried to work out where that *if* had come from. Of course they would reach land safely. He forced his mind back to the conversation. "I'm sure you'll be successful."

"Hope so." Halli stood up, walked over to the window and stared out, as if he expected to see something other than the infinite ocean. In profile he looked despondent and Ægir wondered if the young sailor also had his doubts about their chances of reaching home safely. "I sure hope so," Halli repeated.

Lára shifted impatiently on the sofa, annoyed with Ægir for butting in on the conversation. She licked her lips as was her habit when she was considering her next move. "Do you know what the weather forecast is like, Halli? I was thinking of taking the girls up on deck for some fresh air, so I was hoping this storm would die down soon."

Halli didn't look round. "I reckon it'll stay like this all day. That's what generally happens. It's the good weather that changes quickly."

Ægir reached across the sofa and tentatively took Lára's hand. She didn't reject him and that was the sign he had been waiting for, the sign that soon he would be forgiven. Exactly how the process worked remained a mystery to him; he was simply grateful that his punishment was over. The situation on board was disastrous enough without his having to tiptoe around Lára as well. He risked moving closer to sit beside her and was relieved when she didn't object. Daring now to take the next step in the reconciliation process, he cuddled up to her and whispered an apology in her ear, adding that he needed to tell her something that was rather serious but not dangerous. This last comment went completely against his intuition; given recent developments, it looked as if they might indeed be in very real danger on board.

It had been bad enough that there was a body in the freezer, but at least its presence there had seemed to be unconnected to them. But now that an unknown person had taken the trouble to throw the body overboard, it was clear that the culprit was still on board and that he was trying to protect his interests. Perhaps he had needed to dispose of the body in case it carried traces of his DNA or some other evidence that could implicate him. The thought filled Ægir with such misgiving that, reluctantly, he had decided he would have to share it with Lára. Of course it would be better to pretend nothing had happened, but that would be neither right nor fair: he was so afraid she might unwittingly act in a manner that would cause the culprit to feel threatened. He met her wide, questioning eyes. "What?" she asked aloud, and Halli glanced round, as if he thought she was addressing him. He turned back to the window when Lára ignored him and repeated her question. "What? Is anything wrong?"

"Yes, actually." Ægir forced a wry smile. "The body's disappeared. Someone tipped it overboard while I was diving and it floated past me. I thought I was seeing things but it turns out the freezer's empty."

Lára opened her mouth and shut it again. Her eyes implored Ægir either to retract his words or admit he was pulling her leg. Clearly, she overestimated his sense of humor. "How could that happen?" Without waiting for an answer she leaped to her feet and tugged at him. "Where are the girls?"

"They're below. Where we left them." Ægir rose too, cursing himself for leaving them unsupervised. He had wanted to shield them from witnessing the tension between their parents. When he last saw them they had been sitting up in bed watching a film whose rating neither he nor Lára had had the presence of mind to check. The girls had been so absorbed, and hopefully still were, that it was unlikely any attempt to drag them away would have succeeded. Besides, there was a world of difference between disposing of a dead body and harming living children. "Wait here; I'll check on them." He almost shoved Lára back onto the sofa. Though there was no reason to suspect any harm had come to them, he didn't want her to be first on the scene.

Halli had cottoned on to what was happening and dragged his attention away from the window, which suggested that Thráinn had indeed ordered him to keep an eye on them. When they stood up, he looked around in confusion, as if he was considering forbidding them to leave the saloon. But once Ægir had induced Lára to sit down again, Halli seemed reassured. Plainly, she was the one under suspicion, since there was no way he himself could have thrown the body overboard when he was underwater at the time. Still, he found it so ludicrous that the captain could imagine for one minute that Lára had had anything to do with it that he almost burst out laughing. Then he realized that just as he had automatically assumed that a member of the crew must have been responsible, so the captain had almost certainly sought outside his own ranks for the guilty party. People never suspect those closest to them. But the captain's relationship with his crew was completely different from Ægir's with Lára. They had known each other for a decade, while the crew were strangers to one another who had been assembled to perform a specific task. Perhaps it was a sign of Thráinn's leadership skills that he should automatically side with his men. Or perhaps it was a sign that he was a fool.

"I'll fetch the girls. Don't worry—Halli will wait with you." Ægir walked calmly out of the saloon, quickening his pace as soon as the door closed behind him. He did not run, however. Rationally, he knew his worries were unnecessary. Under normal circumstances he would not even have been moving this fast, but the situation could in no way be described as normal. Only now did he truly acknowledge to himself that something was seriously amiss on board and that the corpse in the freezer was only part of it. This boat was quite simply a bad place. He breathed more easily as he approached the twins' door and heard the sound of the film.

They were still sitting where he had left them, side by side with their backs bolt upright against the headboard. When he appeared in the doorway they muttered a barely audible greeting but did not raise their eyes from the screen. The film must be incredibly gripping since he usually merited at least a grin. "What, not even a hello?" He pulled a sad face.

"It's a really good film. Don't talk to us now."

The yacht lurched suddenly and Ægir grabbed the door frame. "Sorry, girls. I'm afraid you're going to have to turn it off and come upstairs to join me and your mother. You can pause it, can't you?"

They turned their heads, their faces frightened. For the thousandth time he marveled at the magic of genes. He took it for granted that they were identical in appearance but it was beyond him to understand how a cluster of cells could be arranged in such a way as to make the responses of two individual human beings so alike. At times they moved in unison, as if performing synchronized swimming on dry land. This was one of those moments. They even blinked simultaneously, under furrowed brows. "Why?" Uttered with one voice, naturally. "It's nearly finished."

"Because the sea's so rough that we want to have you near us. You can watch the film any time you like; it's not going anywhere."

They ceased to act as one; Arna folded her arms mutinously while Bylgja drew up her legs and said with relentless logic: "If we can watch it any time why can't we watch it now?"

"You know what I mean. Don't twist my words. Your mother's waiting upstairs and she'll be worried if we don't hurry back." He picked up the remote control. "There's a TV in the saloon, so you can carry on watching it there if you like." When he switched off the television, the room was plunged into darkness. "Why have you drawn the curtains? Was the light shining on the screen?"

"No. We didn't want to see out. It was gross." This time it was Arna who answered.

"Gross? That's hardly the right word, sweetheart. The weather may be rough or stormy, but it's not gross."

"We're not talking about the weather."

"Oh?" Ægir was puzzled. "What then? The waves?"

"No." Bylgja shook her head, frowning. "The woman. She fell past the window into the sea. We both saw her when we came downstairs earlier. I'd seen you getting in the water and we wanted to watch you dive. We weren't allowed out on deck so we had to come down here to watch out of our window. Upstairs you only get a view of the deck. But it turns out that our window faces the other way, so we couldn't see you—only the woman falling. We thought it was Mommy at first but when she was lying in thé sea we got a better look and realized it wasn't her."

Ægir swallowed a lump in his throat. "Are you sure you weren't dreaming?" Now at least it was possible to establish that the woman had been thrown from the deck above the girls' cabin. He had been lowered into the sea on the other side of the ship, so for him to have caught sight of it the body must have been pulled under the keel by the current.

"No, we weren't," they replied in chorus.

"There's no woman on board apart from your mother and she's

sitting upstairs in the saloon." Perhaps this was the wrong thing to say; they might have to give a statement to the police later and it was unfair to confuse them like this.

"It wasn't Mommy, it was the woman in the painting. Wearing the same dress and everything." Bylgja shuddered. "Her face looked horrible. Then she sank."

Ægir took a deep breath, making a heroic effort to control his features. If this was true, the woman in the freezer must have been Karítas. He recalled the material of the garment that had been billowing about the gruesome body and conceded that it may well have been the same dress. The colors had looked duller but then the sea would mute them, as it did sound.

"I told you they wouldn't believe us." Arna got up from the bed. "You never believe us."

"Of course I do." Ægir groped for the right words, for some way to distract their attention. His mind was blank. "Why didn't you fetch your mother? Or someone else?"

"We didn't dare leave the cabin at first but when we finally went upstairs Mommy was panicking because she thought you'd fallen in the sea. We tried to tell her you were diving but she wouldn't listen. She didn't want to hear about the woman either." Arna looked doubtfully at her father. "Are you angry?"

"Angry? No, not in the least. But do you know what? It was actually a good thing you didn't mention it. Very good, in fact. I want to ask you to keep this a secret. You mustn't tell anyone—anyone at all. It's really, really important. Do you understand?" He had been overwhelmed by a sudden terror that if it became common knowledge, the person who disposed of the body might think the girls had spotted him. He would have to be a complete monster to attack children, but Ægir wasn't taking any risks. "Not Mommy. And not any of the crew. Okay?"

They exchanged surprised glances. "Why not?" Bylgja had obviously detected something odd in his behavior and her voice betrayed alarm.

"Because this must be our secret. I promise to tell you why after we get home. I promise." He knelt down beside them. "We three know it happened, but nobody else must know. So we won't tell anyone until later."

But of course he was wrong; the perpetrator knew where and when it had happened. And he was one of them: Thráinn, Halli or Loftur. All equally implausible, yet all equally plausible. "What time did you come down here, Bylgja? Was it straight after you saw me lowered over the side?" She nodded, worried that she had done something wrong. Ægir tried to work out what this meant. Bylgja must have left the window and told her sister what she had seen. Then they had spoken to their mother and told her they were going below, before coming down here and taking up position by the window. So about ten to fifteen minutes must have passed between his entering the sea and the body being thrown overboard. Which meant he couldn't even rule out Thráinn or Halli. Although they had been out on deck with him to start with, he hadn't been able to see if they were still there during the time he was underwater.

Ægir rose to his feet. He couldn't stand this, couldn't stand the sea a moment longer or the thought that he had placed his family in jeopardy. The decision to sail home was the stupidest of his life. His eyes strayed to the briefcase leaning against the wall by the desk, which reminded him of what felt almost like a previous existence; the daily grind that may not have put much in his pocket but was at least neither strenuous nor risky. He had been a fool. Looking down at the twins' dark heads, he knew he had failed them. And Lára. And Sigga Dögg, who was waiting for them at home. He clenched his teeth so hard that his jaw ached. They had to get back to Iceland— the sooner the better.

In his mind he kept reciting the names of the crew as if they were a nursery rhyme: Thráinn, Halli, Loftur. Halli, Loftur, Thráinn. Loftur, Thráinn, Halli. Which one had done this? Please God, don't let them all be in on it together.

Chapter 19

The discovery of the body had placed the mystery of the yacht in a whole new light. When Loftur's corpse washed up on shore it had merely lent support to earlier speculation that the disappearance of the passengers must be due to a single catastrophe, but a dead man wrapped in a tarpaulin and left hanging on the end of a rope was quite another matter. This was Thóra's third visit to the police station in the wake of the discovery; Matthew and Snævar had only been summoned twice. Perhaps they would be asked to come back, too, but Thóra suspected the police were daunted by having to question Matthew in English, and Snævar doubtless needed time to recover from the shock of witnessing his friend Halldór in such a horrific state. Strong emotion presumably would not make for a clear statement.

Thóra followed the detective along a corridor that had clearly not been decorated with a view to pleasing the eye. He was the same man she had originally spoken to about the yacht, but this time she herself was a witness and the case had taken a far more serious turn. The officer looked tired and preoccupied; his nicotine gum was nowhere to be seen, replaced by a faint whiff of cigarette smoke. With cuts to the police budget putting extra pressure on her contacts, she imagined they would hardly welcome a complicated, time-consuming case like this. The man didn't let it show, however, and Thóra was grateful. For some strange reason she felt as if she was to blame for the whole affair and kept having to stop herself from apologizing for the nuisance.

The detective halted before the door to a small interview room that looked even less inviting than the corridor. Thóra sat down on a hard chair, feeling very upright and unrelaxed, not because of the chair so much as her own desire to get the conversation over with as soon as possible. The room was hot and stuffy. She undid the top button of her coat and loosened the collar a little so her face wouldn't turn scarlet during the interrogation. "Have there been any developments?"

"Yes and no." The man's face was impassive as he placed a file on the table and took a seat himself. "We've finally had the initial results of the tests on the body samples. As you can imagine, things were considerably delayed by the fact that someone had vomited over the evidence."

"Tell me about it." Thóra was about to share her photocopier experience but caught herself in the nick of time; her cheeks turned pink at the thought that this should even have crossed her mind. "Have you been able to verify that it's Halldór? Snævar was adamant but the body was such a mess that I don't know how he could tell for sure." Pictures of the crew and passengers had just been published; their black-and-white faces had met her gaze that morning as she read the paper over her tea and toast. She had already seen photos of Ægir and his family but this was the first time she had laid eyes on the other three men and learned about the families they had left behind. The captain was a widower with three grown-up children; the other two were unmarried and childless but had parents and siblings. The picture of Halldór had rung no bells.

"Yes, we've received verification." He leafed through the file. "There's no further doubt." He focused unusually intense green eyes on Thóra. Was he wearing tinted contact lenses? He didn't seem the type. His irises were probably naturally that color. "Just as importantly, we've also established the cause of death, though the postmortem results have only complicated matters. You see, it appears that the man drowned, regardless of how he ended up hanging on a rope. That's why I called you in—to consult your opinion on a few details."

Thóra was wrong-footed. It had never occurred to her that the man might have died in an accident. She had been convinced that he had been murdered and that the postmortem would reveal stab wounds or signs of violence. She hadn't noticed any injuries on the part of his body that had been visible; her assumption had been based entirely on the way the corpse had been disposed of. Which is not to say that she had examined him very closely; she had merely gaped at the grisly vision for the instant it took her brain to register the badly decomposed head, then she had looked away to avoid following Snævar's example. Her stomach turned over at the memory. "Ah. I was thinking something new must have come to light."

"Quite. We haven't made this public yet. And I trust you won't discuss the matter with anyone apart from those working on the case with you?"

"No, of course not." She couldn't exactly see herself posting the news on Facebook or gossiping about it with her friends.

"I'm glad to hear it. The postmortem results are indisputable: the man drowned and there's nothing to suggest coercion. His body showed grazing and contusions but not in the places you'd expect if force had been used. What's more, he seems to have incurred these injuries at an earlier stage because they'd already begun to heal by the time he died."

"I see." Thóra didn't really expect an answer to her next question. "Have you made any progress in finding out how he came to be wrapped in canvas and sunk in the sea?"

"Well, I can't go into any detail," the detective replied, "but rest assured that the investigation's in full swing. Though it doesn't help that all the people involved are either dead or missing. It's going to be tricky, but we hope to get to the bottom of it eventually."

"I hope you do." Thóra undid another button on her coat. The police budget cuts did not seem to extend to the central heating.

"I don't know if you're aware but when we boarded the yacht after the crash, the only door we found locked was the one to the storeroom where Halldór's body was suspended from the hatch. It's hard to tell if it's significant but the key was discovered in the corner of one of the stairwells."

Thóra had not heard this before but regarded it as of secondary importance. "What about Loftur? Was he drowned as well?"

"The same applies to this as to what I told you before; you must treat the information as confidential." Thóra merely nodded. "His body was in pretty bad shape after being immersed for so long in the sea, which means the postmortem results weren't as unambiguous, but we've established that he drowned as well; the question is how he managed to do so in chlorinated seawater."

"Chlorinated?"

"So it appears. We had to send some tissue samples abroad for testing to be absolutely certain and we haven't had those results back yet, but I'd be surprised if they contradicted the earlier findings."

"What about Halldór? Did he drown in chlorinated seawater too?"

"No. His lung tissue and other physical evidence indicate that he drowned in the usual manner." The man linked his hands behind his head and tipped back his chair. "Do you remember the Jacuzzi on one of the smaller decks?"

Thóra realized what he was implying. "Loftur drowned in that?"

"In all likelihood. In fact, it's the only real option." He lowered his arms, sat up in his chair and moved closer to the desk. "Of course it could happen to anyone, especially if they're drunk, but that wasn't the case with Loftur. There was next to no alcohol in his bloodstream. Yet somehow the poor sod ended up drowning, stone-cold sober, in one meter of water."

"Are you suggesting he was given a helping hand?"

"No. Not necessarily. It's possible, but of course it's also conceivable that he had some kind of fit when he was in the tub and passed out, or couldn't save himself for some other reason." The policeman seemed to be waiting for her to comment. When she didn't, he added: "Aren't you going to ask what he was wearing?"

"What was he wearing?" Thóra took the hint; if Loftur had been wearing clothes, he was unlikely to have died from natural causes. Nobody would get into a hot tub with their clothes on.

"He was fully dressed." The man arched an eyebrow. "Which is rather odd, as people don't usually bother to dress corpses. And how could he have come to fall in the sea after drowning in the Jacuzzi? It seems clear to me that somebody else was involved. And perhaps that person killed the others on board as well." He clicked his tongue and smiled. "Or not, as the case may be."

Thóra was silent. The news had filled her with horror and for a moment she forgot how hot she was. "I can hardly bear to think about those little girls. It was bad enough before but everything looks much blacker now. Somehow it's easier to accept the idea that they died in an accident than that they fell victim to a murderer." She sighed. "Though the outcome is the same."

"It's certainly not looking good." The policeman's expression was grave again. "But to get down to business, your part in the case seems straightforward, so I see no need to ask you any further questions. Unless there's something you want to add?"

"No." Her first interview had been long and rigorous, and the police had extracted all the information that mattered or that she was able to tell them. Not that she was hiding anything out of confidentiality to her clients, sadly. If she had been it would at least mean that she had some inkling about the fates of the passengers.

"Our interests are not incompatible—would you agree?" he continued. Thóra nodded; their goals might not exactly coincide but the difference was negligible. She needed to provide persuasive grounds for believing that Ægir and Lára were dead, and in order to do so she had to acquaint herself with as many details of the case as possible. The police needed to go a step further; probability was not enough for them, they needed to prove what had happened beyond reasonable doubt. The detective continued: "So we were wondering if we should join forces. I'm not insisting that you work for us since that would be inappropriate for both parties, but we were hoping you'd keep us abreast of any information you uncover that might be of relevance to our inquiry. That way we won't have to keep hauling you in for a grilling. I don't believe this arrangement would be in conflict with your duty to your clients. In fact, I assume it's in all our interests to solve this case."

"Yes, I agree." Thóra paused before continuing: "Of course, I'll need to inform my clients, but I assume they won't object. It's not as if I'm working on anything major; I'm merely trying to establish that the missing couple are dead. Since my last visit to the police station I've sent the insurance company formal notification of their presumed death and explained that a report will follow. I don't know whether to expect a response before they receive the full report but we'll soon see. I'm not exactly optimistic that they'll accept the documentation as sufficient proof, in which case we'll have little option but to take the matter to court. But obviously it would be better if we could avoid that by presenting a watertight case to start with. It's quite possible that my investigation will uncover something that might be of benefit to you."

"But you do take my point? We can't pay you for your time, and anyway it's your public duty. You're a lawyer so I need hardly remind you of article 73 of the Act on Criminal Procedure." He cleared his throat and for a moment Thóra thought he was going to quote the whole article from memory, but her fear proved unfounded. "You are obliged to render assistance to the police in their investigation of matters in the public interest. And it's also important to bear in mind that you're required to surrender any documents and other items in your possession should the police request them for their investigation."

"I assure you I'm not sitting on any evidence. I've already handed over copies of all the papers Snævar gave me connected to his hospital admission and flight tickets; that's all I've acquired so far. In the next few days I'm expecting to obtain documents relating to Ægir and Lára's finances, as well as a declaration from their GP that they were both in good health. It goes without saying that you can have copies of those too if you want. Then I'm going to try to persuade Snævar to obtain a certificate from an Icelandic doctor stating that his broken leg made him unfit for work, as confirmation that the crew was one man short. I won't do that immediately, though, as I want to give him a chance to recover from his shock." Thóra had the uneasy feeling that the detective suspected her of concealing evidence, though nothing could be further from the truth. "Just to be completely clear about this, there are exceptions to the article you cited, as I'm sure you're aware. I only raise the fact because I might have to resort to them at some stage and it would be better to establish from the outset that I reserve the right to assess each point on its own merits. But of course I'll help as far as I can."

The detective seemed satisfied, perhaps even more satisfied than if she had simply acquiesced without reservation. "Fine. It would be good to receive copies of everything you get hold of. Better too much than too little." He turned back to the file. "About the box or case you mentioned in your statement following the discovery of the body;

it transpires that it wasn't among the items we removed from the yacht. So it looks as if it must have been taken by the person or persons who broke in. Perhaps they mistook it for a jewelry case."

"Perhaps, but it wasn't locked. They would only have had to open it to realize there were no valuables inside."

"Are you sure? Did you go through all the contents? Valuables don't necessarily consist of gold or money."

Thóra was forced to admit that she had not made a very thorough inspection. "There's one thing I forgot to mention. I noticed a safe in one of the wardrobes in the master bedroom. Were you aware of its existence?"

"Yes. We had it opened but it was empty. It wasn't stuffed with handy clues, more's the pity." His tone was ironic. "Before I let you go, I'd like your opinion on a couple more matters that you must keep to yourself for the time being. They're unlikely to have any bearing on your case, but you never know. Perhaps you'd keep your eyes open for any evidence that might relate to them."

"Absolutely."

"Good." Before going on, he met her eyes searchingly, as if scrutinizing her for proof of her honesty. When he stared intently like that his green irises appeared even more unnatural. "You said the body was only partially uncovered, so all you saw was the head. Is that correct?"

"Yes and no. It's correct that all I saw was the head, because I looked away at once. I gather from Matthew that Snævar tore the canvas off in a frenzy, then threw up. I can't stand corpses or people being sick, let alone both together, so I only caught a glimpse of the body. And that was more than enough. If I explained badly during questioning, I assure you it wasn't deliberate."

The man was reading the page in front of him, which probably contained one of the statements she had given. "No, no. It's all down here. I just couldn't quite recall." He looked up again. "So you didn't notice that an attempt had been made to dismember the body?"

"No. I wasn't aware of that." Yet again she found herself completely thrown. It was bad enough that the yacht mystery should have developed into a murder inquiry, without people being chopped up as well. "Matthew didn't mention it either."

"He may not have noticed or the canvas may have concealed the lower half of the body. We have photos from the scene, so I can easily check. But that's not the issue. What I wanted to know was whether you remember hearing a splash as they were hauling the bundle on board." He drew a deep breath and fiddled with his shirt collar, apparently feeling the heat as well.

"No. Should I have?" Confused, she couldn't grasp what he was driving at.

"It appears that someone intended to dismember the body but was either disturbed in the act or abandoned the attempt for some other reason. At any rate, he or she managed to sever the legs at the knee and they're missing. I suppose they could have been amputated accidentally, though it's hard to see how. At present we're assuming human agency, but it would be easier to establish the cause if we had the legs. We've had divers out dragging the sea around the yacht but with no success. I was trying to find out if you remembered hearing anything that might indicate that the legs had fallen out of the tarpaulin. It's not crucial, but if they were thrown overboard separately, it begs the question: Why not the whole body? It seems illogical but hopefully we'll find an explanation. We had forensics inspect the boat again for traces of this . . . procedure. Even if Halldór was already dead, there would have been a considerable amount of blood, and we believe we've found the place, though the perpetrator cleaned up afterward. It's pretty clear that the dismemberment was carried out on board."

Thóra tried weakly to imagine the sequence of events. "Where?"

"Below decks, in an out-of-the-way corner between the water tanks. Which suggests that the culprit was at pains to hide the fact."

"Implying that one or more of the others were still alive at the time?"

"Exactly." His gaze was almost hypnotic. Perhaps he *did* wear lenses, just to achieve this effect. "That's the theory we're going with for now. But as I said, we're not a hundred percent positive; the blood may have resulted from a completely different incident. We've also found traces elsewhere, but it had been more carefully cleaned up, so it's harder to work out what was going on. We're currently running tests."

"Where was this?"

He drummed his fingers on the desk. "All over the place, to be honest. On the bridge, by the exit to one of the staircases and in the saloon. Although we can't find any sign of it now, chances are that the deck was running with blood too. But the sea would wash away the evidence pretty fast. The yacht hit bad weather and there would have been a great deal of spray, not to mention rain. The man's legs may have been cut off on deck, for that matter. If you think about it, that would be by far the most logical place."

Thóra remembered that most of the deck was overlooked by one or more of the yacht's windows. "Wouldn't the others have noticed?" She corrected herself before he could reply. "Ah, not if it was night, of course, when most people would have been asleep. But why do it in the first place? Wouldn't it have been simpler to throw the body overboard? Out in the middle of the ocean like that, surely it would have sunk without trace or been eaten?"

"You would have thought so."

"One more question. Is it possible that the captain was referring to Halldór's body when he contacted the British vessel? Could he or one of the others have surprised the murderer in the act, meaning he didn't have a chance to finish the job?"

"It's conceivable. But the message referred to a woman—unless that was a misunderstanding. The connection was poor and when you factor in the language difficulties it wouldn't be surprising if the sense had been muddled."

"I have to confess I'm totally mystified."

He gave her a friendly smile. "If it's any comfort, we're having just as much trouble getting our heads round all this. Why was the body hung overboard? There are any number of places on board where it could have been hidden without being spotted or given away by the smell."

Thóra couldn't immediately think of anywhere that a man's body could have been concealed, though she recalled from the plans that there were storage spaces and tanks on the bottom deck where they had found the blood stains. "Could it have been hidden in one of the water or oil tanks in the keel?"

"We're examining the water tanks. But I gather the oil tank's out of the question." He tapped his pen on the file. "Perhaps I should share one more bizarre detail with you."

"I doubt I'll faint, if that's what you're afraid of. Nothing would surprise me now."

He ceased his tapping. "The postmortem revealed that the body had suffered frost damage."

"Frost damage?" Thóra had to admit that in spite of what she had just said, she was nonplussed. "Did the temperature drop below freezing at any point during the voyage?"

He shook his head. "No. There was a storm but no really cold weather. A more likely explanation is that the body was stored in one of the freezers on board. But since we've found no traces of DNA or fibers from the tarpaulin, there may be some other explanation. Alternatively, the body may have been wrapped in plastic. Since I've told you this much, I may as well add that the woman's body was apparently found in a freezer—if the captain's message was understood correctly. But forensics can't find any evidence of that either."

Thóra would have given a great deal to see her own dumbfounded expression in a mirror. "I don't know what to say. Nothing I've discovered has suggested anything like this." She longed for some sensible, concrete information. "Do you know when Halldór died?"

The detective shook his head again. "I'm afraid not. Most if not all of the methods used to establish time of death take account of conditions after the person has died. In this case the body seems to have been stored in a variety of environments, so we don't have much to go on. It's been submerged in the sea, kept in a freezer and maybe in a crate as well, so unfortunately the time of death is very imprecise. He could have died at any point on the voyage, though it's obvious he couldn't have been murdered after the yacht reached harbor. The postmortem showed too advanced a breakdown of various biological compounds that I'm not qualified to explain. So it couldn't have been submerged there for long, at least not while the yacht was moving, or it would have been in a much worse state. In fact, it would be a miracle if it had still been there when the yacht reached the harbor."

"I'm afraid this is outside my area of expertise." Thóra was boiling by now and experiencing a desperate desire to fling off her coat.

"Of course." He studied her as she sat there, her face scarlet, dreaming of the cold air outside. "Well. That just about wraps up what I have to say, so now I can get on with reprimanding the officers who conducted the original inspection. I try to do so at least once a day." His eyes gleamed. "It beggars belief that not one of them noticed the rope or realized it didn't belong there. Of course, they should have taken along an experienced sailor or at least someone who was remotely acquainted with boats, but I don't tell them that because I enjoy giving them an arguement. It's good for the circulation." He stood up and escorted Thóra to the door.

She drove up Skólavördustígur in a daze, then went into her office and sat there for a while deep in thought. Eventually, she leaned over her desk and shouted: "Bella! Could you pop in here a minute?" It was time to abandon all conventional approaches. Since common sense had proved nothing but a hindrance in this case, it was time for some muddled, left-field thinking, and when it came to that Bella was an expert.

Chapter 20

Mother and daughters were deep in slumber in the big double bed. They lay cuddled up together, their hair mingling on the pillows so that Ægir couldn't tell their locks apart. Their cheeks were flushed, not from fever but almost certainly because someone had finally turned up the heating to compensate for the onset of chillier weather. Ægir had no idea who had done so and, to be honest, he didn't really care. Beside him lay his family, the only thing that mattered. Arna murmured but he couldn't distinguish the words. Her eyes were quivering under their pale lids and her legs twitched. Then all was quiet again. He hoped she wasn't having a nightmare. He and Lára had done their best to behave as if nothing was wrong, masking their fear and apprehension, but perhaps their manner had seemed too forced. Neither could bear the thought that the girls might sense the sudden seriousness of their situation. At least not yet. Soon, though, they would be forced to tell them exactly what was going on, to ensure the girls never left their side.

Ægir listened to the sound of footsteps overhead. He stared up at the ceiling as if he expected the man to start sawing through it at any minute, showering them with plaster. Although the cabin door was locked, the security it provided was illusory as a full-grown man could easily force his way in. Besides, they must keep a master key somewhere safe; perhaps on the bridge. If the man wanted to get in, he wouldn't need to break the door down. But Ægir was not worried about this eventuality; he didn't believe the man had the slightest interest in them—for the moment.

More than seven hours had passed since he had dragged Lára and the girls down to the cabin where they had locked themselves in. In all that time no one had so much as knocked on the door or called out, as if the crew had forgotten their existence. Which suited them fine. Even though it would mean going hungry, Ægir was almost prepared to lie low in their cabin until they reached port. The water in the bathroom taps would be sufficient for him, but he was less sure about the girls; they probably wouldn't be willing to go without food for days on end. Besides, he would have to put in an appearance at some point, not to appease his daughters' complaints so much as to prevent the crew from wondering what was up. If they did, someone was bound to put two and two together and conclude that the family knew more than they were letting on. It would be pathetically easy for that person to finish them off here in the cabin, especially when they were defenseless in sleep.

The footsteps ceased and Ægir felt the adrenaline start to course through his veins. When the man stood still it was even worse than when he was pacing. It suggested that he was plotting. Ægir knew the idea was ludicrous but that didn't change how he felt. He even held his breath while he waited for the man to start moving again. Nothing happened. Then there was a scraping sound from what he took to be a chair or sofa, and he tried to work out which room was directly overhead. Most likely the saloon, which suggested that there were two men up and about, one on the bridge, the other busy with something in the saloon. Ægir sat up and pushed the duvet aside gently so as not to wake his wife and daughters. It might make sense to go out and talk to the men; then the family wouldn't have to show their faces again until lunchtime tomorrow. Their absence must appear as natural as possible; for example, he could go up at regular intervals to complain that the girls were seasick. That way he would be able to fetch the necessities—as long as he disciplined himself to appear relaxed, as if nothing had happened, as if it hadn't occurred to them that one of the men must be linked to the dead woman in the freezer. Although such naiveté would seem pretty far-fetched in the light of recent events, it would have to suffice. If he betrayed the slightest fear, there was a danger he would do or say something with irreversible consequences.

He climbed out of bed and balanced for a moment to accustom

himself to the motion. About an hour after they had locked themselves in, the engines had abruptly kicked into life again. Perhaps the crew had managed to free the yacht from the container, or the captain had simply decided to chance it before the situation on board deteriorated even further. There was no question now of hanging around in the middle of nowhere, waiting for rescue: with their communications system crippled, they couldn't even send out a distress signal, and it was so long since they had seen another ship that Ægir believed, admittedly without good grounds, that they might wait there for weeks without being spotted. Then he remembered the emergency button Thráinn had shown him, which was designed to transmit an SOS with their location. Thanks to that, their fate was unlikely to consist of drifting over the ocean for the rest of their days. Perhaps he should simply go up to the bridge and activate the button right now, and take the gamble that the foreign crew who responded to their call would believe him. But supposing they weren't convinced and refused to take the family on board? In that case it would be better not to chance it. If things got any worse, at least there was security in knowing the button was there.

Ægir scribbled a quick note to Lára, explaining where he was going and stressing that neither she nor the girls should come looking for him. Then he slipped on his shoes and quietly left the cabin. As he was closing the door, he wondered if he ought to wake his wife. She and the girls had been sleeping for over two hours and might find it hard to drop off tonight if they slept for much longer now. Their eyelids had begun to droop during the second film and Ægir alone had managed to stay awake. He would have liked to have followed suit but felt compelled to stay on guard in case one of the crew tried to enter the cabin. How he was to make it through the night was another matter; clearly, he couldn't stay awake for days on end and even if he did, he would be of little use exhausted if it came to a fight. Lára would have to share the watches with him, so it would be better to allow her some more sleep now. The incident with Karítas's perfume bottle had shaken her badly. When she had gone to fetch it in order to convince him that the smell was the same as the one in the freezer, the bottle had gone. What's more, it was nowhere to be found in their cabin or bathroom, and Lára had started imagining all kinds of conspiracies. Ægir, on the other hand, had signaly failed to work up any concern. He had other, more pressing matters on his mind than missing perfume bottles. As he closed the door, he took care not to click the lock too loudly.

On his way upstairs he found himself keenly aware of every step. Until now his body had moved about the ship on autopilot, but now he sensed the gleaming wood under his soles and was acutely conscious of lifting his feet. For the first time he noticed the handrail, cold and hard under his palm. The sounds that carried from above also seemed more distinct than before, though none were particularly loud or penetrating: a squeak; a low humming which, though his ears had not picked it up until now, had no doubt been there since the beginning of the voyage; the scraping of a chair. This sudden hypersensitivity must result from a primitive urge to protect his family, for he quickly realized that his taut nerves were not for himself; all that mattered now was to bring his wife and daughters safely home. The realization gave him courage and he walked up the stairs full of a new self-confidence. The man who was not afraid for himself had a definite advantage.

He decided to check the pilot house first. There he would at least learn what progress they were making and what the weather forecast had in store. Despite hoping fervently that the crew would have found some means of repairing the telecommunications system, he knew this was unlikely. It was a safe bet that whoever had thrown the body overboard had also sabotaged the equipment. It would have been too great a coincidence otherwise. And that was a bad sign. How was the perpetrator intending to enforce their silence after they reached land? There was only one sure method that Ægir could think of.

Thráinn turned out to be alone on the bridge. He sat in the pilot's chair, staring into space as if in a trance. Ægir had to cough to attract his attention. The older man looked round, his eyes bloodshot. There was no sign that he had gone for a rest after lunch, which meant that he must have been awake for thirty-six hours straight. "Hello. I'd begun to think all of you weren't going to show your faces again." Thráinn stretched and rubbed his jaw as if to loosen it up for conversation.

"Lára and the girls are a bit under the weather. Seasick again."

"Right." Thráinn was not deceived. "Let's hope they feel better soon."

Ægir saw there was no point in trying to convince him; he would believe whatever he wanted to. "Yes, let's hope so. I was just fetching them some Coke and a bite to eat in case they get their appetites back, so I decided to look in and see how it's going. Find out if there's any good news for a change."

Thráinn grunted. "Good news." He shook his head slowly, suppressing a yawn. "As you've no doubt noticed, we're under way again—that should count as good news."

"Yes. I realized. What happened?"

"The container sank. Presumably because you loosened the door. It must have shaken open with the movement, letting the air escape. So you fixed it. Bravo." From the taciturn Thráinn, this was high praise. "Anyway, the main thing isn't how it happened but the fact that we're on our way home. I'm going to push her faster than I have up to now, since it's vital we get to port as soon as possible."

Ægir opened his mouth to ask if he was referring to the discovery of the body and its subsequent disappearance, but the answer was glaringly obvious. "How far have we got left?"

Thráinn reached for the chart and showed him their most recent position. Iceland was further away than Ægir had hoped; in fact they were more or less equidistant from all the nearest landmasses, which meant they would have nothing to gain by heading anywhere but home. "All being well, we're about forty-eight hours from home." Thráinn put down the chart. "All being well." He regarded Ægir levelly. "Actually, I'm glad you came up. I was thinking of looking in on you. We need to have a chat."

"Oh?" The yacht plunged sickeningly and Ægir gripped the handle on the wall.

When the captain finally released Ægir's gaze, he turned back to stare at the black expanse of glass that extended the width of the bridge. "As you're aware, we're in a serious situation. There's something very strange going on and, as matters stand, I can't trust Halli or Loftur."

"So?" Ægir hoped Thráinn wasn't going to propose they join forces to overpower the other men and lock them up. He had no way of determining which of the three crew members was guilty. What on earth would he do if there were only the two of them left and it turned out to be Thráinn? Tackle him with Lára's help? Hardly.

"I haven't a clue who moved the body and chucked it overboard—Halli, Loftur, your wife? The girls?" He silenced Ægir's protests with a wave of his hand. "All I know for sure is that it wasn't me and it wasn't you. I didn't leave the rail the entire time you were underwater, but Halli did, and so did Loftur, who had come to watch. I know nothing about your wife, though I admit it's far less likely that she was responsible than one of the boys, if only because your daughters seem to follow her everywhere. And they can hardly have done it."

Ægir chose not to mention that the twins had gone below at around the time the body ended up in the sea. If the captain was planning to take action, the last thing he wanted was to cast suspicion on Lára. He knew it was crazy to imagine she could be involved but his gut instinct was unlikely to satisfy Thráinn. "Were Halli and Loftur away long enough to have done it?"

"Well, Loftur wasn't around to begin with, so he would have had the opportunity then. And Halli went off for a while but I didn't take any notice because there was no reason to. If you'd told us right away that you'd come face to face with the dead woman in the sea, I'd have taken a different view of his absence."

"I've told you already—I thought I was seeing things."

"All right, I know I shouldn't be bawling you out; I'm just tired. So tired I can't be bothered to be polite." He spoke as if manners were usually his strong point. "Never mind that. What I'm trying to say is that I know you can't be involved because you were diving, so you're the only person apart from myself that I can trust. Since I can't stay awake for the next forty-eight hours, I wanted to see if I could persuade you to help me get this ship to port. All you'd have to do is stand watch while I bunk down in here—you could give me a nudge if there were any problems."

"I see." Relieved as he was that the request had not involved tackling the other two men, Ægir was still uneasy. "What about Lára and the girls? Where are they supposed to be in the meantime? I'm not prepared to leave them alone while I stand here gawping out of the window."

"No. Fair enough." The captain scratched his stubble and yawned again without even trying to suppress it. "They could stay in here with us. The mattress is in the back room, so I wouldn't be in your way." He gestured to a door behind him. "It may be cramped but there's no need for them to be uncomfortable. We could easily move a small table and chairs in here."

"Yes, I suppose so." Ægir surveyed the pilot house. "Still, I don't know."

"Well, don't waste too much time thinking about it. I need a rest and if you're not manning the bridge, whoever disposed of the body is bound to do it. I don't know about you but I'm not too thrilled with that prospect."

Ægir lost his temper. "And what about you? How can I be sure you're innocent? You could have done it yourself for all I know—I couldn't see if you were at the rail while I was underwater. And what then? If I help you, I'd be siding against the others who may well be innocent. I'd rather stay out of this; concentrate on keeping my family safe and leave you lot to sort it out among yourselves."

"I'm afraid that's out of the question. If you barricade yourselves in your cabin, the next time you come out there may be one less person. Then two less. Where will you stand then? And your wife and daughters? I'm not sure you'd enjoy that." The captain's expression, which had hardened at these words, mellowed again and the signs of fatigue returned. "As captain I could of course order you to keep watch—I assume you realize that? But I expect I'd be more successful if I managed to convince you without resorting to threats." Thráinn smiled faintly. "Though don't think I'll hesitate to use force if pushed."

The sailing course hadn't covered the captain's remit in any detail, so Ægir had no idea what the consequences of disobeying his orders might be. "And if I still won't obey? Will I be made to walk the plank?"

"No. Nothing that dramatic. I'll simply tell Halli and Loftur to lock you up. And I don't mean in the cabin with your family. Your wife and daughters would be free to come and go. And as you know, the company on board is not exactly desirable. This is no joke, my friend."

Ægir was afraid to speak for fear he would hurl a storm of abuse at the captain and find himself under lock and key as a result. In other words, the captain was saying, either he helped him or they would separate him from Lára and the girls. If the man didn't get his own way he was actually prepared to expose them to danger. Ægir's rage subsided. For Thráinn this was only a means to an important end: to make it home safe and sound. "I'll help." He didn't smile or give any other sign that he approved of the plan. "I'd better fetch Lára and the girls. They're asleep below. You'll have to stay awake in the meantime."

"No problem." Thráinn made no more effort than Ægir to restore the fragile rapport that had recently been established between them. "I've stayed awake longer than this in my time."

Before Ægir could respond, the door opened and Halli appeared in the gap. Neither Thráinn nor Ægir spoke and at first the young man did not seem to sense that anything was amiss. Then he picked up on the atmosphere and his face reddened, either from embarrassment or anger. "What's going on?"

"I was asking Ægir to take over for a while. I need some kip and I reckon you do, too." Thráinn looked straight at Halli and Ægir couldn't help admiring his seemingly indomitable spirit. He betrayed no sign of awkwardness or nerves when it came to informing one of his subordinates that he was out in the cold.

"I see." Halli's red face clashed badly with his dyed hair. He jutted his chin. "If you think I had anything to do with it you're mistaken. Badly mistaken."

"No one knows anything for sure, so there's no point discussing it. Everyone will simply have to obey my orders for the next couple of days; that way we'll make it home safe and sound. I assume we're all agreed that that's our goal?" said Thráinn.

Halli clenched his teeth, his jaws whitening. "Of course." Then relaxing slightly, he looked puzzled. "Where's Loftur?"

"Loftur?" Thráinn repeated wearily. "As you can see, he's not here.

Last time I saw him he was going to fire up the hot tub. I expect that's where he is now."

"Oh?" Halli dithered in the doorway, unsure whether to stay or go. "From what I could see the tub still had its cover on. And he's not below."

"Could he be in the saloon?" Ægir's words came out in a rush as they tended to in fraught situations. "I heard someone there earlier."

Halli shook his head. "That was me. He hasn't been in. I checked his cabin but he wasn't there either." He licked his lips repeatedly. "Perhaps we missed each other. Or he's out on deck."

"What the hell would he be doing out there?" Thráinn rose from his chair. Going over to the console, he fiddled for a moment with his back to the two men. Careful not to meet Halli's eye, Ægir feigned interest in the captain's back. Thráinn turned again, having finished whatever he was doing. "We'd better look for him." He glanced at each of them in turn. "We'll stick together."

Neither objected. In silence they followed the captain out of the pilot house, their clumsy movements betraying the lack of trust between the members of their little party. It did nothing to lessen their paranoia when they finally found Loftur: submerged, fully dressed, under the closed lid of the Jacuzzi.

Chapter 21

The darkness inside was pierced by a sunbeam. Motes of dust glittered in the ray of light, vanishing where it faded out. As she breathed in the stagnant air, Thóra was struck by how quickly buildings betrayed the signs of being uninhabited. After their three-week holiday last summer her own house had greeted them with cold, dry air and an unfamiliar musty smell; not until they had given it a good airing and then turned up the radiators had it felt like home again. Ægir and Lára's house had stood empty for the same amount of time, and although this was her first visit she was sure they too would have made a face on entering the hall.

"Shall I turn the lights on?" Margeir stood in the doorway, looking bemused, momentarily arrested, like Thóra, by the play of dust in the light. "Or should I just open the curtains?"

"Turn on the lights. It would be better." Thóra adjusted a sock that had been half pulled off when she removed her leather boots. "We should take the precaution of touching as little as possible, though of course we'll have to rummage around in drawers and so on. But with any luck we'll find the bank statements and other stuff straight away, so that won't be necessary."

"They were over the moon when they bought this house." The old man groped disconsolately for the light switch. "I helped them with the painting before they moved in."

Thóra was at a loss how to reply. The whole situation was so depressing that words would be inadequate plasters for the man's wounds. Besides, the decorating job didn't really deserve any praise. The house boasted a monochrome color scheme of the type popular among young people. Yet unlike many similar homes now on the market, here the couple had not spent much on the furnishings. Most of the furniture looked like standard IKEA issue, and there were no paintings on the walls, only a few prints, which were probably wedding presents. Thóra was glad at any rate to see no evidence that the couple had been living beyond their means. That made it less likely that they had serious money troubles, unless the interest rate on their mortgage had recently shot up. And if their finances were in order, it would strengthen her case.

They began by sorting the mail from the newspapers that lay piled up in the hall but, with the exception of a recent credit card bill, found nothing of interest. The family had gone abroad at the beginning of the month and there was still a week or so to go before the end. No doubt bank statements would pour in then but Thóra would rather not wait for these if she could use older ones to establish their financial situation. Mortgage payments didn't rise that much from month to month. "Do you have any thoughts about how we should do this? Like whether we should start upstairs or downstairs?" She averted her gaze from a withered potted plant that was crying out for water. There was no point in prolonging its death struggle by a few more days.

"I'd rather start down here. I'm not sure I can face the bedrooms. I couldn't cope with seeing the twins' empty bunks." His head drooped. "This is all just unbearable."

"I know. It's awful." Thóra looked around for a suitable place to begin. "Should we start in the kitchen? Perhaps they stuck their credit card statements to the fridge door?" It was a long shot; she certainly wouldn't display her own in such a place. She wouldn't want Sóley, let alone a visitor, to see the sums that went on paying off loans and other expenditures every month. But they might be kept on top of the fridge or somewhere else in the kitchen. Neither she nor Margeir were keen to prolong this visit.

"If we find the bills, will that give you enough evidence for the court?" Margeir led the way into the kitchen. She suspected him of talking as a way of distracting himself from the empty husk of the missing family's life.

"Yes, as far as that side's concerned. It's essential to be able to demonstrate that they weren't in dire straits financially because this will undermine any attempt by the insurance company to claim they've absconded. After all, what would they have to gain if everything was fine at home? Details like this will weigh heavily with the judge, if we have to go down that road. It's also worth including this information with our request to have their property recognized as their estate."

"It's preposterous that anyone could believe they did this deliberately. Preposterous. If I were in better shape, I'd sue the insurance company for putting such disgusting insinuations on paper."

"Unfortunately, the insurance company has probably had direct experience of similar cases where people have done a runner. Ægir and Lára may have been honesty personified but there are others who have no scruples about making fraudulent claims. By raising objections, the company isn't trying to blacken your son and daughter-in-law's reputations. But it's a great deal of money and they can't pay it out unless they're entirely satisfied that Ægir and Lára really are dead. If our application to the court is successful, they'll accept the verdict and release the money. Who knows? They might even pay up right away."

Instead of answering, Margeir started opening drawers at random and shutting them again immediately without even examining their contents.

Using a clean knife she found on the kitchen table, Thóra opened the envelope containing the credit card bill. The transactions covered two sides but the total was within normal limits, neither strikingly high nor low. If their debit card and cash transactions showed the same pattern of spending, the couple's outgoings could be deemed relatively modest. She ran her eyes quickly down the payments, most of which were to supermarkets or petrol stations. There were also several to a company whose name Thóra didn't recognize, but the amounts were small. A separate summary of overseas transactions was printed at the bottom. Thóra couldn't identify any of the recipients so she had no idea what the payments entailed but it seemed fair to assume that they all involved food and drink. None of them was particularly high, except the payment that was processed the day they left port, which was almost certainly the hotel bill. "I don't know if you'd like a look but their credit card bill is pretty modest. You'll need to contact the bank about paying it off, as well as covering the interest on any loans they have. If you like, I can talk to them. I'm sure they'll be amenable, despite the fact that they refused to release the bank statements. All you need to know is whether there's enough money in their accounts to cover the payments. I can speak to the resolution committee too and find out if they'll be paying Ægir's salary as usual next month."

"Thank you, that would be helpful. I don't really know what to do if there isn't enough. We haven't got any savings; they ran out a long time ago."

"I doubt it'll come to that. This is an unusually complicated situation and I'm sure everyone will be willing to take that into account." Thóra walked over to a large white fridge covered with a motley assortment of drawings and notes, among which were two bank transfers, one for a magazine subscription, the other for the dentist. "The girls liked drawing, didn't they?" She detached a picture signed by Bylgja and showed it to her grandfather. It was the typical offering of a contented child, depicting the five family members all smiling broadly and holding hands, standing on a line of green grass. "Do you think I could borrow this? It's useful evidence that they were a happy family, though naturally it wouldn't be sufficient on its own."

"Take it. Take anything you think will help. Of course, it would be nice to have it back afterward but we're not intending to sort through their things any time soon. It's still too upsetting." He reached out for the picture and studied it. "They both loved drawing. Used to occupy themselves for hours with their crayons, ever since they were tiny. Sigga Dögg's the same, though she's too unsettled at the moment. The poor little thing, she can sense that something's terribly wrong."

"Have the child protection authorities been in touch at all since I had a word with their lawyer?" Thóra looked back at the picture, which Margeir had put down on the kitchen table. The figures' black eyes were staring at the ceiling, their scarlet mouths grinning crazily. The sight was somehow disturbing and she felt an impulse to cover it up with the credit card statement. But they would continue to smile and nothing would change. She tried to rekindle the hope inside her that the girls would be found alive; perhaps they'd been taken ashore at Grótta and hidden away, or secretly conveyed abroad. The hope was faint, but it was there, nonetheless.

"Yes, I think so." The old man took hold of another drawer handle and dithered, unable to remember if he was opening or closing it. "Sorry, my memory's not working at the moment. They keep ringing. My wife's on the verge of collapse and I feel as if I'm heading the same way. I keep being overwhelmed by a feeling of hopelessness; we're not capable of raising her in the long term, and we should just force ourselves to accept it. The money won't make much difference. There'll come a point when we open the door to those people and hand her over. It's so hard when your love for someone harms the very person it's supposed to protect."

Thóra laid a hand on his shoulder. "I do think it's true that she would be better off with a younger couple. But it's equally clear that it would be in her best interests to have as much contact with you as possible. You're her only link to her family and it'll be incredibly important for her to have you there." She withdrew her hand and continued, "I've been promised a meeting this week with the head of the relevant social services department and I'm optimistic that we'll be able to arrange things to be as painless as possible for you and Sigga Dögg, while being for the best in the long run. The authorities would have to be heartless to deny you access. Not only heartless: stupid."

After that they said little. Margeir sat down at the kitchen table, excusing himself on the grounds that he needed to rest for a moment. Thóra continued to search the kitchen but without finding any paperwork relating to money matters. It was the rotten food in the larder that caught her attention; half a loaf of bread covered in green mold and two flat-cakes in the same condition. She closed the door at once but the sour smell lingered in her nostrils. "I wonder if it would be okay to chuck out the old bread and stuff?" She opened the fridge. The situation there was less grim; nothing looked obviously spoiled, though the date on the milk cartons didn't exactly whet the appetite. "I let the police know we'd be looking in and they didn't object. Apparently they haven't been round yet and it didn't sound as if they were planning a visit any time soon. But it would be unfortunate if we threw away something that turned out to be important."

"Why should they want to see the house? It's not as if there's anything of relevance here." Margeir sounded as if he had rallied again; his anger at those who were trying to cast aspersions on the family blazed up, momentarily overshadowing his grief. "Anyway, I can't see what difference an old loaf of bread could make."

Thóra closed the fridge again and smiled. "No. It's not immediately obvious. Unless to prove that they haven't been here recently, or to confirm when they left the country." Her words sounded so lame that she wished she could add an intelligent comment, but nothing sprang to mind. "I'm going to take a quick look upstairs. There's nothing here."

Margeir nodded but made no move to stand up. "I'll be here when you come down." Thóra suspected that if she left the house without telling him, he would remain sitting at the table for hours, alone with his thoughts and memories.

Upstairs the carpeted landing muffled her footsteps, making it seem even quieter than the floor below. She walked past four open doors, peering into the rooms as she went. There were two fairly tidy children's rooms, one with bunk beds, presumably the twins' room, the other full of baby things, which must belong to Sigga Dögg. It contained no bed, only an old chest of drawers and a white-painted table with two small matching chairs. She saw no reason to enter the children's rooms as it was highly unlikely that she would find what she was looking for in there. The clothes and toys she had promised to fetch for the little girl's grandmother would have to wait until her main search was over. It wouldn't help to have to lug around two bursting shopping bags.

She also left out the large bathroom that had apparently been shared by the whole family. It was a mess, which seemed to furnish the most convincing proof that the family had intended to come home. Personally, if she had been planning to abscond she would have washed all the dirty laundry, not left the basket overflowing with socks, T-shirts and underwear. She would also have tidied up the shampoo bottles and thrown away the empty toothpaste tube that lay by the sink, its top on the floor. All the indications were of life being carried on as normal.

The master bedroom seemed smaller than it was due to all the furniture it contained. A cot, its bedclothes unmade, had been fitted in beside the king-size bed. Thóra squeezed between them to reach the bedside table. It didn't take a genius to work out that it had been used by Lára; on top lay a cheap necklace and reading glasses with pink plastic frames that no man would have been seen dead in. The two drawers contained nothing of interest, only an empty pill container and some dog-eared romantic novels with pictures of muscular men embracing long-haired beauties on their covers. No bank statements.

Ægir's bedside drawer proved more rewarding. Under some foreign magazines featuring watches and sports cars, she discovered not bank letters but all kinds of work-related papers. Conscious of their fate, Thóra felt that the couple should have used the bed for other activities besides reading love stories, car magazines and work documents. She leafed through the pile of papers in case any of them related to the family's accounts but found nothing. Instead, she was brought up short by a drawing. It looked like the plans of a ship that bore a striking resemblance to the yacht. Summoning up a mental picture of the cabins on board, she decided that this was indeed a plan of the different decks on the *Lady K*. The yacht's name did not actually appear anywhere, but the page had been badly photocopied: the drawings were at a slant and it was possible that they had been part of a larger sheet. She sifted through the rest of the papers more attentively, noticing a few other pages that struck her as odd. All contained information about the yacht's furnishings and equipment, and it was hard to imagine why an employee of the resolution committee would have been reading them in bed. She decided to take the whole pile of papers with her to study in more detail; if there was an explanation for this, it wasn't immediately obvious. Perhaps Ægir had been required to study the make and design of the vessel for the valuation. But in bed?

When she put her head round the door of the last room on the landing, she hit the jackpot. It had been used as a study and she glimpsed a stack of bills on the small desk beside the computer. Flicking quickly through them she found bank transfers for two mortgage payments and the interest on a car loan. The balances on the three loans were higher than she had hoped, but not alarmingly so. Next she scanned the shelves where she spotted several files marked "Tax—home," together with the year, and took away the most recent, which turned out to be full of receipts and bank statements.

When she went downstairs Margeir was still sitting in the kitchen. A battered wallet lay on the table and he was gazing at a photo in a clear plastic pocket. "Is that a picture of the girls?" Thóra put down the file and took a seat opposite him. The chair creaked as if weakened by standing idle for three weeks.

"Yes, the twins." He turned the wallet so that Thóra could see the photo properly. When she picked it up, the smooth, shabby leather felt slippery to the touch. She focused on the picture.

"Which one of them is this?" She pointed at the solemn little girl standing beside her exact replica, who in contrast was smiling and had slung an arm round her sister's shoulders.

Leaning over to see, Margeir replied: "Bylgja."

"Did she always wear those glasses?" Thóra pointed at the bright-red frames on the child's nose.

"Yes. They were almost identical except that Bylgja was very short-sighted. She hated wearing glasses but she was too young for contact lenses or a laser operation. Her mother went to great lengths to find a pair she was reconciled to. Cheerful, don't you think?" Thóra smiled stupidly and agreed. Failing to notice her odd expression, Margeir carried on talking: "But there aren't many pictures of her wearing them. She generally took them off when the camera came out. That's why I'm so fond of this picture; it shows her the way she usually looked."

Thóra took another glance, then returned the wallet without comment. Although the photo was small and the quality poor, the red frames were beyond a doubt the pair she had found in the wardrobe on board the yacht. How on earth could they have ended up there? What was the child doing in the cupboard? Almost certainly hiding. The question was: from who?

Chapter 22

"I'm not wasting your time. They were there." Thóra stood crimson-faced behind the police officer as he rooted around in the artfully fitted wardrobe with his backside in the air. The fragrance of citrus wood did nothing to alleviate her discomfort, nor did the mirrors on the cupboard doors, which reflected her embarrassment back at her. "It was a red and orange cocktail dress and the glasses were tangled up in some dangly bits on the hem."

"Could you be mistaken about the color?" His voice emerged muffled from among the evening gowns.

"No. Definitely not. I remember thinking it was hardly surprising the glasses hadn't been spotted because they were almost the same color as the dress. But I was preoccupied with Karítas at the time—it didn't occur to me that they could be significant." He didn't respond, merely continued to dig around among the clothes. "You see, I assumed the glasses must have ended up there before the yacht was repossessed."

The officer extricated himself and rose stiffly to his feet. "You should have informed us immediately."

Thóra blew the fringe out of her eyes, annoyed. It was at least the tenth time he had mentioned this since she met him by the yacht. The same went for his colleague to whom she had reported the discovery of the glasses. She missed her friend with the green eyes and suspected that this man and the one who had answered the phone were the officers he had bawled out for their oversight in relation to Halldór's body. That would explain their conduct toward her; they must be pleased to be in a position to offload the blame onto somebody else.

"As I explained, it slipped my mind. I didn't work out the connection until this morning when I saw a photo of the girl wearing the glasses. She didn't have them on in the few other pictures I'd seen of her. To give you an idea of how little importance I attached to them, I didn't even check to see if they were still there the second time I came aboard—even though I opened the closet."

"You should have let us know anyway. It's not up to you to decide what is or isn't significant."

"No. You're right about that." Thóra gritted her teeth and tried to keep her cool. She was aware of a throbbing behind her eyes that threatened to develop into a full-blown headache if she didn't leave the boat soon. She was clearly not cut out to be a sailor if she was in danger of feeling seasick in port. "Of course, I should have rung and told you about every single thing I saw, shouldn't I? Like the towel in the bathroom. Two towels, actually. But I forgot."

The policeman stood up straight and although Thóra was tall, he towered over her. The cabin may have been luxurious but it had a low ceiling, which had the effect of accentuating his height and making him seem almost a giant. "There's no call for sarcasm."

"No, sorry." She relaxed her jaw. If she didn't want to ruin her good relations with the police she had better find a way to lighten the atmosphere. Better drop the matter and get to the point. "Anyway, I don't understand what can have happened to the dress." She opened the wardrobes one after the other and peered inside, though they had already conducted a thorough search. "Someone must have taken it." She took a step back to get a better view of the one that was open. "I couldn't swear to it, but now I come to think of it some of the other dresses may be missing as well." She rubbed off the fingerprint powder that had coated her hands when she opened the doors. A forensics officer had gone round first, taking prints from the cupboards, light switches and the chest of drawers in the cabin, in case any new ones had appeared since the initial examination of the yacht. He had also vacuumed all the wardrobes in search of biological material which might prove that Bylgja or Arna had been hiding inside them. While he was working, Thóra and the policeman had

been forced to cool their heels in the corridor, exchanging small talk
that became increasingly strained with every moment that passed.
Perhaps that was why, once they entered the cabin, they had quickly
begun to get on each other's nerves.

"They took photographs in here when the yacht first arrived in
port, so it shouldn't be too difficult to find out." The man looked at
the sea of color suspended from the hangers. "Though I don't understand how you can tell. The wardrobes are so full it doesn't look
as if there'd be room for anything else."

"There were more dresses." Thóra stepped back still further and
made an effort to picture the contents as she had originally laid eyes
on them. There was still only one empty hanger, but the garments
did not seem as tightly packed. "Yup, there were definitely more
dresses." She closed the door.

The policeman surveyed the cabin with a frown. "If you're right
and there are dresses missing as well as the glasses, the question is
who could have removed them?"

Thóra smiled at him patiently, feeling her headache intensify.
"These are designer clothes—some of the dresses are worth a fortune."

"But they're used. Who wants secondhand clothes, even if they are
expensive?"

"It's not unheard of, you know." Personally, she would not have
wanted any of the dresses in that cupboard, not because they were
secondhand but because she never had the occasion to dress up in
glamorous, floor-skimming evening gowns. "I'd hazard a guess that
the owner of these clothes or somebody close to her would be the
most likely suspects. How have you been getting on with tracking
down Karítas and her PA?"

"I wouldn't know."

"I see." She kept her thoughts to herself. Bella had had no luck in
contacting Karítas, let alone finding out where her assistant, Aldís,
was living. At least she had succeeded in discovering the latter's full
name, by pestering Karítas's mother with phone calls until the woman
had caved in and taken the trouble to dig out Aldís's patronymic.

Thóra suspected she had in fact known it all along. But when Thóra had used the information to contact the girl's family, they seemed utterly indifferent, claiming they often didn't hear from Aldís for months as she was kept very busy by her employer. Bella was not exactly known for her psychological insight, but even Thóra had to agree when she said there was clearly no love lost between the PA and her family. However, the fact that she hadn't crawled home with her tail between her legs could indicate that she was in Brazil with Karítas. Another possibility was that both women had come to a sticky end. And a third, that Aldís had played a part in Karítas's demise. These things did happen. This conjecture was lent more substance by the expression of hatred Thóra had seen on the young woman's face in the photo where she was helping her employer into her dress. She'd looked as if she'd rather be planting a knife between Karítas's shoulder blades than doing up her zip.

"Do these numbers mean anything to you?" Watching Snævar struggle to decipher Ægir's almost illegible handwriting, Thóra was disappointed by his blank expression. She had felt considerably better once she was back on dry land, but her headache still lingered in spite of the painkillers she'd swallowed on returning to the office a good two hours ago.

"No. I doubt they're connected to the yacht. Maybe it's a registration number. Though not like any I'm familiar with." As he put down the piece of paper he looked as frustrated as Thóra. He had agreed at once when she rang to ask him to drop by, and it was all too apparent that he was fed up with sitting at home alone. Few young men would have jumped for joy at the prospect of visiting a lawyer, even a female one.

"Thanks for coming in, by the way." She hoped he would sense how important it was for her to be able to call on him for help. She wasn't well enough acquainted with any other seamen to approach them about such matters, so a sailor marooned on shore by a broken leg, one who actually knew something about the yacht in question, was a godsend. "I really appreciate being able to consult you about Ægir's case, but of course you're free to refuse any further meetings." She smiled at him.

The figure slumped in the chair facing her sat up a little. He looked smarter than he had last time, in a much more presentable sweater, properly shaven. Only the grubby tracksuit bottoms were the same. "It's really no bother. I'm going stir-crazy at home, so I'm glad of any excuse to leave the house. I just wish I could be of more use."

"Oh, I've only just started, don't you worry." She realized she hadn't offered him any coffee. He looked as if he could do with some. In spite of the extra care he had taken over his appearance he was still rather pale and drawn. "How have you been coping since finding Halldór? It must have been horrific for you."

"Oh, you know." His response was as one would expect; he avoided meeting her eye and his fingers twitched in his lap. She didn't need a degree in psychology to see that he was having a tough time.

"Have you received any trauma counseling, Snævar?"

"No. They offered but I refused. I can't really see what use it would be." He sniffed and shifted in his chair. "It's just something I have to deal with on my own."

"I see." It was blindingly obvious that he wasn't dealing with it at all well. "You should talk to an expert anyway. Better late than never. You'd be surprised how much it can help, and it certainly couldn't hurt."

Snævar made a noncommittal noise. Thóra decided to leave it and ask about something more specific. "How's your leg, by the way? Improving at all?"

"I'm supposed to stay in plaster for six weeks." He slapped the plastic splint that jutted out from under his tracksuit bottoms, wrapped in yet another shopping bag, this time from the Nóatún supermarket chain. "I reckon I'm about halfway through, but I can't deny I'm looking forward to being back on two feet. And to wearing what I like instead of the only clothes I can get into." A grin transformed his face.

"You'll be rid of that thing before you know it." At the sight of Snævar looking brighter Thóra's own mood lifted. "That reminds me.

Here are the papers from the Portuguese hospital. You'll probably
need to take them along when you go to see the doctor. Sorry I didn't
return them to you earlier."

He held out a hand for the documents. "No problem. I still haven't
gotten round to it, so it doesn't matter. I really should get a move on,
though."

"I could give you a lift if you like, or get someone else to. The thing
is, I should have asked you for a note from your doctor confirming
that you weren't fit to work because of a broken leg at the time you
were supposed to sail home."

"But I could have sailed home."

She tried to hide her irritation, which was directed not so much at
him as at herself and her gnawing suspicions about Ægir. "Yes, no
doubt you *could* have, but you didn't, and I need confirmation that it
was because of your broken leg. The Portuguese papers aren't enough
on their own." She would prefer not to tell him why. "I could always
ask my ex-husband, who's a doctor, to look in on you. He owes me a
favor." Gylfi had gotten the job on the oil rig and was due to start as
soon as he had finished his final school exams. In three months her
life would change irrevocably. "Then you wouldn't need to leave the
house."

"Oh no, no need. I'll go to my doctor. No problem." Judging by
his expression, he was not at all keen to receive a visit from her ex.
He cleared his throat. "Are they any closer to finding out how Halli
died?"

"I don't think so." It was not her place to reveal what the police
had confided in her. Although it was evident that Halli had drowned,
the details surrounding his demise were so bizarre that it would be
best to say as little as possible. "I'm sure it'll become clear in due
course."

"I see." It was obvious he didn't entirely believe her.

"Have you had any further thoughts yourself about what might
have happened?"

"No." He seemed to realize he was slouching again, and made a
visible effort to look more alert. "Of course, I keep going over it in
my mind and I reckon it must have been a combination of factors.

Since we know now that two of the three crew members are dead, I'm guessing the captain copped it as well and after that the family took the idiotic decision to abandon ship." He flung out a hand. "But that theory doesn't work either when you think about it, since who can have programmed the autopilot and set the course first to Grótta, then to port?"

After acquainting herself with the criteria for the pleasure craft competency certificate, Thóra had immediately discounted the possibility that Ægir could have learned how to use an autopilot on the course. Admittedly, it was conceivable that one of the crew might have taken the time to teach him or Lára to use the system but that wouldn't explain why they had set a course for Grótta. The most obvious option would have been to direct the yacht straight to Reykjavík harbor. None of the alternatives that occurred to her made any sense. There were too many unanswered questions, too many unsubstantiated theories. "One more thing, Snævar." He regarded her hopefully, as if pathetically keen to give her the answer she wanted. "Is there any chance there could have been a stowaway on board?"

From the way his face relaxed, it looked as if this could be answered with a straight yes or no. But it turned out not to be that simple. "I doubt it, but I couldn't rule it out. He'd have had to be bloody clever. And quiet. Every nook and cranny on board is used to the max, so he'd have had to be incredibly lucky for no one to spot him. I guess someone could have hidden in an empty cabin, though it would have taken a hell of a lot of nerve."

"What about in the engine room or storage spaces on the bottom deck? Is there nowhere to hide down there?"

"I suppose there could be. Not in the engine room, though, because they inspect that regularly. If I was going to hide on board, I'd steer clear of the engines and bridge as you'd almost certainly be spotted there."

"So it would be feasible, with a bit of luck?"

"Well . . . I guess so. If you knew the yacht inside out." Snævar grimaced and shifted his injured leg, which seemed to be causing him discomfort. "But who could it have been? And why the fuck would they do it?" There was no disguising the anger in his voice and Thóra could only hope he wouldn't be the first to track down the stowaway if he or she turned out to exist. If he did, they wouldn't have a hope in hell.

"I haven't a clue." In fact, she had already formed an opinion but wanted to avoid rousing his suspicion. If someone had stowed away on board, that person must surely have been linked to the former owners. It was the only logical conclusion. Karítas, Aldís—even the owner, Gulam. Or a henchman he had hired to recover the yacht. The last scenario was a long shot, however, as they would have little to gain by stealing the boat. "Not a clue."

Once Snævar had left, Bella came in and plonked herself down in front of Thóra. "Look, I know I couldn't sort out the photocopier before the weekend, but would you be prepared to trade the upgrade for information about Aldís?"

"What?" Thóra asked eagerly. "Where did you get it from?"

"I rang a girl who used to work with Aldís before she took the job with Karítas. A sort of friend."

"And how did you find out about her?"

"I rang Aldís's mom and asked. Told her we wanted to check if she'd been in touch with any of her mates because we needed to get hold of her urgently. She gave me this girl's name and I tracked down her number."

"Damn it, Bella, you did this here in the office during working hours. I shouldn't have to bribe you to do your job. Anyway, I'm afraid Bragi and I decided the other day not to install a high-speed connection after all. We'll review the situation in ten years." Thóra couldn't resist winding her up a little. "I'm sorry."

Bella pushed her chair back. "Okay, fine. No worries."

"Hey, you can't leave. Tell me what the friend said."

"What friend? I don't know what you're talking about. Try asking me again in ten years—perhaps I'll remember then." Bella heaved her bulk out of the chair.

"For goodness' sake, come on—I was only teasing. We're going to organize the stupid upgrade. I've been waiting for a good moment to tell you. I just didn't want it to look as if I was giving in to black-mail."

"It wasn't blackmail. It's called a trade-off." But the news of the upgrade had brought out the best in Bella and she sat down again, her face shining. No doubt she was daydreaming about how fast she could now jump in with last-minute bids on eBay. "Well, according to this girl, Aldís wasn't exactly the sociable type. She was a bit of a snob, but all right really—she just had dreams of being rich and famous, though mainly rich."

"Famous for what?"

Bella gave Thóra a pitying look. "Where have you been? You don't have to be famous for anything these days. She just wanted to be a rich celebrity. But her plans were going badly, so she was getting a bit pissed off. Her mate thought things would change for the better when she started working for Karítas, but no such luck. She said she couldn't understand why on earth Aldís stayed on if she was so fed up."

"Was the pay bad?"

"The friend didn't say, so maybe she didn't know."

"Why was she so fed up then?" Aldís sounded to Thóra like one of those girls who becomes an au pair, dreaming of foreign travel, only to discover that washing dishes in another country is just as boring as it is in Iceland.

"If I understood her right, Aldís was totally pissed off with run-ning around after Karítas. And with Karítas herself, as well."

"So she couldn't stand her?"

Bella rolled her eyes. "Duh . . . what do you think? Aldís was al-ways talking down to her. The friend said Aldís was forever ringing her to let off steam. She couldn't talk to any of the other staff in case it got back to her boss. They weren't especially close but the friend felt sorry for her because she seemed so disappointed. I bet she thought she'd be allowed to go to the parties and join in on all the fun, but that was way off the mark."

Thóra understood. She had been to drinks receptions at offices and ministries where the young waiting staff had forgotten their place and started mingling with the guests. That could only happen in a soci-ety where everyone was equal, at least in theory. In countries with deeper class divisions the picture was probably very different, as poor Aldís seemed to have learned the hard way. "So she was at best a PA, or at worst some kind of maid?"

"Yes. I gather that's what she was paid for. And it sounds like she found it hard to swallow."

"Did she mention anything to this friend about wanting to resign?"

"I didn't ask. But I did discover that her mate hasn't heard from her for weeks, which is much longer than usual." Bella fiddled with the ring on her finger, which was so huge that it resembled a piece of armor. "Do you reckon she was mixed up in this case? Maybe even bumped off Karítas?" Her face radiated schadenfreude.

Thóra was disturbed by her gloating. "I doubt it, but it bothers me that we can't get hold of either of them. It's a bit too much of a co-incidence and I'd like to know what's going on." She opened the window. Fresh air flooded into the room and the splitting headache that had afflicted her since her visit to the yacht receded a little. "There's a chance that finding out won't help us at all, but it's still frustrating not to know."

Bella filled her lungs, as grateful as Thóra for the fresh air. "But you're wondering if Aldís killed the people on board."

Thóra's headache returned with a vengeance and she felt a sudden longing to go home. "I'm not wondering anything of the sort. Just whether either or both of them could conceivably be linked to the dis-appearance. Not necessarily as the perpetrators. But indirectly."

Bella went off in search of Bragi after being assured that he would arrange the upgrade, and Thóra was left massaging her temples in an attempt to relieve the pain. Perhaps Aldís had no connection to her employer's alleged death. She called the dates to mind and worked out from the information provided by Karítas's mother that her daughter could well have been in Lisbon when the crew arrived. She could have become involved in an altercation with one of the men when they refused to let her on board, perhaps, or because they were confiscating the yacht that she may still have regarded as rightfully hers. It was not difficult to imagine how a row like that could have gotten out of hand. But what then? Had Ægir, Lára and the twins inadvertently stumbled onto the truth, maybe by catching the culprit or culprits in the act of throwing the body overboard at a safe distance from land? Could that have led to their being disposed of in the same way? However hard Thóra tried, she simply couldn't picture this chain of events. Surely no one would go to such lengths?

Chapter 23

"It's unlikely to achieve anything but I propose we do it anyway." Even seriously sleep deprived, Thráinn still commanded respect. Ægir wondered for a moment what it would be like to be a captain with authority over everyone on board, like the dictator of a mini state.

"There's no other explanation. Let's hunt down this maniac, then get the hell home." Halli was breathing fast and couldn't disguise his relief that they had agreed to act on his suggestion of overpowering the stowaway. It was hardly surprising; as the prime suspect, he had the most to gain from their standing together. Either that or he would be left to confront them alone. However, their newfound solidarity depended on their finding the uninvited guest who Halli insisted must have thrown the body overboard and murdered Loftur. He steadfastly maintained his innocence and, like Thráinn, was very persuasive. Ægir could only hope that he himself sounded even more convincing about his own and Lára's lack of involvement. He kept quiet about the fact that he had been awake for over an hour while his wife and daughters slept. Otherwise he would find himself in the same predicament as Halli—desperately trying to make Thráinn believe that it was not him.

"How are we going to do this?" Ægir shuddered at the thought of walking alone through the corridors, peering into every dark corner, with the risk that the murderer—whether it was Halli, Thráinn or the putative stowaway—might be lurking behind the nearest door. Ægir was inclined to believe that Halli was the guilty party but he could not entirely discount Thráinn since none of them were qualified to calculate Loftur's time of death or ascertain exactly how he had met his end. Both Thráinn and Halli had been alone for most of the afternoon and there was no way of knowing which of them was telling the truth when they protested their innocence. Thráinn was calm, Halli on edge, and Ægir lacked the experience to determine which was the more normal behavior for a blameless man. Perhaps there was no such thing as normality in a situation like this. He himself was still in shock from the sight of Loftur's dead body and kept being assailed with the desire to break into hysterical laughter.

When they had reached the Jacuzzi, steam was rising from under its padded cover and all three had stood there at a loss for a moment until Thráinn decided to lift it off. Neither Ægir nor Halli had taken a step closer or offered the captain any help as he struggled with the heavy, slippery lid. And no one had said a word when it was finally removed and they were confronted by the sight of Loftur, submerged fully dressed in the hot water, his eyes and mouth wide open. Countless silvery bubbles clung to his hair like a tiara, rendering his death mask even more grotesque. It would be a while before Ægir could bear to enter a hot tub again after witnessing Loftur's blank gaze. The memory of how the water had trickled from his nose and mouth after they heaved him out and rolled him over onto his back only made it worse. "I'm not sure I want to leave my family alone."

"We're sticking together, the three of us. It's not up for discussion." Despite stifling a yawn, Thráinn still spoke with authority. "Your wife and daughters can wait here in the pilot house. It's lockable from inside and there are windows in all the doors, so they'll be able to see anyone who wants to come in."

"How will it help to see who's outside if the man's intent on breaking in? If he even exists." Ægir's mind was racing; he knew this was his only chance to detect any flaws in the plan that might cost his wife and daughters their lives. His love for them was the only thing that mattered. To hell with the money, to hell with it; to hell with everything except them.

"It wouldn't be that easy to break in. The plastic in the windows is specially toughened to withstand gales and waves far more powerful than any human being. But if it comes to that, they wouldn't be defenseless."

"Oh?" Ægir's voice sounded almost shrill and he paused to get a grip on himself. Laughter welled up inside him again over the absurdity of it all. Lára had never had any reason to resort to a weapon in self-defense. Normal life seemed more remote than ever: shopping for food, replacing the washer on the bathroom tap, having their parents round to dinner, changing the batteries in the smoke alarm. It all seemed so ridiculous now that it made his chest ache. He was on the brink of losing control. "What, are you planning to give Lára the axe?" He gestured to the weapon that was hanging on the wall of the bridge but his hand shook so badly that he quickly lowered his arm. It wouldn't do for the other two to see what a state he was in.

"No." Thráinn was as imperturbable as Ægir was agitated. "I'm going to lend her a revolver."

Unable to help himself, Ægir finally began to giggle. Soon it had spiraled into helpless laughter that reminded him of his short-lived experiments with smoking grass in college. Pointless, self-propagating mirth. The other two men stared at him until he couldn't laugh any more and broke into noisy hiccups. "She doesn't know how to use a gun." Another brief gust of wild hilarity followed.

"It's not exactly difficult." Thráinn looked concerned, doubtless more over Ægir's state of mind than Lára's ability to use a firearm. "She just has to point and pull the trigger."

"Is that a good idea?" Halli blurted out the words before he realized how they could be interpreted—that he would rather she were unarmed and therefore easier to overpower. "I mean, she might be a danger to herself or shoot the girls by mistake."

"I reckon she's too sensible for that. I'd sooner trust her with the gun than you two." As Thráinn studied them both he seemed to be drawing no distinction between them.

It dawned on Ægir how pathetic they must appear. It was some comfort to think that Halli, constantly licking his lips and shivering, cut no better a figure than he did himself. The captain was right; Lára couldn't fare any worse than them. "Shall I fetch her and the girls?"

"Yes. We'll wait here." Thráinn pointed to a seat and ordered Halli to sit down. Then he turned the pilot's chair round to keep him in view. "Get a move on. Don't dawdle."

On the way to the cabin Ægir wiped his eyes, which were still wet
from laughing. He took several deep breaths and hoped he would recover his self-control. It was essential to keep calm while talking to
Lára because if he showed the slightest hint of nerves, he would infect the twins, and no doubt her as well, with his anxiety. It was the
first time since finding Loftur that he had admitted to himself how
he felt. He was not just shaken or alarmed; he was terrified.

Before entering the cabin, he cleared his throat and rubbed his face
in the hope of obliterating the marks of fear. Then, smiling weakly,
he opened the door. His wife and daughters were awake and sitting
up in bed, though still under the duvet. Three identical pairs of eyes
stared at him and in each he read that he had failed to conceal his
fear. "What? What's the matter?" Lára flung off the duvet and got
out of bed.

"Nothing. But something's come up and we need to go to the
bridge. It's nothing to worry about, though. We're going to search
the ship and we want you to wait in the pilot house in the meantime.
You too, girls." He signaled to Lára that he needed to speak to her
alone. "Collect up your books and cards, then come along. Your
mother and I will be outside in the corridor." The girls looked surprised but said nothing.

Lára hurriedly slipped on her shoes and threw a cardigan over her
shoulders. "You needn't hurry. We're happy to wait," she said to the
girls. She looked anything but happy, however, and as soon as the door
swung to behind them, she made her feelings known. "Please don't
tell me if something bad has happened. Please, just let me believe that
everything's all right and that we can count the hours till we're home.
Please." Her eyes were beseeching and she hugged the cardigan to her
as if she could hide inside it.

Ægir felt as if the words were being torn from his throat. He wanted
to lie to her and say it had only been an excuse to get her to himself;
that if they were quick they could take each other here and now
in this overblown burgundy corridor. "I really wish I could." He told
her about Loftur, that it was urgent to find out whether there was an
uninvited guest hiding on board and that while they were searching

the boat, she would have to wait alone on the bridge with the girls. He waited for this to sink in before telling her about the gun.

"Gun? Have you gone out of your mind?" She slapped him. The blow was not hard or intended to inflict pain but it was the first time physical violence had ever been used between them.

"Lára!" Ægir was speechless.

"What if this stupid search of yours doesn't reveal anything? Well?" She didn't wait for an answer. "What am I to do if it's not you who comes back but Thráinn? Or Halli? Am I supposed to shoot them?"

"No." Ægir hesitated, cursing himself for having told the girls they needn't hurry.

"What if Halli claims he became separated from you and wants to come in? Am I supposed to shoot him in front of the girls? Be standing over his bleeding corpse when you and Thráinn come back? Are you all out of your minds?"

"No." Ægir couldn't meet her eye; couldn't cope with this. He wished Thráinn was here to convince her and had to restrain himself from tearing open the cabin door and yelling at the girls to get a move on. The captain would make Lára see sense. He took himself in hand. "If anything like that happens, you mustn't let Halli in. And if Thráinn and I don't reappear soon, you may have to decide what action to take. And if Halli—or Thráinn or this imaginary stowaway—tries to break in, at least you'll be armed." He felt relieved, convinced by his own arguments.

"But what if Thráinn's behind all this? Do you really think he'd give me a loaded gun? Do you know the difference between blanks and live ammunition?" She observed his consternation. "I thought not."

Mercifully, the girls now appeared with their arms full of books and other items that he and Lára had taken down to the cabin when they locked themselves in. They knew something serious was happening and kept quiet. Ægir made a lame joke about their not being short of stuff. They were to go straight up to the bridge and before they knew it they would be captaining the ship and finally things would start going right. Nobody smiled and they made their way in silence up to the pilot house where Thráinn and Halli were waiting.

The captain took Lára aside and spoke to her while Ægir showed the girls the yacht's steering system. He kept glancing over to see what was passing between his wife and the captain, and gulped when he saw Lára receive with trembling hands a parcel which must be the revolver, wrapped in a gray cloth. She stuck it clumsily into her waistband and pulled her top over it with a pained expression. Ægir turned away at once and made some meaningless remark to the girls.

"Is the ship sinking, Daddy?" Bylgja put her head on one side as was her habit when she wasn't wearing her glasses. She was carrying them in her hand in case she wanted to read.

"No." It came out more sharply than Ægir had intended, but the anger in his voice was directed at himself, not her. "Good heavens, no. There's nothing wrong, everything's going to be fine." He was saying the words Lára had wanted to hear.

"Will we drown if the yacht sinks?" Evidently he had failed to convince his daughter.

"She's not going to sink and even if she did, no one would drown. Do you remember the lifeboats?" They both nodded doubtfully. "Ships carry lifeboats so that no one will drown even if they do go down. But this yacht is unsinkable, so there's no need to worry."

"Then why does it carry lifeboats?" Arna interjected, without sarcasm. It was an entirely logical question that demanded an answer.

"Because it's obligatory, sweetheart. All boats and ships have to carry lifeboats. It's the law."

"How silly." Arna ran her finger over the radar screen. Ægir was glad he hadn't told them what it showed; it was such a stark reminder of their isolation. If they needed help, it appeared there was none to be found nearby.

"You know what they say, darling: better safe than sorry." He noticed that Thráinn was signaling to him. Lára stood a little way off, avoiding his eye. There was a conspicuous bulge at her slender waist. "Better safe than sorry."

"I swear I didn't lay a finger on Loftur. Why would I have asked you where he was if I'd just killed him?" No doubt the question had

sounded sensible when Halli formed it in his head but spoken aloud,
it was meaningless. Now that it looked as if they were going to come
up empty-handed, the young man seemed on the brink of despair.
The three of them were down in the engine room, having scoured the
other two levels without finding any trace of a stowaway. They had
given Halli's cabin, which adjoined the engine room, a thorough
going-over, as well as the small workshop next door. "Perhaps the
murderer has moved while we've been searching." Halli was breathing rapidly. "I didn't go anywhere near Loftur. I swear it."

"Methinks the laddie doth protest too much." The marks of strain
were showing on Thráinn's face and the weariness in his voice was
audible. He lowered himself onto a wooden crate by the wall and
leaned backward until his head encountered the steel bulkhead with
a low thud. "I'm going to let you two search in here. Call me if you
find anyone. I'll sit tight."

Halli turned to Ægir, having clearly given up all hope of persuading the captain of his innocence. "You believe me, don't you?"

"I don't know who to believe. I'm working on the assumption that
you're both equally dangerous. It's the safest option." Ægir ran his
eyes over the engines that stood in the middle of the room. He was
fairly sure that in addition to the ship's engine there were two gener-
ators, one probably for backup, and some pumps. "Where shall we
begin?" He took a couple of steps away from Halli, who had come
unnervingly close. "This is your domain so you must know it inside out. It's not as if there are many hiding places here." He
glimpsed a door at the back of the room, behind one of the genera-
tors. "What's that?"

"The door to the storeroom. Might as well start there." Halli now
sounded subdued, as if he had given up trying to win Ægir round and
would simply accept whatever happened. The effect of this was unexpected; for the first time Ægir was inclined to believe that Halli
might actually be innocent. Which meant what? That Thráinn was
the one to watch? They walked toward the storeroom, staying ludicrously far apart, as if each expected any minute to be stabbed by the
other. Abruptly, Halli halted, and Ægir almost cannoned into him.
"I can smell perfume."

Ægir sniffed and became aware of the familiar heavy, sweet odor that had filled the air outside their cabin on the first evening. Perhaps the fragrance emanated from the yacht's air-conditioning system, though it was highly unlikely that they would use air freshener in the engine room. Perhaps the bottle Lára had been hunting for had found its way down here and smashed. It wouldn't be the first time on this trip that something peculiar like that had happened. "Where's it coming from?" He sniffed hard, noticing as he did so that his sense of smell was becoming numbed to the scent. It was still present but there was no way of guessing its origin.

Halli turned in a circle, trying to work out the source. "For fuck's sake. I definitely smelt it."

"Perhaps the mystery passenger is a woman," called Thráinn, who had been eavesdropping on their conversation from where he was sitting. It was hard to tell if he was joking or serious. Neither of them replied.

The storeroom was larger than Ægir had expected. Inside were stacks of toilet paper, cleaning products and linen folded on shelves. Against one wall stood a wine cooler and a chest freezer, and he shivered at the thought of lifting the lid. Halli, on the other hand, went straight to work, reaching behind the shelves to bang on the walls in case there was a hidden compartment behind them. Ægir aimlessly pushed aside some cardboard boxes; they were far too small to hide a person, but he felt he should be doing something. "No one here." Then he braced himself and opened the freezer. He was met not by a blast of cold air but by a disgusting stench that mingled nauseatingly with the perfume that seemed to be growing stronger again. Holding his nose, Ægir peered inside. It was crammed with vacuum-packed meat and vegetables that would never be eaten now. "Shut the lid on that bloody thing." Halli held his elbow over his nose. "We turned off the electricity supply to that bugger to save energy. Close it before I throw up."

Ægir dropped the lid, then stepped out of the storeroom and walked over to Thráinn. "What now? We've been over every inch of the yacht. There's no one here."

"We haven't been down to the bottom deck where the tanks are yet." Thráinn was so red-eyed with exhaustion that he looked like a vampire. "We should probably take a look down there. Otherwise there's little to show for our efforts."

"Let's get on with it then." Ægir may not have been awake as long as Thráinn but he was shattered too. It ground one down having to be constantly on the alert. "I want to get back to Lára and the girls."

"They're fine. The person they've got to fear is almost certainly down here with us. *One of* us, more to the point." Thráinn closed his eyes briefly, then slapped his thighs and stood up. "Best get this bullshit over with."

Ægir turned to call Halli but was stopped in his tracks by an extraordinarily loud, penetrating crack that reverberated around the room. "What the hell was that?" When he turned, he saw that Thráinn had set off at a run toward the exit. Without looking back, the captain shouted: "A shot. Presumably from the bridge."

The sickly sweet smell of perfume intensified until Ægir thought it would suffocate him. He raced after Thráinn as if the devil were at his heels.

Chapter 24

Photocopies of the ship's log lay strewn over Thóra's desk. They had arrived in a muddle from the police, which meant she had to try and work out the chronology from the context. Although the entries were dated, it complicated matters when a day extended over more than one page. Nor did the missing leaves help, since they were probably the very ones that had contained the most significant information. It seemed odd that whoever was responsible for tearing them out hadn't simply tossed the whole book overboard.

She had been disconcerted to discover that the log was written by hand; it felt somehow macabre to be puzzling over the handwriting of a man who was missing, presumed dead; to read his comments from the beginning of the voyage on the satisfactory condition of the engines and the yacht in general; his reflections on the weather forecast and his list of the crew and passengers—people who had believed they had five days' pleasant cruising ahead of them. Nothing in the first entry gave any indication that their fates had been decided in advance; on the contrary, everything seemed to have been in good order. To be fair, the captain did mention that the seal placed on the door by order of the resolution committee had been broken, but he did not seem overly concerned by this, noting that there was no sign of a break-in or sabotage. However, since neither the captain nor the other crew members had any experience of forensic investigations, they might well have failed to notice important evidence. For example, it apparently hadn't occurred to the captain that the person who broke the seal might have had a key. After all, why break in if you could simply unlock the door?

Next came a brief explanation of the passengers' presence on board, accompanied by a few words of concern about the necessity of ensuring the two girls' safety during the trip. Although the captain did not actually curse Snævar for his accident, his displeasure was easy to read between the lines. He was far from happy about allowing Ægir to step into the breach, but had been constrained to fulfill the conditions of the minimum safe manning document and to keep to schedule. These initial entries were excellent news for Thóra's case. It was plain not only that Ægir had been enlisted by complete coincidence but that it had been at the captain's behest rather than his own. Indeed, it was hard to see how Ægir could have planned a life insurance scam that would have required a complete stranger to propose that he sailed with the *Lady K*. There could be no arguing with that.

Neither did the final entry in the logbook presage any abnormal turn of events, though presumably the situation must have changed shortly afterward since all the subsequent pages had been ripped out. The captain had recorded that the communications systems were malfunctioning and that the crew were working to fix them. At that point the yacht had still been able to make contact to a limited extent by radiotelephone. But apart from the captain's barely intelligible conversation with the British trawler a day later, no one was aware of having heard from the yacht. If things had gone to hell at the point where the pages ran out, one would have thought the crew would at least have tried to transmit a distress signal or report the problem. But they had not, and it was disturbing to think that one person may have remained alive; the one who had sailed the yacht close to Grótta and from there to Reykjavík harbor with that strange detour out into Faxaflói bay. It was possible that the boat had taken this extraordinary route because the person who set its course had not known how to program the autopilot or GPS. And that did not look good for Thóra's case; the only people on board with little experience of boats were Ægir and Lára—and the twins, of course, though she had to assume they couldn't possibly count.

Thóra's eyes ached from poring over the entries in the hope of spotting something that was missing, or of gaining a deeper insight into what had happened. She gathered the pages together, feeling frustrated yet again by the absent entries. What she wouldn't give to know what they had contained, to learn from the captain's illegible, old-fashioned script the answer to the flood of questions that plagued her; the explanation for the body he had reported over the faulty radio, and a description of the events leading up to the passengers' disappearance—if that is how the situation had unfolded. Perhaps catastrophe had struck without warning, but if so it was hard to understand why the pages had been torn out. Unless it had been done for another reason—to plug a hole, for instance, or even to use for drawing pictures on. Neither explanation seemed plausible but there was little point wasting time on wondering; the missing pages would be floating somewhere in the sea by now or lying on the ocean floor where the fish would try in vain to interpret their secrets. The remnants of the ship's log, the certificates of seaworthiness and other relevant documents would have to suffice for her report. Whether this would satisfy the insurance company's queries remained to be seen.

After adjusting the report to include this new information, Thóra read it over for what seemed like the hundredth time before sending it to the printer in Bragi's office, feeling dispirited. Its contents were so over-familiar by now that she could no longer determine how well she had succeeded in her task. It was time to take a break and clear her head with a cup of coffee. After that she would decide whether to send it to Ægir's parents in its current form.

"Fucking weather," growled Bella from reception. Melting snow dripped from the shoulders of her anorak and flakes glittered in her hair.

Thóra dodged to avoid a shower as the secretary shook herself like a dog. "Where have you been?"

"I had to run out to the district court with some stuff for Bragi." Bella stamped her feet to dislodge the compacted ice from under her shoes. Two dark footprints showed for an instant on the light-colored parquet but quickly lost their shape on the warm wood. "I had to park a damn number of miles away, so I happened to drive past Faxagardur on my way back. It looked as if the police were sniffing around that yacht of yours."

"Really?" Thóra didn't know why she was surprised. The investi-

gation might have uncovered a new detail or perhaps they were repeating their tests or subjecting a larger area to detailed forensic
analysis. "Could you see what they were up to?"

"No, I just noticed two police cars parked right beside the boat and
a cop wandering around on deck. Maybe they were having a go in
the Jacuzzi."

Ignoring this, Thóra decided it was time for some fresh air.

The coffee provided by the resolution committee was far superior to
the law firm brew and Thóra felt her dissatisfaction receding, despite
having had a wasted journey so far. Ægir's parents had been out when
she called and only with considerable difficulty had she been able to
cram the report into their letterbox. Papers and envelopes projected
from the opening at all angles, like a failed flower arrangement. It was
not hard to understand why: What could possibly come in the post
that would matter to them now? In the end she had been forced to
weed out some of the contents—junk mail and other unimportant-
looking items—to make room. To ensure they received the report, she
would have to ring them and let them know it was there. It would
not do for the envelope to languish unnoticed among the yellowing
newspapers for the duration. In addition, she needed to pass on the
information that Ægir's salary would be paid as usual, and that her
conversation with social services about guaranteeing access had
proved encouraging. It made a change to be the bearer of good news.

"Are you making any progress?" Fannar asked. "We're doing our
nuts here over the lack of information. The police keep giving us the
brush-off." He was sitting facing her in a small meeting room, smartly
dressed as usual, looking for all the world like one of the young bank-
ers who used to swagger around the city streets and bars in the days
before the crash. "Have they managed to clarify things at all?"

Thóra took another sip of coffee and shook her head. She was no
better than Bella, inadvertently spraying the room with drops of water. Some landed on the gleaming table and she put down her cup to
wipe them away, not wanting to be reminded of her insufferable secretary. "No, sadly. The only fact that seems incontrovertible is that

Ægir and his family are dead. Nobody's holding out any more hope
that they could have survived."

Fannar did not look particularly moved by this news. "Did anyone really believe that?"

Thóra shrugged; carefully, to avoid another shower. "Well, people
tend to cling to hope for as long as they can. But now that two
of the seven have turned up dead, it's greatly reduced the chances
that the others could have been saved—and time is passing." She
kept quiet about the possibility that one or more of the people might
have made it ashore. She had no intention of sharing with Fannar
any details that were not in the public domain. The trick was to give
the impression that she was revealing more than she should. "But
you'll keep that to yourself, won't you?"

"Absolutely. You can count on me." A gleam entered Fannar's eyes.
"Nothing we discuss here will go any further. That's why I chose this
room. Inevitably, everyone's dying to know what's happening because
Ægir was one of us." He must think she was a complete idiot. Before
she even reached her car he would have shared this new information
with at least one or two of his colleagues. And by the time she got
back to her office on Skólavördustígur, those one or two would doubtless have started spreading the gossip, and so it would snowball.

"When I collected the papers from you, they included a page with
Karítas's name and phone number. Do you know why? I've been
meaning to ask you but keep forgetting." She held out a copy of the
page in question.

Fannar seemed surprised but was quick to assume a smile again.
"Oh, that." He picked up a sugar-lump and popped it in his mouth.
"That note was among the documents in Ægir's file on the loan and
the yacht repossession. I've no idea where he got the number or what
he was intending to do with it, but I included it anyway."

"Was Ægir acquainted with Karítas at all?"

Fannar stopped sucking the sugar-lump for a moment. "No. I'm
almost certain he wasn't."

"Could he have needed to contact her for work reasons? To get her
signature or notify her of the seizure of her property?"

"It's unlikely. The loan and the yacht were both in her husband's name. There'd have been no reason to contact her, unless he meant to ask about her husband's whereabouts."

Thóra drank some more coffee and wondered what this could mean. The yacht-related documents that she had found in Ægir's bedside table could indicate that he took his job seriously or that he had become obsessed with the case. Or something worse. "Do committee employees work outside the office at all? I mean, would you take your files home with you when there was a lot going on?"

"No, absolutely not. Naturally, we carry around information on our laptops but taking documents home is frowned upon. Why do you ask?"

"I was just wondering if there might be more paperwork relating to the case at Ægir's house—if there'd be any point in going round to check." Again she decided it would be better not to reveal the whole story.

"I wouldn't have thought so. At least, I'd be very surprised. Ægir was highly professional—not the type to smuggle files home with him. Anything of substance should be here and we've already given you and the police copies of everything that isn't subject to bank confidentiality. I can't see how information relating to the former owner's financial situation can be relevant to your case."

Thóra smiled noncommittally and finished her coffee. She longed for a refill but didn't ask. "Would you be able to find out if Ægir rang Karítas's number? I'm assuming he'd have called from the office since it's work related."

"Um, I don't know. We don't usually keep track of phone calls but the bills are itemized and long, expensive calls are sometimes charged to a specific project. I can have it checked if you like. It rather depends on how busy the secretaries are, so it might not happen today." He held up the photocopy. "Can I keep this? Then I won't have to hunt for the original."

"Sure." Thóra sincerely hoped no such call had been made. It would only complicate matters and they would probably never find out what it had entailed.

"Right." Fannar darted a glance at the ostentatiously expensive watch on his wrist, which was half-hidden by a sleeve fastened, inevitably, by a flashy cufflink. "Oh. One more thing." He looked up quickly. "Had either of the bodies they found been shot?"

"Shot?" Thóra thought she must have misheard. "I'm pretty sure they hadn't. Why do you ask?"

"I've just sent the police some new paperwork that came in yesterday. They called right back, anxious to know if there had been a gun on board or if we'd had it removed before they embarked. I hadn't a clue; it's the first I've heard of any gun."

It was the first Thóra had heard of it as well. "And they didn't explain why they were asking?"

"No. The guy hung up off as soon as I'd answered his questions." He swallowed the rest of the sugar lump. "But it occurred to me that it might be connected to the documentation I'd sent them, and I was right."

"What was the document?" Thóra felt absurdly jealous at not having been entrusted with the same information.

"It was a survey we had arranged in connection with the valuation of the yacht, which revealed that there was a revolver kept on the bridge. I asked around and apparently the captain has to be provided with one in case of a pirate attack. Can you imagine? Pirates!"

"Apparently they still exist." She wondered if pirates could have boarded the yacht, killed the passengers and sailed away on the boat they came on, all without leaving a trace. "There was no mention of any gun in the inventory I received. Is this a different list?"

"Yes, the list you have dates back to when the bank granted the owner a loan to purchase the yacht, so we couldn't use it for the latest valuation. The new inventory only came through yesterday. We'd booked an overseas agent to do a survey on the boat a few days before she left Lisbon and the bastard took his time about compiling a report." He sighed. "Not that it'll be much use to us now. The yacht's damaged goods—not just the hull but her reputation too. Unless you can sort that out." He smiled.

Thóra returned his smile automatically, her mind on other things. "Could I get a copy of the new inventory?"

"No problem. The police have requested a better version. I sent them a scan by e-mail but the quality wasn't good enough so they want a hard copy. I'll have another made for you at the same time."

While Thóra was waiting in reception, a police officer arrived to collect the inventory. It was the man with the green eyes. If he found it odd to encounter her there, he didn't show it. Too impatient to observe the formalities, she immediately asked him about the gun. At first he plainly had no intention of revealing anything but then he changed his mind. Apparently the gun listed in the most recent inventory was nowhere to be found on board. The original inspection of the yacht had turned up a small case of ammunition in the pilot house but this had been dismissed as insignificant since no gun was known to have been on board. The new inventory had changed all that. There was no forensic evidence that any shots had been fired on the yacht but six rounds were missing from the case. This indicated that the revolver had been used since the surveyor's visit, because in his report the case had been full and the gun unloaded.

Thóra received her copy of the list and put it in her bag. Before she left, the detective asked her to drop by after lunch as he wanted to discuss a matter concerning one of her clients—Lára. Although he didn't reveal any further details, Thóra could tell from his face that the news was bad.

So far the phone call had revolved around how tragic the whole affair was and how much Lára's co-workers missed her. Thóra kept trying to guide the conversation back to the topic she had called to discuss but without success; the woman was far too upset. While the resolution committee was directly linked to the circumstances of Ægir's disappearance and therefore to the police inquiry, Lára's colleagues were completely out of the loop and had received no news except via the media. Yet the woman was not motivated by nosiness; her questions revealed a genuine concern for the future of Lára's little girl and the terrible grief her family must be suffering. Only after some considerable time did Thóra manage to get a word in edgewise. "The reason I'm calling is that I may need to ask one of Lára's colleagues—someone who was well disposed toward her—to provide a character witness that would put an end to all speculation about her faking her own disappearance."

"Faking her disappearance?" The woman's tone conveyed all that needed to be said.

"It's just a formality. No one's seriously suggesting that she did. Might you be willing to provide one? You seem to have known her quite well."

"I certainly did. We sat at neighboring desks, so you could say we knew each other better than anyone else in the company. Though actually there are only five of us in Accounts and Payroll." The software firm where Lára had worked was fairly large, so Thóra had been fortunate to be put through to such a close colleague. "Anyway, as I was telling you, I really don't know what to say. Just when everything was going so well and Ægir was enjoying his job at last . . ,"

Thóra interrupted: "Didn't he enjoy it before?"

"Oh, yes. Well, sort of. He used to work for the bank that collapsed—the one the committee was appointed to wind up—but he wasn't too happy there; lots of the guys he graduated with had been promoted above him and had more money to play with. Lára told me he'd been held back by the twins; when the girls were small they used to take it in turns to fall ill and he and Lára had to split the child-minding between them. It wasn't well regarded at the bank—unlike here. At our office it's taken for granted that parents have to take time off when their kids are sick. What are the banks planning to do if people stop having children? That's what I'd like to know. Lend money to people in their graves? What sort of bonuses would they get then?"

Thóra ignored this digression. "But you said he was happy in his new job?"

"Yes, or at least Lára gave that impression. His work for the resolution committee was quite different. He didn't have to listen to his colleagues endlessly boasting about their extravagant lifestyles. I only met him a few times, at work parties and so on, but he seemed a really nice guy. In my opinion he wasn't the type to chase after money. But it was a good thing fate intervened when it did so he didn't have to work there any longer; you never know what effect that kind of atmosphere will have on people in the long term. It's bound to bring out their materialistic side."

"But he got away in time?" Thóra prayed that the woman would agree. She really wouldn't be able to cope if any doubts were raised about his honesty at this stage. Nor would his parents.

"Yes, I think so. Luckily. They didn't make any rash decisions and lived within their means, unlike many in his position. The only nonsense I heard about from Lára was the life insurance policy he took out."

"She mentioned that, did she?" Thóra sat up.

"Yes—that was several years ago. He was still working for the bank at the time and one of the things his friends were bragging about was the size of their life insurance policies. Can you imagine anything so ridiculous?"

Thóra couldn't. She couldn't picture herself boasting about anything like that to Bragi. Or Bella, for that matter. But this was good news. "So he took out the high insurance policy to save face among his colleagues?"

"Yes. But then he could afford to. He'd have a fortune after his death."

Chapter 25

Lára looked terribly small, lying face down in a black puddle on the cold steel deck. A trail of blood led back to the bridge. From the instant he had caught sight of her to the moment he discovered that she was breathing, albeit fitfully, Ægir's world had lost its soundtrack. All noise was muted as if he were underwater; he could see Thráinn and Halli opening their mouths but he could neither tell nor did he care what they were shouting. All he could think of was how to get the blood back inside Lára. He crawled on all fours, trying to scoop it up, only to watch it trickle away with the violent rolling of the ship. "Hit him." The words sounded so remote that they might have come from beyond the grave; there was no way of knowing who was speaking. "Hit him!" Ignoring the voice, Ægir continued trying to sweep the blood toward him with his hands. The words did not concern him; he had a job to do. Only when a hand grabbed his shoulder and dragged him roughly to a kneeling position did he come round and it was as if the volume had suddenly been turned up again. At least enough for him to hear when a flattened palm smacked against his cheek with full force.

"Get out of the fucking way! You're in the way. Either get a grip on yourself or move back." Halli shoved him violently aside. Ægir fell over, then propped himself up on one elbow and sat groggily on the deck with his legs sprawled out in front of him. Halli pushed his face so close that his features were a blur, though Ægir could see enough to register the man's anger. Halli seized him by the shoulders and shook him. "I said pull yourself together."

"That's enough. Give me a hand." Thráinn's voice was not only weary but defeated, and it was that which finally shocked Ægir back to his senses. "Leave him alone and grab hold here."

Taking a gasping breath, Ægir shifted until he could see what they were up to. For an instant he wanted to yell that they mustn't tread in the blood—Lára needed it. Then the moment passed. Instead he concentrated on breathing, but the sounds and effort involved were more like gulping down water than inhaling oxygen. He stared at the black patches on the knees of the men's jeans, then looked down at himself and saw that his own clothes were soaked in blood. "Oh, God. Oh, my God."

"Shut up." As Halli turned away from Lára to shout at him, Ægir saw what they were doing. They had rolled her over on her back and the captain was pressing down with both hands on her abdomen, with what looked like the full weight of his body. His hands were dark and still more blood welled up between his splayed fingers. Ægir felt faint but this time his collapse was not as total. He had to pull himself together. Halli turned straight back to Lára and Thráinn, blocking Ægir's view. Not that he wanted to watch; the sight that met his gaze was so terrible that it hurt. It felt as if he were being torn apart; the longing to watch was equaled only by the desire to close his eyes and pretend this wasn't happening.

Thráinn looked up from Lára for a moment. "Are you all right?" Ægir wanted to answer in the affirmative but an unrecognizable rattle emerged from his throat. "For God's sake, pull yourself together, man." Thráinn sounded furious and Ægir was filled with shame. He was failing his critically injured wife. "You go to the girls, we need to be here. They're probably still on the bridge."

Ægir staggered to his feet, slipped in the viscous blood and almost fell on top of the two men as they bent over his wife. He knew it was urgent that he go to his daughters but he couldn't prevent himself from lingering briefly. Carefully keeping his balance, he craned over the men to catch a glimpse of Lára's face. It was turned toward him but her half-open eyes did not seek out his. She looked gray rather than white, and a red bubble formed on her lips with every shallow breath; swelled, then burst, swelled, then burst. Ægir made a desperate effort to hold back his tears but one splashed onto Lára's rounded cheek and ran down to mingle with the blood. Her eyes closed and he tore himself away before he broke down completely. For the girls' sake, he couldn't allow himself that. Two strides and Lára was out of sight.

His legs felt as heavy as lead, every step a dragging effort, as he approached the door to the pilot house. A succession of horrifying images ran though his mind: Arna and Bylgja lying on the floor in shiny pools of blood. In his vision the pools were identical; his daughters twins to the last. Nausea mingled with the agony in Ægir's chest until he thought he might suffer a heart attack. If something had happened to the girls as well, he would welcome the chance to die.

But it hadn't, and the tightness in his chest abated, giving way to a dizzying rush of relief.

Arna and Bylgja were standing huddled at the back of the room, their eyes huge with incomprehension and stark terror. They did not run into his arms as he'd expected, and as he longed for them to. He ached with the desire to hug them tight and bury his face in their soft hair, if only for an instant. To hide from what was happening, from what he simply couldn't bear. Closing the door softly behind him, he made a superhuman effort to stay calm. "Are you all right, girls?" His voice sounded absurdly normal, as if they had fallen over while playing in the garden. Their eyes stretched even wider and he realized the effect his appearance must be having on them. "Thráinn and Halli are helping Mommy. It'll be all right." It was the most terrible lie he had ever told them. "Are you injured?"

They shook their heads simultaneously, with a slight lessening of tension. "Where's Mommy? Why isn't she with you?" Arna spoke as if she had hiccups, the tears not far away.

"Mommy hurt herself and Halli and Thráinn are helping her." A bleak future stretched out before him. A future without Lára. He was assailed by ridiculous concerns; who would do the girls' hair, or help them choose what to wear for birthday parties? It was almost impossible to assume a normal, reassuring manner. "But it'll be all right. As long as you're safe, everything will be all right." As he walked over

to them, he realized they had not once looked up at his face; their
eyes were fixed on his blood-soaked clothes.

"Why did Mommy have a gun, Daddy?" Bylgja began to weep. The
tears were not accompanied by sobs but slid down her face in two
rivers of silent grief and fear.

"In case a bad man came, darling. The gun was for protection. To
protect you and Mommy." He had reached them now and crouched
down to their level. Unable to bear the bewilderment in their eyes, he
struggled to make himself meet their gaze rather than hiding from
it; they did not deserve to be let down like that. "What happened?
Did you see what happened?"

They both spoke at once and in his present state he couldn't tell
who said what. The words emerged in a frantic gabble, punctuated
by hiccups and the occasional sob. "Something banged against the
door. Mommy pulled a gun out of her trousers and pointed it at the
door. But it was only a piece of rubbish and she smiled at us and said
she was just a bit stressed. We didn't say anything, we just stared at
the gun and then she looked all strange and went to put it back in
her belt when . . . there was a bang. Mommy's eyes opened very wide
and we could see the whites all round them. Then she coughed and
grabbed her tummy and told us to wait here. After that she went outside, and there was blood." They pointed to the trail that led to the
door from the place where the accidental shot had been fired. Ægir
had smudged the drops when he walked over them; he had seen so
much blood outside that he hadn't even noticed this light spattering.

"My darlings, Mommy has injured her tummy." Ægir's mouth was
dry and his head felt hot. He came close to breaking down again and
stopped speaking while he summoned his few remaining mental re-
serves. "Mommy hurt herself." He pulled them to him so they couldn't
witness his distress. His tears trickled into hair that smelt of the straw-
berry shampoo they had chosen in the Lisbon supermarket. If only
they could be back there; if only he could reverse the irreversible. He
snorted and did his best to get his emotions under control. He didn't
know how to cry; he'd never had any reason to since he was a little
boy.

"Did the gun shoot her?" asked Arna as the sisters' small arms slipped round his waist and clasped him tight, as if to force the right answer out of him. But the right answer was wrong.

"Scratched her, sweetheart. It only scratched her. Not badly, and Thráinn and Halli are making her better." What had Thráinn been dreaming of to give Lára the revolver? And why on earth hadn't he intervened? He should have known it would end badly; nothing could end well in this waterborne hell.

The door opened behind him and Arna and Bylgja tightened their grip convulsively. "Can I talk to you a minute, Ægir? In private." Halli's voice was devoid of all feeling, which only made matters worse.

"Wait here, girls. I won't be a moment; I'm not going far. It's all right." Ægir freed himself from their arms and left them, their faces distraught. "Please tell me you've stopped the bleeding." He wanted to get down on his knees, as if humility could help. "Please."

Halli stared down at his feet. "We moved her into the saloon. You'd better go there. I'll wait with the girls."

"No." Ægir straightened his back and discovered that his fists were clenched. He wanted to batter Halli's face until it was unrecognizable and incapable of telling him what he didn't want to hear. "You're not staying with the girls." His mind raced, his thoughts dashing hither and thither so he couldn't grasp any of them. Lára, the girls. It was *his* job to protect them. Not Halli's. "I'm not taking my eyes off the girls. They'll have to come with me."

"I'm not sure that's a good idea." Halli continued to stare at the deck, as if fascinated with his shoes. "It's really not a good idea."

Ægir opened his mouth to speak, to shriek, but suddenly all the fight went out of him in the cold air. There was no point shouting or striking out; it would change nothing. "If anything happens to them, Halli, I'll gouge your eyes out." He spoke without anger; it was a simple statement of fact.

"I'll look after them. I'd die rather than let anything happen to them." Halli was worldly enough to realize that the man in front of him was teetering on the edge. Awkwardly, he patted Ægir's shoulder, then went into the pilot house, leaving him alone.

He should have stuck his head round the door to tell the girls to wait a little while with Halli while Daddy went to speak to Mommy, but he couldn't do it. He was incapable of focusing on more than one thing at a time, and now it was Lára who lay either dead or dying on a sofa on board a yacht in the middle of the Atlantic Ocean, hundreds of miles from the medical aid that might have saved her life. A great sob burst from his throat when he entered the saloon and saw her lying there.

In his headlong rush he bashed his shin violently against the coffee table, which the men had pushed to one side, and almost went flying. The girls' coloring books were dislodged and some of the crayons rolled onto the floor but the captain managed to grab his arm in time to stop him falling. "Thanks." The courtesy was so incongruous in the circumstances that Ægir almost laughed. His mother's childhood training was so ingrained that even the greatest calamity could not shake it.

"She's asleep." Still holding Ægir's arm, Thráinn forced him to meet his eye. "I don't know what's going to happen. The bleeding's slowed down; I bound the wound as tightly as I could but it may have nothing to do with the bandages: there may simply be very little blood left." He forced Ægir's face back to his when he tried to look away. "I'm no doctor but I do know that it doesn't look good. Sit with her and speak to her if she comes round. Tell her what she wants to hear, and remember that this may be your last chance to talk to her." Thráinn released his head, allowing Ægir to turn to Lára. "Let's hope not—but it's best to be prepared. I'll wait outside."

Ægir couldn't give a damn whether Thráinn stayed or went. He fell to his knees beside his wife and clutched at the brightly colored woolen blanket that they had probably used to carry her inside. He didn't dare take her hand at first for fear of crushing it, for fear of being overwhelmed by rage at the unfairness of it all. Lára had never hurt a fly. She deserved better than this. Letting go of the blanket, he took her white hand in his. To his relief it felt hot and damp; he had been expecting her fingers to be cold. The blanket covering her looked disturbingly like a colorful shroud, so he pulled it off, revealing bare flesh and pink dressings that had no doubt been white when Thráinn applied them. The bullet appeared to have entered her abdomen beside the left hip. Ægir didn't know if this was a good or a bad place, or if anything in the abdominal area was bad.

He squeezed his eyes shut and the tears spurted out. At first he stroked her hand blindly, then he forced himself to look at her again, concentrating on trying to speak, on groping for words that he would be reconciled to afterward. He kissed her on the brow and temple and brushed the limp hair from her sweaty forehead. The fine lines that had distressed her so much seemed to have vanished, leaving her forehead unnaturally smooth. His mind blank of all else, he whispered this in her ear.

She opened her eyes, emitting a low croak that might have been a word, though he couldn't make it out. Everything he had wanted to say came rushing to his lips and he poured out the words in case she could still hear him, though her spirit had departed. But she only stared at him with glassy eyes that would not close, giving no sign that she accepted his plea for forgiveness.

Chapter 26

"The blood turned out to belong to Lára." The detective shot a glance at his colleague who thumbed through the sheaf of papers he was carrying, then handed a page to his superior. This time there was no hint of cigarette smoke or chewing gum. Thóra hoped this wouldn't affect his mood, but the alacrity with which his much younger subordinate jumped to obey him did not bode well. "The test results remove practically all doubt, though there's always a small margin for error. You can have a copy if you like. I imagine this will be helpful for your case."

"It certainly will." Thóra took the paper and scanned the figures, though she understood little beyond the summary of results. "How did you get hold of Lára's blood or DNA for comparison?" She passed the paper back to the younger officer and accepted the offer of a copy.

"They took a blood sample from her youngest daughter and also found some hairs in a brush in her makeup bag on the yacht. The results aren't a hundred percent conclusive, as I said; they never are. But they're good enough for me and any judge." The detective was grave today and the only hospitality on offer was a glass of water, which Thóra had refused. It was just as well; the bitter police station coffee would have ruined the memory of the superior brew she had enjoyed earlier at the committee offices. "Rest assured that we've prioritized the analysis to make up for the fact that the murder inquiry got off the ground rather late in the day." He folded his hands on the desk before him. "Of course, that's because we were originally under the impression that we were dealing with an accident; we can't afford to launch costly investigations unless we're certain that a crime has been committed."

"The blood stains were found on the sofa, you say?" Thóra saw no point in discussing what was too late to change now. Would it have made any difference if the yacht had been treated as a crime scene from the beginning? She doubted it. Every time a new piece of evidence emerged it only served to confuse her more. In fact, she had yet to be convinced that any actual murders had been committed, and the police probably took the same view. "I don't remember seeing any blood on the sofa; in fact, I don't recall seeing a single drop of blood anywhere."

"There wasn't much but it was enough to enable us to run tests. We didn't spot it until forensics conducted an ultraviolet scan of the yacht and discovered traces on two of the four cushions. All from the same person—Lára."

"It doesn't sound as if the bleeding can have been fatal."

"It's hard to say. There were also signs that someone had cleaned up a trail of blood that led from the deck to the saloon. We can't tell whether it was a minor accident or the result of something more serious. At any rate, there are no indications that large amounts of blood were spilled anywhere else on the yacht. But then we don't know if it was an accident at all. Lára may have been stabbed or struck with a weapon of some kind." The policeman relieved his subordinate of the stack of papers. "Or shot, of course. This latest information puts a completely new light on the possible sequence of events."

"You mean the information about the revolver?" Thóra asked, though the answer was obvious. She watched the young policeman awkwardly shuffling his feet; now that he had surrendered the documents to his superior, his role was undefined. With no part in the conversation and no chair available, he was forced to stand there beside his boss, pretending to be occupied. "I don't suppose you've found it?"

"No. We're confident we've searched every inch of the ship but it's always possible the gun's still there. To be on the safe side, I've instigated an even more thorough examination which is ongoing as we speak."

Although the yacht was large, the living quarters were limited and they were prepared to go over the whole place with a microscope. On the other hand, if the gun had ended up in the sea, they hadn't a hope. "Have you had the results of the tests on the blood that was found between the tanks on the bottom deck?"

"Yes. That was Halldór's; the comparison was easier in that case since we have his body."

Thóra began hastily talking to distract herself from the memory of that grisly discovery. "So, you have concrete evidence that Halldór and Loftur are dead, and it's likely that something bad happened to Lára, but the fate of Thráinn, Ægir and the twins remains a mystery?"

"You could put it like that, yes." At his shoulder the junior officer nodded sagely, as if to emphasize his superior's reply.

"And if their fate was the result of criminal action, there can't be many suspects left."

"No." The detective fixed and held her gaze. "And one of those is your man, Ægir." The younger officer's expression grew stern; anyone would have thought his role was to interpret their conversation through mime. Thóra studied him, wondering if she could train Bella to do the same. The secretary should be capable of arranging her features into a far more fearsome grimace than this callow youth. "I don't know if you're aware, but we took a sniffer dog over every inch of the yacht at the outset, with no result. Smuggling had seemed the most likely explanation but there's absolutely no evidence of it. Moreover, the Portuguese narcotics division have confirmed that they received no tip-offs about anyone on board being involved in the drugs trade over there. In other words, we've pretty much ruled out that angle. Though I suppose the drugs could have been stashed in such a way that the sniffer dog wouldn't be able to detect them once they'd been removed. But who could have been responsible? Having said that, it's not hard to guess where they could have brought the stuff ashore if there was any: Grótta. In which case there would have been people waiting to receive the goods and the smuggler, too."

"Have you checked the possibility that there might have been a stowaway on board?" Thóra felt foolish for asking this but she needed an answer. The likelihood that Ægir or Lára would end up under close scrutiny increased with every victim they found, and if the captain washed up on shore as well, the outlook would not be good.

"We've found a considerable number of fingerprints but the results are inconclusive. There were several years' worth, at least in the places that weren't cleaned regularly. Whereas in the public spaces, like the saloon, galley and even on the bridge, we were surprised by how few we found. Chances are that somebody deliberately wiped them off—unless they kept the place unusually clean." The detective scratched his chin, intent on the problem. "What we did find was confusing, as I said, and it doesn't help that we can't be sure if we've correctly identified the prints belonging to Ægir, Lára and the twins. None of them had a police record, so they're not on any register. We're planning to lift their prints from their house but haven't had time yet. However, we did obtain Loftur and Halldór's prints from their bodies. Inevitably, they had deteriorated badly but forensics managed somehow."

"What about the captain, Thráinn? Did you have his prints?"

"Yes. He was arrested about ten years ago after a fight. Nothing serious, but enough to earn him a night in a cell."

"So you haven't noticed anything unusual? Like too many recent fingerprints to fit the profile of the people on board, for example?"

"I wouldn't rule it out. We found two sets of fingerprints all over the place that we haven't managed to fit to any of the passengers. On balance, it seems more likely that they belong to women but that doesn't tell us much. They could easily date from before the yacht was confiscated."

"Do you know who they belonged to? Could it have been Karítas and her PA, Aldís?"

"I couldn't say. Neither are on our register, but we do know they were in Lisbon at around the right time, so they could well be theirs. We haven't yet decided whether to seek permission to lift prints for comparison from their houses or parental homes. As matters stand, we see no reason to cause their families unnecessary alarm with such a request. After all, there's no indication that they were involved. Unless you have reason to believe otherwise?"

"No. But have you verified that Karítas and her PA have left Lisbon? Have you checked the flights and so on?"

The detective studied her with his strange green eyes and sucked his front teeth. The younger man contented himself with assuming an intelligent expression, as if he too were considering whether it would be right to answer her question. "We've checked that, yes. In light of the captain's report we thought it only right to request that information, though we wouldn't usually go to these lengths unless a person was reported missing. We were hoping to be able to rule out the possibility that one of them was the female body on board by establishing that they both traveled on from Lisbon by other means."

"And?"

"The PA flew to Frankfurt the day the yacht left port, but Karítas doesn't appear to have left the city, at least not by air." He clicked his tongue. "Though of course that doesn't preclude other methods of travel. She could have taken the train or driven. Even left by sea, for that matter. Or, since she was within the Schengen area, flown under a different name. I don't know how people like her live their lives; she might have used an alias. But wherever she is and however she got there, she's no longer in Lisbon. Her mother claims to be in touch with her, though sporadically, and insists she's alive and kicking—in Brazil. I'm not so sure; nobody by her name has flown to Brazil during the last month. We checked that as well. You'd need a passport to go there and we believe she's traveling on an Icelandic passport as her mother is fairly certain that she hasn't applied for foreign citizenship. As long as her mother insists she's alive, though, there's little we can do."

Thóra sat back in her chair. She was convinced now that the woman found dead on board was Karítas. It was a relief to have something straight at last. But in reality she was still just as perplexed, since this only gave rise to further questions, such as who had killed her and why? And what was worse—could Ægir have been responsible?

"Does this look like the same handwriting to you?" Thóra held up the two pages to Matthew and watched as he examined them.

"No. That's pretty clear, even though one's only a signature and the other a short text. And people often sign their names quite differently from their normal style." He took a closer look. "But these are so distinctive that it's unlikely they could be by the same person. If I were to guess, I'd say this one was written by a woman and that one by a man." He pushed the papers back over to her.

It was what Thóra had wanted to hear. One of the documents was the last page of the life insurance policy bearing Ægir's signature, the other the photocopy of the piece of paper on which an unknown individual had written Karítas's name and phone number. "That's what I thought. But then who was the woman who wrote this for Ægir? Karítas herself?"

"Not necessarily." Matthew yawned. He had left work early and dropped by in the hope of persuading Thóra to call it a day. Instead, she had dragged him into her office to pick his brains about various problems that were preoccupying her. "It could be anyone."

"Like who?" Thóra stared at the page as if she expected the owner of the handwriting to jump out at her. "You don't acquire celebrities' phone numbers just anywhere. Karítas lives abroad so she's unlikely to be in the telephone directory, and I gather from Bella that she doesn't have many friends in this country."

Matthew shrugged indifferently. "I wouldn't know. Maybe it was her mother. Didn't you say she lived in Iceland?"

"It wasn't her. That's exactly what occurred to me before you arrived, so I rang her. She denied having given Karítas's number to Ægir or anyone else. She was very emphatic about it."

"What does it matter?" Matthew had plainly lost interest. "Even if you do track down the person who wrote it, I don't see why it's so desperately important."

"Maybe not, but I'd be happier if I could be sure that Karítas and Ægir weren't acquainted and had never spoken. If it suddenly emerges that they had met, it wouldn't be hard for the insurance company to cast a dubious light on their connection."

"I don't see why. He was working on the yacht repossession, wasn't he? Would it have been that irregular for him to communicate with the former owners? Perhaps the note dates from when the committee was in the process of confiscating the vessel. He may have wanted to give her the option of settling or paying off part of the debt."

"She didn't have any stake in the yacht, so it would have been extremely unorthodox for him to contact her about the settlement."

"Might *she* have contacted *him*, then? On her husband's behalf—in the hope of talking him round?"

"I don't know." Thóra was trying to ignore Matthew's obvious eagerness to leave. "Maybe Fannar has solved the mystery. I asked him to look into it and he promised to let me know. Would you mind waiting five minutes, just while I ring him to chase it up? After that I'm all yours."

Matthew looked put out but in the end he grudgingly agreed to allow her five minutes. Not ten, mind. Or even six. Five minutes precisely. He stood up and announced that he would wait in the lobby.

As a result, Thóra's request to be put through to Fannar came out rather breathlessly, and she was still flustered as she explained her business to him. Fortunately, he cottoned on immediately and said he had been about to call her on the same subject. Apparently their receptionist had remembered the incident straight away, since it had involved a high-profile figure. When Karítas had called to inquire who was handling the yacht affair, the receptionist had been unwilling to reveal the information, but Karítas had sounded distressed and claimed she needed to go on board to fetch a few personal effects that she'd left behind by mistake. As Ægir was not in his office, the woman had agreed to pass on the request to him but refused to give Karítas his name. Ægir had apparently been astonished when the receptionist gave him the message. Although she hadn't been privy to any telephone conversation between them, she believed they must have spoken at some point because about a week later Karítas had called again, this time asking for Ægir by name. Fannar added that when the receptionist subsequently expressed curiosity about their conversation, Ægir had turned bright red and insisted that he hadn't been in contact with her. The woman had also noticed that after the conversation with Karítas, Ægir had received two or three phone calls from abroad, which had been diverted to her when he didn't answer his direct line. The caller had refused to leave a message, so she didn't know what they were about, yet she clearly remembered Ægir's odd expression each time she had mentioned them to him.

Thóra rose to her feet at the end of the phone call, glad to be leaving work early for a change but simultaneously disappointed not to be able to follow up the lead. This was yet another piece of bad news, since she now had little doubt that the mysterious body on board was Karítas and that she had died in Lisbon—at around the time Ægir and his family were in the city.

On the plus side, at least she hadn't exceeded Matthew's five-minute limit.

Chapter 27

The heavens absorbed the white trail left behind by the jet. Despite its great altitude, the plane's wings and outline were just visible, unless it was his imagination filling in the gaps. No doubt the airliner was full of people; some on holiday, others traveling for work. Ægir envied every single one of them. They were in paradise compared to the hell that reigned here on board the yacht. He shaded his eyes against the sun. It was strangely unsettling to watch the jet recede into the distance, taking with it his foolish dream of salvation coming from on high. Dropping his hand, he looked down.

"Daddy." Bylgja was tugging at the sleeve of his sweater. He had no idea how long she had been doing this but her insistence suggested it had been some time. His dry eyes stung as he looked down at her. Never in his life had he been as mentally and physically exhausted. "Daddy. Your lips are bleeding."

Ægir licked his split lips and tasted iron. No wonder his mouth was dry; it was hours since he had drunk anything. This was not from any shortage of things to drink, as he had ferried a large supply of cans and bottled water down to the cabin before barricading himself inside with the girls. It was simply that he felt neither thirst nor hunger. There was no room for such sensations when his heart was in a thumbscrew that had been tightened to breaking point. His exhaustion didn't help. How long had he been awake? He couldn't remember. It didn't matter. If it hadn't been for the girls he would have thrown himself overboard and become one with the sea, but for their sake he couldn't allow himself that way out. He had to ensure that they reached home safely. And for that he needed to stay awake, which is why they were now standing on deck in the last rays of the evening sunlight.

He had been so overcome by drowsiness in the airless cabin that a quick trip outside had been essential. He took in a great lungful of sea air and closed his eyes. Fog stole into his mind, as if a curtain had been drawn, concealing all the terrible thoughts that had been plaguing him so relentlessly.

"Daddy. Daddy. You mustn't fall asleep." He couldn't tell which twin was speaking. "*Daddy!*"

Ægir started and opened his eyes wide. The fresh air was supposed to have had the opposite effect, to wake him up and invigorate him, not knock him out. "I'm awake." It wasn't working. He would have to find another way of warding off the beguiling drowsiness. If he had been able to trust Halli or Thráinn he would have asked if they had any stimulants in the medicine chest for use in emergencies. But this was merely another example of irrational thinking caused by fatigue, for if he could have trusted either of them, he wouldn't need to keep vigil—they could take it in turns to rest. "Let's go. That's enough."

"Do we have to go below again?" Arna's face was a picture of dread. "What if the ship sinks?"

"It won't." Ægir was too tired to be kind or understanding. He was desperately sorry about this, aware that they needed him to be a father, not just a bodyguard, but he couldn't perform both roles. He would trust himself to stay awake for the rest of the voyage but not to give free rein to his emotions. If he did he would fall to pieces. "Come on. We can watch a DVD."

"We've watched all the films we're allowed to." Bylgja sounded close to tears but this did not stem from the limited selection of videos, as Ægir was well aware. He couldn't discuss the loss of their mother with them now, though. Later he would have time to choose the right words and arrange them into sentences designed to provide solace for their grief. But for now such a task was beyond him. He had explained that their mother had died as the result of an accident and that they would have to be brave. He had stressed that they must bear up until they reached port but after that they would deal with their grief together and face the future without Mommy. It was all he was capable of in that moment. The tears had poured down their small cheeks but his daughters had shown a self-control far beyond their years. No doubt they sensed how much was at stake. "I don't want to watch the grown-up films." Bylgja smothered a sob.

"Then we'll just watch the funniest one again." Ægir scanned their surroundings, suddenly apprehensive about going below. He hadn't been aware of Thráinn or Halli on their way up, or during the short time they had been standing outside on the lower deck, in a corner where no one could creep up on them from behind. The yacht was making good speed, but that did not necessarily mean that the bridge was manned. The men could be anywhere and if either of them wanted to harm him and the girls, they would make an easy target on their way below. Then again, perhaps only one of the men was left alive. Or neither. He desperately regretted his foolish decision to leave the cabin. If anything, it had only exhausted him further.

"We'll have to find something else to do. If I watch another film I'll start thinking. And I don't want to think." Bylgja gazed at her father and he didn't have the heart to contradict her. He felt exactly the same.

"Would you like to do some coloring?" If they said no to this, Ægir didn't know what else to suggest. He was impressed he'd even managed to come up with that. His eyelids began to droop again.

"Yes, please." Bylgja put her hand in his and squeezed. "Don't go to sleep, Daddy."

"The coloring books aren't in our cabin." Arna grabbed Ægir's other hand and he tightened his grip in an attempt to communicate all he wanted to say to them.

"Where are they?"

"In the saloon." Arna broke off. "Where Mommy is." Her fingers writhed in his hand. "I want to see her. To kiss her good-bye. So does Bylgja." Their eyes, fixed on him, were full of anxiety and Ægir detected a hint of fear as well. It was hardly surprising in the circumstances, but what shocked him was that they appeared to be afraid of him. He must look like a madman.

"We can't go in there." He spoke without thinking. "It's impossible. Anyway, Mommy isn't there any more."

"Where is she then?" Large, heavy tears began to slide down Bylgja's cheeks again. He opened his mouth but no words came out. If Lára was no longer lying where she had died, he had no idea where her body could have been taken. He didn't even know what Thráinn and Halli had done with Loftur's body, but they were probably stored in the same place. He felt dizzy at the thought of them lying somewhere side by side, Lára and Loftur. "Will she be thrown in the sea, Daddy, like the woman we saw falling, or Loftur?"

"No." It felt as if his insides had turned to stone and were now slowly cracking. Soon they would disintegrate, leaving nothing behind but dust. He almost looked forward to it.

"We want to kiss her good-bye if she's going to be thrown overboard, Daddy. Or we'll never get another chance." The tears were still flowing silently, making Bylgja's whole face shiny.

"Come on." It was as if their words finally had a galvanizing effect on him and abruptly his fatigue was gone. What had he been thinking of? Where was the gun, for example? And was he really going to leave the body of his wife, the mother of his daughters, to those psychopaths? Not in a million years.

"What if the men come, Daddy?" Arna dug her heels in but Ægir dragged her along with him regardless. "You said we should hide from them." She had started to cry, too, but unlike her sister she allowed herself to make a noise. No doubt she was torn between fear for her own safety and the longing to see her mother one last time.

"It'll be all right. I promise." Ægir had to let go of their hands in order to open the door. Ushering the girls inside, he closed it quietly behind them. Then he laid a finger on his lips to hush them. The terror and grief in their faces were so heart-rending that he was hit by a sudden, urgent desire to seek out Halli and Thráinn and strangle them with his bare hands. He couldn't give a damn if one of them was innocent. Or both; they had never finished exploring the lowest deck of the boat, so it was still theoretically possible that there was a stowaway on board. He led the girls cautiously up the two levels to the saloon and hesitated outside the door, unwilling to barge in when he didn't know what might await them inside. The only way to find out would be to go out on deck and peer in through the window but it was still daylight so they would be exposed to anyone in the room. So he pushed the girls behind him and undid the catch on the door. Then he opened it slowly and calmly, without saying a word, and stuck his head through the gap, ready for anything.

His precautions proved unnecessary. There wasn't a soul inside and the sofa was empty; Lára had vanished along with the blanket she had been lying on. "Where's Mommy?" Bylgja did her best to whisper but it emerged like a shriek in the silence.

"I don't know, darling. We'll find her." Ægir's eyes ached and when he rubbed them he discovered they were swollen from lack of sleep. Harsh stubble scratched his hand as he ran it down his face: his appearance must reflect his inner torment. If he had to resort to threats against Thráinn and Halli, there was no question now that they would take him seriously. Without looking at the girls, he seized their coloring books and crayons from the coffee table and handed them over. "Come on." There was a strange odor in the room that filled him with revulsion; he didn't want it to linger in his nose, guessing that it was connected somehow to Lára's dead body. He wanted to remember how sweet she had smelled when alive.

They made less effort to tiptoe on their way back downstairs. There was no reason to any more since Ægir now actively wanted to find the men. It went against all his previous plans but the thought of Lára's cold body, alone and abandoned, robbed him of his few remaining wits. What did he mean to do if he found out where she was? He didn't know, but one thing was certain; he was not going to leave her behind to the tender mercies of Thráinn and Halli.

On reaching the pilot house, Ægir signaled to the girls to stop. He inched closer to the door, hoping to hear voices or sounds of movement. But his ears were met by silence; either the door was too thickly insulated or there was no one inside. The girls were mutely clutching their coloring books. He beckoned them over, then pushed them behind him as before.

Inside, Halli and Thráinn were sitting face to face, apparently engaged in a staring contest. "Where's Lára?" The men finally broke eye contact and Ægir was shocked when he saw Thráinn's face. The white stubble made him look as if he had aged ten years; his eyes were blood red and the black rings under them would have done a ghost proud. Halli looked little better. His dyed hair was matted, his face puffy.

"What?" The hoarse croaking indicated that Halli hadn't spoken for a long time.

"Where's Lára? And where's the gun?"

"Do you think it's a good idea for you to take it? It's caused enough harm already." Thráinn's voice sounded like the rustling of dry paper. There were no drinks to be seen and the two men had probably been sitting there, parched with thirst, for hours. Neither apparently trusted the other enough to go and fetch water or a Coke.

"Don't you worry about that. And it's a bit late to be careful now— it's your fault Lára had the gun in the first place." The captain didn't react to the accusation. "But if you want to know, I'm going to throw it in the sea. I don't want it and I don't like the idea of you two having it." Even as he spoke, he realized his mistake. It would have been better to let them believe he had the gun. Exhaustion was making it difficult to think straight, difficult to think at all, and he couldn't come up with any convincing way to retract his statement.

"It's in the top drawer." Thráinn pointed to the console under the window. "You can chuck it overboard for all I care."

"What?" Halli made to stand up and grab the gun first but was so stiff that he couldn't get out of the chair properly. "I'm telling you— there's somebody else on board. We might need that gun. Are you out of your minds?" Ægir went to the drawer and opened it. He didn't reply and it seemed Thráinn was not going to either. In the top of the drawer lay an object wrapped in a dishcloth. As Ægir was unwrapping it, Halli spoke again: "And what about the police? They're bound to want the gun when we go ashore." His voice rose to a falsetto.

"If we ever make it to land." Thráinn coughed and rubbed his forehead. If he was feeling anything like Ægir he must have a splitting headache on top of everything else.

Ægir wrapped the dishcloth back around the gun and took the bundle out of the drawer. "Where's my wife?"

"Down in the engine room." Thráinn glanced at the girls and Ægir thought he saw his face soften a little. They were still gripping their coloring books in both hands, watching the unfolding events with wide, terrified eyes. Bylgja's glasses had slipped down her nose but she wouldn't relinquish her hold on her book to push them back into place. "I'm not sure it would be wise for you to go down there. We'll reach land in about twenty-four hours, all being well, and there'll be plenty of time for that then."

"You're not going down there!" screeched Halli, frantic now. "What'll you do if you run slap into the killer? Eh? Surely you're not thinking of taking the girls?"

Arna and Bylgja looked even more petrified and Ægir was forced to intervene before Halli tipped them over the edge into hysteria. They were in a bad enough state already. "None of your business." Going over to his daughters, he positioned himself in front of them, hoping to block their view. But he could feel them peering round him to see what was happening. "I *am* going, and I don't want to see you two again until we reach Reykjavík. Or ever."

"Shouldn't we try to talk?" Thráinn was still massaging his head, his bloodshot eyes reduced to slits. "We're heading for disaster. Can't we agree to take it in turns to sleep? Two stand watch and keep an eye on each other?"

"No." Ægir shoved the girls toward the door. He had to get out before he succumbed to a proposal that sounded so enticing to his tired ears. "I'm going to look after my daughters. You two can go to hell."

"It's the only way, Ægir." Thráinn reached out, as if to seize Ægir and force him to stay put. "The only way."

"Listen to him." Halli was on his feet now, rocking, though the sea was calm. "It isn't one of us. I keep trying to tell you."

"Then you two should be all right here on your own. You can take it in turns to sleep; you don't need me." Ægir opened the door and herded the girls out. "The point is—I don't trust you. Either of you."

"Ægir." Thráinn did not shout or raise his voice, though he must have known this was probably his last chance to try to persuade the other man. His voice sounded devoid of hope. It almost worked. Ægir paused, halfway out of the door. "I activated the emergency button," Thráinn said, "but nothing happened. Someone's sabotaged the wiring and I don't trust myself to fix it. The lifebuoy isn't working either. But the long-range radio is tuned to the emergency frequency, so you could try to get through. I haven't been able to." The captain's voice gave out. Clearing his throat, he managed to rasp out one more sentence: "Take care of the girls."

Ægir let the door slam and they hurried away without bothering with the catch. On the way he hurled the gun, still in its wrapping, overboard without a moment's regret.

"Are you sure they're bad men, Daddy? Halli and the captain?" Arna freed one hand from her coloring book to hold the rail as they descended the stairs.

"Yes. I am."

"I'm not." Arna hesitated on the penultimate step. "What if there's someone else on board, like Halli said?"

"Halli's talking nonsense, Arna. Don't think about it. We'll lock ourselves in and everything'll be okay."

"I want to wait and see Mommy later. I don't want to go down to the engine room in case there's somebody there."

"Nor do I." Bylgja had caught up with her sister and stopped beside her.

"All right." Ægir had to admit that he was relieved. He dreaded descending into the confined space of the engine room where it was possible that a fourth man—or woman—was lurking. "We'll just go back to the cabin and have a rest; have something to eat maybe. Then we'll see. How does that sound?"

Once he had securely locked the door and given the girls a slice of bread and a yogurt apiece, which they accepted but didn't touch, he sat down and let his mind wander. A bitter laugh escaped him when he realized that if the yacht hadn't tangled with the container they would almost be home by now. The girls both regarded him anxiously and he stifled his laughter. He mustn't lose control—for their sake. If only he could lie down for ten minutes. Or even five. It would be enough to take the edge off his exhaustion and afterward he would be in better shape to stay awake for the rest of the voyage. He closed his eyes, all his problems evaporated and he slipped gently into a dreamless, restorative sleep.

When he started awake he had no idea how long he had been dead to the world; the girls were sound asleep fully dressed on the bed, their coloring books open in front of them, the crayons scattered over the rumpled bedclothes. Outside it was pitch dark, but that didn't tell him much as it had been near sunset when they came below.

Ægir rose, thanking God that nothing had happened while he was out for the count. He was furious with himself for failing in his guard duty but his reproaches lacked conviction since he had at least managed to sleep a little without anything going wrong. Yet he did not feel well rested and was seized by a longing to return to his comfy chair and slip back into unconsciousness. But that was impossible. His luck wouldn't hold forever. He heard a noise overhead and wondered if that was what had woken him. It sounded peculiar, like something being dragged across the deck. Then it fell quiet. Suddenly there was a splash from outside the porthole Ægir had opened to air the cabin. He dashed over to see what had fallen into the water.

He felt as if he had been punched in the stomach. On the illuminated surface of the waves a man bobbed up, as if the sea were rejecting him. It was so unreal that it took Ægir a moment to focus. The body was floating face down but just before it vanished into the darkness astern, he recognized the muscular back and gray-streaked hair. The yacht no longer had a captain.

All that separated Ægir and his daughters from the man responsible for this monstrous deed was a flimsy wooden door. His heart lurched as he realized that on the other side Halli would be waiting.

Chapter 28

"What did I tell you?" Bella's attitude reminded Thóra of her mother's reaction whenever she had taken a wrong turn in her teenage years after ignoring a piece of wise parental advice. "You should have listened to me. I knew it all along." The secretary folded her arms across her formidable bosom. "I have an unfallible instinct for that sort of thing."

"*In*fallible." Thóra resisted the temptation to roll her eyes in case Bella noticed. She had been listening to the secretary's crowing for several minutes now and enough was enough. What a mistake it had been to tell her that Karítas had probably never left Lisbon. Bella's obsession with the fate of her old schoolmate had gone into overdrive. The worst of it was that Thóra couldn't help agreeing with her. "It's *in*fallible, not *un*fallible."

"Whatever." Bella did not allow this grammatical nitpicking to put her off her stride. "She's dead, just like I said. It's a no-brainer. I mean, is she meant to have just walked out of Portugal in her Jimmy Choos? As if. And I doubt she has a driver's license."

Thóra's cell phone rang and she answered without even checking to see who it was. No phone call could be worse than listening to this. Bella kept talking, undaunted by Thóra's inattentiveness; she merely raised her voice to drown out the competition. When Thóra hung up, she smiled brightly at the secretary. "Sorry, what were you saying, Bella?"

Bella glared at her. "Are you kidding?"

"No. Not at all. What was it? That you were so clever because you'd always claimed Karítas was dead? Wasn't that it?"

"Yes." Bella smelled a rat. "Why are you looking like that?"

"Only, that was Karítas's mother on the phone. Her daughter's come home." Thóra's smile broadened. "But do go back to what you were saying. You have such an infallible instinct for these things. Please go on."

Bella's arms fell to her sides. "You're kidding me?" Her downturned mouth reminded Thóra of a bulldog's. She had never seen anyone so disappointed by good news.

"I'll soon find out. I told Begga I'd drop by. But first I need to inform the police; I expect they'll be interested in talking to Karítas, too, and I owe them some information. I haven't been keeping up my end of the bargain."

"What, Karítas is willing to meet you?" Bella looked astonished. Plainly she couldn't care less about the information owing to the police. "That's weird, seeing as how she didn't even want to be your friend on Facebook. And she's got hundreds."

Thóra had thought the same thing. "According to her mother, Karítas herself suggested she call me. I don't know why but we'll soon find out. Perhaps she needs a lawyer. If she does, it'll be a wasted journey because I can't act for her while Ægir's parents are my clients."

"I'm coming with you. You don't know how to handle a lowlife like her."

"She's hardly a lowlife," protested Thóra. In all the photos Karítas had looked extremely glamorous; a little plastic, admittedly, but hardly a lowlife.

"That's what you think. I'm coming anyway." Bella rushed into reception to fetch her coat.

"Really? I don't remember you at all." Karítas stared at Bella, stretching her big blue eyes as wide as they would go. It didn't suit her. Instead of the little-girl effect she was aiming for, she came across as a simpleton. She was draped across the sofa in her mother's sitting room, her long legs taking up the entire seat so that Thóra, Bella and Begga had to make do with chairs. "You weren't in my class, were you?"

"No." Bella was sitting upright, making no attempt to appear at all girlish. When Karítas's mother had introduced her as an old schoolmate, Bella had looked uncomfortable; obviously she hadn't wanted this information revealed right away. Yet she had clearly taken umbrage at Karítas's failure to remember her, so it was hard to work out what she did want.

"Amazing." Karítas gave Bella a conspiratorial smile, apparently oblivious to the animosity sparking off her. "That's, like, so weird. Did you used to be skinnier back then? Not so . . . you know?"

Thóra hastily interrupted to prevent violence from breaking out. "When did you get back to the country?"

"I only just got here."

Karítas's mother broke in. Her eyes were red and swollen, her cheeriness forced. "I don't understand how you can look so well, darling, after such an awful journey. All the way from Brazil. We wouldn't look so fresh after such a long flight, would we?" She addressed her words to Bella who stiffened even more.

"Did you come via the States?" Thóra noticed how oddly Karítas had reacted to her mother's words, as if she would have liked to smash the nearby crystal vase over her head.

"No." She did not elaborate but twined her fingers into a lattice, enlivened by slightly chipped hot-pink nail varnish. "Look, I didn't get you round to talk about boring things like flights." She untwined her fingers and rested her hands demurely on the cushions on either side of her. The hot pink clashed violently with the crimson velvet. "You're working on the yacht, aren't you?"

"Not directly." Out of the corner of her eye, Thóra noticed that Karítas's mother was looking embarrassed; presumably she had already told her daughter this. "I'm acting for the parents of one of the men who went missing. So my case is only indirectly linked to the yacht."

"Have you been on board?" Karítas stretched, then tucked her legs under her as Thóra nodded. "Isn't she to die for?"

"Well, my reason for going on board was rather grim, so I didn't really stop to think about it." A shadow fell over Karítas's face and Thóra saw that she had better praise the boat quickly if she wanted to stay on the right side of her. "But, of course, she's . . . to die for." She tried to sound enthusiastic. "Amazing."

"Yes, well." Karítas had apparently seen through her pretense. "Obviously you've never been on board a yacht before but believe me, *Lady K* is totally fabulous." If Karítas realized how boastful she sounded, she didn't seem to care. "She's the reason I wanted to see you. The thing is, I need to go on board. You could fix that for me, couldn't you? I don't want to bother the police."

"The police wouldn't be able to help you anyway. They've concluded their examination, so I don't even know if they have the keys any more. The resolution committee is responsible for her now, so you should really talk to them."

"That's too much hassle." Angry red spots formed on Karítas's cheeks. "It would be much better if you could let me in. It's not as if I'm going to do any damage."

"May I ask why you want to go on board?"

"I've still got a lot of personal belongings there and I want them back. Clothes and so on. I didn't manage to fetch them before the yacht left Europe, though I had a perfect right to. I just didn't have time."

Thóra resisted the impulse to point out that Iceland was part of Europe. "I thought you'd gone to Lisbon to do precisely that. To remove your personal property. Was that a misunderstanding?"

"Yes. I mean no. I was going to but I didn't have a chance."

"You mean you didn't have a chance to fetch your stuff or you didn't make it to Lisbon?"

"You know, I really can't remember. I travel so much." Karítas avoided Thóra's eye. Her words hung in the air during the ensuing silence. The lie was so blatant that in the end she added awkwardly: "Actually, I think I did. I went there but the yacht had already left or something. At least, I didn't manage to get on board."

"Oh?" Thóra felt as if she were negotiating a minefield. If she put a foot wrong there was a risk they would be shown the door. It wasn't the choice of words that was difficult so much as the effort to make one's questions and comments sound innocuous. "I must have misunderstood, because when I looked in the closets I thought one of the dresses had been removed. At least, there was an empty hanger. I know so little about this whole business that I just assumed you must have taken it and left the rest because they'd gone out of fashion."

"Clothes like that never go out of fashion. They're *haute couture*." Karítas's pronunciation owed more to Akureyri than to France. "But the fact is, I haven't had a chance to fetch anything and that's why I wanted to speak to you. To get you to help me gain access. I won't need long." She spoke like a woman used to having her slightest whim obeyed.

"Is it possible that your PA, Aldís, went on board, either at your request or on her own initiative? When the crew arrived to bring the yacht home the seal over the door had been broken. The person who did it must have had keys as there was no sign of a break-in. And if it had been an ordinary burglar, you'd have thought something would have been stolen. There were enough valuables on board."

"I haven't a clue what Aldís did or didn't get in to. She doesn't work for me anymore."

"Did you give her the sack or was it just that you couldn't afford to pay her any longer?" Bella's sudden entry into the conversation came as a relief to Thóra. She could be a loose cannon but it was good to have a moment's respite from her thinly disguised interrogation.

Karítas rounded on Bella. "I can afford staff perfectly well." She flicked her hair back with a quick movement of her head. "If you really want to know, I fired her."

"Why?" Bella certainly didn't beat about the bush.

"*Why?*" said Karítas. "Why wouldn't I? She was lazy and she was nicking my stuff." She was beginning to look distinctly tight-lipped.

"One question, Karítas." Thóra smiled pleasantly. "Were you by any chance in contact with a man called Ægir, from the resolution committee? Your phone number was found among his papers. Did you approach him about granting you access to the yacht, as you're approaching me?"

"Ægir, you say?" Karítas was a terrible actress; it was plain to everyone in the room that she wasn't racking her brains to remember. "Yes, that sounds vaguely familiar."

"He was on board the yacht with his family. I'm representing his parents. His wife and two small daughters are missing as well. It could be significant if you spoke to him. The police will probably be in touch to discuss it. I know they want to talk to you."

"The police?" Karítas finally sat up properly. "What do they want? I haven't done anything."

"Perhaps because there's a possibility that the body of a woman was found on board the yacht. In the freezer, to be precise. At first people thought it must have been you."

"Shit, why would they think that?" Interesting that she seemed less worked up about the presence of a dead woman in the freezer than the fact that the woman had been wrongly identified. "Anyway, what are you talking about? A woman? In the freezer?"

"There was no body in the freezer when I was there." Karítas's mother looked outraged. "What's this nonsense?"

"All I know is that the police are investigating the matter. As I explained, my involvement is indirect, so I may have gotten it wrong. But what were you saying about Ægir? Did he speak to you before going on board? Or meet up with you in Lisbon? You must have been there at the same time."

Karítas scratched her neck, leaving red marks. "No, I didn't see him. But I did talk to him on the phone. That's not a crime. In fact, he called me."

"Really?" Thóra was trying hard to keep her voice friendly. "Was that when he was in Portugal?"

"No, here in Iceland. I rang the resolution committee and the woman who answered the phone told me he was dealing with the yacht. He wasn't there, though, so I asked if he could call me back and gave her my number. He called. Big deal."

"What did you want from him?"

"I wanted to go on board. Like I do now. He had the keys."

"What happened? Did he agree to help you?"

"Sort of. At first he was really unhelpful." She gave Thóra a dirty look. "Like you. But I talked him round and he agreed to arrange it."

"What did you promise in return?" Bella opened her mouth to add a further comment that Thóra feared would be highly inflammatory, but she didn't get a chance.

"I said I'd make it worth his while." Karítas flushed a little when she saw Bella's grin. "Not in the way you're insinuating. I was going to pay him. Pay him well."

"Just to get your dresses back?" Thóra couldn't imagine promising a hefty reward for the return of any of her own clothes.

"Not just them. I need to pick up a few other items too." Karítas's lips thinned until they almost disappeared.

"And what happened?"

"He was going to meet me in Lisbon before the yacht left. But it didn't work out."

"Why not?" Thóra had given up trying to be nice.

"I didn't go. Something came up and I didn't need his help any more. Or so I thought." Karítas bared her teeth in a failed attempt at a smile. "But now I'm hoping you can sort out the red tape for me and let me in. You know, better late than never, and all that."

Thóra studied this woman who had been created in the likeness of an angel, the beautiful outer shell concealing something much darker inside. The missing people were of no consequence to her, merely an inconvenience. It didn't seem to matter that they included two little girls. "I'll consider it if you tell me what it is you want. The police have been over the yacht with a fine-toothed comb. I can't quite see what could be so important to you apart from the dresses."

"You don't need to worry about that. If you're going to get all weird about it I'll pay you. How about that?"

"No, thanks." Out of the corner of her eye Thóra caught Begga's expression of relief and swung round to her. "Is something the matter?"

The woman jumped. "Oh no, nothing. I was just worried about the money. We're in a spot of bother at the moment, you see. Only temporary, mind." She turned to her daughter. "Darling, when it comes to little things like this it makes more sense to trade information than to pay for it. She doesn't want your money anyway." She gazed pleadingly at her daughter, brushing a lock of hair out of her eyes. Her gray roots had not been touched up since Thóra and Bella's last visit.

Karítas was not remotely grateful for this intervention. She shot her mother a spiteful look. "I'm selling this house, Mom. It's not up for discussion. You'll just have to fend for yourself until everything's sorted out." She added to Thóra: "Lawyers handle conveyancing, don't they?" Her mother seemed to shrink in her ornate chair, a symbol of a lifestyle that would soon be history.

"I'm not an estate agent." Thóra caught a smirk on Bella's face. She seemed to be delighted with her employer, for the first time in living memory. "And I'd like to know why you didn't go ahead with your meeting with Ægir, since it was so important to you."

"I told you. The situation changed. I didn't need him anymore and I wasn't going to pay him for what someone else was prepared to do for less."

"Someone else?"

"Yes. I bumped into one of the crew members in town—I recognized him—and he was much nicer than that Ægir. I discussed the problem with him and he was more than willing to oblige. But everything got screwed up because his stupid friend had an accident and he had to help him, so he couldn't meet me as planned. He rang and said he'd sort it when they reached Reykjavík. What was I supposed to do? By then it was too late to try and persuade Ægir to meet me because the captain had arrived and was staying on board. So I had a wasted journey to Lisbon and was forced to wait until the *Lady K* got to Reykjavík." She closed her eyes. "Then everyone goes and disappears, and I'm the one that loses out."

"What was this man called?" asked Thóra, though there could only be one answer if the man's friend had had an accident in Lisbon.

Karítas was silent for a moment, thinking. Then she turned her heavily mascaraed gaze on Thóra. "Halli, I think. He used to work for me on the *Lady K* in the old days. Yes, I'm pretty sure his name was Halli."

Chapter 29

The hardest part, Ægir thought, was not having a clue how far they were from their destination. He had no idea how long he had been asleep; nor could he remember what Thráinn had said about the length of time remaining. Had he said twenty-four hours, or a day? And if the latter, what had he meant by a day? Twelve hours? Was it possible they only had a few hours left at sea? He cursed himself for not having checked the clock at the time or demanded more detailed information. Had he done so, he would have been able to calculate how far the yacht had sailed while he was asleep and plan his next moves accordingly, such as whether it would pay to jump ship in a lifeboat with the girls. The raft might be equipped with an emergency transmitter that would be activated when it hit the water, but Ægir didn't know how far the signal would carry, so this course of action would only make sense if the yacht was nearing Iceland. The ocean surrounding them was so vast that there was almost no chance of crossing the path of another vessel if they were still up to a day's journey from land.

In any case, it was too late now. Thráinn wouldn't be giving any more answers, at least not in this world; and Ægir wasn't about to seek out Halli, as the question would no doubt be his last. He lay back and stared at the ceiling, then closed his eyes and watched the white specks dancing on the lids. Never had so much ridden on a decision of his. Never had he felt so bewildered—or alone.

"Daddy? What's the time?" He looked over at Arna who was sitting up rubbing her eyes. She had fallen asleep on a crayon and it had stuck to her sweater without her noticing.

"I don't know." He didn't wear a watch and hadn't charged his phone since they lost reception. He perched on the edge of the bed beside her and reached for the crayon. It was blood red and the sight of it over her heart disturbed him. "It's nighttime, as far as I can tell."

"When will we be home? My tummy hurts."

"Soon, hopefully." Ægir smoothed her hair but it sprang up again in a mass of tangles. "We might go home in one of the lifeboats. How would you like that?"

"I don't care. I just want to go home." She pushed his hand away. "Then we won't have to be brave anymore."

"You're right." Ægir lapsed into silence, not knowing what else to say. The easiest course would be to lie and claim there was nothing to fear; before they knew it they would be home, where no one would have to behave themselves any more. But that wasn't true; there was no guarantee that they would ever reach Reykjavík and, even if they did, they were unlikely to take any comfort in their homecoming now that Lára was gone. "You've coped so well, Arna. Much better than I'd have dared hope. With any luck you won't need to keep it up much longer."

"Good." Arna lay down again with her eyes open. She regarded her sleeping sister, then asked: "What do you think Sigga Dögg's doing?"

"I expect she's gone to beddy-byes by now." Ægir spoke in a low voice; the thought of his youngest daughter was too painful to bear. She would grow up without a mother and he wasn't sure he was capable of providing her with the sort of care she would have received from Lára. He didn't know how to comfort his daughters, how to brush their hair, choose their clothes or presents, or help with their homework. And he was a hopeless cook. He worked too hard, but then he had to; if he applied to work fewer hours he would soon find himself out on his ear. Not that money would be a problem. Indeed, perhaps that would be the best solution after all that had happened; to retire from work and become a full-time father instead and devote himself to his daughters. But how long would it be before people began to wonder how he was supporting himself and the kids? A year, two years, three? It didn't matter. Sooner or later the time would come. And he would be unable to answer. The sudden thought of

Lára's life insurance policy brought a bad taste to his mouth. It would solve that particular problem. But what would it feel like to see that huge sum appear in his bank account? He had long dreamed of a fortune but it had never occurred to him that he would acquire it like this. He had paid far too high a price.

"Sigga Dögg doesn't know Mommy's dead." Arna closed her eyes. "She's so lucky."

"She'll find out, darling, as soon as we see her again. But I'm not sure she'll understand. She's so young."

"She's still lucky. I wish I didn't know."

"Me too." He would have given anything to have Lára back but, since that was impossible, he wished he could have deceived himself, even if only for a few days or until they reached port. Having to cope with the grief and terrifying uncertainty at the same time was unendurable. He felt as if the chances of a happy ending would be many times greater if all he had to contend with right now was the uncertainty. But deep down he knew it wasn't like that; there could be no good moves in this game.

"Can we go up on deck and see if we can spot Iceland?"

"No," he snapped and immediately regretted how harsh it sounded. He didn't want Arna to suspect that something even worse had happened. "It's too dark. We wouldn't be able to see."

"We would. There might be lights. You can see lights from outer space."

"That only applies to big cities. I'm sure Reykjavík isn't visible from space or from this far out at sea, for that matter." He lacked the energy to explain about the curvature of the earth. "All there'd be is black sea and more black sea."

"Perhaps the captain has binoculars that work in the dark. We could go and find him. I don't believe he's a bad man."

"No, I don't suppose he is, but it doesn't change the fact that only soldiers and commandos have binoculars like that. They cost a lot and, anyway, sailors don't need to see in the dark; they have radar and all kinds of other equipment to do it for them." Ægir hastily steered the conversation away from Thráinn; it was easier to talk nonsense about binoculars. The memory of how the man's body had floated away was too horrible, and somewhere at the back of his mind a voice whispered that the captain had not been quite dead when he was thrown overboard. The voice grew ever more insistent, though Ægir didn't believe it. If that had been true, surely Thráinn would have at least attempted to raise his head out of the water? And what did it matter if he had drowned within reach? Thráinn had given Lára the gun and Ægir would never forgive him for that. It had almost certainly influenced his decision to do nothing as Thráinn vanished into the darkness. The captain was to blame for Lára's death. An eye for an eye, a tooth for a tooth. "Aren't you thirsty?"

Arna shook her head and lay down on her back. She stared up at the same ceiling tile as Ægir had focused on earlier; perhaps like him she found it soothing to have nothing but its blank white surface before her eyes, not reminding her of anything. He longed to lie down beside her and copy her example but stopped himself. There were important matters to think about; such as how to act for the best in their current predicament. A noise overhead made him shoot an involuntary glance at the ceiling. It sounded as if it was coming from the same deck that Thráinn's body had been dragged over. The noise, innocent enough in itself, would not have startled him in other circumstances, but now it reminded him that Halli was still at large and doubtless preparing his next move, which would surely be aimed against him and the girls. "What's the matter, Daddy?" Arna had turned to him and her face reflected his own alarm.

"Nothing, darling. I'm just tired."

"Do you think it's the bad man? The man Halli said was on the boat?"

"No. There's no one else here. It's probably only Halli." Ægir had to make sure that neither Arna nor Bylgja found out what had happened to Thráinn. If they panicked it would make the whole situation far worse. Things were bad enough already. "Or Thráinn." All at once he regretted throwing the gun overboard. If he hadn't, he could have hunted Halli down and killed him. The thought wasn't in the least shocking. On the contrary, it was so tempting that he allowed his mind to play out the sequence of events, a smile rising to his lips as he blasted imaginary bullets into the young man's back. It faded the instant Ægir forced himself back to earth. He must concentrate.

Bylgja stirred and half-opened her eyes. She appeared to be still asleep, though her gaze was resting on the coloring book that lay open in front of her. Arna passed her the red glasses and she sat up, struggling to focus, yawned and put them on. "I dreamed about Mommy."

"I didn't." Arna looked hurt, as if her mother had been showing favoritism from beyond the grave. "I didn't dream about anything."

Ægir tried to block out his daughters' chatter and concentrate on the sounds outside. Halli must need to sleep at some point as he'd had no more rest than Ægir. Even if he'd seized the opportunity while Ægir was dozing, a short nap like that would not have been enough to overcome his fatigue. But if Ægir could find out when next Halli went to sleep, he would have a chance to act to secure his daughters' safety. For that he would need a plan, though. So far the only idea that had occurred to him was to escape in a lifeboat. Perhaps that would do. He didn't have time to consider all the options and assess which was the right one. After all, there was no right decision.

They heard the door to the corridor open, then slam shut. Ægir gasped, feeling his heart miss a beat. What if there was another gun on board and Halli had gotten hold of it? What point would there be planning their getaway or trying to defend themselves? "Who's that, Daddy?" Arna whispered anxiously. She must sense that he felt threatened by whoever was out there. He laid a finger on his lips. The girls' eyes widened and Bylgja clasped her hands over her mouth as if to prevent herself from screaming. Ægir came close to emulating her when he pressed his ear to the door and heard somebody walking along the corridor, systematically trying the handles to the cabins. Adrenaline coursed through Ægir's veins for the split second that he doubted he had locked the door. But when their handle was grasped from outside, the door remained shut. All three stared transfixed at the handle, which remained motionless for a moment before someone turned it again, more forcefully. None of them said a word or moved so much as a little finger, as if they were actors in a film that had been paused. Not until they heard footsteps retreating down the corridor and the door at the end opening and closing again did they draw breath.

"Who was that?" Arna eyed the door as if she expected it to burst open any minute. Ægir felt the same. Although the corridor seemed empty, it might be a trap. And who *could* it have been? Halli knew precisely which cabin Ægir and Lára had been occupying and he also knew which room the girls were using. So why had he walked all the way down the row? Was it not Halli after all? The more he considered this possibility, the more his doubts grew. Surely Halli would know where the master key was kept, unless there was no such key on board? Perhaps it *was* Halli and he had gone to fetch the axe from the bridge in order to break down the door. Or perhaps it was someone else entirely.

"Who was that, Daddy? Was it the bad man Halli was talking about?" Arna wasn't going to let her father get away without answering.

"I'm sure it was only Halli. He's tired like I was earlier, so perhaps he can't remember which cabin he's in." Ægir immediately regretted telling the girls what they wanted to hear rather than what they needed to know. If they were to come through this alive, they would have to be aware of the danger. It wouldn't do for them to run to Halli when or if they encountered him. If he caught one of them, Ægir would go to pieces and that would be the end of them all.

"It wasn't Halli." Bylgja wrapped her arms round her narrow ribcage as if to keep warm, though it wasn't cold in the cabin. "I'm sure it wasn't Halli."

"How can you tell?" It sounded as if Arna couldn't decide whether she wanted her sister to be right or wrong.

"It just wasn't him." Bylgja shifted closer to the headboard. "Why don't we go up and talk to them, Daddy? Halli and Thráinn might be able to help us and catch the bad man."

"Not now. We'll go out presently, but not quite yet." They left it at that, though neither twin seemed satisfied. Ægir wasn't either, but it couldn't be helped. While he didn't know who was out there or whether that person was still on the prowl, there was little he could do. Then again, he wouldn't find out if he stayed in the cabin. But he couldn't bring himself to confront this fact just yet. It was better to sit tight and hope for the best. Wasn't it?

Ægir had succumbed to sleep again. He woke from his dreamless state with such a violent jolt that he was lucky not to fall out of his chair. Something had changed, and in his horror at having fallen asleep on guard again he thought at first that someone had entered their cabin. But it turned out to be the long-desired silence that had woken him. Previously the deep throbbing of the engine had been constantly in the background but now all was quiet. The yacht was no longer moving. "How long is it since we stopped? When did it happen?" He tried to keep the despair out of his voice. This did not bode well.

"A while ago." Arna rolled over and closed her coloring book. "We didn't want to wake you because you were so tired."

"How long is it since I dropped off? Did it happen straight after that or only just now?" The girls exchanged glances; clearly they had no idea. It was still pitch dark outside, so assuming he hadn't slept for twenty-four hours it must be the same night. "Has anyone tried to get in again?"

"No. No one." Bylgja laid aside her book as well.

Ægir rose and went to the door. There was no sound from the corridor outside. Perhaps this was the chance he had been waiting for; he might not get another. There was no need to shut down the engines in order to go to sleep, but perhaps, just perhaps, this indicated that Halli—or whoever it was—was resting. Perhaps he was afraid of oversleeping and entering Icelandic territorial waters while he was dead to the world. It was entirely possible that he had pressed his ear to the door just as Ægir was doing now, and, hearing that Ægir was asleep, judged it safe to take a nap himself. "Was I snoring, girls?" They nodded. He vacillated. If he could make a dash for the bridge to fetch some emergency flares and the axe, or simply to find out where in the world they were, they would be much better off. He could set off a flare if he heard or saw any other ships. "Okay. Now

I need you two to be brave one last time." They looked far from happy. "I'm going up to see what's happening. You must wait for me here in the meantime. You mustn't leave the cabin, whatever happens. Do you think you can do that?"

"We don't want to stay here alone." Bylgja looked at her sister in hope of support. "What are we to do if someone comes in while you're away?"

"No one's going to come in. You'll lock the door behind me."

"But what if he pretends to be you?"

"No one can pretend to be me. You know my voice." Reluctantly, they accepted this, though it was obvious from their expressions that it was the last thing they wanted. They needed him. He was their father. But it couldn't be helped; he couldn't take them with him when God alone knew what awaited him upstairs. "Perhaps you should hide in the wardrobe just to be on the safe side. If anyone looks in here, they'll think you went with me and go away again."

"But then we won't hear you when you knock."

"I'll knock extra loud." He put his ear to the door again and listened intently. Still no sound. "And I'll be very quick." He meant to seize the door-handle and leap into action before he lost his nerve but was filled with a powerful longing to kiss his daughters one last time before he abandoned them. Their cheeks were soft and warm and the scent of their young skin was the best thing he had ever smelled. What had he been dreaming of to think they needed more money for their life to be perfect? You couldn't improve what was already perfect; you could only ruin it. His eyes fell on the briefcase that was still leaning against the wall where he had left it and he wanted to scream until his vocal cords gave way. Instead, he looked sadly at his daughters, so lost, so desperately fragile and vulnerable. "Hide in the wardrobe and wait there until I knock. I'll call out my name so you won't be confused." He gave them each a lingering kiss on the brow.

The corridor was deserted and Ægir met no one on his way up to the bridge. Every muscle, every nerve and sinew was tense, ready to confront the murderer, whether it was Halli or a stranger. Of course he hoped it wouldn't happen, yet part of him desired nothing more than to find the man and beat him to a pulp. Although he'd never had any real experience of fighting, he was fairly sure he would succeed. No matter what was driving the other man, Ægir had hatred on his side. The sight of his face reflected in the pilot house window brought him to a standstill; rage had contorted his features. He hoped with all his heart that he hadn't looked like that when he said good-bye to the girls; if anything happened to him, he didn't want that to be their last memory of him.

Inside the bridge there was no one to be seen; all the lights were off but the glow from the computer screens and instrument panels provided enough illumination to preclude anyone hiding there. Nevertheless, it was with extreme caution that Ægir opened the door and went in. Closing it behind him, he headed straight for the GPS. According to this, the yacht was still worryingly far from land. Because the engine had been turned off, the data about their course, which had previously been displayed at the bottom of the screen, had now vanished. As a result, there was no information about how long it would take to reach their destination. But he didn't really need it; he guessed they had approximately ten hours' sailing time left, but every hour the yacht remained motionless was another hour at sea. Perhaps he should start her up again? He and the girls couldn't abandon ship in these waters and he suspected they wouldn't be allowed to remain undisturbed in their cabin for the rest of the voyage. On the other hand, if he started the engine, the killer would be aware of his presence and might take steps to deal with him. Ægir was terrified that the killer would head straight for the girls and get to them first. That was unthinkable.

Abandoning the console, he began to hunt for flares. If he did try to start the engine again, he would do it last, before racing back down to the girls. He soon unearthed the flares in a white cardboard box in a drawer; he would just have to hope they were in working order. But the axe had vanished from its place on the wall and the realization reduced him momentarily to panic. Then, pulling himself together, he went back to the drawers and began searching for a possible weapon. Finding a suitably heavy wrench, he took it with him, though it wouldn't be much use against an axe. The weighty metal bar felt so good in his hand that he actively looked forward to having a chance to use it. He wouldn't hold back. He tightened his grip and resolved to go out on deck and check that the lifeboats were still in place. If he had time, he would work out how to launch them—should they be forced to escape in one, he would have to act fast and there would be no room for mistakes. Once he had done this he would return to the bridge and try to get the yacht back on course. Then he would fly back to the girls as if the devil were at his heels.

A bracing gust of sea air hit him as he emerged on deck. Oddly, it carried not the tang of salt but a waft of perfume, and Ægir paused inadvertently to sniff the air in the hope of detecting its source. The yacht was facing into the wind and he peered warily round the corner of the pilot house toward the bows to discover whether the smell emanated from there. The lights had been switched off on the foredeck, yet he could see enough to tell that there was nobody about. The perfume was unquestionably coming from there. Instinct warned him to leave well alone but his curiosity proved stronger. It was a woman's scent; no man would wear such a heavy, sweet floral fragrance. And if it was a woman, two things were clear; one, that there was a stowaway on board and, two, that he would almost certainly prove the stronger should it come to a fight. If he tracked her down and overpowered her, they would be able to sail fearlessly to port, instead of having to risk their lives in a flimsy life raft.

Creeping stealthily round the pilot house, Ægir tried to follow the scent. But before he had gone far he was met by a sight that caused his heart to miss a beat. Two legs were protruding from under the white bench that ran around the bows. Instantly he recognized the shoes that Halli had been wearing throughout the voyage. And he could not be asleep, that much was certain. His legs were lying at such an unnatural angle that they must be broken. Forgetting all caution, Ægir sprang toward the bench and bent down for a better view. The stench of perfume was so sickening that he would never be able to smell it again as long as he lived without retching. It got worse when he tugged at one cold limb and realized that it had been severed from the body. When he finally forced himself to look, he discovered that the rest of Halli's corpse was nowhere to be seen. He snatched back his hand and leaped to his feet. He was not safe here, whether the killer was male or female. This person was clearly insane.

All thoughts of starting the engines again evaporated as he ran for the stairs that would take him back to the twins. He wanted to scream out their names, to tell them to be careful, that Daddy was coming. But he was silent, saving his breath for the sprint. Even as he opened the door he realized he needn't have bothered. He would never reach his daughters now. That thought was almost more agonizing than the axe that sank into his belly. It was dragged out and driven in again, under his chest. As his muscles ceased to obey him he dropped the flares and wrench, which fell with a series of thuds onto the steel deck. His last rational thought was not of the pain or his daughters, now left on their own. Rather, it was puzzlement as to how on earth this could be happening. Perhaps, after all, the dead could rise from the grave?

Chapter 30

"So you knew nothing about this? Your friend Halldór didn't say a word about meeting Karítas in Lisbon?" Thóra had to raise her voice to be heard over the music that was blasting from the sound system behind her. She didn't know the band and had no wish to become any more closely acquainted with them. The bass was turned up so high that her body seemed to throb with it and she was almost afraid her heart would start beating in time to the insistent drumming.

As soon as she and Bella left Karítas and her mother, she had called Snævar and asked to meet him. She had taken care to reveal nothing about their errand, merely hinting that she wanted his opinion on a few small things. He had agreed and suggested she come round to his place as his leg was particularly bad that day, which made it hard to leave the house. If she wanted to see him at her office, it would have to wait until tomorrow. Thóra felt it was too urgent for that, so she and Bella drove straight from Arnarnes up to the suburb of Grafarvogur where Snævar lived in a long block of flats that could have done with some exterior maintenance.

Inside, Snævar's flat was little better. Thóra hoped for his sake that the squalor could be blamed on his broken leg. As it was, he was lucky not to have tripped over the piles of rubbish that littered the floor and broken the other one. He apologized casually for the mess. It was obvious that he was glad of the company; perhaps it was a sign of his loneliness that he should be willing to receive guests in the midst of all this noise and chaos. But his pleasure visibly faded when Thóra accused him of having held back information. "Though to tell the truth, I find the whole thing rather far-fetched," she added. "And I'm fairly sure the police will, too."

Snævar stared blindly into an empty mug with a congealing ring of coffee froth around the inside. "I didn't want to tell anyone. I was so afraid people would suspect Halli. None of you knew him so you're bound to believe the worst of him. Even if he did speak to her, he didn't do anything. I can't and won't believe it."

"You obviously don't have much faith in the police." Thóra pushed a robot vacuum cleaner away with her foot in order to make more legroom. The poor thing had obviously run out of power and been prevented from reaching its recharging point by the obstacle course on the floor. "You can trust them to find out the truth."

"How can they, when there's no one left to tell the tale? Surely you must see that?" Snævar shoved an embroidered cushion behind his back for support. It looked like an heirloom from his grandmother's house. "Anyway, nothing happened. I broke my leg and Halli had his hands full coping with me and preparing the yacht for departure. There's no way he would have had time to help Karítas, so I didn't think it was relevant."

"It's not up to you to decide what is or isn't relevant. Not as far as the police are concerned, at any rate. But you don't have to answer *my* questions unless you want to."

"I do want to." Snævar seemed agonized by this turn of events and kept glancing from Thóra to Bella in the hope of eliciting sympathy. "I can't begin to describe how much I regret not having mentioned it before."

"You didn't mention it now either." Far from being irritated by all the mess with which she was sharing her chair, Bella seemed extraordinarily at ease. "You'd have kept quiet about it if Karítas hadn't said anything."

"Look, surely you can understand? Once you start telling lies or leaving things out, it's difficult to stop. And I can't see how it changes anything."

"Would you please just tell me what happened?" Thóra had lost patience with his excuses. "The police are interviewing Karítas as we speak and I expect they'll come on here straight afterward. Then you'll have to talk, so why not tell us first?"

Snævar turned pale and the dark shadows under his eyes became even more marked. "Of course I'll talk to them but there's no harm in telling you as well. It would be better to hear your questions before I meet them."

"You mean you want to practice your story on me?"

"No. I didn't mean that." He seemed wounded by this but continued nonetheless. "Karítas was in Lisbon all right, but there's no way Halli knew that beforehand or that she went there because of him. He ran into her completely by chance."

"Were you there?"

"Yes." The color was slowly returning to his cheeks. "It was on our first evening. We went on a pub crawl and she was sitting in one of the smarter, more expensive bars. We'd have walked out again if Halli hadn't spotted her and wanted to say hello. I didn't mind; we weren't having any luck pulling girls and I thought we might be more popular if we were seen in the company of a classy bird like her. She was friendly, too. Very friendly. She seemed over the moon to see Halli again; she remembered him well."

"Did she know what had brought you to Lisbon?"

"Yes, Halli told her before we sat down. I remember because I thought she'd be pissed off to be reminded of her husband's bankruptcy but not a bit of it. She didn't seem bothered. She just thought it was a funny coincidence."

"So when did she bring up her request and what exactly did she say?"

"We'd just gotten our drinks, so it must have been pretty soon. She asked Halli if he could do her a little favor and he reckoned it shouldn't be a problem." Snævar paused, as if searching his memory, then carried on: "She said she needed to get into the yacht to fetch some stuff and wanted to borrow the keys."

"So you lent them to her?"

"Yes. I think so."

"Really?" Bella exclaimed, earning a sharp look from Thóra, though she tried not to let Snævar see. She didn't want him to find out right away that his story was inconsistent with Karítas's admittedly rather vague account. People were often caught out by the small flaws in their statements.

"Yes, as far as I recall. Though I could be wrong." He gave Bella a questioning look. "Why, did she claim she never got them?"

"She didn't mention it," Thóra intervened hastily. "We were discussing the matter from a different angle. Let's just assume that you're right."

Snævar seemed confused for a moment. "Well, we sat there for a bit, then we left. She took our phone numbers and said she'd be in touch the following day. Halli told her she'd have to go on board before the captain and the fourth crew member turned up. Loftur, I mean." He hesitated but when neither Bella nor Thóra commented, he went on: "Then nothing happened except that she called the next day and spoke to Halli, though I don't know exactly what she said. All he told me was that they'd arranged to meet up the following day. I broke my leg that same evening, so I don't think they could have. Halli was busy helping me all the time that he wasn't carrying out preparations on the yacht. Thanks to me, he had to manage all that on his own. He wouldn't have had time to run around for Karítas, that's for sure."

"Did she mention what it was she wanted to fetch?"

Snævar shook his head. "No, not in any detail. Just some of her crap. Clothes, stuff like that."

"A big fuss to make about a load of old clothes, don't you think?"

"Don't ask me what goes on in women's heads. Maybe they were all her favorite things."

"Maybe." The music ceased abruptly as Thóra was speaking and the second half of the word came out as a shout. Mercifully, the disc seemed to have finished and she lowered her voice before continuing, though she was ready for the next track to start booming out of the speakers any minute. "She seems to have gone to an awful lot of trouble over a few dresses. But tell me something else. Was Karítas's assistant over there with her? A young woman called Aldís."

Snævar seemed momentarily thrown; he shifted uncomfortably on the sofa. "I wouldn't know."

"So she wasn't at the bar and her name didn't crop up in conversation? I imagine you asked Karítas if she was there alone? At least, that would seem to me a natural question if I bumped into someone I knew abroad."

"Maybe we did, or rather Halli did. I can't remember. Can't remember if she mentioned her either. Why do you ask?"

"She can't be traced." Thóra watched his Adam's apple move up and down. "Which is rather odd. Yet she was definitely in Lisbon. The police have checked up on the two women's movements. They both flew there but only one of them came home." She wasn't about to tell him that the PA, not Karítas, had taken a plane out of Portugal. Which in itself was peculiar given that Karítas had come home, however she had managed it. Thóra suspected that when the CCTV recordings from airport security were examined, it would transpire that Karítas had traveled under her assistant's name. No doubt the police had that covered.

"How can they know that?" Snævar was looking very uneasy. "They can hardly have checked with every airline in the world?"

"I don't know but that's what I'm told." Thóra caught Bella's eye. "Maybe we should be going. I'm keen to hear what the police have to say now that they're getting to the bottom of this." She turned back to Snævar. "Do you know what I think?" She didn't wait for an answer. "I think there was money or other valuables on board that Karítas wanted to get her hands on. Maybe her husband had hidden away a fortune on the yacht in case of emergency, and he didn't have a chance to remove it before he was forced to surrender the keys to the resolution committee. Whatever the truth, either he asked Karítas to recover it or she took it upon herself to do so. She needed to get on board somehow and that's when you two drunken idiots fell into her lap. I reckon that when he sobered up your friend Halli began to suspect that she was after more than just clothes and jewelry, so he decided to take either all or part of it for himself. You were out of action, so there was nothing to stop him hunting for it. After that something happened and Karítas's PA had to pay the price, perhaps because she'd come up with the same idea. It seems likely that Karítas was involved in her demise since she used Aldís's air ticket to leave Lisbon. The truth will emerge. Perhaps she simply lost her own ticket or accidentally mixed them up. Who knows?"

"Not me." Snævar moved to the edge of the sofa, as if to be ready to make a break for it. "Halli would never have harmed a woman. I'm telling you the truth."

"But you've told me so many things, hardly any of which seem to have any foundation in fact. So permit me to go on with the story. This mess created by your friend and Karítas almost certainly cost my clients their lives. And their daughters." Thóra dearly wished she'd brought along a photo of the twins that she could shove in his face. "Presumably whoever killed Karítas's PA stuffed her body into the freezer, hoping to dispose of her once the yacht was out at sea. Then perhaps the couple or one of their daughters came across the body or the money, or worked out by other means that there was something strange going on. So it became necessary to get rid of the family."

"Halli would never have done anything like what you're implying. Never."

"Maybe not. But how do we know that someone else wasn't there with him? Or on board on their own account? Nothing much was heard from the crew after they left port, so there may well have been other passengers on board, whether they were aware of the fact or not. It's a big yacht."

"Like who?" Snævar narrowed his eyes. "No one could hide there without the crew noticing. I've already told you that. You'd have to know the yacht inside out and even then you'd have to be incredibly lucky not to get noticed. It's a crazy idea. Completely crazy." Turning to Bella, he asked: "You don't believe this bullshit, do you? You remember what it's like on board. Do you think either of you would be capable of hiding there?"

"No, maybe not. But then we don't know our way around. I bet there are plenty of other people who could." Bella shrugged.

Thóra leaned as far back as she could without touching the damp towel that was draped over the back of her chair. "I assume the police will look into that. And once the culprit has been found and confessed to the truth, it'll be much easier for a judge to rule that my clients are dead. Then I'll be able move on to other things, unlike their family who will have to struggle with their grief for the rest of their lives."

Snævar sat back in the sofa again. "No stranger could have stowed away on board. You'll never get me to buy that."

"No, maybe not. But could Karítas have done it?"

"Oh, do me a favor." Snævar looked incredulous. Perhaps he thought women were incapable of stowing away. Or committing murder.

"Or maybe somebody quite different," said Bella.

"Like who?"

"Like you." As soon as Bella had uttered these words, Thóra felt uncomfortably aware of the smallness of the room and their vulnerability to attack. No doubt Bella had intended it sarcastically; perhaps she had wanted to needle the man sitting opposite them, who was now racking his brains for a suitable reply. But big mouths often blurt out the truth, and all of a sudden Thóra realized that Bella could be right. As far as she knew, no one had checked Snævar's claim to have flown home, and he could well have been on the yacht, in spite of his broken leg. Her eyes dropped to the plastic splint that projected from under his trouser leg, concealing the cast. From what she could see he was wearing a sock underneath it, and in a flash she understood his reluctance to procure a doctor's certificate. No doctor with a modicum of self-respect would give a healthy man a certificate confirming that he had a broken leg.

Rarely, if ever, had she been as eager to get outside into the open air.

Chapter 31

Thóra had dressed up that morning out of respect for Ægir's parents, but as she sat at the table in the small kitchen, she realized it would have made no difference what she was wearing. Such matters were trivial in the face of the news she had brought them. The couple sat opposite her, their haggard features expressing a heartfelt wish that she would stop talking; that she would get the harrowing story over with as soon as possible. They listened attentively, saying little, their eyes fixed on the pattern in the tablecloth. Every now and then one of them would adjust the teaspoon in their saucer or smooth out a wrinkle in the cloth, as if the events Thóra was describing were so unreal that they needed to touch something solid to reassure themselves that this was not a bad dream.

"So, at the end of the day, it all came down to money. I suppose it's not really surprising." Thóra tried to make eye contact but neither of them would look up. "There was a fortune on board; millions of U.S. dollars that the owner of the yacht had stashed in the safe. Or so it's claimed. No money has been found but both Karítas and Snævar swear blind that they didn't take it because, although they had the security code, they couldn't open the safe. They may be telling the truth for all we know. I doubt we'll ever find out. The fact that they didn't simply program the yacht to sail off into the Arctic Ocean and never be seen again suggests they genuinely believed the money was still on board. They broke in after her arrival in Iceland to make yet another attempt on the safe, but came away empty-handed, though Karítas couldn't resist the temptation to grab some of her clothes and a box of personal papers at the same time. Next she tried to persuade me to let her in, presumably for one last crack at it." Thóra automatically lowered her voice for what she had to say next. "It appears that Ægir got in touch with the American manufacturer of the safe, apparently on behalf of the resolution committee. Once he had managed to convince them of the change of ownership, they provided him with the code that would reset the lock. But he kept this information to himself, so he alone would have had access to the contents. If there were any."

"Ægir?" Margeir's face was unreadable. He avoided looking at his wife who did not seem to have grasped the implications of Thóra's words.

"Yes, but, like I said, we're not sure there was anything inside when he opened it, though it's clear that somebody had used the code. We'll probably never know what happened, so it's best to assume it was already empty—at least until further evidence comes to light. So much is still unresolved."

Although many of the questions about what happened on board remained unanswered, the circumstances were much clearer now. The police were still working on the inquiry but the officer Thóra had talked to the day before had thought it unlikely that much more would emerge. Snævar and Karítas had both given extremely one-sided accounts, and the detectives were having to try and piece together the probable sequence of events from their statements.

"What we have established is that two of the crew members ran into Karítas by chance in Lisbon and she persuaded them to help her go on board to retrieve the money. Not that she actually admitted what she was after; she pretended all she wanted was to fetch some belongings that had been left behind by mistake. They lent her the keys and that same evening she sent her assistant Aldís to pack up her clothes. She herself intended to go on board the following morning to empty the safe." Thóra allowed this to sink in before continuing: "Snævar and Karítas give conflicting versions of what happened next. She claims she paid an unexpected visit to the yacht that evening and found the keys in the lock but her assistant nowhere to be seen, so she concluded that the girl must have emptied the safe somehow and changed the security code. Whereas Snævar alleges that Karítas caught Aldís messing about and trying on her clothes.

When, on top of that, the safe wouldn't open, Karítas attacked the girl in a rage and pushed her—probably without meaning to—with the result that Aldís banged her head on a sharp marble sink surround in the bathroom."

"Which of them is telling the truth, in your opinion?" Margeir's question seemed perfunctory, as if he didn't really care about the answer.

"My money's on Snævar, but they're waiting for the results of tests on the marble surface, which should decide the matter. Until then we'll just have to rely on their evidence, and his story fits with the captain's report about finding a dead woman. Whereas Karítas's statement is full of holes and she's unable to explain why she took a flight out of Lisbon under Aldís's name. The police believe she did it to give the impression that the girl had fled the city. If necessary, she wanted to be able to back up her story that Aldís had tampered with the safe and possibly even emptied it."

Outside the window a postal woman walked by, towing a red trolley that looked half empty. She was holding some envelopes that she checked briefly before continuing on her way, past Ægir's parents' house. Perhaps she couldn't face trying to force any more letters into the couple's mailbox, which was still bursting at the seams. "If Snævar's account is to be believed, it seems that Karítas lost her nerve and rang his friend Halldór to ask for help. She promised him a big reward if he'd dispose of the body once the yacht was out at sea."

The couple's faces radiated disgust mingled with disbelief; Margeir's forehead creased into a mass of wrinkles. His eyes begged Thóra to stop talking and leave at this point. Trying not to let this deter her, she persevered with her tale: "But Halldór refused to get involved, though he agreed not to report her to the authorities. He believed her claim that it had been an accident and also bought the idea that he and Snævar were somehow implicated because they had lent her the keys that had been entrusted to them. Yet this wasn't enough to make him do what she wanted and no doubt everything would have turned out differently if he had only kept the matter to himself. But he didn't. That evening when he and Snævar were out boozing, Halldór confided in him about Karítas's request."

Thóra paused for breath. Her audience seemed more disorientated with every word and she wasn't sure they were following her any longer. "Do let me know if there's anything you don't understand and I'll try to explain it better."

"I understand the words all right." The woman fiddled with the buttons of her cardigan. The wool was worn and frayed at the seams, and Thóra wished she herself hadn't come dressed as if for the courtroom. "I just don't understand them. What kind of people are they?"

"Deeply flawed. Each in their own way." Thóra licked her dry lips. She could have done with a glass of water but didn't want to put her hosts to the trouble. They had enough to cope with at the moment. "Anyway, to go on, Snævar became very excited and tried to talk Halldór round. Karítas was offering a big sum of money as a reward and he thought it only natural that they should share it. But Karítas had omitted to tell Halldór that the money she had come to retrieve was locked in a safe that refused to open, which made it unlikely she would ever be able to pay them a penny of it. In fact, unbeknownst to her, the safe was completely empty. However, Snævar believed she was capable of paying and in the end he told Halldór he would do it himself and keep all the money. Halldór reacted badly and forbade Snævar to make contact with Karítas, threatening to go to the police with the whole story if he went ahead. According to Snævar, they were both pretty drunk by this point and started a fight which ended up with Halldór falling into the road, getting hit by a car and breaking his leg. He was so plastered that he couldn't give a coherent account of his accident when he was admitted to hospital, and that wasn't only because of the alcohol. You see, Snævar had lent him his European Health Insurance Card because Halldór hadn't had the sense to apply for one before he left home. As they were about the same age and there's no photo on the card, the staff at A & E didn't doubt for a moment that he was Snævar, so Halldór couldn't reveal the full story behind his injury. In addition to which, he was in such pain that his priority would have been to see a doctor and get medical attention as soon as possible."

Thóra paused for breath before carrying on. "Karítas and Snævar give contradictory statements about what happened next. She asserts that Snævar killed Halldór, whereas he insists that *she* murdered him. I doubt the mystery will ever be solved, any more than many other details of this case. It's clear, though, that after Halldór's leg had been put in a cast, Snævar took him back to the hotel where he slept it off for most of the day. Meanwhile, Snævar rang Karítas from his friend's cell phone and they agreed to meet down by the yacht. There Snævar set to work, cramming the PA's body into a large bin-bag and hiding it at the bottom of a big chest freezer. They made a deal that he would throw it into the sea in return for a share of the cash, unaware that this would never be forthcoming. The police believe that after Halldór woke up to find himself in a plaster cast, he went down to the harbor and discovered what was going on. He was furious and threatened to report them, after which one or both of them shut him up by drowning him. He may simply have fallen in during the struggle and been unable to save himself because of his injury. Instead of helping him, they didn't fish him out until it was too late. Presumably, with the body in the freezer, they were eager at all costs to avoid the unwanted attention that a drowned man would attract."

"Which of them is more likely to have killed him?"

"I'd guess Karítas. She had much more to lose at this stage. But it could just as well have been Snævar. In any case, Halldór's body ended up on board like the PA's."

"My God." The woman rubbed the corners of her eyes behind her glasses. "I didn't know people like that existed."

"I'm afraid so." Thóra deliberately didn't remind them that Ægir himself had probably succumbed to the temptation of Karítas's money while he was in Lisbon with his family. Thóra was fairly convinced that the safe had turned out to contain a fortune in cash and that he had removed it. She hadn't a clue what he had done with it but it was quite possible that the money had influenced his decision to travel home by ship, since it would have been easier to smuggle it back to Iceland by sea than by air. But his parents didn't need to hear any of this. Things were bad enough as it was. "Their next actions can probably be blamed on the fact that they were in a state of shock; they decided that Snævar should join the crew, posing as Halldór, throw the two bodies overboard during the voyage, and keep up the pretense that nothing was wrong. Karítas dyed his dark hair blond to make him look more like his friend. The other crew members hadn't met either Halldór or Snævar before, so he had a good chance of getting away with it."

"What were they thinking of? How could they imagine it would work?"

"Apparently, their original idea was that just before the yacht reached land Snævar should jump ship, making it look as if Halldór must have fallen overboard and drowned. Accidents like that aren't particularly unusual, so it was unlikely to have aroused much suspicion. Then Snævar would pretend that he had been waiting at home with a broken leg after flying back from Lisbon. As it turned out, it never occurred to anyone to check his alibi. After all, Snævar's leg appeared to be broken and he had papers to prove it from the hospital in Lisbon because Halldór had used his health insurance card. No one thought for a moment that he could have been involved." Thóra hesitated. "And he would almost certainly have gotten away with it if Halldór had been the only one to disappear. The investigation of one missing person is nothing compared to a case in which an entire yacht-load of people have vanished into thin air."

"I don't know if I can bear to hear any more." Margeir's expression was grim. "These people are sick."

"If you don't want to hear the rest, I can leave it at that. But when this despicable pair are called to the dock, you won't be able to avoid reading about the case or seeing it on the news. It'll be impossible to block it out." She had resolved beforehand to leave out various details, such as the fact that Snævar had decided to chop off Halldór's legs, reasoning that it would be best if his body washed ashore as proof that he had fallen overboard, but at the same time needing to disguise the fact that he had a broken leg. As bodies washed up by the sea often have a limb or two missing, he reckoned it wouldn't look suspicious. But he alone knew why he had amputated both legs rather than just one. Perhaps he thought it would look more plausible as sea damage if both were missing. After this, he had stolen Halldór's splint and plaster cast to bind round his own leg.

Thóra also left out the description of how Snævar had originally

tried to hide Halldór's body in his own cabin. When the smell of decomposition grew increasingly obvious, Snævar had to find a new
place for the corpse. First he tried to disguise it with perfume that he
had filched from Lára and Ægir's room. But when that failed to mask
the stench, he stuffed it into a freezer that was located in a storeroom
adjoining the engine room. There the body remained until Snævar
wrapped it in canvas and hung it over the side of the ship so that when
he eventually chucked it overboard, it would look as if it had been
immersed in the sea rather than deep-frozen. First he removed the legs
using an axe that was kept in the pilot house, taking the precaution
of putting his own shoes on the feet in case they got caught in a fishing net or washed up somewhere. This was to ensure that those who
survived the voyage would identify the legs as Halli's. Then Snævar
turned off the ship's main engine so that he could push Halldór's body
out through a hatch which couldn't be opened while the vessel was
underway. The navigation computer confirmed that by this point they
were only a day's journey from port.

But Snævar made a fatal mistake in the final stretch. After tether-
ing the body outside the hatch, he locked the storeroom behind him
in case Ægir thought of trying to escape with the girls on one of the
Jet Skis. On his way back upstairs to dispose of Halli's legs, he ran
into Ægir and apparently murdered him, losing the key in the struggle. By the time he realized this he was too close to shore and had no
time to search for it. As a result, he was unable to jettison Halli's body
as planned.

After his return home, the news of the police examination of the
yacht and the collection of forensic evidence had driven Snævar frantic with anxiety that he would be betrayed by the presence of his
DNA on Halli's body. His chance of removing the evidence when he
and Karítas went on board was thwarted by an inquisitive nightwatch-
man and they were forced to flee. So when Snævar was offered the
opportunity to go on board with Thóra, he planned to pretend to
stumble on Halli's body by chance, in the hope that this would explain any forensic traces linking him to the corpse. As it was, his friend
was in such a horrific state of decomposition that he didn't need to

force himself to vomit; the reaction was involuntary. And his plan had worked.

"I want to hear the rest." Sigrídur jutted out her chin as if she could handle it, though her wet eyelashes told a different story. "Go on."

"Unfortunately, not much more can be established with any certainty. Snævar insists that he had no part in any other death, and is sticking to his story that all he did was deal with the bodies for Karítas. She, on the other hand, claims that he gave her a very different account after his return home, in a long phone call that his telephone company confirms took place. According to her, Snævar killed Loftur because Loftur had worked out that it must have been Snævar who threw the body of the woman in the freezer overboard. It wasn't hard for him to guess, since only two people could have done it, him or Snævar—or rather Halli, as he was calling himself. When Loftur accused him of this, Snævar drowned him in the Jacuzzi, which Loftur was in the process of heating up at the time. After that Snævar invented a story about a mysterious stowaway but the others weren't convinced, so when the net began to tighten around him he killed them, too—the captain, Thráinn, when the poor man fell asleep on watch."

"How did he kill . . . ?" Margeir couldn't finish the sentence but there was no need. Thóra was well aware of what he was asking.

"According to Karítas, Lára died as the result of an accidental shot. No one knows if that's yet another lie but the gun that should have been on board is missing. Snævar told Karítas that Ægir threw the weapon overboard, but I very much doubt that. The police believe that Snævar murdered her as well as the others."

"And Ægir?"

"He supposedly killed him last. Karítas claims this was unintentional. Snævar had hoped that Ægir and the girls would stay out of the way below deck and that he himself would be able to keep a low profile once they reached Iceland. Ægir would believe that Halli, who had vanished, was the murderer and no one would ever find out that Snævar had been posing as his friend on board. However, I find it hard to believe that he'd have taken such a risk, so I'm guessing that he killed Ægir to save his own skin. If everyone on board disappeared, people would put it down to an accident and no one would suspect a man with a broken leg whose only connection with the yacht had been before the vessel had left harbor. Apparently he went around the ship and removed all the cell phones and cameras he could find in case he appeared in any pictures. Then he flung them all in the sea. During his time on board he had taken care to touch as little as possible and to wipe away his fingerprints when no one was looking. So there weren't many prints to give him away. In fact, his actions seem to have been carefully premeditated, which suggests that he wasn't just Karí-tas's innocent dupe as he would like us to think."

"How did he get ashore? He was waiting with us on the docks when the yacht put in." Sigríður's voice was angry, as if she had let herself be tricked and should have seen through him from the beginning.

"He set the autopilot to bring the yacht close enough in for him to jump into the sea and swim to shore. He was wearing a wetsuit, which he apparently knew how to use, and reached land safely without be-ing noticed. He had brought along a change of clothes, the splint and the plaster cast in a waterproof bag, along with the crutches that had been lent to Halldór in Portugal. Afterward, the yacht continued on its pre-plotted course, sailing in a large circle in Faxaflói bay to give Snævar time to be waiting on the docks when she entered the harbor. The whole thing had been planned to prevent suspicion from falling on him. He even wore a woolly hat to hide his freshly shaven head; I don't know if you remember that."

"Yes." They both nodded, but the woman still had reservations. "The harbor may not be far from Grótta but it's still quite a distance on two feet, let alone on crutches. And he wasn't out of breath."

"He waited until the last minute to put on the cast, which was only loosely fixed round his leg. As for his journey from Grótta; Karítas had ordered her mother to park her car in the neighborhood with the keys under the seat, two days before the yacht reached land. It was the plan she and Snævar had originally made, when only Halli was sup-posed to go missing. She kept up her end of the bargain and claims she had no idea what lengths Snævar had gone to during the voyage. Her mother has since confirmed the part about the car; she was under the impression that some mechanic friend of her daughter's, who supposedly ran a garage in the area, was going to service the car. But in reality it was for Snævar. He changed his clothes and fastened the sawn-off plaster cast round his leg with adhesive tape and string. Then he tied a plastic bag over it and drove down to the harbor where he took up position as if nothing had happened."

"God, I wish we hadn't met him there. I wish we'd never gone to meet the yacht; that we'd never set eyes on that man." Margeir rubbed his forehead as if to obliterate the memory. "We were just so excited. I'd asked my cousin in the Coast Guard to give us a shout, whatever the time of day or night, when the yacht appeared on their radar. We were worried because we hadn't heard from them, so we were immensely happy and relieved when we got his call."

"Snævar sabotaged the communications equipment, as well as the emergency button that could conceivably have saved them. He disconnected the aerials, with the result that the radios hardly had any range, though we know that at least one ship tried to contact the *Lady K* to warn them about a container that had blown off a vessel near the area they were sailing in. They didn't think they'd gotten through."

Thóra saw that this was enough horror for one day. These people needed some good news, though she had not yet answered the most important question about the fate of those on board. Nevertheless, she felt it would be better to break it up before going any further. "I've sent the insurance company the court's verdict that Ægir and Lára are presumed dead, along with a declaration from the police stating that the investigation into their disappearance is in its final stages and that everything points to their having been murdered. The company may send you another letter trying to object, but only for form's sake. I'll reply on your behalf. All going well, the insurance money should be paid out in the next few months." The couple murmured at this but didn't say anything aloud. Money mattered little in comparison to what they had lost. Fortunately, however, she had more good news for them. "It seems you've also passed the Child Protection Agency's evaluation with flying colors and I've been informed unofficially that you'll be granted very generous access rights to Sigga Dögg. A proviso will be made that whoever adopts her should be fully apprised of the tragic circumstances. So you'll continue to play an important role in her life as her grandparents. In that respect nothing will change."

"Nothing will change. So you say." The woman shook herself and shivered. "But nothing will be the same either." Thóra didn't reply. The woman was quite right; of course nothing would be like it was before.

Her husband coughed and turned his head to look out of the window. "What happened to the girls? I notice you avoided mentioning them but I need to know. As little as I want to."

Thóra stared down at the table. "It's not clear. Snævar flatly denies having laid a finger on them and swears that they simply vanished. He says he searched high and low for them but with no success. As matters stand, nobody knows if he's lying, but the yacht did circle for a while as if looking for something that had fallen overboard and the location fits more or less with his statement."

"What about Karítas? Didn't he tell her during their phone call?" Margeir stared even more intently out of the window. The street was empty and there were no passing cars. It was as if the neighborhood had come to a standstill out of consideration for the old couple's loss.

"Karítas backs him up. She says he told her the girls had simply vanished."

"Do you believe that?"

"No, I don't. But then no one will ask my opinion."

"God will ask." The woman fumbled under her cardigan and her hand reappeared clutching a small silver cross on a modest chain. "And lies won't help them then."

Shortly after this Thóra took her leave, promising to ring at the end of the week, or earlier if anything new emerged. On her way out she passed the door of the sitting room where Sigga Dögg sat on the floor watching a cartoon. Tom and Jerry were involved in a chase around a boat that rocked violently, causing the cat more problems than the mouse. The episode was almost over and as Thóra stood watching the child, both cat and mouse fell overboard. They splashed around in the sea, still fighting, their open mouths full of water. Next the pair appeared clad in white robes, complete with wings and halos, floating up from the surface of the sea to heaven; the mouse beaming from ear to ear, the cat looking thoroughly fed up. Perhaps this was the explanation for the child's words about her sisters and parents. She knew they had been on a boat and when they didn't come home, she may well have concluded that they had gone the same way as poor old Tom and Jerry.

"They used to be Arna and Bylgja's favorite programs. I'm afraid the tape will wear out." Sigrídur smiled faintly. "Not that my granddaughters will mind now."

Sigga Dögg looked round at the sound of her grandmother's voice. She studied the two women calmly for a moment, then turned back to the screen. The next episode was starting; life went on, though some had fallen by the wayside.

On the way home Thóra couldn't stop thinking about this shattered family and the fate of the two little girls, which would perhaps never be known. Although not religious, she sent a silent prayer of thanks to the higher powers for her own family's good fortune. Yet the thought of Gylfi's imminent adventures in Norway filled her with trepidation, reminding her that nothing could be taken for granted. The future could never be pinned down. Abruptly, she decided against going back to the office where Bella was sitting glued to the computer with its new high-speed connection. Instead, she turned the car and drove to Orri's nursery school. She would pick him up early and enjoy the rest of the day with him. The sun peeped out from behind the clouds and suddenly the world seemed a brighter place.

Chapter 32

"He's not coming." Bylgja had long since stopped crying. Her cheeks were dry, not because the flow of tears had ceased but because the fringed hem of the dress that was pressing, cool and soft, against her face had soaked them up as they fell. It was almost as if she hadn't cried at all and this made her feel even worse. As if she had betrayed Daddy and didn't care about him. "What do we do if he doesn't come? He didn't tell us."

Arna shifted in the narrow space and the dresses rustled as if joining in with their whispering. "I don't know."

"Should we stay here until the bad man finds us?" Bylgja adjusted her position as well since Arna's elbow was now sticking into her stomach. She didn't care about the discomfort; they would rather be squashed up together than alone in separate wardrobes.

"I don't know. Maybe he won't find us."

"He'll find us if he looks."

"Maybe he isn't looking for us." Arna sounded as if she was still crying.

"Maybe." Bylgja was all for closing her eyes and concentrating on something other than the trouble they were in. She wanted to think about the holiday cottage her mother had been dreaming of, and the advertisements she sometimes let them study with her to help her choose which one they would buy if they were incredibly rich. If she closed her eyes and put her hands over her ears she could imagine they were sitting together at the kitchen table, looking through the papers in search of the nicest. A cottage with a deck, and little trees that would be big by the time she and Arna were grown up. But even when she shut out all she could see and hear in the dark cupboard, she couldn't block out the heaving motion of the yacht and that ruined everything. "Are you thinking about Mommy?"

"Yes." Arna started wriggling again.

"Do you think the bad man has thrown her in the sea?" Arna didn't reply. "You must answer. I want to hear you talk."

"I can't talk about Mommy; in the sea." Arna sniffed. The dress next to her was probably covered in wet patches. "Let's talk about something else."

"I want to get out of this cupboard." Bylgja groped for her glasses, which she thought she had put on the floor. "I feel awful and I want to look for Daddy."

"But what about the bad man?"

"Perhaps there is no bad man. Perhaps it was all a mistake and Daddy's forgotten about us and is talking to Thráinn and Halli. Remember how tired he was? I bet he's fallen asleep. I'm so fed up with whispering. And maybe we'll use up all the air in the cupboard and suffocate." It grew suddenly brighter and Bylgja put her hands over her eyes: Arna had opened the door. They scrambled out and after a moment the light stopped hurting their eyes.

"What shall we do?" whispered Arna. She glanced around, her gaze lingering on the signs of their father. A shirt on the chair by the dressing table, the briefcase on the floor and the book he had been reading at the beginning of the voyage, which was lying face down on the bedside table. She didn't want to think about whether he would ever finish it. Even the Coke can he had been drinking from produced a peculiar sensation in her tummy, a sharp pain that traveled upward as if aiming for her heart. "Let's go. Let's go out on deck."

"Do you think it would be all right?" Bylgja suddenly regretted being responsible for making them leave the cramped interior of the wardrobe. They had been safe in there. For the moment, at least.

"Yes. I think so. Remember, we went out on deck with Daddy when he was tired and it was all right then. I don't think he'd tell us off."

"Are you sure?"

"Yes. We can always come back down here if we want to." Arna went over to their father's bedside table, picked up his paperback, folded over the corner of the page and closed it. "I'm going to take Daddy his book."

"If we find him." Bylgja squinted. She thought about making another attempt to locate her glasses but decided against it. It wasn't worth it. She didn't want to see anything on this horrible ship, so she'd be better off without them. She envied Arna for thinking of taking the book and looked around for something she could bring along. "I'll take his briefcase. He'll be glad to have that too."

They both yawned and smiled at each other. "Let's go," said Arna.

They tried their best to move quietly after leaving the cabin but their constant shushing of each other made more noise than their light footsteps along the corridor and up the stairs, or the sound of their opening and closing the doors. They were completely unprepared for the blast of wind that struck them as they emerged into the open air; Arna dropped the book and it fluttered along the deck, driven by the gale, until it halted by the rail. Arna ran after it, but the book lifted into the air and vanished into the darkness. There was a faint splash.

Arna ran up and peered over the rail. As Bylgja followed, it dawned on her that the yacht was stationary. It was wallowing in the waves but not making any progress. She slowed down as she considered this, so arrived after Arna at the rail. "Can you see the book?" She squinted into the night but could see nothing. The boat's lights did not reach far enough. Arna did not reply. She was standing rigidly, pointing at something that Bylgja couldn't make out. "What? What is it?"

"Daddy!" Arna's voice was filled with utter despair but the wind whipped her shriek out to sea.

Bylgja spotted a long, black shadow floating close to the side of the ship. Grateful that she wasn't wearing her glasses, she recoiled from the rail before she could distinguish any details. "I don't want to see him," she said, turning away. Arna copied her example and they stood side by side, their backs to the horrific sight floating on the surface of the sea below. Their world had fallen apart and there was nothing left. No one would miss the book and there was no one left to take care of them now. They had no father or mother and nothing would ever be good again. Neither of them were aware of how long they stood there contemplating their wretched fate. They no longer felt the cold, and the wind that tore at their hair did not bother them.

When Arna eventually spoke, Bylgja wished more than anything to be left in peace. It would be best if they could stand there until they caught their death of cold.

"Bylgja, do you remember Tom and Jerry?" Arna's voice sounded normal, although tears were pouring down her cheeks.

"Yes." Bylgja couldn't move, couldn't weep, couldn't scream or do anything but answer mechanically. It was as if she were no longer herself but a different person.

"They fell in the sea, then went up to heaven. Perhaps we should do that too. Become angels in white dresses with wings, and see Mommy and Daddy again."

"I don't care."

"I don't want that bad man to kill us, Bylgja. If we jump in the sea we'll escape and be with them. Mommy must be there too somewhere."

"Yes." Bylgja felt Arna take her hand and lead her to the rail. She was still carrying her father's briefcase but now she raised it aloft and threw it over the side. The case opened on the way down and countless pieces of green paper flew up in the air over their heads like a flock of birds.

They clambered onto the rail and perched there briefly. "Are you cold?" Arna took her sister's hand again.

"No. You?"

"No. Just tired. I want to be with Mommy and Daddy."

"Me too. I don't want to stay here any longer."

Their eyes met and they smiled.